PRAISE FOR

Solomon's Crown

"Riveting, haunting—two powerful rulers in a battle for love and respect."

—Tamora Pierce

"Absolutely captivating and wonderfully romantic . . . I didn't want to put this book down, even when it had ended."

—Rainbow Rowell, #1 *New York Times* bestselling author of The Simon Snow Trilogy

"Glorious, heart-wrenching, and, above all, hopeful, *Solomon's Crown* is a meditative, startlingly lovely examination of love, rivalry, and what makes a legacy, and Natasha Siegel has crafted a triumph of a debut."

—Grace D. Li, *New York Times* bestselling author of *Portrait of a Thief*

"An utterly delightful reimagining of medieval Europe, where a romance between two kings unfolds across enemy lines . . . Natasha Siegel's sweeping tale full of heart and historical optimism will make you believe the impossible."

—C. S. Pacat, *New York Times* bestselling author of *Dark Rise*

"I savored every page. These two kings will wreck your heart, and you'll ask them to do it again. Natasha Siegel's is a voice I craved in historical fiction."

—HEATHER WALTER, author of *Malice*

"*Solomon's Crown* has the mixture of sweeping scope and lush sensory detail that makes for the best historical fiction. I turned the last page and immediately itched to read it again, more slowly, so that I could roll around in the aching romance and assured prose. This is a joyful debut from a remarkable talent."

—FREYA MARSKE, author of *A Marvellous Light*

"A breathtakingly intimate love story set against a sweeping historical backdrop . . . an unforgettable delight."

—S. T. GIBSON, author of *A Dowry of Blood*

"*Romeo and Juliet* meets Oscar Wilde in twelfth-century Europe. *Solomon's Crown* is a work of supreme imagination, wit, and forbidden love that feels timeless, and Natasha Siegel's lyrical language sings. This is truly a unique work and one to be savored."

—MARGARET GEORGE, *New York Times* bestselling author of *The Splendor Before the Dark*

"Captivating . . . Siegel's smooth, gorgeous writing deliciously evokes the era and establishes her well-drawn characters. This will be catnip for readers who like their historical romance to come with a deep political slant."

—*Publishers Weekly*

Solomon's Crown

Solomon's Crown

A NOVEL

Natasha Siegel

DELL

NEW YORK

A Dell Trade Paperback Original

Copyright © 2023 by Natasha Siegel
Book club guide copyright © 2023 by Penguin Random House LLC

Published in the United States by Dell, an imprint of Random House, a division of Penguin Random House LLC, New York.

DELL is a registered trademark and the D colophon is a trademark of Penguin Random House LLC.
RANDOM HOUSE BOOK CLUB and colophon are trademarks of Penguin Random House LLC.

LIBRARY OF CONGRESS CATALOGING-IN-PUBLICATION DATA
Names: Siegel, Natasha, author.
Title: Solomon's crown: a novel / Natasha Siegel.
Description: New York: Dell, [2023]
Identifiers: LCCN 2022027932 (print) | LCCN 2022027933 (ebook) |
ISBN 9780593597842 (trade paperback) | ISBN 9780593597859 (ebook)
Subjects: LCSH: Richard I, King of England, 1157–1199—Fiction. |
Philip II, King of France, 1165–1223—Fiction. | LCGFT: Alternative
histories (Fiction) | Gay fiction. | Romance fiction. | Novels.
Classification: LCC PR6119.I325 S65 2023 (print) |
LCC PR6119.I325 (ebook) | DDC 823/.92—dc23/eng/20220621
LC record available at https://lccn.loc.gov/2022027932
LC ebook record available at https://lccn.loc.gov/2022027933

Printed in the United States of America on acid-free paper

randomhousebooks.com

2 4 6 8 9 7 5 3 1

Book design by Caroline Cunningham
Title and part-title tree silhouette: AdobeStock/EVGENIY

To my mother, Caroline

The House of Plantagenet

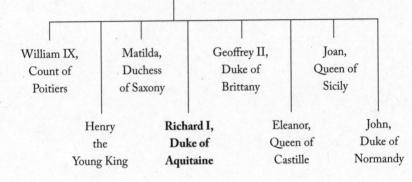

Henry II — Eleanor of Aquitaine

William IX, Count of Poitiers

Henry the Young King

Matilda, Duchess of Saxony

Richard I, Duke of Aquitaine

Geoffrey II, Duke of Brittany

Eleanor, Queen of Castille

Joan, Queen of Sicily

John, Duke of Normandy

The House of Capet

Louis VII — Adela of Champagne

Marie,
Countess of
Champagne

Margaret,
Queen of England
and Hungary

**Philip II,
King of France** —
Isabella of Hainault

Alix,
Countess
of Blois

Alys,
Countess
of Vexin

Agnes,
Byzantine
empress

HISTORICAL NOTE

This is not a historically accurate novel. It takes enormous liberties with its setting: adding wars that didn't happen, removing wars that did, ignoring deaths, changing clothing and geography, and portraying medieval battles with such flagrant disrespect for reality that any military historians who read it will probably throw the book into their fireplaces before they manage to finish it. In particular, Philip and Richard have been made entirely distinct from their historical counterparts; they aren't intended to reflect the real-life Philip and Richard in any meaningful way, except their political positions and family ties.

That being said, many of the places, people, and events described in this story were inspired by reality. In the High Middle Ages, France, England, and the duchy of Aquitaine were entangled in a grand drama of dynastic rivalry and intrigue. In 1152 CE, Eleanor, Duchess of Aquitaine and the most powerful woman in Europe, left her husband King Louis of France. She then married Henry, the Duke of Normandy and future king of England. She and Henry had four sons: Henry the Young King, Richard, Geoffrey, and John. Of those sons, three would lead a failed rebellion against their father during his reign, and two would eventually become kings themselves. Meanwhile, Louis also remarried, and his only son from his third wife would become Philip II of France, one of the most successful medieval monarchs to have ever lived. These two families were inextricably linked: their members were enemies, rivals, allies, and lovers; they made war against each other and with each other; and their choices changed the face of Europe forever.

Both Philip II of France and Richard I of England are now legendary figures. Philip is known alternately as "Dieudonné," or "God-Given," and as Augustus; Richard is, of course, the Lionheart. When it comes to those so heavily mythologized, it is difficult for even historians far more discerning than me to distinguish fact or fiction. However, in their youth, the two had been close enough that they were reported to have been sleeping "in the same bed" by a chronicler. Many historians in the past few centuries have bravely stepped forward in defense of the kings' heterosexuality, arguing that this doesn't prove a romantic or sexual relationship between them. Maybe it doesn't, but assumptions have certainly been made about heterosexual relationships on the basis of far less evidence.

The real Philippe Auguste and Richard the Lionheart left behind complex legacies befitting of two kings ruling almost a thousand years ago, in an era of crusades, antisemitism, Islamophobia, and misogyny. They were not good men by any modern standard, and this novel has no interest in redeeming them. The Philip and Richard contained in these pages, and the imaginary Europe they live in, are above all else fictional. But I hope that—at least in some part—this story does reflect one element of reality: that throughout history, people loved one another and persevered.

Solomon's Crown

Richard

Mine was an easy birth. It was a birth my mother would later tell me was fit for glory, fit for a prince. I was born early, as swift and as keen as a sword. My mother lay down to deliver and I emerged three hours later. The moment I had air in my lungs I screamed and I screamed, and I kept screaming until the entire court was raw with it. I was the sixth child, the second son still living. I had no right to cry with the entitlement that I did. But I did. I wailed as if the weight of the crown was already upon my head.

It was not so with Philip. Philip was born in high summer, just outside of Paris. His mother must have broiled in the birthing chamber as she awaited him, swaddled in sweat-soaked linens, the sun beating at the warped glass of the windows with impatient fists. Eight hours into the ordeal, she was rolled in a blanket, lifted off the bed, and tossed from side to side in a desperate attempt to draw him out. When he was finally tugged into the world, slippery and pale and silent, it took the frantic hands of a physician to rouse him. Even afterwards—or so he described it to me—his voice was thin and reedy, his breaths uneven, and his parents feared he would not survive the winter. But still, it was enough. Philip was no warrior, but something greater. He was a boy, as his father had wished four times before: a first son. One day, he would be king.

Church bells tolled for the entire week; people danced in the streets; France sang his praises to the heavens themselves. "Philip the God-given" he was called. I can only imagine how my father must have laughed at this, ruling from his throne in England, with three princes already to his name. I was with my mother at the time. But I remember her sitting with me, petting my head and murmuring into my ear. She often repeated these words as I grew older:

"Richard," she told me, "although this child may become a king and you will not, you must never forget who you are. You are the grandson of an empress, the son of the king of England, and the future Duke of Aquitaine. You yield to no man."

I told Philip what she had said, years later. In hindsight, I doubt he believed me. But the way he smiled when I recounted it, his fingers curled around my wrist, my lips over the shell of his ear—*our little secret, Philip*—I like to think that he wanted it to be true. It hadn't mattered, not really. Nothing had mattered, with a pair of thrones between us, and my heart clutched like a rosary between his hands.

Part One

DESCORT

CHAPTER ONE

Philip

At thirteen years old, I almost died.

I had gone riding with the court and ventured out too far. The forests outside of Paris are lovely in the spring, carpeted with bluebells, sunlight weaving between the oaks; but as night fell that day, and the clouds roiled, the trees became a labyrinth of clawing fingers. Stumbling between them, the flowers tugged at my feet, pulling me into the mud. I could do little but sit curled-up amongst the roots of a wizened beech, praying I would survive the storm. I remained lost in the darkness with only the torrential rain to keep me company; and when they found me in the morning I was coughing and shivering, clinging to consciousness.

I was only half formed at that age, and the sickness came quickly. I was laid out upon my bed, flushed and trembling, sprawled like a prisoner on the rack. I spent most of my childhood swaddled in luxuries—furs, tutors, vellum—but when I think of my youth, the first thing I remember is the tang of my sweat in the air, my mother digging her nails into my forearm as she chanted prayers, the bitter taste of herbs and the fog of fever.

I made the perfect picture of a martyr. Outside the wind shrieked and rattled at the windows in zealous accusation; the foundations of the castle groaned with me. Physicians came and went like visiting pilgrims. They bled me until my pallor became corpselike, and they argued incessantly over courses of treatment; they all wanted to be the one to save the life of a future king. One recommended my head be shaved; another thought I ought to be as warm as possible, to draw the fever out; and a third, hardly a doctor at all, loomed over me murmuring in funereal Latin. In my delirium, the layer of sweat on my skin became a horde of insects. I scratched and clawed at myself, scoring scarlet lines over my arms. I was slathered in a paste of stinking moss, which soon dried to a thick green crust. I must have looked like a leper.

My father never once came to my room to see me. Instead, he departed on a pilgrimage to beg God for my recovery. Of all places, he went to a shrine in England. He was aging and infirm, but still, he went. He was never the same when he came back, remaining silent for hours upon hours. I think the strain of the journey pushed his addled mind a step too far. And yet it worked; by the time he returned, I had improved. Whether by grace of God or blind luck, my fever broke. I awoke one morning frail, half starved, but blessedly alive.

It took another week before I could leave the bed. I had lost so much weight it was almost comical; when I walked, I wobbled awkwardly, like a dancing bear. I should have been relieved, but the world I returned to seemed dull and underwhelming. The experience left me bone-weary and afraid. It felt as if time distended around me, and I aged years in the weeks I had been away.

I went to visit my father soon after my bedrest ended. He had been taking private Mass ever since his homecoming. When I first saw him, I wondered if he had been eating nothing but communion bread; his wrists were even leaner than mine, his bones bursting from their skin. The fire in his chamber had been stoked to heaving, and the scent of the smoke mingled with incense. The dim light cast his cheekbones into disturbing relief. His breaths were so shallow they seemed entirely absent; only the languid, occasional movements of his eyelashes were proof of his living. I watched him from the doorway, unable to step into the room. But he soon noticed my presence, and he outstretched his hand to greet me, fingers trembling.

I knelt before him to receive his blessing.

"My son," he said, and I rose. He was sitting in his wooden chair, the one with wide, high arms that forced his shoulders beside his ears. He was clutching a cup of wine in his other hand, and I could see the liquid quivering in his grasp. I had to stoop to look him in the eye.

"Father," I said. "Are you well?"

"I am well," he replied, perhaps believing it, "and you are well also. Praise be to God."

"Praise be."

"My son—"

"Yes, father?" I asked.

"You must give thanks, Philip. Give thanks to God."

"I shall," I replied. "I have."

As much as I wish it were different, this is what I remember most about my father: how desperately he clung to his saints and his epistles, like a hanged man scrabbling at the noose. Louis the Monk, some called him. I saw more of his back as he knelt to pray than I ever did the front of him. When I was very young, I idolized him, fancying him a someday-saint. As I spoke to him, I would imagine the relics his bones would make. That evening he whispered to me in the soft rasp of a dying man, and all I could do was stare at his skeletal fingers, imagining them shut in a reliquary box.

"You are a good boy, Philip," he said, offering me a faint, papery smile. "No, not a boy. You are a man. My son." He dropped his wine to the floor—the warm liquid splashed the front of my slippers—and he surged forward, grasping my hands with sudden strength. "You will be king, soon enough," he told me.

"Father—"

"We have no choice. You know as well as I."

"Know what, Father?"

"We must—" His grasp became more insistent, his upper lip curling back to reveal a row of shrunken gum. "We must— I am not as I was. Our lands are not as they were. England has diminished us."

"England," I echoed. I imagined England as an enormous, gaping maw, making its slow, interminable gulp towards us: closing its teeth around the entire continent, Calais to the Pyrenees. "What shall we do?"

"You must be crowned."

When I thought of kings, I thought of the man sitting before me. I wanted nothing less than to become as he was. Louis was only a half person. The soul was gone, and the rest was skin and muscle and bone.

I could do nothing except kneel and bow my head in expectation of his blessing. He did not bless me. Instead he stooped over, clutching my head in his hands. His eyes were welling with tears. He had black eyes, glazed matte, like ink. My own were blue and glasslike, and I had spent years learning to lower my lids, knowing their transparency; but at that age—surely, Louis must have seen how afraid I was. He pressed his thumbs into my cheekbones. His grip was weak, but his fingers seemed to threaten some sudden surge of strength, to press my skull so tightly it might rupture into shards. I was trapped there, on the floor of his chamber, with the roar of the fire behind me.

"My son," he said. He closed in, pressing his forehead against my own. "You are already a king."

"I am?" I asked.

"You are. What makes a monarch, Philip?"

"Blood."

"Blood," he said, satisfied. "Royal blood. My blood. With it, you will become a great king. A pious king. A new Augustus."

"I shall try, Father."

"You were born for this. Remember that."

Louis withdrew. He reached down to take the cup from the floor, cradling it in his palms. His gaze skittered across me, and he peered into the empty cup, frowning.

"Shall I give you leave?" I asked, still on my knees.

"Yes," he murmured. "I have need of more wine. Fetch some wine, boy. Fetch Eleanor."

Eleanor was his first wife. He was now on his third.

I stood. He did not look at me as I left him there, hunched and vacant, clutching his cup, in the same position as when I'd arrived.

~·~

The year passed. Medicine holds that those who are cold and dry in the body are melancholic, an affliction I was treated for numerous times during my childhood. The physicians would placate my parents by listing all the great leaders of history who suffered a similar malady: Charlemagne and Julius Caesar both had such temperaments, they would say, as they ground me pastes of astringent herbs to swallow each morning. Silent and

sullen, I spent evenings wrapped in coarse wool to promote heat.
I was served only foods deemed warm and wet: meaty stews,
fennel-seed teas, wine spiced with sage.

Nothing helped, and the months after my illness, my melancholy grew more and more pronounced. Cinnamon is worth its
weight in gold, and yet it became a daily medicine. It coated
every bite of food I took. My tongue became thick with it. My
little sister Agnes was light and merry, she ran hot. She spun
around the corridors like silk on a loom. Every day we met in the
same hall on the way to Mass. "Have you had a good morning,
Philip?" she would ask me.

"My morning was good if yours was, Agnes," I would respond.

"Then mine was the best morning in the world."

She would laugh and grasp my arm. And when she did, I
would always have the same hope: that perhaps some of that
heat would run from her hand and into my blood.

It never did. I began hiding in the library as much as I could,
taking comfort amongst pages that whispered to me of distant
pasts, of kings and nations that did not know of me and never
would. My mother would have to come fetch me before supper,
and in the doorway of the great hall she would remind me to
smile to the vassals, to finish the food on my plate. "Otherwise,
they will think something is troubling you," she'd say, leaning
forward, so I could smell the chapel incense her confessor favored. She always smelled like a confessional; she bore the guilt
of something I would never know, guilt enough that after my
father's death she retreated to a convent and we never spoke
again. Our interactions were limited to these moments of criti-
cism, when she instructed my behavior, using her thumbs to
push at the corners of my lips. "*Smile*, Philip," she would say.
"Why must you look so sad?"

I was always asked to be happy, even as everything around me emphasized the virtues of suffering. Monks flagellated themselves into woodcuts, stripping themselves raw before God. The Tragedies instructed me to count no man happy before he was dead. I asked my confessor whether there was wisdom in these words. He said to me, "You are not yet a man, Philip. You are young. Be joyous in your youth." Was I expected to be happy now, knowing that someday I was destined for sorrow? "Yes," he replied, as if that made perfect sense and I was simply too young to understand why.

But the more I understood of my position, the expectations upon me, the scarcer that hope became. It was the map that haunted me most, hung above the desk of my tutor's rooms. There was shown the hollowing of France, in great strokes of red ink: all the land once ours, snatched with hungry hands by England during my father's reign. It was the fruit of his folly, a pair of shackles waiting to descend. My lifetime would be spent redeeming his lifetime of surrender, and no amount of cinnamon could change that.

<hr />

I was crowned less than a year after my illness. It was a dry month, a cold month, a melancholy month. There was very little rain, but the air was abrasive with frost. I knelt at the altar of the church, hearing the dry, cold wind whistle outside, feeling the dry, cold click of my throat as I swallowed. There were so many people, lost in the pile of faces and expensive fabrics. My father, barely sensate, was propped up at the front row. He had not spoken in weeks. My mother sat beside him, her fair hair piled heavily at her neck, bowing her head as if the weight were too much. The archbishop struggled to keep balance in his towering hat. Behind my parents stood the king of England, Henry, watching me. He was tall, colorfully dressed, a vivid stain on the crowd. His gaze was like a bowstring pulled taut. I wonder what he thought of me, calf of a prince that I was, struggling to wrangle my hand from my sleeve.

The archbishop swiped too much oil upon my face as he anointed me, and I went cross-eyed watching it drip off my nose. Then came the prayers and the hymns, and meanwhile I gripped my scepter so tightly that my knuckles went white. Even inside, the chill was such that the tips of my ears went pink beneath the crown. By the time it was all finished, I felt entirely numb, and it hardly registered when the archbishop presented me to my subjects. I stood and raised my eyes to the vaulted ceiling, rather than return the attention of my audience.

There was a feast afterwards, of course, in honor of a monarch who resented his own throne. The frigid air was inescapable, the light faded to a frozen twilight, and the rushes on the floor had been stamped thin by the crowd. I was sat next to the king of England. He stared at me and chewed thoughtfully, while I fiddled with my cutlery.

"We have much to speak of, you and I," he said to me. He had a small chunk of bread in his hand. As he spoke, he began to pick at its crust, causing flakes of it to fall upon his plate. He was a handsome man, carrying his age well; tanned, wide-shouldered, with an impressive head of red-blond hair.

I nodded, and he smiled. Frowning, I looked away from him to spear a parsnip with my knife.

"We could be friends, Philip," he said, as I pushed the vegetable around my plate. I disliked the sound of my name in his mouth. I had to force myself not to flinch.

"I am glad if that is true," I replied.

He laughed at that, and he returned the bread to his plate. The weight of several curious glances fell upon us, but a cursory

conversation within the hall continued, granting us an uncon-
vincing illusion of privacy. On the opposite side of the table, the
Count of Blois had no such compunctions. The count had always been one of my father's most troublesome vassals; he had
no more respect for my authority than he had Louis's, it seemed,
and he was glowering at me as if I had offered Henry my kingdom along with his meal.

"You are skeptical of my intentions," Henry said, glancing between myself and Blois with open amusement.

I put down my own knife. "My father has fought with you for
decades."

"Your father was angry at me for stealing Eleanor. Surely you
do not suffer the same jealousies?"

Henry had married my father's first wife after their divorce,
and Louis had always been bitter; but this was a ridiculous
claim. A facile attempt at manipulation, even if directed at
someone so young. I said, affronted, "You have stolen our land.
It is hardly a matter of jealousy."

He raised a brow. "You are bold, Philip. We are allies, are we
not?"

"Yes. But only when we must be."

He smiled again. His face was deceptively expressive, a sort of
false openness that invited complacency. "I thought you your
father's son," he said. "You seem now to be little alike."

"Fathers and sons often differ."

The grin grew strained. "Sometimes. My sons and I are reconciled."

"Of course, my lord," I said.

"With no thanks to France, who funded their rebellion."

I ate the parsnip, chewing it to the point of disintegration,
giving myself time to consider. "Would you have done differently?" I asked finally. "Than what my father did, I mean?"

"No," he replied. "But you are king now, Philip. And it is you who must accept the consequences of his actions."

"How so?"

"My sons were content, until your father taught them otherwise," Henry told me. There was no grief for their betrayal, in the cynical press of his lips—a whisper of a grimace, nothing more. He continued, "My second son, Richard, has lands upon your border. Aquitaine, greater in size than France itself."

"I know," I replied, frowning.

"It should trouble you. Have you not wondered where he is? He is a powerful lord. Should he not be at your coronation?"

"Yes, he should."

"But he is not," Henry said. "He is quarrelsome. He will not bow to you. Your father has fueled his discontent, and now we both must pay for it."

"It is no concern of mine if you quarrel with your son."

"It should be. Think of this as a warning, Philip. We both have land he might wish to claim. Which of us is the easier target?"

I shrugged. Henry's words were empty, we both knew that. It was him who cast his shadow across the Channel, even if it was Richard's land upon my western border. There would never be a genuine alliance between France and England, not as long as their rulers had heads on their shoulders and armies to lead. There was an ancient elm which stood directly upon the border, Normandy to its north, Vexin to its south; its neighbors' kings had met beneath its branches many times, and not once had they brokered a lasting peace. Our hostility had deep roots. The fickleness of princes did not change that.

And *still*, I thought, what threat could Richard truly pose? A prince who could not be bothered to make an appearance at a king's coronation, who allowed his father to speak ill of him unheeded; he seemed to me a foolish sort of man, to be so flippant with his reputation. But I knew I could not say this to Henry without seeming hopelessly naïve. Instead I simply sat there, little king, clutching my knife in my fist. I smiled thinly at him, widening my eyes in an affectation of innocence. "Thank you for the advice," I finally managed. It was something of a surrender, and he looked pleased.

Henry could be forgiven his smugness, sat beside a fourteen-year-old boy in his too-big crown. How ridiculous we must have looked to the others at the table, kings in contrast. *What makes a monarch?* I thought to myself, seeking comfort in the words, repeating them like a psalm. *Blood makes a monarch. There is glory in my veins.*

It is these words that have sustained me in the years that have followed. It has always held true; all kings bleed the same. Our family trees are as tangled and thorny as a briar patch. King of England, king of France; a pair of thrones in a tapestry of genealogies. It is impossible to unpick one thread without the entire thing coming apart. But on that day, as Henry sneered at me, the seed of a defiant idea found soil.

I could pick at those threads. I could cause the tapestry to unravel, and remake it in my own image.

I would let the map haunt me no longer. I would be a wise king, a great king. I would be a new Augustus.

Blood makes a monarch, I thought. *But glory is earned.*

CHAPTER TWO

Richard

When I was fifteen, I went to war.

Even at that age, battle was a joy. On the field, I felt a leviathan, all of those around me clinging to my ankles as I marched forward; sometimes they felt like weights around my feet, there to prevent me from striding. But the sense of magnitude I gained was worth the struggle, and so I fought not only willingly, but *gladly*, ravenous and unafraid. It was a rebellion against my father, waged alongside my brothers and the king of France. We demanded more power, more autonomy, more land. In truth, I cared little for the terms of our victory. That was my brothers' concern. They fought the battle for the battle's end. None of them knew the joy of it, as I did. No one else craved it.

What a sight I must have made, at the apex of my pride, unmarred by surrender. I had grown fast, I was taller and stronger and more furious than I had any right to be, more of a king than the king of England himself—and I wanted everything to be louder, faster, *greater* than what my father had. I wore livery in gold brighter than the sun. I drank wine from silver pitchers. I would dream of the swing of a sword; I spent all my waking hours listening for the song of it in the air. I found minstrels whose drums sounded like the march of infantry, men who sang ballads and built me into a legend, stone upon stone, battle upon battle, until everyone in France and England knew my name.

And yet we were losing. By the summer of that year, our surrender seemed almost assured. I found myself spending more time in the library than on the battlefield. It was an awful place, that French library, with its stink of vellum and moldy leather. King Louis would watch with an acerbic expression as I argued with my brother Geoffrey, who was younger than I and yet insisted on speaking to me as if I were a child. Meanwhile, Harry, the eldest of us, was as insipid as he ever was. He would lounge on a bench and do absolutely nothing productive, drumming his fingers on his thigh, his too-tight doublet warping over his chest. Really, who could be surprised that we lost? Too much time stabbing at maps and snapping at one another, and the English troops had us routed. We were left humiliated, forced to answer to a father who despised us, and who we despised in turn.

I might have tolerated surrender, even then. But our mother, who had supported the revolt, was imprisoned. This was the greatest blow of all. I had spent my childhood with her in Aquitaine, while my brothers and father remained in England. She had raised me, and her sudden removal from my life felt nothing less than an evisceration. My disappointment shifted to grief, and then to fury. I returned to my duchy, bruised and baying for retribution, but revenge had to give way to practicality. Until opportunity came, I would have to hide, and hide I did; I remained there, in Aquitaine, out of sight of my family. It was necessary, unavoidable, but it still felt like cowardice.

I needed to distract myself from my anger and my shame. So, I turned distraction into an art form: building myself a cult of chivalry, dancing from place to place with a court of minstrels. I was a poet, a knight, a lover, but not a soldier. I could never be a soldier, not while my father kept my mother in chains. Instead, my war was one of decadence. I wanted to wield my freedom like a lance. I wanted to be admired. I wanted everyone to know the Duke of Aquitaine, in all his virtue and depravity, basking in his liberty. See how his spirit remains unbroken! See the leviathan unbound!

Still, each moment of joy was tempered by fury. Each year I spent free, my mother spent another fettered; in my imagination, my father's image steadily grew more and more grotesque, a gargoyle peering at me from the buttresses. I wished to visit her in her confinement, but I could not stomach the thought of Henry waiting at the gates, grinning as he turned me away.

What I needed was an opportunity. I needed a chance to go to England when I knew my father would be unable to stop me. That chance came years later. Louis had given up. There was a new king in France, and Henry was unavoidably detained at the coronation. There would be no better time for it. For the first time in three years, I would see my mother again.

❧

I arrived at the fortress with only a small retinue. Our horses' hooves squelched in the wet grass as we approached the tower. The sky was grey, the gelding I was riding the same; England was devoid of color, as it always would be, night or day, winter or spring.

I hated this place. England was my father's country. Being there made me feel disoriented, unanchored. But I told myself seeing my mother would be worth the trip. In a family of vipers, she was the only one without venom in her bite.

I slipped off my mount, sinking into the mud, grinning at the guards upon the battlements. They stumbled about quite comically in response, baffled by my unexpected arrival. What were they to do? We all knew Henry would not want me here. But I was a prince, a duke in my own right. They could not defy me.

After several minutes of waiting, the gate was winched open. The others with me—about fifteen men in all—began to dismount. The first to approach was Stephen. His umber skin was glossed with the damp of the air, the clouds casting silver reflections on his cheeks. Now knighted, he was the highest-ranking man in the group apart from myself; the only one with the confidence to complain, and he did so immediately. "I assume you expect us to wait in this muck, Richard?" he asked, kicking at a puddle. A wet wind ruffled his black curls, as if to retaliate. "I do so enjoy the places you take us to."

I slapped him on the back, and he stumbled at the force. "Much suffering to you, my friend, soon to languish in the presence of my mother's ladies."

He grinned. "Eleanor keeps lovely company, that is true."

In the courtyard, the ladies had already come to greet us. They were dressed fashionably in the French style, their colorful silks too light for the weather, the bell sleeves of their gowns trailing the ground. At their head was Adelaide, a Poitevin by birth and a favorite of Eleanor's. Adelaide had always been indulgently beautiful, dark-haired and brown-skinned. When I had been younger, I had fancied myself quite in love with her. She flashed her green eyes at me, and I briefly wondered if I might love her again, but the impulse passed just as quickly as it came. I was not who I once had been, at my mother's court in Aquitaine, and neither was she. The years had changed us both. Sometimes I wondered if I was still capable of the devotion she had once inspired.

"My lord," she said, dropping into a neat curtsy. The other

ladies did the same, tittering at my men, who were doffing their caps with exaggerated deference. Once Adelaide rose, she continued, "Your mother awaits you inside."

"Lead the way," I replied. "I am certain the others can entertain themselves while we are gone."

Adelaide nodded, and I followed her into the bowels of the castle. The place felt neglected. The air was musty, the torches managing merely a half-hearted glow. They lit small green patches of the fabric of Adelaide's gown, the rest of her defined only by her silhouette and the measured movement of her footsteps. She led me to the second floor, where the damp was less persistent. The chill here was still enough to make me shiver as we passed through the corridors. There were no wall hangings to insulate the stonework.

"It has been a long time," I said to her, and she cast me a bashful glance over her shoulder.

"Three years," she agreed, her voice soft.

"You look well."

"As do you, my lord."

"As lovely as ever," I continued, and she smiled. "Even amongst this . . . squalor."

"We make do, my lord."

"My mother is a queen. She shouldn't have to 'make do.'"

"God willing, she will be released soon."

"God willing," I agreed.

Adelaide stopped in front of a large oak door and pushed it open, gesturing for me to enter. When I did so, she did not follow, and it shut behind me with a decisive click. Inside, my mother sat beside the fireplace, a book in her lap. She placed it upon the table and stood to greet me.

"Richard, dear heart," she said, opening her arms.

My mother was nearly sixty, still with all the striking beauty that had famed her across Christendom. She had aristocratic features, with high cheekbones and arched brows; she was tall, as I was, but that was where the resemblance ended. My coloring was my father's. Eleanor's looks—whip-thin, auburn hair, green eyes—had gone entirely to my brother Geoffrey. I had always been jealous over it.

Seeing her again, I found I was too moved to speak. I embraced her. She smelled of the lavender she kept dried by her bedside, and her grip was warm and familiar. When I pulled away, she sat down once more, spreading her skirts around her, lifting her chin imperiously. She gestured for me to join her.

Instead I crouched beside her, taking her hands in my own. I could feel them trembling. "Mother, are you well?" I said, alarmed.

"I am overwhelmed, Richard," she replied, "but I am in good health."

"Overwhelmed?"

"For years, I have not seen you, my dearest son. I had feared that I had lost you. That your father had turned you away from me."

"Never," I said, placing my forehead upon her knee. "Of course not, Mother. Every day, I pray that you will be released."

Her hand passed over my head, in a blessing. "It gladdens my heart to hear it. Now, sit. We have endured so long with only letters between us."

I sat opposite her. She examined me, assessing, and then she smiled. "You look strong," she said. "Healthy. I am glad."

"I hunt often. I eat well. The air is good in Aquitaine."

"It always is. You have timed your visit well, to avoid your father while he is in France. But surely you will be missed at the coronation?"

I shrugged. I was certain that Philip would manage without

me, *God-given* as he was. I had never spoken to the young king, or seen him for more than fleeting moments—he was kept away from my brothers and me, when we were at Louis's court—but on my journey to England, I had often wondered about him, now he was both anointed and unchallenged. His father was not yet dead, but so close to it that he had simply *offered* his son the entirety of his birthright, with no war nor brothers to worry about in the process. I was consumed with envy at the ease with which the crown had fallen upon this stranger's head. I did not regret missing the ceremony, not at all.

"Richard," Mother said, her tone disapproving, "if you are to play the game, you ought to play it well. There will be talk. Philip may be insulted."

"Philip is too young to be insulted."

She laughed. "On the contrary, boys his age find every opportunity to hold a grudge. How charming that you speak as if he is so much younger than you. He will be married within a year, and you have yet to make a match."

I flinched at this. "I will see him soon enough. I can apologize then."

"You underestimate him. He is king."

"You know Louis," I said. "You know what their family is like. What do I have to be afraid of?"

Her lips tightened in distaste. "Certainly, you should know better than to judge men by the quality of their fathers. And regardless of his character, you would do well to endear the king to you."

"How so? What need have I of him?"

"If you and your father quarrel again, you ought to fight one army, not two."

"France is a skeleton. Louis starved it dead."

She replied, "France is an ancient kingdom, and it has suffered more than this. Philip is better an ally than an enemy."

As always, I could do nothing but agree with her. "Perhaps," I said, but my tone made my reluctance clear.

Amused by my contrariness, she smirked, leaning back in her chair. "Now, tell me of your brothers."

I scowled. "Why? I have not seen them in months."

"Indulge me, Richard."

"Harry is much the same. Still a senseless dullard."

"Does he quarrel with your father?" she asked.

"As much as he is permitted," I said. "He has not the courage to cause serious trouble."

"And what of John?"

I had not met my youngest brother in years. "He is still father's pet, I assume."

"And dear Geoffrey?"

Even the mention of his name caused an instinctive sneer. "He is well enough."

"When did you last see him?"

"A year ago, in Anjou."

"He could be an asset to you," she said, "if you would allow him to be."

"I doubt that, Mother."

She sighed. "There will come a time when you have no choice, Richard. You will have to accept his help."

"I can find my own friends."

"Can you?" She leaned over, placing a hand on my arm. "I worry, dear heart. You are isolating yourself. For now, you are content to hunt in Aquitaine, to be young and merry. But your father does not trust you. Your land is my gift to you, and he has coveted it for years."

"I know that."

"Good. Remain cautious. Recklessness can ruin you." She turned towards the fire, sending shivering shadows across the walls of her prison. "I know that better than most."

She reached her hands out to warm them, her skin translucent and her lips pale from the chill. Fury coiled in my stomach.

"This is intolerable," I said. "Mother, return with me. I will take you home. I can keep you safe."

Her face softened. "Richard, I wish desperately that I could."

"You do not belong here. If not Aquitaine—the French court could offer you sanctuary—"

"With Louis still there? He would never allow it. Besides, it would be as good as declaring war upon your father." She shook her head. "Darling boy. I have always admired your bravery. But we both know how prone you are to rashness. Do not risk everything we have been working towards out of pity for me."

"I want to help you."

"You feel powerless, and that makes you angry. But you are not powerless, remember that. You are the grandson of an empress, the son of the king of England, and the Duke of Aquitaine in your own right. You have centuries of royal blood running through your veins."

"So does Harry, and Geoffrey, and John," I said. "So does Louis, and so does Philip. So does my father."

"But they are not Richard." She placed her hand on my chest, over my heart. "You were born to lead. I have known it since you first held a sword. The dynasty began with your father. But it is you who will make it great."

I embraced her again. "I am grateful for your faith in me, Mother. Always."

"Faith is important." She pulled away, tucking her hands in

her lap as they trembled. "In times like these, what else do we have?"

And so, we sat together in England, surrounded by the grey and the chill. Meanwhile, in France, Philip sat upon his throne, and the winter laid sheets of ice across the Channel. We built the fire higher and higher to keep the cold away.

I did not know, then, what would come to pass—how could I have? But sometimes I wonder what might have happened, had I gone to the coronation instead. My heart was such a wizened thing, so full of bile. Without the relief of my mother's forgiveness as it was granted to me that day, I might have spewed my vitriol across the altar as the king was anointed; I might have leapt across the nave and throttled my father where he stood. Thank the Lord I did not go. Thank the Lord I came to England instead, and found some measure of absolution.

~᪣~

As the afternoon darkened to evening, Mother's countenance lightened. After sunset, she gathered all of us into the great hall, where she had the fire stoked and the candles lit, coloring the entire room gold. We sat and drank French wine as my mother's ladies danced a rondel for us. Adelaide was singing the main refrain, spinning as prettily as a seed in the wind, her green skirts blooming around her.

"If you won't try it, I will," Stephen said. He glanced quickly at my mother to gauge if she could overhear. She did not react, but that was no guarantee that she was not listening.

I rolled my eyes at him. "I doubt Adelaide would come within a foot of you, Stephen."

"Why? Is she too high-blooded for a baron's son?"

"Too high-blooded for anything but the holy bonds of matrimony, I suspect."

"Or a duke," he muttered.

"Or a duke." I toasted him with my cup and took a sip, smirking. He huffed and looked back to the dance. Taking pity on him, I put my wine down, leaning my forearm on his shoulder. "Take heart," I said. "You are spoilt for choice. Should my mother's ladies fail you, the grounds are replete with washerwomen."

"And stable boys," he said.

"And stable boys," I replied, serene. "How kind of you to remind me."

Stephen snorted and opened his mouth to reply, but whatever he intended to say was cut short by the end of the song. We whistled our approval at the dancers as they finished. The servants arrived with the evening meal, and the ladies came to sit at the table.

Adelaide stopped across from us. She was still flushed from the exertion of the dance, and she dropped into a curtsy as pretty and precise as an embroidery stitch before sitting down. Stephen gave me an assessing look, but I made no move to converse with her. He immediately fell into flattery. The remainder of the meal was spent watching them trade shy glances, and I followed their flirtation with a dulled curiosity.

I stood from the table the moment my mother did, bending to kiss her cheek in farewell.

"Sit with me in the solar, Richard?" she asked, resting her hand on my arm.

"Tomorrow, perhaps. I thought to take some air in the courtyard."

"You will catch your death in this chill." Sighing, she dropped her hand to release me. "Good night, then."

"Good night, Mother," I said.

As I moved to leave, some of my men stood up to accompany me. I gestured for them to stay behind. They sat with little resistance; they were used to my solitary evening walks. Besides, my mother's ladies were still at the table.

Outside the cold was almost unbearable, of a grating intensity that provided immediate clarity. The air was damp and earthy, and breathing in was like taking a bite of the soil. I went to the back side of the tower. It was in much worse condition than the front. Patches of moss and frosted-over weeds crawled partway up the walls. The stonework itself was already showing patches of wear, despite having been built only two decades prior. I dragged my hand across one slab that was beginning to crumble; when I pulled it away, my fingertips were covered in black sediment.

That was when the clarity became unwelcome. I recalled how I had once thought myself a dragon slayer; how I had once gone to war convinced that I would tear my father's serpentine heart from his chest, and in doing so free myself and my mother from his clutches. But now, years later, that day had failed to come. Instead, the walls of this tower had grown taller and taller, and the insult of it had driven deeper and deeper, until it pained me as much as the imprisonment of my mother did.

Perhaps it was selfish of me, to resent my wounded pride as much as her suffering. But resent it I did. And as I stood there that night in England, I could feel that resentment staining my very soul, like the weathered stone before me, going black in the wind and the rain.

CHAPTER THREE

Philip

My father died when I was sixteen. I had been ruling for more than two years in my own right. His had been a second death, a death of body, long after his mind had gone. His last words to me were "God be with you." He had spoken them only hours before he died. I stood dry-eyed by his bed and knew it was the end. He was no longer a father by then, no longer a man. He was only a warning: failure made flesh.

After I left his side, I went to the library and sat by the fire, reading a book whose pages were blurred—not by tears, but by eyes pinched near shut with exhaustion, as I had not slept the night before. I stayed there, fingers tracing over the indents the quill had left on the page, until the door opened. The steward entered. He fell to his knees.

"My king," he said.

I looked at him kneeling before me, head bowed, and I knew what had happened. I found I could do nothing but laugh, in panic and regret.

I grieved Louis, of course; what son would not grieve his father? What subject would not grieve his king? I grieved his loss, and I grieved France's misfortune. My country, my burden, my inheritance: shackled now to a young boy who was scared and alone, who laughed at his father's death because he had never been taught how to weep.

Louis was gone, but his influence on my rule lingered. My vassals were petulant and quarrelsome, resistant to any edicts I tried to pass; they saw me as a failure's son before they saw me as their king, and they afforded me no more respect than they had my father. Furthermore, when I was a child, Louis had betrothed me to Isabella, the daughter of the Count of Hainault. In the eyes of God, and my vassals, Isabella and I were already considered husband and wife. Even once I was crowned, I was powerless to stop the wedding. I delayed the ceremony as long as I could, but by the time I was eighteen, I had to acquiesce to the demands of my council. Isabella came to Paris that September.

My new wife was taller than I was, though I was nearly five years her senior. She made no sound throughout the entire affair, save for a cold's sniffles. Her red curls had been braided with militant tightness against her scalp, and each time she frowned she winced in pain, which caused her to frown further, which caused her further pain; then her entire face would scrunch up like a finger that had been in the bath too long. She stood stooped over as the priest spoke, and she couldn't stop shaking, either; she shook throughout the entire Mass, and the feast afterwards, and when we were led into my bedroom and tucked under the covers. I would have shaken also if I were the sort to do so, but instead I held myself with such rigidity I might have shattered. I lay frozen beside her while the priest swung his censer over our heads like a flail. She flinched violently at the sound of the door closing behind him as he left. I could feel it from across the mattress.

Once we were alone, I sat up and blew out the candle by the

bed. I stayed seated instead of lying back down, my hands
clutching the sheet. All I could hear was Isabella's breathing,
coming faster and faster the longer I refused to move.

"Are you well?" I said to the darkness. The words were quiet—
too quiet for them to mean anything genuine.

"I am honored to be here," Isabella responded, so quickly it
sounded a single word.

"Thank you," I told her, and then winced at how stiff my voice
was.

"My lord, I am very young," she said.

"Yes, I—I know."

"I am very young," she continued. Her delivery was stilted, as
if she were reciting from memory. "It is my duty and honor to
bear you an heir. But as I am very young it would be impru-
impudent to risk a pregnancy because—because I am very
young. It would put the b-baby at risk."

I tried to look at her, but my eyes had yet to adjust to the
darkness. All I could see was a misshapen lump at the other end
of the bed, curled up to make itself as small as possible. "Did
your mother tell you to say that?"

"Yes, my lord."

"I know that you are very young," I said. "Everyone knows
that you are very young. I imagine that it isn't—it isn't expected
of us. Not yet."

"Y-yes, my lord," she stuttered.

There was a moment of utter silence. She must have been
holding her breath. "Are you afraid?" I asked her.

"Yes, my lord."

"I am sorry that you are afraid."

Isabella shifted, compacting herself smaller under the covers.
The entire room seemed to shrink with her. I extended a hand
across the mattress, intending to pat her on the shoulder, as I

sometimes had to comfort my sister; but I ended up pausing mid-reach, and I dropped my arm back to my side.

"I am tired," I said, lying down. As I pulled the covers up, I felt a cold hand brush over my elbow, and then withdraw reflexively, as if I were an open flame. I recoiled at the touch, turning my back to her. "I am tired," I repeated, "and I should like to go to sleep."

"My lord?"

"Sleep."

"Oh! Yes, I—thank you."

I wanted to thank her also. I thought to myself, with some amusement, that my father must have angered God somehow. Why else would he have produced a son who felt relief when his wife asked him not to touch her? For all the hair shirts and fasting, for all the terror and fury; the sum of his efforts now lay huddled on the edge of his marriage bed, flinching away from a thirteen-year-old girl. I could, at least, take some vindictive pleasure in his mistake—as I knew, of course, that there was a mistake there. Although my wife was young, her presence was a reminder of some absence within me, a slip in the hand of my creator that had carved away the *correctness*. It had replaced it with something I had yet to name.

Several minutes passed as I thought of this, and I was almost relieved when Isabella spoke again. She was whispering, her tone almost conspiratorial, as if she feared someone might overhear us and tell us off for talking. "Did you like your present, my lord?"

I huffed and turned to face her. "What?"

"Your—your present."

"Which one?"

"Um. The dog."

"Oh. The hound?" I asked.

She said, "Ye-es?" drawing out the word to several syllables.

After supper I had been presented with a puppy; sand-colored and lugubrious, with ears halfway down its neck and a nose like a ripe cherry. "Yes, I did like him," I said. "Thank you. Pardon, I did not thank you earlier."

"There were many presents."

"There were."

"What will you name him?"

There was something in the trepidation of her tone that made me pause. "Have you named him already?"

"I have been calling him Galahad," she mumbled. Beneath the blankets, she wriggled her feet back and forth, as if she were trying to swim in the bed. "I like Galahad. The knight, I mean. In the stories."

"I like him also."

"Is he your favorite? He is my favorite, and my mother's favorite. He is the greatest knight that has ever lived. Even Arthur said so."

"My favorite is Gawain, actually."

"Gawain," she repeated, scandalized. "You can hardly name him *Gawain*. His name is *Galahad*."

"Very well. We shall call him Galahad, then."

"Good," she whispered, and she yawned.

"We ought to sleep."

"Yes, my lord."

"Then—good night, Isabella."

"Good night, my lord."

I turned away once more, so that our backs were facing each other. I could hear her fidgeting with the sheets, her breathing loud and stilted. Several minutes of this passed.

"You cannot sleep?" I said, exasperated.

"Pardon, my lord."

"Call me Philip," I told her. And at that moment I realized that no one else did, now that my mother and my sisters had left Paris. So, I continued, "Please."

"Pardon, my—Philip. It is only that . . . my mother always read to me before bed."

The idea of this—that someone might sit with their child every evening until they fell asleep—seemed so outlandish that it caused me to lapse into silence.

"M-my lord?" Isabella asked.

"What did your mother read to you?"

"The Bible," she said. "Romances, sometimes. And she has been reading me *The Aeneid*. But we never finished it. Do you know of it?"

"I know it. I had to memorize it for lessons."

"Really? Do you remember it?"

"Some," I replied.

"Do you like it?"

"Yes. Where were you, in the story?"

"Aeneas was entering the underworld," she said, with hushed excitement.

I knew that section well, and I murmured a line of it to the ceiling, gauging her reaction. Isabella shuffled towards me to listen, so I continued. Every so often, she would interrupt to ask about a Latin word she did not know; otherwise, she was the most attentive audience I had ever had.

As time passed, her breaths became deeper and deeper, until they were slow and steady. My recitation fell quiet. I felt a bone-deep relief.

───── ୨୧ ─────

Eventually, I slipped out of the bed. I was unaccustomed to having another body beside me, and there was something disarming about my new wife's vulnerability as she slept. Feeling restless and unwelcome, I pulled a robe over my nightclothes and left the bedchamber, thinking to visit the kennels.

When I came into the outer rooms, I was surprised to find that only one servant was present, warming himself in front of the fire.

"Where are the others?" I asked him. My entry was silent enough that he jumped in surprise, nearly falling off his stool. He stood and bowed.

"Ah—preparing rooms for our visitor, my liege."

"Visitor? What visitor?"

"The Duke of Aquitaine."

"The Duke of Aquitaine," I repeated, incredulous. "Why wasn't I told he had come?"

"The steward said you were not to be disturbed, my liege. The duke only just arrived."

"I should have been informed immediately," I said, coldly, to the horror of the servant, who was unable to respond with anything but half-mumbled apologies. "Where is the duke now?" I asked.

"I believe he is still in the southern courtyard, my liege."

I swept past him, the movement of my robe causing the flames to sputter at the hearth. As I marched down the hallway, I saw several people carrying sheets and firewood towards the guest lodgings, all stopping to bow as I passed; I paid them no mind, and once I was outside, I began to make my way towards the courtyard. The journey was eased by the clear sky, the moon lighting the path, but at this time of night the chill was such that I regretted not retrieving a cloak. I began to shiver, so I took the time to stop and force myself to still before continuing. A king should not be seen trembling.

Guillaume, my steward, came to meet me as I was walking.

"My liege," he said, struggling to keep up with my brutal pace. His long, thinning hair fluttered weakly in the breeze. "I was told that you were awake—"

"Yes, and most fortuitous it is that I am, considering that one of the most powerful men in Europe has appeared at my gates. Why was I not told?"

"My liege, it is your wedding night," he replied.

"Guillaume, I am expected to sleep with my wife every evening. An audience with the Duke of Aquitaine is rather less frequent." I turned the full force of my scowl upon him. "In future, I am to be informed of important arrivals the moment they occur. Understood?"

"Yes, my liege."

"Excellent. You are dismissed, then."

"But—"

"You are dismissed," I said. "Is the duke still in the court-yard?"

"I believe he is approaching, my liege, in the direction of the guest rooms."

I quickened my pace, leaving Guillaume behind. I came to a halt as soon as I saw a group of torches farther down the path, pulling my robe across my chest with the grim determination of a jouster buckling his breastplate.

It was an exercise in futility, trying to look imperious, half dressed and still shivering from the cold. But what else was I to do? Considering who the duke was, who he one day could be, I had no choice. He was a stranger, admittedly; I had seen only glances of him when he was at court years ago, during his rebellion. I had never once spoken to him. But still, I knew of him, as everyone did. He was Richard the Lionheart, already granted the name for a battlefield ferocity somewhere between cruelty and magnificence. No one trusted his truce with his father. No one trusted his peace with me, the king at his border, whom he had never visited nor acknowledged. Richard was a problem, a tool, a contingency. For this reason, I had planned for this meeting many times over. An arrival at this time of night seemed odd for such politics, but I was prepared. I had to be.

"My Lord Aquitaine," I said, loudly, as he approached. The duke was easy to identify. Tallest of all of them, he led the group by several paces, dressed in his duchy's red livery. He stopped, turned back to one of his companions, and said something inaudible. At the response, the duke stiffened and took a step forward. Even as he came closer it was difficult to distinguish his features, the light too dim to do so. I could see the harsh line of a jaw, a red-blond curl at the nape of a neck.

"My liege," he said amiably, his voice clear and confident.

I felt a stab of annoyance at his easy tone. I shuffled my feet, slippers suffering in the dirt. "What brings you to Paris?" I asked.

"I am journeying to Rouen," he replied, "and we required lodging. Besides, congratulations are in order, surely?"

"If you are here for the wedding, you have avoided the ceremony."

"What a shame."

"Your absence was widely commented on," I said.

"It is good to know I was missed."

"Indeed," I replied, and I cleared my throat. I had been expecting a lack of deference, but still his manner disquieted me; he spoke very quickly and effortlessly, as if the conversation was merely a diversion. It gave me little time to formulate my responses, or to assess his intentions.

"Shall we enter?" the duke asked, inspecting my clothing with a critical eye. "You must be cold."

I scowled, but he breezed past me without further thought, and I was forced to follow him as he continued down the path.

His pace was swift: not hurried, but still purposeful. We soon pulled ahead of the others.

"I am sorry we interrupted your wedding night, my liege," he said. "I had expected you would greet me in the morning."

"Will you be staying long?"

"Only until tomorrow. I am running late as it is."

"Why do you continue to Rouen?"

"I am meeting with my father."

"Was your journey pleasant?"

"Are we to make small talk all evening?" he asked.

"In Paris, we make a point of being polite."

Amused, he replied, "In Aquitaine, we only ask questions we require the answer to."

"Well—" I choked, and then I swallowed my frustration. "*Regardless,* it would be good of you to stay for longer."

"Why?"

"You have avoided court for years, and we have much to discuss. Surely, that much is obvious? I thought you only asked questions you required the answer to."

He laughed. "Pardon. I had assumed you would wish to avoid such distractions, so soon after your marriage."

"Hardly," I said. "Matters of state must take precedence."

"Is that so," he murmured. He had a low voice, and when it went quiet, it approached a growl.

We approached the entrance of the castle. The torches on the walls strengthened the light. I looked up at him, in order to examine him properly. He had his father's Norman coloring: fair hair, brown eyes. His features were asymmetrical, right cheekbone scarred, ears too large for his face. But that did not seem to matter, for he had the immediate and arresting appearance of someone utterly confident in his own attractiveness. I felt entirely bewildered by the strength of his skull beneath his skin, the force of the furrows in his brow. My own presence felt piti-fully small.

He noticed my examination, and he smirked at me in re-sponse. His eyes held mine instead of moving back towards the path. I opened my mouth to speak, but my mind had become strangely silent. It was as if the duke had wiped it clean of thoughts, as one would condensation from a pane of glass; the sounds of the night grew louder—the distant rustle of trees, the gust of the wind, our footsteps trading echoes—and it felt to me, suddenly, that we were alone. That I was at the mercy of this stranger, isolated with him, in an empty courtyard of an empty castle, with only each other for company.

"I—well—" I said, disturbed. "It—it is not relevant."

"What isn't?" he replied. We stopped in front of the doorway, the others yet to catch up. Neither of us made any move to enter.

"My marriage," I said. "It is not relevant to what we need to discuss."

"What do we need to discuss?"

"Your intentions."

"My intentions?"

"How you mean to govern."

"Oh, *that*," he said. "By that you mean, am I going to war against my father?"

"Yes," I said. "Or myself."

He grinned at me. "I am recovering, still, from my last con-flict. I had to clean up a revolt in Périgord—a revolt which was your fault, by the way. I know your men gave money to the reb-els. But—ah, no, you mustn't look at me like that, my liege. Never fear, I have forgiven you already."

The revolt had been funded by Blois, actually, without my consent; it was a sound strategy to support the rebellion, and I'd have helped him, had he asked, but he had not. The duke did not need to know that, of course. No need to give him cause to doubt my grip on the throne. "I did not ask for your forgiveness," I said to him.

"And yet you have it. Surely you should be grateful?"

"I shall be *grateful* when the king of England is not breathing down my neck."

He laughed. "Then you will only be grateful once he is dead."

"But there shall be a king of England still," I observed. "So perhaps, not even then."

"Perhaps," he agreed.

The servants finally reached us, most of them carrying baggage. I stepped away from the door to leave them room to enter. The duke opened his mouth to say something further, and I lifted my hand to stop him. He stared at my raised palm with bewildered amusement. "Shall we have a *constructive* discussion this evening," I said, "or are you here merely to be a nuisance?"

"I suppose that depends on what you mean by *constructive*."

"Why stop in Paris at all, my Lord Aquitaine? We both know there are other places to stay."

"Perhaps I finally wanted to see you in person," he said. "You are king, after all."

"Now you have seen me. Are you satisfied?"

"I should say so."

Instead of replying, I took a step forward to look at him more closely. He raised his eyebrows, but he did not react apart from squaring his shoulders, exaggerating his height over me. He was broad in build; if I wrapped my hands around his neck, I doubted that my fingers would meet. Perhaps I ought to have been threatened by that, but there was something pleasant in how outwardly his power was displayed. There was so little artifice in the slapdash scatter of the stubble on his jaw, the deep furrows of his brow, the harsh square of his chin. His was not a face made for deception. As I watched him, I maintained a passive expression, and we each remained in silence, waiting for the other to display some discomfort. I felt like Canute standing on the shore, ordering the tide to halt.

Eventually, he glanced away. I noticed the network of veins surrounding his pupils, inflamed from exhaustion. The duke was less at ease than he first appeared, and his surrender made me content to stand down. "Will you take wine before bed?" I asked him.

He bowed his head in a parody of courtesy. "If you would be so kind."

I took him the long route to the guest rooms. It forced him to follow me through several of the best corridors, the ones my father had not emptied of their opulence. If he was impressed by the lodgings, he did not show it. His step was so much heavier than mine—so much less inclined to silence—that anyone listening to us pass must have assumed the duke alone walked through the halls. Every so often, I would glance sideways at him, and he would always meet my eye readily; he kept his hands folded behind his back, his pace measured, like a general wandering through an army camp.

The fire in the sitting room had been stoked to blazing. I poured myself some of the wine that had been left for him, and I settled into a chair. He did the same opposite me, staring at me with casual curiosity, as if I were an interesting illustration on a manuscript.

"I missed your coronation," he said. "Years ago. I never apologized for it."

"Will you apologize now?" I asked.

"Do you wish me to? It seems a pointless gesture."

Bemused by his bluntness, I shook my head, taking a sip of

my wine. "You said you are going to Rouen to speak with your father?"

He sighed. "Yes. We are to have an argument."

"Oh?"

"He wants me to swear fealty to Harry—my older brother. He would have me fall to my knees and pledge my allegiance to him in front of the court."

"Why?"

"To show submission. To acknowledge England's authority. But I will not do it, and my father knows that."

I frowned. "Is your brother not a king already?" I asked. "Why must you prove this further?"

He shrugged. "They call him a *junior* king, actually. Imagine that! In England we have two kings, a big one and a little one. Henry and Harry." As he spoke, he illustrated with his hands, causing his wine to slosh dangerously in its cup. "I never know which one I ought to answer to."

"It seems that you answer to neither of them, my lord."

"Yes, that is a fair assessment. And Henry knows that; he starts these arguments only to spite me. He isn't particularly fond of me, I'm afraid." He smiled at me over the rim of his cup, eyes glittering. "Still sore about the rebellion, I suppose."

"And your brother? Harry? He insists you swear fealty also?"

"Hm. Only because my father does." He sighed. "You are lucky for your lack of brothers, I think. They are about as dangerous as the pox, and twice as difficult to get rid of."

I almost laughed at that, and I cleared my throat. The deflection failed; he noticed my amusement, and his smile widened. He leaned forward in the chair, resting his chin on his fist. "You ought to call me Richard, I think," he said. "Let's be finished with all this *lord* and *liege*ing. I shall call you Philip, in return."

"Shall you?"

"Why not? It will save time."

"I am not in a hurry," I replied.

He laughed. "You remind me of your father. I called him Louis, once, and he looked as if I had pissed in his pottage."

"I am *not* like my father," I replied, and my tone was sullen enough that I felt a flush of embarrassment. I turned my eyes towards the fire. A spark leapt from the flames, mocking me for the outburst.

"There are some similarities," Richard said.

I looked back at him, galled. His lips were curved slightly upwards. It was not quite a smile, but a promise of one; it threatened to slip into another laugh at any moment. His pleasure at my annoyance only served to make me more frustrated.

"You are . . . courting me, hoping to turn me against my family," he continued. "Your father did so also."

"Only because it is a good strategy. If you were in my position, you would do the same."

"And if you were in my position, Philip? What would you do?"

"That depends."

"On what?" he asked.

"On what my intentions were."

"Ah, intentions again," he said.

He was testing my patience. "Why did you come to Paris?" I demanded. "Why are you here, when you might have stopped anywhere else?"

"You already asked me that."

"You did not answer."

"I suppose that is true," he said. "Why don't you tell me? As you seem to think you know the answer already."

"Fine," I snapped, and he *laughed* again, delighted, as if my irritation were charming. "I shall list the possible reasons, then; since you are apparently unable to."

"Please, enlighten me."

I began ticking off on my fingers. "The first is that you wish to make a request of me; the second is that you expect me to make a request of you; the third, as absurd as it may be, is that you are here for no reason but curiosity. But if this were the case—if you were really so *curious* as to come uninvited—then your delay is inexplicable."

"Is it?"

"Yes," I said. "Why wait years to meet me? Perhaps you are lazy, or a fool. But I doubt that either is the case."

"You flatter me."

I chose to ignore that, and continued, "You are in a comfortable position, as it stands. As comfortable as your position can be. Your father, as much as he dislikes your hold on Aquitaine, has been busy with scuffles in England. Your reign remains stable. You might wish to begin another rebellion, but without your mother to engineer an alliance with your brothers, you have neither the troops nor the opportunity. My help alone would not amend this."

"So . . ." he prompted.

"So, you came because you wanted *me* to want something from *you*," I told him. "As ludicrous as that sounds. You thought that I, cowed by your success against a rebellion I funded, might wish to simper to you and request a formal alliance. You thought you might come here, extract from me an apology, and put me in your debt. You thought that I feared you."

Richard leaned back in his seat, his posture relaxed. "Is that so surprising?" he asked. "Louis feared me. My lands rival your own."

"I am not afraid of you, Richard."

"And why is that?"

"Because I know what it is like to hate your father," I said. "I know that you are no threat to me, because I know what Henry has done. I know the lengths you will go to, to amend it. I know it is *he* who should fear you, not I."

Richard was too stunned to respond. His brow furrowed as he stared at me, jaw clenching. Meanwhile, I hid my smile in my cup; finally, my move had been made. Whatever strange discomfort it was that had settled during our conversation, the triumph of this sudden shift had erased it entirely. I now held control.

When the silence stretched too thin, I prompted, "He has wronged you."

Richard groaned. His frown became a scowl. "Henry keeps my mother like a criminal," he said. "Until we are at arms, I can do nothing to release her."

"I will not start a war for your sake. Not until you have something to offer."

"Yes, *that* much is obvious," he replied.

"I am a king. I must act on France's behalf, not yours. Do not resent me for ruling."

Richard huffed and took a sip from his cup. Around the stem, his fingers whitened with the tightness of his grip. His eyes met mine, narrowed, thoughtful, and his lips pursed. I noticed that the corners of his mouth were flushed red with wine. Feeling suddenly disoriented, I looked down to my own glass, but it was empty.

"I thought not to only hear your apologies, Philip, when I came here," he said. "There was curiosity also."

"Curiosity?"

"I wanted to meet you at least once, before my brothers or my father got an alliance out of you."

"Was it worth the trouble?" I asked.

"Certainly. To think, I had feared you might be *dull*." His eyes trailed languidly over my face, from my hairline to my jaw; a cataloguing, exploratory sort of gaze, one that felt almost violating. "I thought you might be tedious, as your father was. But you are not."

"What am I, then? If not dull?"

"I do not know," he replied. "A contradiction. An enemy, an ally. A question and an answer."

I did not know how to respond to that. I watched him warily, empty cup balanced precariously on the arm of my chair, fire spluttering in its last gasp of life; all was tentative—unbalanced—and though uncertain of what I intended to say, I opened my mouth to speak. But the words caught in my throat, as a sudden wave of exhaustion hit me, and I had to snap my mouth shut to suppress a yawn.

Richard must have noticed the clenching of my jaw. "It is late," he said, "and I have kept you from sleeping. I did not realize."

"There is time to sleep yet."

"Is your new bride not bereft, without you in her bed?"

"I doubt she will notice."

Richard chuckled at that, much to my chagrin. He stood up. "Even if I cannot compel you to bed," he said, "I must sleep regardless. We leave at dawn."

"So soon?"

"You have given me much to consider." Seeing my dissatisfied expression, he added, "Perhaps I shall return, on the journey back from Rouen. If you would have me, of course."

"Of course," I echoed. My gaze slid away from him, back to the last dregs of the fire. "Safe travels."

"Good night, Philip."

"Good night, Richard."

I kept my eyes on the hearth as he turned away, and I did so until the door closed, focusing instead on the slow pulsing of light beneath the embers. Richard left silence behind him, but I could still hear his movements inside the other room. It is laughable, how intently I listened. I heard the interminable back-and-forth of his footsteps, the repetitive swing of a cupboard door. I was too fixated upon it. I was too fixated upon *him*. I knew that I was. But, drowning out that accusatory whisper, the triumph of memory remained. I remembered the hint of a grimace on Richard's lips as he told me, *Henry keeps my mother like a criminal*. It was the same expression as his father's had been at my coronation: the Angevin sneer. For them, it was a moment of weakness, betraying their resentment. For me, it was the promise of opportunity.

I waited for Richard's movements to stop, but there was a restlessness about him that he maintained even in private. It is unlikely he ever went to sleep at all; eventually I had to return to Isabella, and my own bed. When I woke up the next morning, he had gone.

CHAPTER FOUR

Richard

The meeting with Henry in Rouen went badly.

There had never been much chance of it going well; I had known that before I left Aquitaine. Still, my father and I had spoken for less than an hour before the fury between us had cracked its whip and sent us bolting away from each other. It had been a spectacular failure, on both our parts. Each time we met, we tolerated each other less. Soon no words would pass between us but those spoken by swords.

At least my retinue was now making its return earlier than expected: towards Aquitaine and home. The journey south was usually a simple one, but that autumn was wet and cold and grim, and it did its level best to slow us down. The more progress we made, the more the horses sank as they walked, and the more the sky gathered the clouds so low they seemed likely to fall.

"It will rain again," Stephen said, as his palfrey picked its way along the track. A leaf still wet with yesterday's shower bowed over him and dropped a fat, baptismal drop of water directly upon his head. I chuckled while he shook himself, doglike, in disgust. He continued, "We might have stayed in Rouen longer."

"We might have," I agreed. "We were hardly in a rush, since my father did us the favor of leaving early."

"You say that as if he left by choice, and you did not force him into such a rage that he started *spitting blood*."

Remembering it—remembering Henry hacking scarlet into his kerchief—brought a dizzying moment of vindictive satisfaction. I did not feel ashamed by my pleasure, although perhaps I should have. "He has always had a sensitive stomach," I said to Stephen. "He gets ulcers every second week. It is hardly an achievement."

"Such humility!"

"I am Sir Richard, the virtuous, after all," I said, laying a hand over my breast, "famed for his temperance and his modesty; knight of valor, champion of the faith, slayer of fathers, ravisher of fair maidens and stable boys, et cetera."

"Charlemagne bows before him," Stephen said, his voice flat. Then he sighed. "We might at least lodge in Paris again. Everyone is exhausted."

"We can't lodge in Paris again. It is only a little farther to Montlhéry. No more complaints."

"But *why*?" he asked. "Was the king really that awful?"

"I am afraid of him."

"Pardon?"

"I am afraid of Philip," I said. "He was terrifying."

Stephen laughed. "*You* are terrified?" he repeated. "Of *him*?"

I could understand his derision. I hadn't recognized Philip at first, when he had stumbled down the path towards us in his bedclothes. I had turned to Stephen and asked if he knew who he was—*That is the king, I believe,* he'd said. The king! It seemed absurd that this wisp of a man, half dressed and half asleep, should be a ruler of any sort. Philip hardly seemed to have any presence at all, fading into the cobblestones. When he came into the light of the torches, he looked a slender, uncertain sort of creature, as slight and skittish as a finch. He was pale and dark-haired, with wide, solemn eyes; his features were delicate, apart from a prominent, aquiline nose that made the rest of him seem frailer by comparison. He was rather lovely, yes, if one were so inclined—which, admittedly, I was—but he also seemed exactly as his father had been: small, insipid, and easily led.

As such, I had been quite unprepared for the resistance my examination would meet. Philip had a mind like a scalpel, and he wielded it with all the brutality such an instrument required. In one conversation, he had stripped me raw. He had cut away the bluster to show the bitterness beneath. I resented and admired it in equal measure.

I told Stephen, "He was—quicker, than I had expected him to be," in a response so entirely inadequate that he laughed at me.

"Quicker," he echoed.

"Yes, he is quick. Smart. *Intelligent,* Stephen. It was unexpected. I thought it better to return once I have something to offer him."

"Something to offer him? Like what?"

"Oh, I don't know. Land? Loyalty?" A raindrop slid down my cheek, and I glanced to the sky. "My father's head on a pike?"

"Will he side with you, do you think?" Stephen asked. "If it comes to war again?"

"I can't be certain." There came a slow roll of thunder, and another raindrop. Stephen groaned. I ignored him. "He is further inclined to me than Henry, I believe. Or—he is very good at convincing me that he is."

"He sounds—" Stephen said, but he was interrupted by something snarling a hair's breadth beside my ear. I ducked instinctively, pulling my horse up short, and I heard the portentous clunk of an arrow hitting the tree trunk behind me.

Stephen, despite his posturing, had not secured his position for lack of competency. It took mere moments for him to see the plume of the arrow protruding from the bark. Stephen pulled his horse up short and hollered "An archer! Protect the duke!" to the others. He spoke with enough volume that a blackbird was sent tumbling into the sky above us. The group formation was quickly broken as those behind us surged forward, some breaking away in pursuit of the assailant.

Who? I thought wildly, and names began to process like pageant players—*Henry, Harry, Geoffrey, Philip*—there were so many with the means and motive to see me dead. Such as it had always been, since the moment of my birth. It was surprising, really, that something such as this had not come sooner. This was the price for my lack of caution, and it seemed one exceedingly dear; for if the arrow had struck, and I was to fall, what was to remain? What would I have left behind, except a corpse buried in wet leaves, and the thunder, and the beginning of the rain?

But panic lasted only briefly. Then I let the reality of it fade, and instead there was the surge of savage joy that came to me in times of danger. I ducked once more, tilted, and dismounted to the forest floor. My boots sank into the ground with an unpleasant squelch. It was the sort of sound that made me think of English bogs, the smell of peat, the rotting walls of my father's castles.

"It *is* troublesome, traveling this time of year," I said, grinning, heart thundering with the sky. I turned to look at the arrow embedded in the tree, approaching to inspect it more closely.

Stephen had been peering around the trees, following the progress of the soldiers in pursuit. When I began to move, he lowered his head to look at me, as did the rest of my men. "Richard, get back here—*Richard,*" he hissed, but I was now beside the tree. I pulled the arrow out as gently as I could, in order to keep

the shaft intact. It took some strain, but eventually I held it in
my hands. It was plumed with white goose feathers, crudely
made, iron head curved and broad.

"A hunting arrow," I said.

"What?"

"It is a hunting arrow."

I waved it in the air at them, and then I turned it around and
jabbed its blunt tip into my palm. The youngest of us, Bernard,
flinched as I did so; he was the fifteen-year-old son of a baron,
with a sparse patch of hair on his upper lip. As the sharp end of
the arrow dug into my skin, the half-moustache warped with his
grimace. "Oh *dear*," he warbled, shifting in his saddle.

Stephen turned to stare at him with an expression of supreme
distaste. Precluding an argument, I said again, "A hunting arrow."
And I laughed. "For deer or boar, it seems. A rather awful one,
too."

"It still might've wounded you," Stephen replied, ducking his
head as the rain began to fall more heavily.

"It might have. But what assassin uses an arrow like this?"

"One that would have it seem an accident."

"It is more likely to bruise than kill. It is duller than you are,
Stephen."

He snorted. "The relevant issue is that someone would attempt to murder you, not that they are doing so *badly*—"

"Why, certainly it is relevant," I said. "I am worthy of a crossbow, at the very least."

He opened his mouth, no doubt to insult me, and then a hol-
ler came from the trees. Stephen's shoulders relaxed. "They have
caught him," he informed me, as if I could not already tell.
"Please get back on your horse, and stop being awful."

I tossed him the arrow, and he nearly fell out of his seat trying
to catch it. Instead of remounting, however, I walked forward to

stand in front of the horses. Three of my men appeared soon after, dragging between them a boy of perhaps thirteen or fourteen years old. He had a quiver at his back, and he wore the undyed wools of a peasant. He looked about ready to soil himself.

"Oh, I see," I said in a paradoxical rush of disappointment and relief. The boy was thrown at my feet, falling with the grace of a sack of stones. One of the men tossed a hunting bow to the ground beside him.

"Poaching, are we?" I asked, and the boy looked up at me. His face was grubby, streaked with tears, snub-nosed and unremarkable.

He let out a stream of panicked French in response—at least, I presumed it was French, since we were still in French territory. His dialect was so far from anything heard at court that it was impossible to decipher, particularly at the speed with which he was speaking. "I do not understand you," I said. "Speak slower. Do you understand me?"

He paused, and then he nodded.

"Do you know who I am?"

He looked at my clothes, and the livery on our horses. He said, very slowly, "A knight?"

It was not an unfair assumption. "Yes," I said, because it seemed much simpler to do so. "These lands are a reserve of Count Theobald. Did you know that?"

"No, my lord, upon the Virgin and the saints I—" was all I managed to catch before he dissolved into formless blubbering.

"Right." I looked up at my men, in vain hope that one of them might be able to understand him. They all seemed mystified. I turned to the boy once more. "Right. Look. Is this your arrow?"

Stephen brandished the arrow at him. The boy shook his head no.

I rolled my eyes. "You are wearing a quiver, and there are three identical arrows inside it."

His lip wobbled, but he did not reply.

"You almost killed me. Do you understand?" I sighed when he remained silent. "You are poaching also. What is the penalty for poaching in this area?"

I asked the second question to my men, but it was the boy who responded, lifting his left hand. His smallest finger had been removed at the joint. "Mercy," he whispered. "I beg, sire."

"They will hardly be so lenient again, if we turn him in," Stephen said. "Take his weapon and be done with it. He is likely to go hungry, that is punishment enough."

I scowled. "And the next time he shoots a man in the throat, we shall have his blood on our hands."

"Richard—"

There was another roll of thunder, and the boy flinched. Despite the noise, the rain was still perfunctory at best. I raised my hand to silence Stephen, and I gestured to the boy to stand up. He did so, staring at his boots.

"What is your name?" I asked him.

"Richard, sire," he mumbled.

I chuckled at that, which only seemed to make him more afraid. "Had you killed me, Richard," I said, "you would have been put to death. We could very easily put you to death regardless."

"Please—please, *mercy*, sire."

"This is not simply poaching. This is a well-used trail. You know that as well as I."

"Please, mercy." He took a trembling step forward, and then he stumbled on the uneven ground, falling to his knees. One of the men behind him put his hand on his sword hilt—perhaps in response to the boy's movements, or perhaps preparing for my order.

I remembered, suddenly, Philip's face in the firelight as he had said *I am not like my father*. He had not bothered, afterwards, to ask if I was like mine; perhaps the answer had been clear enough already. We looked enough alike, and I had enough of Henry's malice, that I doubt I could have denied it. But it occurred to me then, looming over this other Richard on his knees, that I had created a sort of malignant court—even if only momentarily—that rivaled any in England. I stood ready to judge this boy, in vile mimicry of how my father judged me.

I did not have the stomach for it. I turned away. "Release him," I said, and I approached my horse. Behind me I could hear the boy gasping, as if my attention had been drowning him and he had now reached the air; Stephen offered me a searching look, but he said nothing until I mounted. By then, the men had tugged the boy back to standing. They pushed him away, and he half ran, half crawled back into the woods.

"I feared you would have him killed," Stephen said.

"Do I seem capable of doing that?"

"I do not think so. At least, I hope not."

"I also hope not. I wish to be merciful."

"You were merciful."

"I know," I said. "But I wish—I wish I had found it easy. I wish I found it easy to be kind."

"Does it matter if it is easy? You have been kind. Is that not what matters?"

"Yes, perhaps. I hope I continue to manage it. Kindness is a virtue, after all." I spurred my horse forward, and he followed. Attempting levity, I said, "Let the Lord strike me with an arrow, should I ever stray."

Stephen cast a nervous glance to the sky; whether it was aimed towards the thunder, rain, or heaven itself, there was no way of knowing. "You are a good man, Richard," he said, perhaps for his own comfort more than mine, and it seemed something to which I could not respond. So, I fell silent, and we continued untroubled as we passed the edges of Paris.

~⤸~

We soon reached the manor at Montlhéry, and it was evident that my plan to avoid Philip had failed quite spectacularly.

"Brilliant," Stephen said, peering at the tangled mass of horses and baggage at the entrance. "You are a master strategist, indeed. That *is* the royal heraldry, is it not, Richard?"

"Yes, Stephen, it is," I said.

"So, the king is here, then. Shall we run away?"

I did not service him with a reply. Instead, I dismounted my horse and straightened my clothing, running my fingers through my damp hair. I pointed to an empty patch of courtyard, where the morning rain had left a large, despondent puddle. "Wait there with the others," I said. "Do *nothing* until I retrieve you."

He made a rude gesture at me. I ignored it, approaching the royal servants. "Excuse me," I said to one boy, who was fiddling with a pile of rolled-up linens. "Are you packing, or unpacking?"

"Packing," he replied distractedly, and then he turned to see me properly. Noticing my clothing and my retinue behind me, his eyes widened. "—my lord."

"Do you know where the king is?" I asked.

"I—no. But he might." He pointed to another man across the courtyard; he was older, clothes severely tailored, face stern. He was watching over the proceedings with impressive contempt, tapping his foot in an immaculate rhythm against the cobblestones. "That is the steward, my lord."

"Right," I replied, clapping the boy on the shoulder. He cowered as if I had made to slap him.

I walked purposefully across the courtyard towards the steward. The man seemed to recognize me immediately, and he bowed. "My Lord Aquitaine," he said; his voice was thin, somehow both obsequious and scornful. "We were not expecting your arrival."

"I was not expecting you to be here when I arrived," I replied.

"The king makes progress to Blois. We leave imminently."

"I would speak with him. Where is he?"

"He is taking the air in the gardens, my lord. He wishes not to be disturbed. We are to fetch him when we are prepared to leave—if you wish to meet with him you ought to—"

"I will find him," I said.

"But—"

"Thank you very much for your help, er—"

"Sir Guillaume."

"Sir Guillaume. Excellent work." I saluted him and retraced my steps, back to where my men were standing by the courtyard wall.

"How do I get into the gardens?" I asked Stephen.

"How in God's name would I know?"

"I think it is through that gate," Bernard said. "Over there. But it is locked. If you went through the house—"

"If I went through the house, I would have to speak with the lord of the manor."

Stephen frowned. "You shall speak with him anyway, Richard, if we are to stay here tonight as you planned."

"I hardly have time for that," I replied. "Philip might leave while I am distracted."

"I thought we were avoiding Philip."

"We *were*. But now we have come across him entirely by chance."

"What difference does that make?" he asked.

I shrugged. I had never been one, particularly, for superstition. And yet a lifetime of poetry and romances in Aquitaine had made its mark. There seemed something lyrical in this coincidence. It would be such a *shame* if I did not surrender to it.

"He will discover our presence, regardless," I said. "And besides, I . . ."

"You what?"

"I am curious," I said. "Help me up. It isn't very high."

"You will break an ankle, Richard."

"Preferable to spending more time with you, certainly."

"Arse," Stephen replied. But, sighing, he complied, pushing me up so that I could scramble over the wall.

I managed to land with a minimum of fuss on the other side. I found myself in a small herb garden. Although reduced by the season, it was still clearly the pride of the manor: plots and trellises were arranged with mathematical precision, and stone benches had been set along the path to allow visitors to linger. It reminded me of the gardens in Poitiers. I would have allowed myself a moment of reminiscence, strolling around the flower beds, had Philip not been sitting on one of the benches. He was remarkably composed for someone who had just seen the Duke of Aquitaine fling himself over a garden wall. He stared at me blankly, clutching a small sprig of rosemary between thumb and forefinger. The moment my eyes caught his, the tip of his nose went a little pink, and he dropped the rosemary as if it had offended him.

The hazy, overcast light of the afternoon softened his edges, like watering down ink. My stomach tightened. "My liege," I said, bowing low.

"My Lord Aquitaine," he replied, as he stood from the bench. "Is the gate broken, or do you make a habit of vaulting over walls?"

"Only when you are on the other side of them."

He ignored this. "It must be an urgent matter," he said, "if you must arrive unannounced while I am traveling—"

"It is a coincidence, Philip. I am going to Chinon. I intended to lodge here, with my men."

"A coincidence," he murmured. He cocked his head at me, owlish, displaying the side of his throat. His skin was the color of marzipan, and it had the same delicate quality, as if it might begin to dissolve in the damp air.

"Yes, a coincidence," I said.

"You have nothing in particular to request of me?"

"Not particularly."

"You were not looking for me," he asked, "when you climbed over the wall?"

I smiled at him. "I was looking for you, of course."

"Of course."

"But not to make a request."

"Why, then?"

"Well—to greet you."

"To greet me," he repeated.

"Yes," I said. "Hello."

At that, Philip glanced sideways—as if I might have been speaking to someone else—and then he looked back to me. "Hello," he replied. It was a confused echo, rather than a genuine greeting, but it served my purposes well enough.

I walked over to him and sat down. I gestured to the space beside me invitingly. Instead, he sat delicately on the other end of the bench, leaving as much room between us as he could manage.

He frowned at me. "I shall be leaving once we are packed."

"I know."

"If you have anything to ask of me, you ought to ask it now. I know that you saw your father—"

I blew a raspberry, which sent Philip into a near paroxysm of disdain; his eyes went very narrow and his mouth twitched. It was the most expressive I had yet seen him. "Never mind my father," I said. "I shan't say his name. Talk of the devil, and all that."

"The meeting did not go well, I presume?"

"It went exactly as expected."

"You will not swear fealty to your brother?" he asked.

"Of course not. And Henry will not demean himself to *request* it of me. Only to demand it, and grow more and more furious each time I refuse."

He nodded. "What of your younger brothers—Geoffrey and John. Do they support you?"

"Hardly. They would push me off a cliff if our father told them to."

Philip watched me intently. There was a good measure of scorn in his face. I could not tell how much of it was merely his natural expression. "It is a petty argument," he said.

"I shan't deny that," I replied. "My family and I seize any reason to despise one another."

"It is particularly foolish on Henry's part, when you are such a threat to his position. He ought to be incentivizing your loyalty, not punishing you without cause."

"Is that what you intend to do, Philip?" I asked. "Incentivize my loyalty?"

"Do you wish me to?"

"That depends. What sort of incentive would you offer?"

The flirtation was too blatant, and Philip frowned, perplexed, shifting on the bench. "There is very little I could not provide you with, were you to make it worth my while."

"The situation remains as it was. I need nothing from you. Not yet."

"Then why are you *here*, Richard?"

"I thought it might be pleasant to speak with you," I replied. "I thought we might have a conversation without politics. Is that so strange?"

He rolled his eyes as if the question were idiotic. It seemed the only emotion capable of breaking his composure was contempt. "Of course, it is unusual," he said. "It is quite unbelievable, in fact."

"Do people always require something of you, when they speak with you?"

"Is it not so with you? Duke of Aquitaine, prince of England?"

"Often. But there are also those whom I consider friends. Those who have no ulterior motive."

"Everyone has an ulterior motive," he said.

"Not everyone."

"Yes, everyone," he repeated. "Including you. Including me."

"Then you must tell me yours first."

Philip smiled. It was only the most minuscule twitch of his lips, but unmistakably a smile, all the same. "If I told you, it would not be ulterior."

I grinned back at him. "I will discover it, someday."

He hummed in thought. I allowed my gaze to wander from his face; towards the back of the garden, a gust of wind passed over one of the trellises. The plant—it looked like mint—was doing well despite the chill, the leaves a soft silver-green. When I was younger, I had been encouraged to eat candied mint as a remedy for my hot-blooded temperament. I had acquired quite the taste for it. There seemed something preordained in the way it now framed Philip from behind; some encouragement to shift closer, inch by inch, until his eyes widened and his cheeks began to darken.

There was no real intention behind it, except to gauge his re-action. I risked nothing from my flirtations but his disgust: I was a duke and a prince, after all, and I answered to no one but God. If He could forgive all the other hell-worthy sins I had committed, my occasional dalliances were hardly relevant. Besides, my attraction to Philip still had some level of detachment. He seemed quite unlike a real person. His beauty and composure had made him into a doll sort of man, planned and constructed; something to put on a shelf and admire.

Then I moved closer to him, and I saw him grow flustered at my proximity, become *affected* by it, as if my admiration were returned. Suddenly, whatever veil had been obscuring Philip from me was pulled away. His presence became tangible—I realized that if I were to reach out, I would be able to touch him, flesh to flesh—and this sudden strike of comprehension left me mute. I paused in my movements, staring at him.

Philip felt the change as much as I did. He stood up, increasing the distance between us. "I think . . ." he began, but he was so disquieted he struggled to continue. He had to pause to collect himself. "I suppose I needn't know what you want from me, Richard," he said finally. "If you are so reluctant to tell me, it can hardly be that important."

"Philip—"

"If you would speak with me properly, you ought to come to court in Paris, instead of ambushing me here. I cannot understand what you hoped to achieve by it."

"It was a coincidence, as I said."

"And yet you are so determined to see me," he replied, "that you would climb over a wall—"

"Yes," I said, and I laughed. "*Yes,* because I had an impulse. I heard you were here, and I wanted to see you. Surely you have impulses, sometimes?"

"Of course, I do. But I *resist* them if necessary. I can hardly just—*fling* myself into things."

"Perhaps you ought to try it," I said. "Flinging, that is."

"And perhaps *you* ought to try having some common sense."

"Common sense? Me? Never."

Philip raised his eyebrows in surprise, and then he covered his mouth with his hand. I realized, delighted, that he was attempting to suppress his laughter. When he lowered his arm, his lips were pressed very firmly together. "I begin to believe you really have come on a foolish whim," he said, "since you are so unable to explain your own reasoning."

"Indeed, my liege, I have been utterly irrational, as always."

"Some would say you have wasted my time."

"Perhaps I have provided you with some entertainment?"

"Some," he said. Then he murmured, "You were better than the rosemary, at any rate."

"Between sage and parsley, perhaps, if one were to employ such a scale."

"That would be a generous estimation."

I placed a hand over my heart, as if wounded, well prepared to tease him further; I was interrupted by the sound of someone coughing loudly. Guillaume was standing at the garden gate, peering down his nose at us. He was too far away to hear us properly, but his low, impatient bow made it clear why he was there.

Philip looked at me. "I must leave," he said.

"I know."

"Richard—"

"Yes, Philip?"

"Find me in Paris," he told me, and he flushed again. I felt that flush in the tips of my fingers; a slow sting, like the ache of your teeth when you grit them against the cold. "That is—if you wish to speak of serious matters—at court—"

"Of course, my liege," I replied, inclining my head. "It would be my honor."

He nodded. He began to walk slowly down the path. Halfway towards the gate, he turned back to look at me. When he did, I offered him a smile sharp enough to puncture. I would have been gratified to see him blush once more, but this time he was prepared. His brow furrowed, his lips pursed, and his eyes narrowed to shards of blue: crystallizing, brittle and cold. I wondered what he could see in my face. I wondered what, exactly, I was seeing in his.

"My liege," Guillaume said, impatient—loud enough that I could hear him—"My Lord Blois insisted we reach his court by sundown. If he takes our delay as an insult . . ."

Philip nodded curtly, and he turned away from me. I watched him leave in silence, as I sat alone on the bench by the rosemary. I knew it would not be long before I sought him out again.

CHAPTER FIVE

Philip

Every night since our marriage, Isabella and I alternated reciting *The Aeneid*. During the day, I would find her poring over the text, committing the Latin to memory. It was something of a blessing, to have a wife who took as much solace in our chastity as I did. We spent our nights lying beside each other in grave, funereal poses, arms gently folded over our chests to prevent any accidental touching of skin. I gave her gifts: miniature tapestries and embroidered belts of Dido, tiny Roman heroes suspended in thread. It felt a small way to reassure her, defining our marriage with trinkets. I did not tell her how much it reassured me also.

My trip to Blois, and my meeting with Richard, had formed an uncomfortable interruption in the otherwise humdrum routine of kingship. I had not expected to see him so soon after our introduction. Without my castle's defenses, or a cause to further, our second conversation had been by his lead. I considered it his victory. I let that be a source of shame to me over the next few months. In that way it was helpful, as it hardened my resolve. When I felt overwhelmed by responsibility, I recalled the twist in my stomach as he leaned towards me, and I thought, *Never again*. I had never felt such attraction to anyone. It being a man was tolerable, perhaps even somewhat expected, at that point in my life; I'd certainly never desired a woman, and I expected I never would. But it being a prince of England was another matter entirely.

The task of ruling remained my primary concern. It had to be. I spent most of my time embroiled in brief, petty fights with my subjects, pushing and pulling at counts and barons until my mind frayed at its edges. My Lord Blois, ever discontent, insisted on meeting upon meeting, demand upon demand, coin upon coin; and the threat of a rebellion from him or another vassal alienated by my father's disastrous reign loomed ever nearer. Meanwhile, as always, I kept an ear to England. I listened for news of its king, the dissatisfaction of its princes; I wrote missives and read offers; I plotted and calculated and *waited*. It felt as if exhaustion had burrowed into the very marrow of my bones.

Such was the depths of my boredom that I almost missed the letter when it arrived. Within the stack, it was a small envelope, the wax seal warped by heat and the weight of the documents above it. I tore it open expecting nothing of consequence. The contents were routine but significant, forewarning a new arrival to court. Another of Henry's prodigal sons: Geoffrey, Duke of Brittany. Richard's younger brother, third in line to the English throne.

Brittany had once been French land, although my father had lost it in war with England. Ruled by a young and unmarried duchess, it was easy enough for Henry to ensure it stayed within his dynasty. With four sons, there had been more than enough candidates for her hand. It had fallen to Geoffrey, whom I had never met, nor heard much of. He had kept himself quiet in the

years since the rebellion, and had done little to insert himself
into politics. That was either a sign of wisdom or cowardice; I
couldn't tell.

Isabella had been stitching in the same room when I opened
the letter. She had a habit of reading over my shoulder, and she
came to hover. "What is it, my lord?" she asked. Her manner
with me vacillated, still, between precocious curiosity and crip-
pling shyness. Today was the former. Her hair was down, and
she wore no shoes. She was now older than I had been when I
was crowned.

"A letter from the Duke of Brittany," I said.

"What does he want?"

"I do not know," I replied. "But do you see how he finishes the
letter?"

She squinted at the writing. "With loyalty and gratitude," she
read.

I folded the paper and put it back in its envelope. "An important lesson to learn, Isabella," I told her. "If an Angevin pledges
loyalty, they are certain to request something in return."

"And if they are grateful?"

"Then they already expect that you will give it to them," I
said. "And God help you, if you do not."

~⁊~

I received the Duke of Brittany in the throne room, with a host
of courtiers present. I had seen a little of Geoffrey before, from
brief meetings in childhood, but I had clearly remembered him
wrong. I had expected someone with Angevin looks—blond,
broad, brash—but the man who knelt before me was all finesse,
lean and long-limbed: a knife to his brother's axe. He was beautiful, too, with a sweeping, poetic face. His hair was a shade of
auburn that caught the light like dying embers, and he held

himself with a subtle, compelling grace. But he also had the narrowed eyes and careful smile of a politician, and I distrusted him immediately.

"My liege, greetings," he said.

I raised my hand to acknowledge him. "Rise, Lord Brittany."

He did so. Lacing his hands together behind his back, he bowed with practiced ease. "I bring grave news," he told me. "I am too long gone from court, I know, and I ought to pay homage. But I fear it is urgent. Will you hear me?"

Murmurs amongst the courtiers. The duke gave them an arch look. As carefully deferential as he was, he remained a prince, and that single glance was enough to show his presumption of superiority. "I will hear you," I said. I stood from the throne. From her seat beside me, Isabella craned her head, no doubt pleading to accompany me; I had no choice but to ignore her. "In private," I continued, and he nodded.

Descending the steps, I found that the duke towered over me, as his entire family seemed to. Richard's height had been natural to him, another way to express an innate advantage; Geoffrey seemed to bear his more consciously. As I led him out of the hall, he performed a dance of tiny steps, shortening his pace to match mine. It was an elegant movement, but a strange one, all the same.

"You were at my coronation, years ago, I believe," I said. "But I have not seen you since."

"I was there, my liege," he replied. "But we did not speak. Pardon."

"It is I who should apologize."

"You had many guests."

"But few who were princes."

He laughed. "Yes, that is true. Might I enquire where we are going?"

"My study."

"And why is that?"

"My ledgers are there. Clearly, you intend to negotiate something, and I thought it best to have the numbers at hand."

He went quiet to consider this. He lifted a finger to tap his chin, slowly, in a sort of performative musing. "I have avoided court," he said. "I did not come to your wedding. Has that offended you?"

"No. You needed nothing from me, and I needed nothing from you."

"Indeed," he replied, pleased. "But I know that Richard visited after the ceremony. It would be a considerable shame to be a lesser neighbor than he."

I opened the door to the study. "I do not judge my neighbors by their courtesy calls, or lack thereof."

"A sensible choice."

We entered. There was a strong wind outside. Its whistling cut through the otherwise suffocating silence of the room, which had neither a fire nor an occupant. My papers were neatly stacked upon the desk, beside a half-played game of backgammon: the dregs of a morning spent with Isabella. I went to pack the board into its box, allowing Geoffrey to stand awkwardly beside the chairs, unable to sit without permission.

I waved my hand to him as I closed the lid. "Please, sit," I said, and he did so. I took the chair opposite his.

He glanced over my shoulder. "Backgammon?"

"Yes. My wife is fond of it."

"As is mine," he replied. He laid his palms flat across his thighs, cocking his head. His movements had an almost eerie gentleness. "I bear news of my brother," he said. "News, certainly, that you will hear soon enough, regardless of my visit. But I bring it to you now, as a gesture of goodwill; and because, as you said, I intend to negotiate."

"News of your brother?"

"Yes. Harry, the oldest of us."

"What is it?" I asked.

"He has the flux," Geoffrey said. "He shall be dead within weeks. I was meant to visit him last month, but when I came his court was in disarray. I learnt the truth before I was intended to."

"It is certain?"

"It is."

Geoffrey's placid expression belied the tragedy of his brother's imminent death. It was too soon to show shock, but the prospect of this change in Europe's foundations formed a worm of panic in my gut. I breathed deeply. "I am sorry to hear it," I told him, carefully maintaining my composure. He replied with a nod: it was a controlled, decisive movement, with little consideration for grief.

"Fortune's hand is fickle," he murmured. "Such as it always has been, and such as it always will be. With Harry's death, all of Christendom shall be shaken. My father's heir will change."

"Richard," I replied, and the worm squirmed.

"Richard," Geoffrey agreed. I would have expected resentment in his tone, but the word was as soft-spoken as all the rest. "Richard will become king of England, as well as Duke of Aquitaine."

I pictured borders realigning, the strings of Europe snapping and rewinding, tangling France within them. "It is a significant increase in power," I said, and Geoffrey nodded once more.

"It is a *detestable* amount of land for one man to hold," he replied. "Detestable not only to us, but to my father also. Henry never wanted Aquitaine for Richard—that was our mother's doing—and this serves him a perfect excuse to take it away. No man can be king of England *and* Duke of Aquitaine. Our father will not stand for it. He intends to give the duchy to John. He has told me himself."

"To *John*?" I asked. I knew nothing of John, the youngest Angevin, but for the fact that he was generally considered irrelevant.

"He is the only one of us not a duke. And he is my father's favorite son also, since he did not rebel."

If Geoffrey was vexed by this, it was expertly masked. I asked him, "Will Richard surrender the duchy, if pressed?"

He shrugged. "He would die before he does. Our mother raised him, and she crowned him duke herself; to surrender would be to betray her, and he would never do such a thing. But Henry has her in his custody, and he still has the greater army. Richard's defeat would be inevitable, without an ally."

"And with an ally?"

"It would come to war," he told me, with a vicious satisfaction. "Civil war."

A war between Aquitaine and England, with France caught in the middle. The sort of bloody, frustrated conflict that had defined my father's reign—and now, it would seem, would define mine.

"Richard feeds on battle, but our father grows weary," Geoffrey continued. "Henry will delay. Negotiate. Bully. Use our mother as leverage. His army is larger, true, but his levies have depleted since the rebellion, while Richard's have only grown. He will not fight until it is the only option."

I understood, now, what Geoffrey intended. "You would have us involve ourselves," I said.

"Of course. We would be wasting an opportunity otherwise. Surely you realize that?" I nodded. Satisfied, he leaned back in his chair. "And you have administrated your realm far better than your father ever did. Considering the defenses you've built, and the state of your treasury, your armies must now match Henry's. You have more men than I, my liege. More men than Richard also. You could determine the outcome of the entire war." Geoffrey tipped his head towards me, the picture of deference. "I would not raise a sword against you."

The question was, of course, which side he wanted us on. I considered the issue myself, as we stared at each other; then I said, "Richard."

"Richard," Geoffrey agreed, and I swallowed a sigh of relief. "My brother prioritizes Aquitaine above all else. He shall be easy to extract promises from, and he is likely to keep his word. I cannot say the same of my father."

"And what promises do you intend to extract?" I asked.

"I want the duchy of Normandy."

"An extraordinary demand."

"He will have no choice but to agree, not if he needs my help," he said. I nodded reluctantly. "And for you, Anjou," he continued.

My fingers tightened around the arm of the chair. "Anjou," I repeated. A province once the heartland of the kingdom, another step towards the western sea. It had been one of my father's greatest losses.

Geoffrey leaned towards me. His nose flared like a hound catching the scent. "The prizes of war," he said, coaxing. "Ours to take. I could offer allegiance to Richard, but without France—without *you*—I cannot ensure his agreement."

I hummed in thought. "My aid alone," I replied, "might be enough to win him the war, with or without Brittany's armies."

"That is true."

"Then why do I need you, my Lord Brittany?"

"Why wouldn't you? Richard would never give you the land I am asking of him. From you, I ask for nothing at all, except your agreement. In exchange I offer my loyalty and my armies. With my men on the field, yours are far more likely to succeed. I only wish to ensure that you consider me a partner, rather than a pawn. You will be glad of my help, once all is done."

I almost laughed at that. "You are so confident in your usefulness?" I asked.

"I know my brother," he returned. "I know how to manage him. There is no one better suited to aid you."

As I considered this, I examined his face: looking, in sheer fascination, for something of Richard in it. I sought some proof that these men were brothers. It was a difficult task. Not impossible, when studying a certain sharpness of his jaw or the slightly pointed tips of his ears, but difficult, all the same. Geoffrey was undeniably the prettier of the two. His features were unscarred and elfin, an artful scatter of freckles across the tip of his nose and cheekbones. When he caught my gaze, I saw that his eyes were an unusual shade of green, light enough to tend to grey. But there was something disaffecting about him, something uncomfortable and cold, that prompted you to look away. Where Richard was familiar, overly so, Geoffrey had elected to emphasize his detachment. He would be a dangerous ally to make. A worthy one, perhaps.

I stood. Returning to the desk, I smoothed my hand over the walnut of the backgammon box. It was as good an excuse as any to hide my expression as I considered. I recalled Richard in the herb garden, with his strange, furious sort of naïveté, as he demanded we be friends; I wondered if he would be angry to learn of this meeting, or betrayed by it. He almost certainly would be. That realization made me pause and remain silent for a moment too long, looking at my warped reflection in the polished wood.

He was to be king now. I would have to treat him as yet another piece on the board. I could not allow myself the indulgence of conversations in gardens, or glances that lingered for too long, or stifled laughter behind palms.

Geoffrey gestured to the backgammon box. "Would you like to play a game?" he asked, and I nodded.

"In celebration," I said, "of our partnership."

He smiled at me briefly—he had a smile like oil on glass—as I laid the board on the table. "May it prove fruitful for both of us."

I took the black counters, and he the ivory.

"I have always had more of a mind for backgammon than chess," he said to me.

"And I the opposite," I replied.

"A compromise, then. Should I win the backgammon, we will play a game of chess, and you may defeat me in turn."

"A sound plan."

We played mostly in silence. We were still mulling over our agreement, measuring each other. It was pleasant that Geoffrey did not force small talk, and I found that I was enjoying myself.

"I must admit I am relieved," he said, eventually, as we neared the end of the game. "I thought that Richard might have convinced you to avoid my company. He does not trust me."

"Why is that?" I asked.

"Because he makes decisions in a manner fundamentally different from my own," he said. "And when my decisions run counter to his, he takes it as an insult."

I raised an eyebrow at him. "How does Richard make decisions, then?"

"With his stomach. He is a creature of instinct. It often leads to . . . disagreements. But he is my brother still, and I wish him to succeed. I would put him on the throne, after all."

I scrutinized his earnest expression. I was not inclined to put much importance in Geoffrey's words; whether they were true or not, he wanted Richard to be king for his own gain. If he stood to benefit from Richard's downfall, his offer would have been much different. In this way, the sentiment mattered little, and we both knew that.

"One might not fault Richard for being cautious," I said.

"In our family? No, of course not. Betrayal is in our blood. Our crown was taken by treachery, after all. My father stole the throne from his cousin."

"If you felt it would be the right decision to betray him," I said, "would you?"

His gaze caught mine, unflinching. "Yes."

"Even though he is your brother?"

"Of course." He rolled the dice. "I wish no harm upon him, but sometimes such things are necessary."

"And once he is king?" I committed to memory the brief grimace that crossed Geoffrey's face as I said the words. The distraction of the game had succeeded in cracking his composure. I continued, "Will you feel the same?"

"Yes," he said. Then, before I could reply, he added, "Oh, look. I have won."

I looked at the board, clear of white pieces. "So you have."

Geoffrey shifted in his chair, examining my expression, gauging how I was responding to the loss. I caught his eye, impassive, as I gathered my pieces.

"I suspect that you threw the game," he said.

"Why would I do that?"

"Perhaps you wanted to know if I would be willing to beat you."

"Perhaps you are the better player," I said.

"I doubt that." He steepled his fingers under his chin, leaning on his elbows. His expression had a sudden keenness to it, an arrowhead "V" appearing between his brows. I could not tell if he was angry or pleased. "At first, I had thought so, but now I suspect the opposite."

"I told you I had no mind for backgammon."

"But we were playing more than backgammon, were we not?" he asked.

"Were we?"

He smirked. "Very well. I shall accept my victory. But now we must play chess, I should think, if our deal is to be maintained."

I nodded and stood. "Will Richard *want* the throne?" I asked, as I returned the backgammon board to its shelf. "You seem to think he will not."

"He will want whatever is contrary to our father's wishes. He will want our mother safe."

"But he has no innate ambition," I said, and I turned back to Geoffrey. "No desire for glory."

"Oh, he is *ravenous* for glory. He simply wishes to find it by the sword, rather than by politics."

"And you?"

"I take an opportunity when it is offered. A conversation is safer than a battle, and usually twice as effective." I nodded in agreement. He continued, "A lesson learnt as a third son, in a household where I was as irrelevant as a daughter. When one rules by cunning, blood ceases to matter."

"Be that as it may," I replied, "I am not here to be ruled, through cunning or anything else."

"Yes, that has become clear enough."

"Good." Carrying the chessboard, I walked back to the table. "Then I am certain we shall work well together, Geoffrey."

He smiled. It was the first genuine smile I'd seen from him, savage instead of civil. "Oh, yes," he said, as his incisors flashed against his lower lip. "Philip, I believe this alliance may prove even more valuable than I had expected."

~⁂~

Upon Geoffrey's leaving, I went to look at the map in my desk drawer. It was an unusual thing to find maps of this sort, which had land drawn as a single mass of towns, cities, and borders. It showed all the immensity and complexity of Christendom, in a manner I found dizzying. I traced my finger across the border of Anjou, remembering Geoffrey's words. A prize of war, he had called it. A prize indeed.

It was not only land. Once France had territory stretching from west of Brittany to east of Croatia, and its kings had sat on the throne of emperors. I had made a promise to myself, on the day of my coronation, and I would keep it: one day, I would reclaim that which my father and forefathers had lost. It was an ambition borne of fear. I did not want to be another step to the kingdom's dissolution; I did not want to be a failure. Forgotten, perhaps, but not remembered with contempt.

I could not think of myself as my own man, not without pulling all the Capetian blood from my veins. As a king in a line of kings, I did not have to know who I was. I was only ever as much as I needed to be: a conqueror, a diplomat, a servant. Geoffrey had come to add another task to that list. He had offered me a new mask to wear. I was to lead armies, for the first time in my life. I was to take up a sword and douse my hands in blood. I was no warrior—that I knew—but I trusted my knowledge of strategy. I trusted my generals and my men. I trusted that this was what was expected of me, as king, and I trusted that I could win.

I had to be confident of my victory. I had to be willing to *die* for my victory, if that was what France required.

It did not matter if I survived it, in the end: war awaited, as habitual and expectant as an evening's rest. When it was done, I would have another piece of land for the map. I would be another step further from my father's legacy. I could ask for nothing more.

CHAPTER SIX

Richard

There is a flower that grows in the south, with leaves like arrowheads, white petals small and sharp. It blooms in the winter, and it bends over in an arc, cowering, deferential; it is known as Solomon's Crown. My mother was very fond of it. She had seeds brought from Provence, and she planted them in the courtyard of our palace in Poitiers. I had always loved the way they bowed to me as I passed them by, the paleness of their color, how they shuddered and stooped under the weight of the snow.

Once warmth comes and the earth goes dry, Solomon's Crown ceases to bloom. There is a moment—a matter of weeks—when the flowers remain aboveground but start to die, going brown and shriveled. My mother, when she ruled Aquitaine, had them culled as soon as their color began to darken. I always tried to do the same. The spring when Harry was sick was the first year I had forgotten to give the order, and although I could be forgiven for it—I was occupied, after all—I still felt as if I had made some inexcusable error, when I looked down at the dead flowers rusting the grass.

I turned away from the window. Stephen and I were in the study. I had stabbed a knife into the desk earlier that day, in a moment of frustrated impulse, and Stephen was currently trying to extract it from the wood, attempting to avoid any damage to the map it was holding in place. Unfortunately, the county of Touraine looked unsalvageable.

"The flowers," I said.

He looked up at me. "What of them?"

"They are dying."

"Yes," he replied. "They do that every year."

"I know. It still seems a shame."

Stephen paused in his work. He looked at me with cautious sympathy, hand resting gently on the hilt of the knife. "We shall soon hear news."

"It has been weeks of nothing." I pulled out a chair and sat down, putting my feet on the table. "Lord, I was hardly told anything in the first place. What was it that my father wrote to me? *Richard, your brother is indisposed.* The letter might as well not have come. He desires I live in ignorance. Harry could have a cough or the plague, I would not know."

"He shall recover."

"I would be surer of that if I knew what the problem *was*."

Stephen managed to pull the knife free, but he overestimated the force necessary. The blade skidded across the table, bisecting the map into neat halves. He sighed.

"Harry has never been dear to me, nor I to him," I continued, "but we are brothers, are we not? Surely I deserve more than *this*? I am kept out of everything, always. Father sets me aside, like a bird in a cage. Throw on a blanket, keep it quiet."

Stephen pushed the two halves of the map together, attempting to align them. "He keeps the peace," he said. "Better a quiet bird than a dead one."

"Better a dead man than a helpless one."

"You have never been helpless, Richard. Not really."

"Apart from when we met," I said.

He looked up to smile at me. "Apart from that," he agreed, and we shared a moment of mutual nostalgia for our first meeting: a summer eight years ago in Bordeaux, when I had climbed a gnarled olive tree in his uncle's garden. I had looked down to see an unfamiliar boy grinning at me: dark skin, coarse, curly hair, no shoes—*Bet you can't jump!* he said. And I did, of course. I landed beside him, my foot went one way, the rest of me another. I had to put my arm around his shoulders as he dragged me back to the manor. For the rest of the week my ankle was red and swollen as a beesting, and I had to use a stick to walk. Every time I limped into the room, Stephen had laughed so much he doubled over.

There was a knock on the door. Stephen went to open it. When he returned, he held a letter out to me, very slowly and carefully, as if I might bat it out of his hand. When I saw the seal upon it, I realized why.

"Oh," I said.

"You must read it."

"I know."

"He might have news of Harry."

"I know," I repeated.

I had anticipated that someone would write to me eventually. But the seal was that of my younger brother Geoffrey, the last person I had thought to receive such a letter from. We had never gotten along. While my relationship with my other brothers was strained largely as a result of circumstance, the dislike between Geoffrey and me had always felt intensely personal, an incompatibility of character. The malice between us had only ever compounded itself as we grew older.

"Read it," Stephen repeated, extending the letter closer. I snatched it away from him, breaking the seal.

Richard, it began, *it aggrieves me greatly that I must write to you under such circumstances. Tragedy strikes our family. Now, more than ever, we must put petty grudges behind us. It has been too long since I last spoke to you, and I fear we have forgotten the ties of blood that bind us together. I intend to come to Poitiers. There is a matter of utmost urgency I must speak to you of, concerning Harry, and concerning ourselves. I come not as an enemy, but as a friend and brother . . .*

He continued for some time, enough that his writing covered both sides of the page. When I was done with it, I threw the letter onto the table, making a noise of disgust. "He wishes to come here," I said, "to Poitiers. To 'speak' with me about something concerning Harry."

Stephen went quiet. He realized, as I did, that this meant Harry's life was in danger. There would be no other reason for Geoffrey to come.

I swore. Tension traveled from my closed fists to my shoulders, and my posture became hunched. It always took me time to comprehend such monumental news. My body responded before my mind did. Grief, confusion, anger, all came like a barrage of needles. My skin prickled, muscles tensed.

I turned back to the window. Outside, the dead flowers rustled gently in the wind, mocking me for my earlier consideration. Some satire of a man I had been: bemoaning the maintenance of his garden, as his brother reached for the grave.

"Will you let him visit?" Stephen asked.

"He has given me little choice in the matter." I stalked over to the table and picked the letter up. "Geoffrey shall arrive," I said, as I began to tear the parchment, "and he shall tell me of Harry, and he shall speak of how we have wronged each other, how he is willing to reconcile. And he will do so in the knowledge that I shall never forgive him, nor him me. Then I will lose my temper, as I always do." I opened my palms, allowing the remains of the letter to flutter to the floor. "And he shall leave, absolved of his trespasses, for I have become the aggressor. He is always the victim. Saint Geoffrey, the penitent."

"It has been two years since you last saw him face-to-face, Richard," he replied. "Consider, at least, that you remember him unkindly."

The last time I had seen Geoffrey had been his wedding, in Nantes. I could recall the ceremony very clearly: the stiffed-back, obsessive etiquette of it all, the pomp and ritual. Geoffrey and Constance had already been in love, unable to disguise the adoration on their faces as they clasped hands. It was not the sort of dreamy devotion that one might expect—never something so romantic or impetuous for my brother—but instead the intense focus of a pair locked in mutual anticipation. They both knew what the marriage would give them: power, influence, prestige. The sorts of things that matter to such people.

I walked to the door. "No matter. I will deal with him when I have to."

"Where are you going?" Stephen asked, frowning.

"To find the gardener."

"You could leave them, you know," he said. "The flowers. They will be gone in a few weeks anyway."

"I do not care," I replied. "I can hardly stand to look at them."

And before he could respond, I slammed the door shut behind me.

~⁀~

That spring quickly became one of the loveliest in my memory. The temperature was warm and pleasant, it rained very little, and where dead vegetation was cleared violets and poppies came in its stead. The evening my brother finally arrived, I met him in the gardens, sheltering beneath my mother's favorite plum tree. When I was young, she had read poetry to me there: *chansons de geste* about brave knights and faraway lands. Sometimes I still dreamt of those stories, and of her singsong voice narrating in Occitan as armies clashed and dragons roared.

But my mother was not with me that day. It was only my brother and me, brought together by tragedy. He had only a small retinue with him—armed, of course—and there seemed some attempt at intimacy in that, some pretension of friendliness. But his posture was rigid and formal, and his clothing was as meticulously tailored as it always was, buttoned up to the chin.

"Geoffrey," I said, as soon as he was near enough to hear me. He straightened his shoulders and lifted his nose towards me, like a snake rising upwards.

"Brother," he replied, tone cordial. As he stepped towards me, he lifted his foot over one of the plum roots, his expression one of patient disgust. "You are well?"

"I was surprised when I received your letter."

"You were expecting to hear from someone else?"

"I was not expecting to hear from *you*," I said.

He paused to consider this, his eyes narrow and vulpine. When he spoke, his tone was cautious, each syllable equally measured. He had always spoken like that, as if words were a currency he was bartering with. "Are you disappointed that it was I who contacted you, Richard?" he asked. "Would you have preferred to hear from Father, or from John?"

"Perhaps."

He sighed. "It has been so long. I had hoped that you might be more welcoming, considering the situation."

"Welcoming?" I repeated, incredulous. "Geoffrey, we despise each other, *situation* or no. Surely you have not forgotten. When I would not swear fealty to Harry, you threatened *war* against me."

"I chose to side with the king of England. You can hardly fault me for that."

"Of course I fault you for it," I said. "It was an insult."

Geoffrey rolled his eyes. "You are far too concerned with insults," he replied. "You were being foolish. I had every right to support our brother and father against you, and I will not apologize for it."

Despite the affectation of pride, Geoffrey's lips curled slightly as he spoke, as if he were amused by the words. I knew he intended for me to notice this and feel injured by it; suppressing my frustration, I said, "Why *are* you here, then, if not to beg for my forgiveness? You have news of Harry?"

"I do." His eyes swept around the garden. "Shall we sit?"

"I prefer to stand."

"Very well." He cleared his throat. "Harry is dying, Richard."

I had imagined these words for weeks, but hearing them was still painful. Flinching, I leaned more heavily against the tree. There was a phantom barb within my throat, making each swallow painful. I tried to picture Harry's face, as I had many times since I was told he was sick; I found that now, for some reason, I could not. Perhaps it had been too long since I had last seen him.

"He has the flux," Geoffrey continued slowly, when it became clear I would not respond. "He will be gone before the month is out. Father has endeavored to keep you in ignorance, until it was certain. It is certain now."

"Harry is still in Limoges?" I asked.

"Yes."

Not far. But— "He will not see me."

"Of course not."

And now, finally, I could picture Harry, as he had been the last time I saw him, more than two years ago: junior king, Young Henry. He was always second to our father, always determined to compensate for it with loudness and confidence and too-tight clothing. Harry had lacked the brutality others in our family had—my mother, father, brothers, and I; he had no stomach for cruelty, soft as he was, simple as he was. He loved sport and music and wine. We were friends when we were children, before I moved to Aquitaine. He had once been my favorite of my brothers, for all that meant. It meant very little, especially now.

"We have not always been on the best of terms, Richard," Geoffrey said, "but perhaps now it is time to mend things."

"Why?"

"You are to be king, one day."

"No," I said, nonsensically, reflexively; I could see Geoffrey suppressing a laugh.

"Yes, you will be," he replied.

"I am Duke of Aquitaine."

"And now, eventually, king of England. Surely you realized this?"

"Realized, but not—I had not *thought* of it. I—"

"You are glad, surely? Mother will be ecstatic. Imagine, Richard of Aquitaine on the throne. Eleanor of Aquitaine released from our father's clutches. A queen again."

"Quiet," I snapped, somewhat feebly. "I am not glad that our brother is *dying*."

Geoffrey grasped an elbow with his opposite hand, tapping it with his index finger. He tilted his head to the side, and he inspected me with the vacant curiosity of a physician. "You were never close," he said, "Harry and you. Remember him, of course, as I shall; but you are a fool if you think there is time or cause for grief."

"You are as monstrous as ever."

His lips pressed thin. "Be that as it may, you must listen to reason. Harry's death will mean more than death alone. The tides have changed, Richard. They pull you across the Channel. Father will despise you having both the crown and the duchy. It is too much power."

"Of course he will despise me. What will that matter?"

Geoffrey seemed amused by my ignorance. "It matters," he said, "because he will try to take Aquitaine away. He will try to give it to John."

"To *John*?" I repeated.

"Father has already told me so," he replied. Here, finally, he allowed his tone to show the viciousness of his character; the words were spat like cherry stones. "And so, I have come to warn you. He will not give it to *me*, since I am already a duke. But his youngest son is his favorite, as you know, and his youngest son needs land. Why not give him yours?"

"Henry will not take Aquitaine from me," I said, my hands curling into fists. "War it shall be, if he insists on that."

"War, with only your armies against the whole of England? All of Henry's allies, his fortresses in Normandy—you would risk your head upon such a victory?"

"I would rather lose my head than my duchy."

"Nonsense," Geoffrey said. "You will not have the duchy if you are *dead*, Richard. So, then, you will fight, and you will surrender, and you will lose Aquitaine, along with your reputation."

"I can find allies."

"Indeed, you can," he agreed. "And you shall have to, if such a fate is to be avoided. That is why I am here."

"You would help me? Over our father?"

"With just reward? Of course."

"That is—you—" I said. Then, unable to finish, I began to pace the base of the tree.

Geoffrey's lands were substantial—he was Duke of Brittany, after all—and his aid would be invaluable, if war was to come. But how was I supposed to think in such terms now? How was I expected to consider *cost* and *reward* at a moment like this? My brother had come with news not only of Harry's impending death, but also my own. I had always been Richard, Duke of Aquitaine. I was not English, nor was I a king. To take the throne, whether I remained duke or not, would be to kill the version of myself I knew; to become someone else, a stranger wearing a foreign crown.

I turned to Geoffrey. "You do it," I said. "You become king. I do not want it."

"You are now eldest son. That is a choice, regrettably, that neither of us could make."

"But—why help me? Why not watch me fight and be humiliated?"

"Because I have nothing to gain from your humiliation," Geoffrey said, frowning. "My only hope would be that you died on the battlefield, leaving me England; but considering your talents as a soldier, such a thing would be unlikely."

This was the closest Geoffrey had ever come to paying me a compliment. I blinked at him, wordless, paralyzed by confusion.

"There is much to consider," he said. "I understand. But once we succeed, Richard, we can go to Mother. We can free her."

"Stop—stop pretending you are concerned about *anyone* other than yourself, you little *rat*," I snapped. "I can hardly believe you would say such a thing, when you have visited her not *once* since her imprisonment."

"And you, only a handful of times."

"I was forbidden by Henry! How could I risk visiting England, while he was there? You had no such restrictions, and yet you did not go. She has been *alone*—"

"Whose fault is it that you argue with our father?" Geoffrey asked. "You hunger for conflict and judge others for doing the same." I could say nothing in response to that, true as it was, and Geoffrey shook his head. "Let these petty arguments go, Richard. You need my help, and I am offering it. But know this: I will fight only if France does. We have little chance without Philip's support."

"And your 'just reward'? What of that?"

"I want Normandy."

"Normandy!" I repeated.

"Yes."

"Even our father knows better than to allow you two duchies."

"Father might not allow it, but you will, if you want my backing," he said. "You will keep Aquitaine and Anjou. It is a fair request."

"It is a ridiculous request."

"Those are my terms. You know them now; it is your decision."

"I do not need you," I told him. "I would do well enough with Philip's aid. Our combined forces—"

"*Would* he aid you, knowing that Brittany stands with England? Knowing that you will be busy defending your northern border, while he bears the brunt of Henry's forces?" Geoffrey made an incredulous sound. "He would pay a heavy cost for such a war. You have met Philip, have you not? Did he really seem that naïve?"

Philip had certainly not seemed naïve. It was my own complacency I was concerned about. All he needed to do was blush, and I tossed any misgivings directly into the Seine. And yet, despite my weakness around him, Philip had begun to seem a path to salvation, unspoiled as he was by the rot of Angevin blood. In my desperation I clung to this thought with sudden and unwarranted conviction. I recalled the momentary softness of his gaze as I had leaned towards him on the bench, and in my mind's eye, that softness spiraled into an unspoken promise. Surely Philip had felt, as I did, the sense of inevitability between us; the tidal tug of something yet unnamed, but still significant. It *was* significant. It had to be.

"He might," I said. "Philip might help me, even without you."

"Go to him, then. See if he will. You know where to find me when you fail."

Geoffrey's smile was as painfully genial as it had ever been. He had a face as smooth as glazed clay, unscarred and unknowable.

"I do not want this," I said. "England—the throne—I do not want them."

"That does not matter," Geoffrey returned. "This is the fate of princes, Richard. Our lives follow a trail of blood begun thousands of years before we were ever born. Whatever happens, we persist." For a moment, he gave me a look of genuine sympathy. "We must always persist."

"I want you to leave, Geoffrey," I said.

"I have only just arrived."

"You have said all that needed to be said. I want you to leave."

He bowed to me. "We shall soon meet again."

"Must we?"

"We have no choice. But for now, farewell, brother. I shall pray for your good health."

I said nothing as his retinue navigated out of the garden. Sun sinking, the light was now blue and gold. It was beautiful, in a taunting sort of way. The plum tree blurred before me. Stephen split off from my men and approached, coming to lay a hand on my arm.

"Richard?" he said softly. "I am sorry to hear of your brother."

"I am sorry, too," I replied.

"Shall I—"

"I need to be alone, Stephen."

"But . . ."

"Go!" I snarled through gritted teeth, and Stephen took a faltering step back. He knew me too well to be insulted, but his look of concern as he left the garden with the others was somehow worse; I have always found nothing more repellent than to be pitiable.

I was left standing alone by the plum tree. Once I was certain they were all gone, I allowed every ounce of anger and grief I had struggled to repress rise up and consume me all at once. I reached for the lowest bough—it was slender, but not insubstantial—and with all my strength I snapped it from its trunk. The tree had blossomed late that year, and the bough brought with it a shower of pale flowers; I swung it at the tree with a satisfying crash, and then again, and again. With each hit more flowers fell until I was covered with them. My palms were scraped raw by the bark of the branch, sweat dripping down my neck. I sat down in the dirt and I thought of Harry's face, when he was thirteen and I was ten: one of my few winters in England, when he had hit me on the knee with a wooden sword during combat training. I could hear his warbling voice, crying, *Sorry, Richard! Sorry!* It was the last time that a brother of mine had apologized to me, crouching beside me with genuine contrition, because he had meant to do it—he was angry that I was a better fighter than he—but he hadn't meant to hurt me, not really. I had not responded with equal kindness. I had lashed out at him, fists flying, and our father had to pull us apart.

Now I was here, more than a decade later, hitting things with tree branches like a barbarian, while Harry lay dying. He would die an ignoble death, riddled with flux, in a puddle of his own shit. And I wondered, who deserved their fate more, him or me? Because Harry was not the one who was a blasphemer or a traitor. Harry had been a good son, in the end, and a good Christian. He had loved his wife. Once, perhaps, he had loved his brothers, too. Now I awaited the crown, and Harry awaited a tomb in Normandy. Was that justice? Was that faith? Should I thank God for that?

I needed to tell my mother. The letter might only reach her after he was dead, but it had to be done all the same, before she could hear the news from my father rather than me. She and Harry had never been close, but he was her son, and she would mourn him.

I stood and brushed the flowers from my shoulders and hair, dropping the branch onto the ground. Today, I would write to my mother. In the morning I would leave for Paris. Small steps, taken with purpose. I would do nothing impulsive. I would leave Harry and all his legacy behind, to drain into the soil, culled like Solomon's Crown.

CHAPTER SEVEN

Philip

Geoffrey wrote to me that summer, after he had seen Rich-ard. *He was possessed,* the letter said, *by fear and grief and anger. He is desperate. You shall have little trouble making demands.* But Richard himself had yet to contact me, out of desperation or otherwise. I ought to have been concerned, perhaps, but I was occupied by the state of my court. Two barons had written demanding an easement of their tax levies, and my refusal had caused a spiral into threats of rebellion. My councilors favored military action; I did not. In our last meeting, Blois had stormed out halfway through the discussion. "A man who cannot hold a sword should not lead armies," he had said in his typical, gruff bark, "whether towards a battlefield or away from it." I ought to have responded with anger, or ordered him to stay—but I hadn't the authority, not really. He was an accomplished general, with more years of military experience than I had been alive. The crown did not change that.

After the council meeting, I went to sit with Isabella in the castle grounds, seeking distraction. We sat atop a small hill, sheltered underneath a large oak. Summer that year was dry and hot, and I felt too sluggish to work with any sort of efficiency. My tax papers were laid uselessly in my lap. A group of court ladies below us were braiding flowers into one another's hair. The air was heavy with the scent of dry grass, and the cicadas maintained a steady drone from their perches on the trees. Beside me, Isabella had her head bowed, hair loose. Her cheeks were sunburnt to a lurid pink. In her lap, she was weaving daisies into a chain.

"My lord," she said, as her fingers twisted the stems, "may we go swimming later?"

"I'm not certain," I replied, frowning at the incomprehensible handwriting at the bottom of the page. It was my own, from two days prior, but that did little to help me decipher it. "Where?" I asked.

"The pond?"

"The water is too stagnant. You'll catch something from the bad air."

"Oh." She turned her head to look at me, imploring. "The lake? On the other side?"

"I suppose," I said.

"Will you come?"

"I am busy."

"Tomorrow?"

"Perhaps," I said. "Not if it is sunny."

"Are you worried about getting burnt?" She raised a hand to her cheek. "It hardly hurts."

I sighed. "That is a lie, Isabella. You complained of it all morning."

"I—not *all* morning. It's fine now." She slumped dramatically against the tree. "You are so busy."

"I am king."

She tossed her daisy-chain—now looped into a crown—at

the sky. It spun in the air, then fell into her lap. "Well, I am queen," she said, "and I have nothing to do."

I paused in my reading to look at her properly. It had been obvious from her demeanor in recent weeks that she was tiring of her routine of poetry and stitching.

"Would you like lessons?" I asked her.

"Lessons? What sort of lessons?"

"Philosophy?"

"Philosophy? Who would teach a girl philosophy?"

"Anyone, if I ordered them to," I said. "You would like it. I used to tell Agnes of my lessons, and she enjoyed it."

"Really? Then, yes, I suppose. I think I should like to learn philosophy."

"Good."

"May I start tomorrow?" she asked.

"What about swimming?"

"Oh. In the afternoon?"

"Possibly," I said. "I will lend you some books first. We will see if it interests you."

"Thank you, Philip." She took the daisy-crown from her lap and leaned forward, placing it on my head.

I smiled at her; it was rare that she referred to me by name. I was so surprised by it I failed to object to the daisies. Isabella returned the smile and leaned back again. She was sitting entirely in the shade except for her legs, which were extended into the sunlight. Her pointed red slippers were peeking out of her skirt. They made her feet look like rose petals. She closed her eyes, content.

I glanced down at the ladies on the hillside. Agnes would have been with them a few years ago, but my abundance of sisters had now entirely abandoned me. I looked back at the paper. The numbers written upon it had been so imprecisely measured that they were hardly of any use at all. I considered telling Isabella we could go swimming in the lake.

"My liege!" someone cried. It was a messenger, huffing desperately as he made his way up the hill. When he fell to his knees before us, it was impossible to tell whether it was an act of deference or exhaustion. "My liege, visitors."

I had received no word that anyone would be coming today. "Who?" I asked, already suspecting what the answer would be. Anyone else would have bothered to forewarn me of their arrival.

"Aquitaine," he said, "and attendants."

"Ah." I paused, considering. "Escort them here."

"You wish to receive them *here*, my liege?"

"Yes. I see little reason to move, when the weather is so pleasant. And my wife is resting."

I saw a brief smirk flicker on Isabella's face, but she kept her eyes closed.

"Very well," the messenger said.

He went puffing back down the hill. The ladies giggled as he passed them.

"Aquitaine?" Isabella mumbled. "The prince?"

"Yes," I replied.

"He is important, isn't he? Won't he be insulted that you're making him come to the garden?"

"He needs to know that I prioritize my comfort over his."

"Oh. Because you are the king?"

"Exactly."

In the distance I could see horses. They came to a halt at the base of the hill, and I surveyed the tops of their riders' heads; one was taller than the rest, a burst of red-blond hair over scarlet livery.

"Shall I leave?" Isabella asked.

"No need." I stood, moving into the sun, and I offered her my hand. She took it and lifted herself up. Worrying nervously at her skirts, she stepped behind me.

"My apologies for arriving unannounced!" Richard called, as he walked up the hill. His attendants waited with the horses. His expression was decisively unapologetic: a wide, handsome smile that pressed a deep dimple into each cheek. It seemed he had been traveling for some time, since he had stubble on his jaw and dust on his cloak and shoes. The general dishevelment helped mask the exhaustion on his face, but not by much. His smile was less convincing the longer I looked at it. I felt a moment of pity, which I forced aside.

As he reached us, he bowed deeply, and said to Isabella, "The queen, I presume. My lady, it is an honor." He kissed her outstretched hand before turning to me. His grin widened as his eyes flickered to my hair. "Philip, you look well. Have I missed yet another coronation?"

Flustered, I pulled the daisy-chain from my head and dropped it to the ground. Curtly, I said, "Are you to make a habit of arriving without informing me first?"

"If I could give you greater forewarning, I would," he replied, in a blatant lie. "How long has it been since I saw you last?"

"I saw you in October, in Montlhéry."

"Oh, yes. Rosemary."

"Rosemary," I echoed, and Isabella cast me an inquisitive glance.

Richard sighed. He rubbed at the back of his head and allowed the smile to drop. "Might I bother you for a drink? I've been riding for some time."

I nodded. "Isabella, would you fetch us some wine?"

Isabella flashed me an expression of profound gratitude, then nodded awkwardly to Richard. She scuttled down the hill at a pace fast enough to be an impropriety.

Richard watched her progress, amused. "Quite young, is she not?" he asked.

"You may lodge your complaints about the match with my dead father, as he was the one who made it."

"I did not mean to offend."

I made a short sound of acknowledgment, tugging at my collar. "Might we return to the shade?"

"Of course," he said.

I sat down at the base of the tree. After a moment's pause, Richard followed. "You dislike the heat?" he asked, watching me.

"Somewhat. Why are you here, Richard?"

"Well, to see you."

"Obviously. Why?" I asked. "Another impulse?"

"Unfortunately, no." He drummed his fingers on his knee. "You have heard the news, I presume."

"Of your brother, you mean?"

"Yes."

"I have heard. He has been unwell for some time."

"He has." His expression was pained, twisting with sorrow and frustration. He did not have the masterful control of Geoffrey, but there was something just as disarming about his earnestness. "He seems likely to die."

"I am sorry to hear it," I said. "I do not know what it is like to lose a brother, but I imagine . . ."

I did not know how to finish. Richard's shoulders slumped. "I do not know either," he said. "Perhaps I never will. My family produces brothers only by blood. We grew up together, but once I left for Aquitaine . . . it was never the same."

I was woefully underqualified to respond. "I assume that you did not come here for comfort," I said, regretting it immediately after.

Richard's eyes narrowed. "Oh, of course not," he replied. "God forbid I should ever be permitted *that*."

"Pardon."

"No, it is no fault of yours. It is only—never mind. You know why I am here. I shall be heir to the throne."

Rather than meet his eyes, I looked away, remaining impassive. "Yes. You shall."

"My father despises me," Richard said. "He would have me concede Aquitaine to John."

"And you will not?"

"I will *not*," he snarled. "Aquitaine is my home. My mother's gift to me. I would die defending it."

"You cannot win a war against England. Not alone."

"I am aware."

"So, you will negotiate with your father?"

"I shall have to. I cannot lose the duchy. I have no choice."

"And what if negotiations fall through?" I asked.

His eyes met mine. "That depends on you."

"You want an alliance," I replied, satisfied.

"With the aid of both France and Brittany, my victory would be assured."

"It was not assured the last time," I said. "When you rebelled—"

"When we rebelled, your father was king. He had half your funds and an army already depleted by foreign wars. *You*, on the other hand . . ."

True enough. "Geoffrey has agreed to this?"

Richard scowled, but he replied, "Yes."

I paused, considering how best to navigate the conversation. Across from me, Richard shuffled on the grass, impatient. "Why should I help you?" I asked him, allowing a note of derision into my tone. "What benefit is there to me, to ensure you remain so powerful?"

"An alliance with the future king of England is not enough?"

"No, it is not," I said. "And I will not fight for glory alone."

Richard stood, and I wondered if he was going to leave. Instead, he stepped so that he was in front of me, and he crouched, bringing our faces level. "What would you have, then, Philip?" he asked. "What would be enough?"

I refused to give him the satisfaction of leaning away. I met his gaze directly "I want Anjou," I said. "Anjou—and Normandy."

Richard's brows lifted. "That is a lot of land," he said, which was a vast understatement. The request was truly absurd.

"I know that."

"Some would call it greed," he murmured. I became acutely aware of how close he was to me. I focused on the reflection of the grass in his eyes.

"Greed, ambition," I replied. "They are the same thing."

"Well, then. Ambitious as you are, imagine the advantages for you, to have a friend on the throne rather than an enemy. Should you really be asking for so much?"

"Is that what you are, Richard?" I asked. "A friend?"

"I can be," he said. "But I need more than half promises."

He was easy to read, anticipation in every line of his features, his eyes wide, his lips parted. I knew that Geoffrey had also requested Normandy from him, but I was curious to see if Richard would promise the same thing to both of us. I wondered if he was as immune to Angevin duplicity as he seemed to think.

"Anjou *and* Normandy," I repeated. "Anything else would not be worth my time. And my aid will not be immediate. I cannot intervene until you are openly in conflict."

"That could be years yet," he said.

"Then years you will wait."

He grinned and rocked back on his heels. "You are quite formidable, Little King."

"I would rather you refrain from calling me that."

"Very well. You will have Anjou and Normandy both, should you make good on your bargain."

He was either a good liar, when called for, or Geoffrey had not yet made his demands. The former seemed more likely. Richard clasped my hand in his, in a signal of agreement; his palm was warm and dry, and his grasp smothered my own. When our hands dropped, the heat lingered.

A servant began to climb the hill, juggling wine and cups. We fell into silence as he approached. We did not speak again until he had laid the items down and retreated.

"How long will you remain at court?" I asked. Richard shuffled so that he was sitting in the sun. His hair went the color of straw in the light.

"I am uncertain. I await news of my brother." He poured the wine, first for me, and then for himself. His eyes caught mine over the rim of his cup. Despite the wariness writ in his face, there was no discomfort in his posture; he seemed to fully occupy every space he found himself in, possess it as if he had been born and raised there. "You have a beautiful court," he said to me, motioning towards the ladies at the base of the hill. His gaze swept over them. "Your wife keeps good company."

"Good company indeed," I replied, reproaching, "and virtuous to a fault."

Richard seemed amused by this response. "And you are equally virtuous," he said, "from what I have heard. Your devotion to your wife is inspiring."

My lack of mistresses was somewhat unusual, considering the circumstances of my marriage—but not exceptionally so, and I did not understand why Richard felt the need to comment on it. Defensively, I replied, "Perhaps once you are married, you will be considered my equal."

He said, "I have a great horror at the thought."

"Of what? Being my equal, or being married?"

He smiled, but he did not answer. His hands fiddled idly with the hem of his shirt, rolling fabric between his fingertips. "You are a good king, Philip," he said. "I would be glad to match your competence."

"I have not been king long."

"Six years is enough. You have achieved more than your father did in a lifetime. You have negotiated new land and rebuilt your army."

"Expected tasks for a new monarch," I said.

"Ones well executed, all the same. Impressive, considering your age."

"I am not much younger than you."

"That is true," he said. "I apologize. You know, I was surprised when we met after your wedding."

"How so?"

"I was expecting a child, really. Instead, you were—" he broke off and took a long pause, sipping his wine. "You were all righteous fury, standing in front of me in your slippers. It was quite a sight."

I rolled my eyes. "I apologize if I scared you," I said, my tone sarcastic, but Richard only seemed to become more earnest in response. He leaned forward.

"On the contrary," he said. "You were quite extraordinary."

I felt my face begin to heat. Fisting my fingers into the grass,

I stared up at the sky, hoping that the blush would go unnoticed. When I looked back at Richard, however, he was staring at me with an odd expression: partly a frown, partly a smile.

"I have embarrassed you," he said.

"You have not. The heat is simply too much."

"I see."

"I—" My fingers dug into the ground, tearing some of the grass from the soil. I dropped the strands back to the dirt and took a long breath. "I would like to return for supper," I said.

He stood. "Of course."

I had thought that, after a moment of such intense discomfort, I might be provided some sort of reprieve. Instead, as we walked down the hill, Richard stood closer to me than was necessary. I had to step sideways to avoid bumping into him. He noticed my nervousness. "It would never be my intention to make you uncomfortable," he said.

"I should hope not," I replied, my tone cold.

"And you must tell me immediately if I am overfamiliar."

"Of course. But—"

"But you must forgive me if I surrender to temptation," he said, interrupting me. "You are so lovely when you are flustered."

It was the first time such a thing had ever been said to me. I was at a complete loss as to how to respond. I stopped walking and turned to look at him, mouth half-open in surprise.

Richard returned my gaze. Despite his affectation of confidence, I could tell he was cautious, watching for signs of anger or disgust. When it became clear I was struggling to reply, he said, gently, "Philip?"

I was saved by the approach of Isabella, running eagerly towards us, barefoot in the grass. She called my name, light-voiced, birdlike, suddenly and wonderfully familiar.

"Excuse me," I said hoarsely, and I walked away from him.

Richard remained where he was, watching as I retreated, his gaze heavy with curiosity.

~ ·o~

I had spent the formative years of my reign ensuring that my court ran on an exacting schedule. My life was extraordinarily efficient. I spent each day in the same manner, and this routine was the source of my equilibrium; I had hours allotted for work, for reading, for chess with Isabella. The Philip I wanted to be, that I needed to be, relied upon this order.

Over the next week, Richard seemed determined to demolish it. I had thought I had the measure of the duke, who, in our previous meetings, had seemed somewhat predictable; who, according to Geoffrey, would be as moldable as wet clay. I felt a fool for it now. I no longer knew what he was thinking, nor why he had remained at court at all. One day he was behind every door I opened, in every room I entered, in every corridor I walked down. The next, he was nowhere to be seen. He showed up for meals either hours early or hours late, but never on time. When he was present, every movement he made seemed to have some unknowable significance. Sometimes I caught him staring at me, and he would turn his eyes away very slowly, as if to ensure that I knew he had been looking. When we took wine together before bed, he would either monologue with a war story, or he would ask me so many questions it was as if he took pleasure merely from the sound of my voice.

I did my best to maintain normalcy, but there was, shamefully, some satisfaction in his attention. He provided me a brief escape from the demands of a court still doubtful of their young, untested king. One night, Blois ambushed me in the corridor after supper, demanding permission to lead an army against the baron we were quarreling with. "A simple siege, quickly done," he said to me, his oval, sallow face sagging beneath the weight of his scowl, "and if it *pleases* you, my liege, we shall burn no buildings save—"

At which point Richard turned the corner, barreled into us, and said, "Pardon, Blois, most urgent business—it's—knights—strategy—England—" and seized me by the arm to lead me away. "Good Lord, what a bloody bore that man is," he murmured into my ear, as we hurried down the corridor. "He's your marshal, isn't he? Say the word, and I shall start a war somewhere far away, so you can send him off and find a moment's peace. Poland, perhaps?"

"Too nearby, I fear," I replied. "Greece?"

"Oh, shall we make him an Alexander? Send him to India?"

"Perhaps he shall exceed Alexander and conquer Cathay."

Richard laughed, delighted. "Cathay it is," he said. "I shall write to the khan and start some argument between us."

Then, inscrutably, he raised my hand to his mouth and kissed my knuckles, as if I had granted him some great favor.

Blois did not approach me again that month, and I was grateful to Richard for offering me some reprieve. But despite each act of service he performed for me, each compliment he paid, his behavior was too erratic to draw conclusions from. The intensity of his fascination with me when we were together might have held some deeper meaning; but his extended absences made me doubt this was anything but a shameful fantasy on my own part. Richard was grieving his brother. He was doing so preemptively, perhaps, but he was grieving, all the same. I was only a distraction. Once the novelty ended—once he finally realized that I was king, that I would eventually be his enemy—his interest in me would disappear. Then he would no longer stare at me with that burning gaze, and I would no longer feel as if I were on fire.

Geoffrey's letter arrived one week after Richard did. After the platitudes, it said only, *I will come to court at once.*

My first thought was to speak to Richard. He deserved, at least, to be forewarned of Geoffrey's arrival. I stood from my desk and untied my hair, allowing it to fall beneath my ears. I told Galahad to stay as I left, but he hardly needed the instruction, as he was fast asleep on my rug.

It was simple enough to find a servant and request Richard's whereabouts. I was directed to the southern courtyard. This was strange, because that courtyard was used only for garrison training. The explanation came when I found Richard there unaccompanied, shooting arrows into a target.

His expression was grim, and his stance was very rigid. He wore his tabard without a shirt, leaving his arms bare—excusable, considering the heat—and he held a plain-looking bow that he must have pilfered from a soldier. He released the arrow with an impatient sort of discontent, reaching immediately for another from the crate without pausing to inspect his success. His aim was fair, if not perfect. There were no arrows in the center of the straw target, but there were many clustered in a ring around it, as if to wreathe the bull's-eye.

I hovered in the doorway to watch him as he took another shot. My eyes followed the shift of the muscles in his arm as he pulled the bowstring back, and I felt something entirely unwelcome slide down my spine in response.

"Richard," I said.

He looked up from the arrow crate. "Philip!" he replied. "Pardon, I did not know you were here. I would have been a better shot, if I had."

I did not know what to say, so I simply stepped forward and offered him the letter. He looked at it inquisitively, and then he noticed the seal. Scowling, he took it from me. As he read, I closed my eyes, allowing myself a moment's peace to enjoy the breeze.

When I looked at him again, Richard had crumpled the letter in his fist. "That is my letter," I said mildly.

"I know. Pardon," he replied. He did not sound apologetic. He dropped the wad of parchment to the ground and sighed.

I said, "Geoffrey . . ."

He waved away my concern. "No use in speaking of it. He will come, whether or not I would like him to. But—it is a shame we have so little time alone together before he arrives."

I frowned at him, perplexed. Richard chuckled, gesturing to the bow he had laid on the crate. "Do you shoot?" he asked.

"Badly," I replied. The last I had attempted it was when my father was alive. He had briefly thought to make me a warrior, but such aspirations quickly departed.

"Do you know the English style?"

"English style," I repeated, skeptically. "I have never heard of it."

"Come, I will show you."

"I do not—"

"Philip, please."

He seemed oddly desperate, and it was only out of some vestige of pity that I allowed him to hand me the bow. He instructed my stance, watching me follow his commands with narrowed eyes. It seemed the English style was much the same as the French one, except that it afforded him the ability to criticize anything he wanted.

"Take off your rings," he told me.

"No," I replied.

He threw his hands up in exasperation. "The Amazons cut off a breast. I believe you can remove your jewelry."

"I am not an Amazon."

"Your grip is suffering." Richard approached to stand behind me. He reached forward, putting his hand over my own around the bow grip. "See?" he said.

"What am I supposed to be seeing?"

"Your rings are loosening your hold."

Now that he was tightening my grip, I realized that this was true. I also realized Richard's proximity, which was already driving me halfway to madness. He did not touch me anywhere other than my hand, because *that* would have been an impropriety; instead, he hovered behind me, with his other hand floating over my hip. It was somehow much worse. I had no excuse to pull back, nor to tell him to move.

I shifted uncomfortably. "I will remove the rings," I said.

"Good," he murmured. He slid his hand down to hold the bow, dragging his fingers along my knuckles. He kept his arm raised there as I pulled my rings off. I could feel his breath along the back of my neck.

Taking the bow back from him, I prepared myself to shoot. He said, "May I correct you?"

"How?"

"Your stance."

I nodded, expecting him to tell me what was wrong. Instead, Richard took my shoulders and began to maneuver me into position. I made a choked sound of surprise and annoyance, which only made him laugh as he continued to push me into place. He used his feet to shove my legs farther apart.

"There," he said. His hands had settled on my sides. Through the fabric of my shirt, his fingers pressed into the hollow of my hips, his thumbs on my lower back. The touch was tentative, but unmistakable in its intent. My breath stuttered, and I found myself stepping back, pressing flush against him. He made a sound of approval. Like this—with his arms bracketing my waist, his mouth hovering over my neck—I struggled to recall why I had come to the courtyard in the first place. I could not remember why I had ever warned myself to keep away from Richard, why I could not drop the bow and turn to him and pull him nearer.

"Now what?" I asked him, voice shaking.

"Now," he whispered, "you shoot."

I glanced down to his hands, and then to his face. Our gazes met. We stared at each other, and his grip on my hips tightened. His eyes fell to my lips. I could have moved forward—I could have pressed my mouth to his and made good on every unspoken promise between us. I could have made my breath his breath, and tasted the uneven corners of his smile. But I did not. I could not move.

You must do it, I wanted to say to him. *I will never have the courage. It has to be you.*

I turned away and took the shot. It was awkwardly done, as I had to pull my arm back almost sideways to avoid elbowing him in the stomach. The bow swung wildly upwards. The arrow sailed over the target and hit the wall behind it, with a pathetic, dying clunk. It fell and disappeared into the bushes.

We stood in silence as we considered my failure. Richard bowed over so that his nose brushed my shoulder, and he began to laugh. "You *are* terrible," he said, muffled by my collar.

"You were in the way," I replied.

"Yes, I suppose that is true."

"But I am also terrible," I admitted, which made him laugh more.

I let him do so, and I let myself stay where I was, even as I knew I would eventually have to move. The tension had broken, somewhat; I had found myself again, somewhere in the haze of my desire, although my presence remained tenuous at best. But Richard's lips were still hovering over my collarbone, and his palms were still pressed against my hips, and I was painfully aware how easy it would be to lose myself once more.

"Richard," I said.

"Yes?" he murmured. He began to rub circles into my back with his thumbs.

"What is this?" I asked.

"Archery."

I turned my head to frown at him. That was foolish, because our faces were now very close. His lips twitched in amusement at my expression. "Stop pouting, Philip."

"I do not pout."

"You do. Very effectively, I might add, so feel no shame for it."

"If you will not answer me—"

"No, I will," he said. "This is whatever you would like it to be."

I stared at him, allowing myself to linger over the messy tangle of his hair, and the scar on his cheekbone, and the ears too large for his face. Then I thought of my father, who had gone half mad grieving the Duchess of Aquitaine after she left him; I thought of the map in my drawer; I thought of Geoffrey and the plans we had made. I reminded myself that Richard's brother was dying, and that Richard was desperate to distract himself from it. Grief can drive desires that we later come to regret.

We could create a thousand grievances between us, for the sake of this single moment. I did not trust myself enough not to disappoint him. Eventually, Richard would realize that I was not what he wanted, and he would resent me for it. That resentment would be dangerous, once we both wore crowns upon our heads.

"I would like it to be archery," I said.

Richard dropped his hands from my hips, taking a step back. "Of course," he replied.

"Richard—"

He shook his head and gave me an uncomfortable, bitter smile. "It *was* archery," he said. "Was it not? What else could it have been?"

"I . . ."

"Terrible archery, yes," he continued, "but archery all the same. I commend you for the effort."

It was an attempt at a truce, even though his teasing tone had an edge of genuine frustration. I nodded. "Thank you for the instruction."

"Shall we go to supper?" he asked, gesturing towards the doorway.

I nodded again. As I put the bow back into the crate, I found myself digging my nails into my palms in some effort of self-punishment. It had been selfish of me to entertain Richard's advances. I had guaranteed his disappointment, and mine.

When I looked up, Richard was gone. He had not waited for me before he had walked inside. I almost gaped in astonishment. I had not been treated with such rudeness since my father was king, and he had forced me to wait outside the chapel while he prayed. Once, I had stood there for more than an hour, in the winter cold. My fingers had turned blue. And yet—somehow—this still felt worse.

CHAPTER EIGHT

Richard

It had become clear enough that my interest was unreturned.

If it were as simple as a rejection, I might have feigned acceptance. But Philip would hardly look at me, even when we were forced together. At mealtimes, he was silent and solemn, staring blankly at his plate, gaze hardening to steel whenever it happened to meet my own. It was as if he wanted us to be strangers, but I did not have the patience to maintain the illusion. I would rather an argument than this tepid truce. Something had to give way: I began to stare at him openly, brushing my knee against his beneath the table, cracking chicken bones to make him flinch. Anything to provoke a response. I wanted him to snap at me, or else give me an excuse to snap at him. I wanted proof that he knew I was *there*. But he had refined his composure to a needle point.

By the end of the week, I was going quite mad, and Philip was only partially the cause. Harry haunted me. I saw him in every reflection. He wore my own face, but not quite my own; he was haggard, grey, eyes hollow with hunger. That was what flux

did, it made food flow through you like water. One might eat
and eat and never be full.

I had dreams, too. I had dreams where Harry knelt with
his head upon the block, crowned with a laurel of thorns. My
father would come, bearing an axe, and cut away his head; he
would lift it up by the hair to display it, as Harry's dead, swollen tongue spilled from his lips. Then he would fling the crown
to me. As I caught it, the thorns pressed into my palms, blood
streaming to my wrists. It was clear enough what such dreams
meant, what fears they spoke to. They were no less terrifying for
it, though, and no milder were the feverish, shivering sweats I
would awake to.

One morning I emerged from such a dream and found myself
sitting up in the bed, as if preparing to rise. The new angle of
viewing made me confused as to where I was; I half stumbled off
the mattress, in a panicked tangle of limbs and feet. I dressed
badly. My shirt was tied sloppily, my boots half undone. I made
little time for anything but escape. When I pulled the door open
to leave, however, I almost collided with my courtier Bernard.
He had his fist raised in preparation to knock.

"My lord, Geoffrey has arrived," he said, realizing from my
expression that I would have no patience for greetings.

"*Geoffrey?*" I repeated, and I stepped into the corridor. Still
bleary with sleep, I scrubbed my face with my hand, as if to rub
the dream away from it. "Good God, he came quickly. Where
is he?"

"In the front courtyard," Bernard replied.

"Has the king been informed?"

"Of course—I came as quickly as I was able, but—"

"Christ," I snarled, and I marched down the hallway, leaving
him in my wake. I made straight for the front courtyard, thundering down the stone steps to the ground floor. When I reached

the door, I nearly tripped on a bootlace. I tucked it into the edge of my shoe, rather than spend the time to tie it. Then I stepped out into the sunlight.

I was too late. In the shade of the walls, I saw Philip and my brother, mired in inaudible discussion as the horses were led away. They were vexingly complementary to each other, both statuesque and slender; they had the same cautious elegance in their movements and expressions, each speaking softly, nodding and frowning as if engaged in some sort of Socratic dialogue. As the door swung shut behind me, they both stopped talking and looked up towards me. Geoffrey smirked. Philip's face remained blank.

Geoffrey greeted me with "Brother" as I approached.

"Geoffrey." I glanced at his companion. "Philip."

"My Lord Aquitaine," he replied.

"You look well, Richard," Geoffrey said.

If he thought I would affect politeness for Philip's sake, he was mistaken. "No thanks to your arrival, dear brother," I responded, and Philip raised an eyebrow. "Why have you come?"

"I have news," Geoffrey said. "Perhaps we should go inside?"

"News? Of Harry?" I asked.

"I—yes. I am afraid so."

It was as good as telling me he was dead. Whatever anger I had felt at Geoffrey's appearance drained away, leaving only a curious emptiness. My hands prickled, palms damp with sweat; as my fingers curled against them, the wetness felt almost bloody, as if I were dreaming again. I took a halting step backward, scuffing my heels on the base of the steps.

Philip glanced between us. I could almost hear the movements of his mind as he assessed the situation, like the winch of a trebuchet. "Inside," he said, and we could do little but follow him into the castle.

He led us to a set of chambers I had never seen before. They were as well kept as all the others but lacking any evidence of recent use. There was a table in the center of the room, surrounded by wooden chairs; there was little else of note apart from the large tapestry hung across the back wall. I went to stand in front of it, unable to look either Philip or Geoffrey in the eye. It was beautiful work, if something of a macabre subject. The many-headed dragon of Revelation was battling against servants of God, lances skewered through each of its throats. Gore flowed from the wounds like tributaries of a river. It was a momentary distraction, and I allowed my head to empty as I looked at it.

A chair scraped against the floor as Geoffrey sat down. Philip approached me. He looked at me, and then the tapestry. He said, "It was my father's."

"Pardon?"

He cleared his throat. "The tapestry. It was a favorite of his."

I looked down at him. His eyes were scanning the tapestry with efficient movements, left to right, top to bottom, as if he were reading words on a page. Their blue color was so clear they reflected the red threads as a mirror would. His gaze lifted and met mine. When he realized I was staring, he flushed and turned away, moving back to the table.

I turned to see Geoffrey watching us with an inscrutable expression. Unwilling to sit, I stood at the table's head, laying my palms flat on the wood and leaning forward.

"I was near Chinon when it happened, and I heard the news quickly," Geoffrey said. "I made haste here, since I knew you were both in Paris."

"How considerate of you," I said.

"I am glad to be the first to tell you, Richard," he replied, "even if you would rather hear it from someone else. Harry has died. He is to be interred in Rouen."

I bowed forward, my arms briefly unable to support my weight. Philip said, quietly, "God rest his soul."

"Amen," Geoffrey murmured.

"Was it—" I began, and then I shook my head.

Both of them stared at me. Words filled my mouth, but I could not speak them. Philip cleared his throat and asked, "Does Henry know?"

"Of course," Geoffrey said. "Harry wrote a confession to him on his deathbed, asking his forgiveness."

"Forgiveness for what?" Philip asked.

"The rebellion."

I scoffed at that, glad for the stab of annoyance I felt. It was easier to speak when fueled by anger, rather than grief. "We were already forgiven," I said. "At least publicly."

"I suppose publicly is not good enough, when one's immortal soul is at risk," Geoffrey replied. "Well. He got what he wanted. Father would not see him, but he sent him a ring as a sign of his favor."

"A *ring*!" I repeated.

"Yes, a ring, with the royal seal on it. It is said Harry cried tears of joy to see it."

Harry had felt such relief to receive my father's mercy, but even on his deathbed he had sent me nothing, and he had asked me for nothing. Our last conversation had been an argument. Our last embrace had been when we were children. He had been absolved by our father with a trinket, gladly so, and yet he left no apologies, not even a letter for the brother once his friend. I said, with astonishment, "And so he shall dance straight through purgatory, no doubt! Since King Henry has cleansed him of his sins with jewelry!"

"Oh, *Richard*," Geoffrey said, making a passable attempt at sounding scandalized. But Philip made a strange cough, clearly attempting to disguise a laugh, and we both turned to him. He shifted uncomfortably in his seat.

"Pardon. Your father is . . ." he began, and then he trailed off. "A ring, truly? Instead of visiting his son on his deathbed? It is almost an insult, is it not?"

I said, "I should think so. He might as well piss on Harry's grave, for all the 'favor' he has shown him."

Philip had schooled his expression into one of stoicism, but there was a curl to the corner of his lips that betrayed his amusement. It was intensely gratifying to see such a fissure in his composure, as tiny as that fissure was. It struck me that he was simply too lovely to be sitting next to Geoffrey: a hyacinth in a patch of hemlock. I stared at him with a newfound, manic concentration. Philip could usurp whatever other images my mind supplied. He could replace Harry's grey, dead face with his own.

Geoffrey sighed, folding one leg over the other. If he recognized my expression, as I stared at Philip, it was of no consequence to him. "It matters very little now," he said. "Henry shall come calling for Aquitaine soon. You have months, at most, before he tells you to give it up. He will not name you heir until you do."

"And we all agree that we shall not allow it," I replied.

"He will attempt to negotiate," Philip said. "Coerce, certainly, if that does not work. He knows this is a fight he is unlikely to win."

Geoffrey agreed. "He will delay as long as possible. It is to his advantage. This—Harry's death, I mean—was obviously unexpected; he is not prepared for battle."

"Neither are we," I said. "The state of *your* army, in particular, Geoffrey—"

He interrupted, "Unlike you, the entirety of my treasury is not devoted to war—"

"And that is cause for regret, brother, for if we now must *go* to war—"

"*When* we go to war, we will have had time enough—"

"We shall go to war," Philip said. Despite his gentle tone, his voice was surprisingly loud, sufficient to cut off my sneering response. I had begun to loom over the table without realizing, and I fell back, chastened. "We shall go to war," Philip repeated. "But some patience is necessary. We all need to prepare our armies. Meanwhile, we must stay the course, and maintain confidence in the alliance. Do not give Henry cause to demand more than he already shall."

Geoffrey tapped impatiently on the table. "And if—when—the negotiations fall through, in terms of land ..."

"You shall have Normandy," I told him, taking a seat. I glanced nervously to Philip, wondering if he might call out my lie. His expression was impassive.

"And you, my liege?" Geoffrey asked him.

"Anjou," he said.

"Only Anjou?"

"Yes."

"Then Richard shall have a kingdom," Geoffrey said.

"A kingdom," I agreed, "and Aquitaine also."

"And Aquitaine, of course," he replied. "Tell me, Richard, how long have you been in Paris?"

"A week."

"Not long, then."

"No."

"You wish to return home as soon as possible, I presume," he said, "now that Harry is dead. You would not leave your lands undefended."

Now that Harry is dead. To hear it spoken so casually was

painful, as if someone had put their hand through my stomach and twisted. "And you?" I asked, strained.

"What of me?" he replied.

"Shall you return to Brittany?"

"I am not under immediate threat." I opened my mouth to respond, but Geoffrey turned to Philip, speaking quickly enough to cut me off. "I shall remain at court," he continued, "if you would permit it, my liege."

Philip nodded. "You may stay as long as you need, my Lord Brittany."

I made a noise of disgust and leaned back into the chair.

Geoffrey smirked. "Pardon, Richard. Is something the matter?"

"No, brother, of course not."

"You seem distressed," he said. "Are you so reluctant to return to your duchy?"

"Are *you* so reluctant to return to yours?"

"There is no fault in visiting the court of an ally, when circumstances permit."

Had there been an appropriate object on the table, I would have thrown it at him. "And the funeral?" I asked.

"Harry's funeral?" he said. "Come, now. As if we would ever be permitted the time to travel. I expect Father has already put him in the casket. He will be rid of him as soon as possible. Yet another failure of the Angevin lineage." His lip curled in disdain. "Fuel for the pyre, nothing more."

This was a fair summation of our father's character, and one I could not respond to without revealing my agreement. I settled for scowling at the table. Philip looked back and forth between us, his lips pursed. I could not fault him for deciding to abandon the conversation. He stood from his chair.

"We have more to discuss, I know," he said. "But I am afraid there are matters I must attend to, before supper. My Lord Brittany, I thank you for bringing us this news. I am sorry for your loss."

Geoffrey nodded. "My liege."

"Philip," I said, by way of farewell.

"Richard," he responded. Then he frowned slightly, as if angry that he had done so. As he left, he neglected to close the door behind him, and it slammed shut.

I stood also. Geoffrey frowned. "Shall we not speak?"

"We have spoken."

"Not without the king present."

"I have nothing more to say to you," I told him. I ran my hand through my hair, tugging hard enough to sting my scalp. "Do you have anything of any importance to tell me, or may I leave?"

"Nothing that you would deem important, regardless of how important it is."

"So, you do not."

Geoffrey waved his hand dismissively in a swift, practiced movement. "Leave, then," he replied. "But answer me one question."

"What is it?"

"We are family, Richard," he said. "We have shared history, shared interests. Will that count for something, in this alliance?"

"What would you have me say, Geoffrey? We are brothers in blood only."

"And Philip?" he asked. "You would trust him more than me?"

"Trust him? Perhaps not. But I like him better, certainly."

"Oh, I'm *sure*," Geoffrey replied, with all the weight of his derision, and all the implication that came with it.

Frustrated by my transparency, I made a rude gesture at him. He tutted loudly, opening his mouth to continue speaking; I said, "Piss off." Then I was already leaving, nearly tipping a chair over in my haste. He watched me go without comment.

Once I reached the sanctuary of the corridor, I took a deep breath, taking a moment's pause to press my forehead against the stone wall. It was cool and dry, a small relief from the warmth of the air.

I briefly entertained searching for Philip, but my mood after my brother's arrival was hardly one of reconciliation. I stared down at my untied laces. My eyes watered with grief and anger. A single tear landed upon the leather of my boot.

I closed my eyelids. Behind them, I imagined the battles that awaited me, the swinging blades and the shouting soldiers. War promised that singular and total absence of comprehension, when a man becomes only teeth and tongue and hand and sword. It would be a baptism of fury: I would enter a duke, and leave a king. Then all this would be a memory, the wound of Harry's passing closed. All this suffering would feel less futile.

I prayed to God, that it would feel less futile than it already did.

⁓

By evening I had summoned my composure, and I sought a servant to request Philip's whereabouts. If I would be return- ing to Aquitaine the next day, I refused to leave things as they were.

I was directed to his study. He seemed to have chosen the room to be as far away from everything else as possible. To reach it I had to walk across a courtyard, through the summer storm that had brewed over the course of the day. I came inside drip- ping wet from the rain.

It was almost as if the door had something of Geoffrey's smugness about it, and I rapped on the wood with more anger than I intended. After I had done so, I feared that Philip would recognize the frustration in the knock and realize who it was; perhaps he would simply ignore my presence and leave me waiting outside. But the door soon swung open.

Clearly, Philip had not been expecting visitors. He had taken off his outer tunic and doublet, exposing a severe set of collarbones beneath his undershirt. He had a blanket draped over his shoulders for warmth. In his left hand he was clutching a small, velvet-bound book, which had a ribbon peeking from its top as a page marker.

If he was unnerved by my presence, the only sign was a slight narrowing of his eyes. "My Lord Aquitaine," he said.

"Philip."

"May I help you?" His tone was not the sort that invited response. He pulled the door halfway shut behind him, as if to prevent me from forcing my way inside. Then he looked at me properly. With some surprise, he said, "You are soaking wet."

"It is raining. Unavoidable, I'm afraid." I gave him my most winning smile. "But a warm fire would not be amiss."

"There is a fireplace in your chambers."

"Ah, but then I would have to run back through the rain. Take pity, Philip, please."

His lips tightened. He gave me a brief, assessing glance, and perhaps he saw some sign of my distress; his expression gentled somewhat. There was no pity there, but still a small impulse of kindness. He took a step back, opening the door to allow me inside.

The room was small but lavishly decorated, with several cabinets of books. In front of the fireplace, a sand-colored hound was curled up on the carpet. It lifted its head as I entered, regarding me with suspicion. In the corner stood a blue lacquered table that appeared Byzantine in construction, and sitting beside it was Philip's wife, Isabella. She looked at me with eyes as wide and as dark as the dog's.

"My lady," I said to her, and I bowed.

"My Lord Aquitaine," she mumbled in return, sliding down from her chair and dropping into a curtsy.

"Isabella, I shall have to send you back," Philip said, as he opened a cabinet. He pulled out another small book, and then put them both on the table in front of her.

"*Two?* Really?" she asked.

"Take care of them."

"I shall." She gathered the books in her arms with exaggerated caution, as if they were made of glass.

"The rain shall ruin them," I told her. "You might wish to wait—"

"She can leave through the back of the tower," Philip said. "It is connected to the rest of the castle. No need to pass through the courtyard."

"Ah," I replied, as water dripped into my eyes. "I see."

Isabella had none of Philip's composure, and she turned away from us, books cradled in her arms, attempting to hide her amusement. Philip watched her, and I watched Philip, as his expression softened to affection. He looked as I imagined brothers ought to look.

"Shall I accompany you?" he asked her.

Her gaze flickered to me, and then back to him. "But—what of . . ."

"I am content to wait," I said. I sat on one of the chairs by the fireplace, stretching my arms above my head. The dog sat up and cocked its head at me. "No lady should wander the castle alone at night. What if a lonely spirit steals her away?"

"A spirit?" Isabella repeated, her tone skeptical.

Philip crossed to the desk, where his tunic had been folded neatly beside the candle. As he pulled it on, he sighed. "There are no spirits. Obviously."

"Perhaps not here, but there are plenty in Poitiers. They keep me up all night with their wailing."

Isabella looked at Philip. "Surely not?"

"It is true," I said. "I must keep guard at all times, lest they pull me down to hell with them, to burn for all eternity."

Isabella let out a surprised "Oh!" at this. The dog stood at the sound and raised its hackles, its ears pinned to its head.

"Galahad, down," Philip snapped. With some reluctance, the hound sat. Philip glared at me. "Isabella, we are leaving," he said to her. He took her by the arm and pulled her to the door.

"Good evening, my lady," I called as they exited.

I caught Isabella's confused farewell as the door closed. Then I was left at the fireside, the dog staring cynically at me.

"Hello, Galahad," I said to it. Its ears twitched, and I wondered if it would approach me. Instead it made a loud groaning noise, lowering itself back to the floor. Uninterested, it seemed. Dogs do take after their masters.

For lack of anything better to do, I stood and inspected the room more thoroughly. It was completely different from the one I had been in with Philip and Geoffrey earlier that day, luxurious in its furnishings and clearly in regular use. I went to the desk first, smoothing my hand over the surface, marveling at the carvings: a repeating motif of a golden swan on blue water, its feathers each individually detailed. On top of it was a stack of documents, tax information of some sort. I was surprised that Philip would take time to read the raw figures himself, rather than request a report from a steward. Mantes, Saint-Denis, and Montlhéry were all listed. Some numbers were underlined, some were not. An inky thumbprint had been left half smudged in the bottom corner. I spent several minutes going through the rest of the papers, but they were all of a similar sort.

Giving up on the documents, I put them back down. I tried to open the drawers, but they were locked. Also on the desk was a brooch, presumably Philip's, which he must have been using that day to pin his cloak in place. It was made of hammered silver, in the shape of an eight-pointed star. Each point was studded with a tiny, round piece of lapis lazuli. I lifted it up and found it was surprisingly heavy.

Shivering from the damp, I returned to the fireside, inspecting the brooch in the light. The dog raised its head to look at me, but I ignored it. I instead found myself entirely fascinated by this object and the traces of Philip it held: I wondered whether it was a gift, or his own purchase; I wondered why he wore it on that day; I wondered why he would choose this shape and not a cross or a fleur-de-lis or a sword; I wondered why he would want silver and not gold, blue gems instead of red; I was overwhelmed, suddenly, by all the details I did not know. Finding myself in a meditative state, I wheeled the brooch back and forth across the flesh of my palm, the points leaving constellations behind them.

"You are prying," Philip said from behind me, and I nearly jumped in surprise.

"Lord, you are quieter than a monk," I replied, turning to look at him. He was halfway into the room. As our gazes met, he allowed the door to close behind him. The dog leapt up to approach him, its tail wagging. Philip lowered his arm to scratch it behind the ears.

"You have dripped water all over the rug," he said to me.

I looked at the floor. The rug beneath me was as extravagant as the rest of the room, dyed a vibrant red, now marred with darker patches where my boots had pressed against it. I looked back to Philip. "It is a lovely rug," I said. "I am certain it can withstand a little rain."

"It is Moorish," Philip replied. He folded his arms. The dog looked between us, decided it ought to leave, and began to whine at the door. Philip let it out.

As he closed the door again, I said, "You have been avoiding me."

"I have," he agreed. "Why are you here, Richard?"

"Distraction, I suppose. It is difficult to be alone, when . . ."

I could not finish. Philip's expression loosened a little, and he pursed his lips in contrition. He walked over to the desk, reshuffling the documents nervously.

"You have looked at these," he murmured.

"The documents? Yes, I did. I couldn't understand them."

Philip began to laugh, and he cleared his throat to prevent it. "I expect I cannot be the distraction you require," he said cautiously.

"Perhaps not. Perhaps I cannot be distracted from this."

"I know you must be upset." He pinched the bridge of his nose. "Pardon. I . . . it is not . . . I do not know what to say."

I shook my head. "It is not your burden to bear, Philip. It is only that—I am returning to Aquitaine tomorrow, and I cannot stand the thought of leaving things as they are."

Philip frowned. "And how would you like to leave things?"

"I would like to be your friend," I said. "We could, at least, have that."

"I cannot be your friend."

"Why?"

"Why do you *think*, Richard?" he said. "We might have pretended friendship, once, but now . . . I do not want to pretend. We shall become enemies the moment our interests do not align. Anything else is an illusion."

"Must you always be so cynical?"

"I am realistic. We cannot—*I* cannot have everything I want. It is important to accept that. This is how things ought to be."

I frowned at him, attempting to decode this new cypher he had laid before me. Philip seemed to have little interest in aiding the effort, and he glared at me, defiant, from behind the desk.

"I think very little of how things should be," I said.

"Perhaps you would be wise to think of it more often."

"Perhaps," I agreed. "But in truth, Philip, all I think of is you."

His eyes widened. His hands gripped the edge of the desk, and his head bowed. A lock of hair fell in front of his face. "Richard . . ."

"Would you have me pretend otherwise? I will if you demand it of me. But it seems a pointless fiction, now."

"You say this because you are desperate," he said. "You are desperate and grieving, and you believe I can make you less so."

"It isn't only that," I replied. "I swear."

"What else is it, then?"

"I have wanted you since the moment we met. On your wedding night, even; I thought about it as we spoke. I thought about what it would be like, to have you in my bed."

He made a choked noise. "You—you cannot have *possibly* imagined we could . . ."

"I did," I said. "And I still do. Constantly."

Philip was undeniably affected by this. His lips parted, but he made no sound. I began to approach him, slowly. He did not retreat. Instead, he remained standing between the desk and the window, staring at me. Behind him, the rain thrummed against the glass.

"You are making a mistake," he told me. "We are making a mistake. I've already decided this is impossible."

I stopped in front of him, laying my hand over his own, where his palm was pressed against the desk. "Then tell me to leave," I said.

"I cannot."

"Tell me you do not want me."

"I cannot," he repeated. "You know that I cannot."

I kissed him. At first, he froze; then he sighed into it, relieved, as if I had absolved him of a sin. I circled my arm around his lower back, pulling us together. His hands skittered across my chest, thrown by the sudden shift in balance. They rose to grip the damp fabric on my shoulders, the heat of his palms burning through the last of the lingering rain.

Tentatively, his tongue pressed against the seam of my lips. I responded in kind, and the kiss grew more heated. I crowded him farther against the window, pushing myself against him. Eventually Philip paused and pulled his head back. His eyes were clouded with desire, pupils blown, but they still narrowed as they looked at me. It was as if he had come to some realization.

"Philip?" I said, unsettled by the sudden sharpness of his gaze.

"Anjou," he said.

"I— What?"

His lips twitched in faint amusement, and he repeated, "Anjou. You promised me Anjou *and* Normandy, when I first agreed to help you."

I winced. "Must we speak of it *now?*" He gave me a withering stare. "Fine. And Normandy, yes. But Geoffrey . . ."

"If you are to lie, Richard," Philip said, "you ought to do it well."

Attempting to mend things, I tipped my head down. His lips parted in anticipation, but instead I brushed my mouth against his cheekbone, his jaw, his throat. He lifted his chin to give me more room. I made a small noise of appreciation.

"I lied to Geoffrey, not to you," I mumbled against his collarbone. "You shall have them both."

"I do not believe you," Philip said. I nipped at his skin, and he shuddered. "And now you are trying to distract me," he continued accusingly.

"Is it working?" I asked.

"I will have Vexin, instead," he said. I paused in my efforts. "My father should never have given it away. It will leave Normandy and return to France. Anjou as well. Geoffrey shall have the rest."

I pulled away to look at him. I could not help but admire his audacity. "Did you plan this?" I asked him.

"Does it matter?" he returned.

"How clever you are, Philip. I would be a fool to agree to that."

"You do not have a choice."

"No, I suppose not." I kissed him again. "I do not care, either way."

Philip pushed his hands up the back of my neck, tangling his fingers in my hair. "You should care," he said. "You are allowing me to manipulate you. Why?"

"Because I want you," I replied.

"But *why*?"

"Do I need a reason?"

"Yes."

"You are as you are, and I want you for it. Is that not enough?"

Philip went quiet, considering this.

"No," he said. "But I want you also. So—for now—I shall pretend it is."

It was permission enough; it had to be. I swept the tax papers away from his desk. Philip made a sound of complaint, but then I lifted him up so he was sitting where the papers had been, and his legs were wrapping around my waist, and he was tugging me forward by the collar so our mouths could meet. I presumed I was forgiven.

The rain grew louder against the window. There was little noise in the room apart from its hum, and the soft gasps Philip made as my hands wandered, and my own heartbeat in my ears—no less a sound of my own creation, it seemed, than any other I could hear; my body, no longer mine, was acting entirely upon instinct, pressing closer to him, *desperate* for him, aching and insistent. My fingers trailed up his thighs. Philip shuddered, and then widened his stance in invitation, arching his back to press us flush against each other.

Someone knocked on the door of the study. Philip pulled away and froze completely, wide-eyed. I groaned and turned to look at it, saying loudly, "What is it?"

There was a long pause. Then came the muffled voice of Philip's steward. "My Lord Aquitaine," he said, "I seek the king—"

"The king is busy."

"*Richard,*" Philip hissed, disentangling himself from me. "Is it urgent, Guillaume?" he called at the door. He was still slightly breathless. It was marvelously incriminating.

"The council requests an emergency meeting. The Baron of Beauvau has sent men towards Craon, claiming to seize the assets he is owed by the crown—"

"Owed!" Philip barked, and he slid off the desk. Bereft, my arms fell to my sides. "An act of rebellion, nothing less. Has Blois—"

"He threatens to withhold support unless his prior concerns are addressed, my liege."

Philip swore. He bent and began collecting the papers I had pushed to the floor. "I'll be there shortly," he called to Guillaume. There came a sound of agreement from the other side of the door, and then footsteps as our intruder left.

"You're leaving?" I asked, frowning.

"I must. Help me with these, won't you?"

I aided him in collecting the papers. "I am departing from Paris today," I told him as we piled them on the desk. "This afternoon. I will prepare to meet with my father. It might be months before my return."

"I know."

"So—could the meeting not wait?"

"Wait?" Philip repeated, mystified. "No, it cannot. My vassals expect me."

"Tell them you will come later. You are king, and they must listen to you."

"That is the issue," he said. His puzzled expression warped into a scowl. "I am king, Richard. I have the weight of a nation upon my back, and a vassal in open rebellion. I cannot put that on hold to—to—"

He made a vague, frustrated gesture at me, and I flinched, wounded.

"Oh, I see," I said. "Pardon, my liege. I suppose I have been distracting you from *important* matters."

"That isn't what I meant."

"No? What did you mean, then?"

He blinked at me. His mouth opened, and then closed. Even his silence felt calculated, as if he knew his astonishment would be crueler than any further insult. The fault was mine, really. I shouldn't have expected him to lend a brief fumble on a desk any significance.

"No matter," I said. "I should leave you be."

"I— Look, I have to prioritize—"

"Prioritize what you like, Philip. I do not care. Prioritize Vexin. Prioritize your council meetings and your taxes and your petty wars. I shall return when I have something more worthy of your time than—" I made the same vague gesture towards myself that he had. "Than *this*."

Philip's shoulders fell, and his face became blank. The only lingering elements of his previous lust were the wide, black circles of his pupils, and they watched me with an empty sort of regret; it almost felt as if I could have fallen into them.

"Very well," he said. "Perhaps you are correct. It was foolish of me to encourage you. Rest assured, I shan't allow it to happen again."

"Fine. I am glad it won't."

He didn't respond. His expression remained impassive, and he watched me with silent vacancy as I spun on my heel and left the room.

My composure held only until I had stepped over the threshold, at which point I closed the door behind me with enough force to make it shudder. It was a childish thing to do, but the violence of it provided some satisfaction, all the same.

Once that satisfaction drained, however, I resisted the urge to sink to the floor and scream into my hands. I wanted to tell myself I had still achieved some small victory by that meeting, as sourly as it had ended; I did not have Philip, but at least I now had the sense I had marked him somehow. I could pretend that my touch would remain with him permanently, a stain upon his lip where my thumb had brushed over his mouth, like the inkblot on his papers. I could pretend that when I returned, even if it was years from now, Philip would still have that indelible trace I had left on him. Perhaps that would be enough.

But I knew, even as I imagined this, that it was not enough. There was no permanent stain. Instead, the only reminder of my time with him was temporary, already beginning to fade: the embossed fleur-de-lis on the handle of the study's door, imprinted on my palm by the force of slamming it shut.

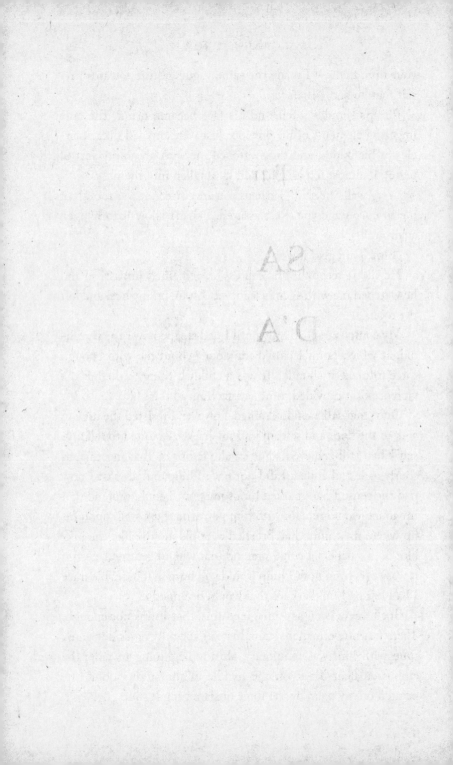

Part Two

SALUT

D'AMOR

CHAPTER NINE

Richard

When I die, I will be taken apart. My family own lands across the continent, and so across the continent we are laid to rest; our bodies buried in Anjou, and our entrails entombed in the place of our death. Titles determine where the heart is laid. Once I became king, and the empire was mine, my heart would be buried in Rouen. It would not be in Aquitaine, my true home.

I did not like Rouen. Rouen was in Normandy, and Normandy was Henry's land. I was only ever there to speak to my father, and I was only ever speaking to my father when he wanted something I was unwilling to give. Everything in the city was his entirely: the winding streets, the stink of the market, the lopsided huddle of its houses. The cathedral felt his in particular, spindly and skeletal in its construction, sneering and smug. But it was, for better or worse, one of the few places in Rouen where I was certain to be alone. My brother was buried there, as I one day would be. I was at least permitted to visit his tomb without fear of reprisal.

It had been more than a year since my last visit to Paris; since

I had last seen Philip face-to-face, and since Harry's death. The time had been passed in Normandy, Aquitaine, and England—in constant talks with Henry, and in constant preparation for war. Now, I awaited yet another meeting with my father. It was a final, futile attempt at negotiation. I was expected at the palace, and I should have already arrived. But I had come to see my brother first.

I stood in silence in the cathedral, staring at Harry's tomb. Inside lay his unmoving heart, embalmed in frankincense. His effigy, a fair likeness if not a perfect one, rested stoically above it. The folds of his robe had been carved with geometric severity. It seemed as if the lines had been made hastily, chiseled deeply across the stone. His face was impassive, and it did not react as I shivered from the chill of the chapel air.

"They have made you shorter than you were," I murmured to the statue. Perhaps I ought to have said a prayer, but he had been offered enough of those already. *They will bury me across from you, Harry.* I could have told him that. *Then you will have to stare at me for eternity. I am certain you will enjoy that.*

I thought of his heart within the tomb, decaying sweetly in its puddle of scented oils. It seemed an ignoble end for the center of the soul, torn out of him and left abandoned in a Norman church. The heart is a sanguine organ. The greater the heart, the more the humors of the body run to heat, to extroversion and compulsion. When I was twelve years old, an English doctor told me I had a heart too large for my chest. Really, to what end had he informed me of this? Was he to remove it and shave it down to size? I spent the next few months wondering if my heart might grow faster than the rest of me, until it weighed me down, and I would have to walk bent over like a hunchback.

That summer, my mother and I went south. We visited a court at the foothill of the Pyrenees, and amongst the courtiers there was a Moorish physician. The local lord feared we would be angry that he had employed an infidel, but my mother instead insisted that the doctor examine us. He was young, with skin the color of cherry wood, and he spoke Occitan with an accent like smoke. When he pressed his fingers over my neck, I had trembled with confused and reluctant desire.

"Your heart is strong, my lord," he said, as if it were a good thing, as if it were something I should be *proud* of. But then he frowned. "You are agitated. I will not hurt you."

"Yes, Doctor," I replied. I made my voice very quiet, so that he would think he was correct; that distress had been why my pulse was so fast. But I spent the rest of our visit watching him, peering at him from behind granite columns and apricot trees. It had been one of my first infatuations. I have always found it easier to fall in love in the south, or during the summer, when the sun can filter through my skin, and pass its heat to my chest.

Now I wondered if the Moorish doctor could have saved Harry. If he had, my brother's heart would still be inside him. I would not be the heir, and I would not be in Rouen. I would be in Aquitaine, or Paris. I could visit my mother, or go on progress, all the way to the Pyrenees.

But there was nothing to be gained from such thoughts. Harry was dead, and I was in Normandy. There was only one reason I was here, and it was not to mourn my brother.

~∽~

I was far too deep within Henry's duchy to be comfortable, especially when we remained on the brink of war. I had to assure myself with the knowledge that I could fall back into French territory, should I really need to, although Philip would be displeased at me for drawing English hostility into his lands. We had been writing letters about the state of negotiations—the extent of our communication, for the past year—and he framed my discussions with Henry as some sort of Saxon epic. *Do not let him scent weakness,* Philip would write, as if my father were Grendel coming to feast.

I clung to these moments of imagination, thinking them proof that Philip and I remained something more than political partners. Perhaps this was a futile fantasy. Considering the argument we'd had when I'd last seen him, I had almost given up hope that my affections were still returned; but a dying fire still burns. I always responded to his messages with dogged familiarity, as if I could erase our disagreements through writing alone. In one of my recent letters, I wrote a small note at the bottom:

P.S. Today, one of my soldiers hit his commander in the foot with a stray arrow. It made me realize how lucky we had been that day, to avoid injury. I suggest you never hold a bow again.
—Richard

I was pleasantly surprised to receive the following response:

P.S. I am insulted to court comparison with an inept soldier. You were in the way, and you ruined my aim.—Philip

I still had this letter with me as I made my way to the ducal palace, where my father and I were to meet. It had arrived only that morning, and thus its presence was only coincidental; besides, it meant nothing, and I would afford it no significance. But I found myself pulling the parchment out of my satchel as I stood on the barge, tracing the harsh sprawl of Philip's handwriting, imagining his fingers as they wrapped around the quill.

The building was a heavy, several-centuries-old construction lying at the crossing of two rivers. The greater of the pair, the Seine, flowed north. If I were to fall into it, pushed off the castle walls by some vindictive gust of wind, I would be swept across Normandy and into the Channel. The smaller river was the Aubette, which would take me west: towards Brittany, and Geoffrey. I did not know which would be the better outcome.

My guard waited behind as I was led into the throne room. Henry did not permit the presence of strangers during our discussions. The door was closed at my back and I was left there alone, facing the dais where my father loomed above me. The light was dim, and I waited for my eyes to adjust. Henry said nothing. He was a shrouded figure on the throne, hungry, vengeful. I had to step closer to look at him. It was only then that I saw John huddled beside him.

Henry had my coloring exactly: red-blond hair, brown eyes, tanned. He had my large ears and wide shoulders. If he were to stand up, we would be the same height to the tenth of an inch. There was no doubt that we shared blood. It was not so with John, who had dark hair; a soft chin; small, sharp eyebrows— like strokes of ink; and pale, yellow-toned skin. He was short, too—as short as Philip and as slender besides. He looked nothing like me, nor Geoffrey, nor Harry, nor Eleanor. I had heard my mother once say that he bore a striking resemblance to my paternal grandmother. It was fortunate that he did, for otherwise his parentage might have been called into question. As it was, John had always seemed out of place in our family: a crow amongst ravens.

It had been a long time since we last met. As I dropped to my knee in greeting, I counted the years. He was seventeen now, or thereabouts, depending on when his birthday was. I did not know. He seemed younger than he was. As I looked at him, I could see his nervousness, his eyes unwilling to meet mine. His hand was laid flat on the arm of our father's chair, as if he might fall without support.

"I greet you, Father, Brother," I said. I raised my chin as I did so, ensuring the deference of my position remained superficial.

"Stand up, Richard," Henry said. "No need for such displays."

I stood. "Come, John," I said to my brother, "it has been so long. Will you not greet me?"

He looked to my father for instruction, and Henry nodded. John descended the steps with his arms raised to balance himself. He stopped in front of me, and then he seemed unwilling or unable to act. I stepped forward and embraced him.

"I have no quarrel with you," I murmured before I moved away. In truth, I had no way of knowing whether John wanted Aquitaine for himself; my father might have decided it without his input. But it did not matter. The outcome of the argument rested on mine and Henry's shoulders alone.

John wrung his hands and took a faltering step back. "I am pleased to see you, Richard," he said. He was so soft-spoken I had to strain to hear him.

"I had expected you to remain in England," I replied. "You are regent when Henry is away, are you not?"

"This matter concerns John, and so John shall have a place here," Henry said. He surged from his chair and marched down the steps, folding his hands behind his back. His skin was starting to sag with age, his forehead creased into a permanent frown. It took nothing away from the sheer presence of him, the captive-lion quality of his movements. He paced around us at considerable speed, with his shoulders pulled back and his head raised. John shrank in his posture, as if ropes were pulled taut around him.

"You come with an impressive guard, Richard," Henry said.

"You come to Rouen—one day *your* Rouen, the capital of your lands in the continent—and you march through the streets with a false army. Are you not ashamed?"

"No, I am not," I replied, clenching my hands. "You called me here, and so, Father, you must have something to say. Say it, and be done with it."

"I shall make you an *offer*," he spat, stopping in front of me, "little that you deserve such a thing."

I was astonished by this. Neither of us had moved an inch on our negotiations since they had begun. I looked to John, to see if this was a surprise to him. It was not. He stared at his feet, frowning, petulant. It was now clear why Henry had brought him. Our father had wanted John to witness this; he had wanted John to know that his wishes were secondary. My brother needed to see what could happen to him, one day, should he betray our father as I had done.

"You will rescind your rights to Aquitaine," Henry said.

"No."

He raised his hand to halt my protest. "You will rescind your rights to Aquitaine," he repeated, "and you will be made junior king, as your brother was. You will have Anjou, and a crown."

"You have offered me this before, and I have refused."

"But I shall also offer you this, Richard. Should you agree, I will pass the duchy not to John, but to your mother. She will rule there again."

John, scowling, turned away from both of us.

"To-to—" I stuttered, and my hands loosened, my shoulders dropped, "to Eleanor? You would release her?"

"I would."

"You would exchange my mother's freedom for Aquitaine?"

"I would." He paused. "She will name John her heir, of course."

"Of course," I echoed.

"But for the rest of her life, it will be hers, and once John becomes duke he will be your vassal."

I said, with the realization bitter on my tongue, "And then my duchy will never be mine."

"No," he agreed. "It will not."

I could look at him no longer. I turned away, and I felt a familiar lance of anger pierce my belly.

"I would rather lose the crown," I said.

Henry gave a brittle laugh. "If only it were possible," he replied. "But I cannot pull your brother from his grave. I cannot make you second son again."

"Then you did not bring me here to offer me a choice. You brought me here to cause me pain, to ensure I would feel the guilt of my refusal."

"Any guilt is of your own devising, Richard."

I turned back to him. "I will not give you Aquitaine," I said, almost shouting, "I will *not*! Eleanor meant that land for me; she raised me for it. She would never abide my surrender!"

"Even if it meant her freedom?"

"Yes!"

"Can you be sure of that?" he demanded, his voice now also raised, and John stumbled back from both of us. "Your mother is older than I, Richard," Henry said. "Will you tolerate her living and dying in a prison, while you continue with this childish crusade?"

"She is your *wife*!"

"She is *not* my wife!" he roared. "No more than you are my son! You both chose this path when you raised arms against me! Did you think I had forgotten?"

There was a moment where neither of us spoke, his shout still ringing in the air. When I replied, my voice was resigned.

"No, I did not think you had forgotten," I said. "It is clear that you have not. You have poisoned us all with your resentment, and perhaps it will kill us, just as it killed Harry. But you *will* forget, one day. You will have to forget, once you have buried every one of your sons, and you are left with nothing but their blood on your hands; or when I bury you, wearing the crown you were forced to give me."

His arm reached out, and his hand cracked against my face with enough strength to bring me to my knees. I struck the stone floor with painful force, but I made no sound. I bowed my head.

My sword was on my hip. My hand came to rest upon its pommel. Henry was unarmored. It would be so easy to stand up and run him through. It was an absurd fantasy; John would run immediately, he would fetch the guard, and when the knowledge of what had happened became public my titles would be forfeit. I would be simply Richard, kin-slayer, not Richard, Duke of Aquitaine, or Richard, king of England. But if I did do it—if I had to flee—the first thing I would do would be to go to the river. I would follow the Seine, against the current, along its banks, through the mud and silt. I would go south; south to Paris, where I could see Philip for a final time; and from there south again, to the edge of the Mediterranean, where I could look across the water and see only ocean and sky. If I could, I would. If I could, I would tear these roots of resentment from my feet, cleanse myself of fury, and make myself a better man.

"You owe me your very *life*, Richard," Henry said. "Remember that. I could have had you killed when your rebellion was finished."

"You should have," I replied.

"Perhaps so."

I looked up at him, and he took a step back. A smile crossed my face when I realized he feared retaliation for the hit. But I did not stand up, remaining on my knees, and after a moment's silence his shoulders relaxed. "I have nothing more to offer," he said. "I shall give you three days to consider. You have an opportunity to make things right. Do not allow your pride to prevent you from doing so."

He walked past me. As he did so, his hand rested momentarily on my shoulder: some mockery of concern, as if he thought his touch could sway me. We both knew it was futile. We both knew I would leave Normandy that very day, rather than refuse his offer face-to-face.

"Come, John," Henry called, and I turned to watch him as he walked out of the throne room. He did not bother to see if my brother was following.

John did not follow. Instead, he approached me. In a slow, hesitant movement, he offered me his hand. I looked up at him. He did not say anything. I took his hand, and he helped me stand.

Our father called "John!" from the hallway. John shook his head, and before I could stop him, he walked past me.

"Farewell, John," I said as he reached the door. He paused.

"Farewell," he replied. Then he was gone.

One of my knees gave a jolt of pain. It was my left, the one I had shattered more than a decade ago in that play-fight with Harry. I must have aggravated the old wound when I fell. It did not usually trouble me so; I knew that it was a memory of pain I was feeling, rather than any real injury. But it was still enough that I sat down once more, legs flat against the floor. I leaned forward, pressing my fingers against my kneecap with as much force as possible, as if I could crush the bone with the pressure. I wish it would have worked. At least, that way, it might have been something a physician could fix.

I did not stay that night in Rouen. Instead, I went to the manor of a baron south of the city. I took as few of my retainers as possible, and I drank until I was sure to be sick the next morning. The baron himself was happy enough to gain the favor of the Duke of Aquitaine; he was happier still to seat his pretty, flirtatious daughter beside me. He chatted with my knights and pretended not to notice as I took his pretty daughter to bed. Perhaps he hoped I would offer her a place at my court, but I was not foolish enough to take a lover with me to Aquitaine. My mother had taught me that much, at least.

Her name was Genevieve, like the saint. She was eager, and cheerful, and honored to be paid the attention. She had blue eyes, like Philip's, but her hair was Norman: white-blond, falling to her shoulders like snow. When we were done, she lay beside me and she went to sleep. It was as simple as such a thing could be. That should have been a comfort, but it was not. When I had complimented her, she had complimented me in return. When I had made a joke she had laughed openly, and she had not turned her face away to hide her amusement. She did not wind her fingers into my hair as I kissed her. She had demanded nothing of me that I could not give.

It was not enough. It was not her fault that it was not enough; no one and nothing could have been, on that day. No amount of wine or sex could have erased the red mark my father had left on my cheek. I left her sleeping in the bed, and I stalked the corridors of the manor in a pair of slippers. The hallways looked similar to those in Paris in the darkness. They were built narrow to keep the heat in, long rugs on stone floors, tapestries on every wall. I traced my way to the guest chambers, and when I went inside the sitting room the fire was still burning. There was enough light that I could see several of my men. They hadn't bothered relocating to their beds. Instead, they were draped drunkenly over the chairs and the floor, snoring sonorously. I stepped over them, almost stumbling in the process, and I went into the master bedroom. There was a lump under the covers— I shoved it, and it groaned.

"Stephen," I whispered. "Get out of my bed."

Stephen shuffled upwards so that he was sitting against the headboard. He said, slurring the words, "Norman arse not good enough for you, Richard?" and then he smirked, as if he had said something particularly witty.

"Bloody—Christ, get *out,* you bastard," I said. I shoved him again, half-heartedly; he had fallen asleep while sitting up. I moaned in complaint, and I crawled into the bed anyway. I pulled the covers off him and wrapped them around myself. The pillow smelled like ale. Stephen's hand rested briefly on my back, and then retreated.

I quickly fell asleep. I dreamt of Aquitaine. It was summer, and I was in the Pyrenees. I sat below a tree, leaning backward to press my hands against its roots where they entered the earth. The ground throbbed under my palms, like a pulse, and I closed my eyes to focus on the sensation.

When I opened them again Philip was there, sitting on my lap. His legs bracketed my thighs. He kissed me. He tasted like blood and apricots, like summer and war. As he traced the bruise on my cheek with his fingers, I stripped him of his clothes. I pushed him down, onto the grass, and then I fell also, over him so that our chests were pressed together. His hands splayed across my back, and he pulled me closer.

I curled my arms around him, and I found that he was hollow, and that I was hollow, too. I had been peeled away, rib cage exposed, taken apart. But there was no blood, only sweet-smelling frankincense leaking out between us. So, as I lay with him, I was part of him, and he part of me, and my lungs were his, and my liver was his, and my heart was no longer too large for my chest. We breathed together, and the sun rose over Aquitaine.

When I woke up, it was still dark. The room swayed when I moved. I was the only one in the bed. I pressed my fingers to my lips, but all I could taste was the sourness of stale drink and the salt of tears. I must have cried while I was sleeping. It did not matter; there was no one here to notice. Staring at the stone wall, I pressed my hand to my knee. I thought of distances. The Pyrenees were far away, but Paris was not. Down the Seine, against the current, Paris still stood.

There, my father could not go.

CHAPTER TEN

Philip

Do you think yourself your father? the letter said. *Or do you think yourself something greater? You are no pretender to Charlemagne, Philip. You are no emperor.*

Leave my sons alone. Leave Angevin quarrels to Angevin blood.

I will not warn you again.

I put the paper down with trembling fingers. Across the table, Isabella peered at me over her embroidery, glancing at the seal on the letter.

"Henry, again?" she asked.

"They are constant."

"They trouble you," she observed. "These letters, I mean. Do you fear him?"

"I fear he is correct."

"I do not know what he is saying, but it is certainly nonsense," she said decisively, and she made a stitch. She had long fingers, slender and delicate. Her movements with the needle were precise and pretty, like a harpist plucking a string. They belied the quality of the work. The thing on the linen was somewhere between a worm and an upside-down mushroom.

I put the letter down, and I gestured to the embroidery. "What is that intended to be?"

"A butterfly," she replied, distressed. The fabric was dropped to accompany the letter. "Oh, why did you let me start another one?"

"I told you not to."

"I shall never touch a needle again."

I smiled and stood up, walking to the fireplace, taking the poker to prod at it. Galahad was sleeping nearby, and he grumbled at the sound of wood shifting. It was a futile effort: the fire was roaring, but the chill that night was unyielding, and outside the countryside was blanketed in snow.

Isabella's hair was now long enough that it brushed the ground as she tipped her head back. She had plaited it with ribbons, green and gold and silver. I approached her and gave the braid a gentle tug. She opened her eyes to glare at me.

"This is dull," she announced.

"I am glad you enjoy my company so, Isabella."

"Not *you*, only—the winter. Especially the evenings. It is always so dark."

"I like it," I said, sitting down.

"You like it because it is quiet. We get so few visitors this time of year."

"Is that truly so terrible?"

"Yes! Visitors are *interesting*."

"We have Geoffrey arriving any day now, I expect," I told her.

Geoffrey had been visiting with increasing regularity over the course of the year, and Isabella had grown fond of him. I, too, had come to know him in some manner resembling friendship, as much as friendship could be built on fundamental mistrust. It was almost pleasant that we both knew how frail the foundations of our relationship were. The pressure to affect kindness—to affect earnestness—was refreshingly absent.

"I know," Isabella said. "I simply . . . well. Never mind what I think." She paused and chewed at her lip. "Philip, my mother has written to me."

"Has she?" I asked. The sudden change of subject was odd, but I did not prompt her to continue. If Isabella wanted to say something, she would say it; I did not need to force it from her.

"She asked if my courses are regular," she told me.

"Your—"

"She wishes to know why I am not pregnant."

"I see," I replied. I did not know what else to say. Isabella tapped a finger impatiently on the edge of the table.

"I am sixteen," she said, frowning. "Almost seventeen."

"Yes, you are."

"I am still young, I know, but—but not young enough, not really. Not for it to be an excuse. And I know that there isn't much— I mean, I know that we are *friends*—but am I so repulsive that—"

"What?" I said, shocked. "No. No, it isn't that."

"Would it really be so difficult? Is it so awful to think of?" She rubbed at her eyes with the heel of her hand, and then she squared her shoulders. "I heard there are ways to make it easier—"

"Isabella, please—"

"Poultices and prayers—"

"Stop—"

"No, I *can't*," she said. "You have no right to dismiss me, Philip. Every moment that I am not pregnant, it is *me* who is judged for it. *I* am the wife, not you. If I can't have a child, then it is *my* failure."

"It is not your failure, Isabella," I replied.

"It is. Everyone will believe it is, and that is what matters."

I stood frozen as I attempted to formulate a reply, and I was grateful to be interrupted by a loud rap on the door. Isabella scowled and looked away from me. I covered my face with my hands briefly, as if the darkness would erase all signs of my distress. Then I went to open it.

My steward Guillaume stood on the other side, and he tipped into a bow as he saw me. He had flakes of snow still attached to his cape and his beard. They sparkled faintly in the light of the torches.

"My liege, good evening," he said. "Pardon, for the interruption."

"Hello, Guillaume," Isabella said sullenly.

"My lady, greetings," he called back. In lower tones, he told me, "We have a visitor. The Duke of Aquitaine."

"Richard," I said, shocked, and Guillaume frowned, perplexed. Richard had been haunting me ever since he left; his furious face after our last conversation seemed chiseled behind my eyelids. The prospect of this ghost made flesh incited immediate panic.

Guillaume mistook my anxiety for confusion, and he began to explain, "He has shown up unannounced—"

"He has never once shown up *announced*, Guillaume." I took a very deep breath, and I turned back to Isabella. "I must leave."

"Why?"

"Ri—the Duke of Aquitaine is here."

"Oh," she said. "Well. I suppose you must, then."

"Yes, I must." I took a step forward to go, and then I retreated back into the room. "Except—one moment."

I shut the door in Guillaume's face. Aghast, Isabella said, "What . . ." but she trailed off as I went to my wardrobe. I brought out a wool cloak, lined with ermine.

"Brooch and comb," I said, "Isabella, if you please—"

She leapt from her chair and went to the jewelry box I kept by the bed. She returned with an ivory comb and a star-shaped brooch, which she used to pin the cloak to my shoulders as I ran the comb through my hair.

"Hat?" she suggested, as she stepped back.

"I have no time to pin it down. If you could have some wine brought to the guest apartments—"

"Of course," she said. "Go, Philip. Be very important and in charge."

"I will try." I was suddenly overcome with affection for her, and I grasped her by the shoulders to press a kiss to her cheek. "Thank you. I am sorry for—for—"

She laid a hand over my own before she stepped away. "Never mind that. We will speak of it another time. Now *go*."

I went. Guillaume led me directly to the entrance of the courtyard. Standing in front of the door, I stared at him, waiting for him to leave. He gave me a brief and grateful bow before scurrying away.

I told myself, *Be the king. You are the king.* Then I opened the door, to find Richard standing on the other side.

We both froze in the doorway, less than a meter apart. The light of the torches behind me crawled weakly across the threshold. The chill of the night air was like a rake of teeth across my face, and I could already feel my cheeks going pink with it.

Richard looked much the same as he had when we last met. He had made even less of an attempt at shaving, something of a half beard shadowing his jaw. But his fair hair was still soldier-short, and his gaze had the same sort of frantic energy, bouncing from my cheeks to my throat to my eyes; he had a snowflake balanced precariously on one lash, and as he blinked it tumbled down his cheek.

"Philip," he said.

"Richard," I replied quite uselessly. Then we both stood in the doorway, and stared at each other without saying anything at all.

He cleared his throat. "May I come in?"

"Ah—yes." I took a step back to let him through. He entered the castle, pulling the door shut behind him. I blinked at it. "What of your retainers?"

"They shall use the other door," he said. He patted down his shoulders, pushing snow to the floor. "It has been a long road from Rouen, and they have been babbling—Lord, *constant* babbling—I am driven half mad. Hungover also. Extremely so."

"You are as much an idiot as you were the last time we met," I said somewhat impulsively. To my relief, he chuckled.

"Indeed, I am," he replied. "And you are just as I remembered."

I did not know what to say in response to that. "What brings you to court?" I asked, for lack of something better, and I turned towards the stairs.

"Politics," he said. "At least—that is what I ought to say."

I paused on the first step to look back at him. "It is," I agreed.

He opened his mouth to speak, closed it, and then shook his head. "Walk the ramparts with me."

"In this weather?"

"You are wearing a cloak. Come, we shall be quick." Without pausing for a response, he opened the door once more, allowing a gust of cold air into the room. He walked into the courtyard.

I called after him, but there was no reply. Grimacing, I curled my cloak tighter around my shoulders, and I followed him.

Outside there was no evidence of his retainers, except for foreign footprints in the snow. It was too cloudy to see the stars, and the darkness would have been absolute were it not for the torches studding the stone walls. The snowfall was light enough that it was not an inconvenience, although by the time we had reached the walls a light dusting of it had turned our shoulders white.

Richard walked ahead of me until we reached the ramparts, and then he fell into step by my side. "We shan't be too long," he said, noting my exasperation. I sighed in response. "Have you been well?" he asked.

I frowned at him, considering how to negotiate the conversation. With so much time passed, we could be cordial, at least. We could ignore what had happened between us, the flirtation and the arguments, each lingering glance and desperate touch—a year would be long enough, surely, to dull the blade of temptation. "Yes, I have," I replied. "Yourself?"

"As well as one could be," he said, "considering the circumstances."

"Geoffrey—"

"Philip, *please,* no."

"He is coming to court," I told him. "Soon. I expect him tomorrow, or the day after."

Richard groaned. "Of course."

"It has been planned for several months. He convinced Isabella we ought to go on a hunt."

"Boar?"

"I do not know."

"It must be boar," Richard said. "They are at their most aggressive in the winter. It is good sport."

"Oh, wonderful," I replied, and he laughed.

"I look forward to it."

"You presume you are invited."

He smiled widely, pressing dimples into his cheeks. I stared resolutely at my feet. "I shall earn my place," he said. "But I shall also hear no more of my family until tomorrow. I've had quite enough of them."

I paused to observe him properly. "What happened?" I asked.

"I—no matter."

"Richard," I prompted. It felt cruel, for some reason, to speak his name. "What is it?"

"I have been to Rouen. My father tried to strike a deal. Aquitaine would go to my mother, and she would name John her heir. I would rescind my claim. Eleanor would walk free."

I stopped. My shoulders tensed. The offer was an act of desperation on Henry's part—he knew the impending war was one he could not win—but it was still a canny strategy, threatening to dissolve our alliance before the battle began. "Did you agree?" I demanded.

"No," Richard replied. "Henry knew that I would not."

"Oh."

"It was a difficult argument to have, and—and a difficult trip to make. After it, I wished to see you. That is why I have come."

"You wanted to tell me of your father?" I asked.

"I wished to see you," he repeated. He turned away from me, and he began to walk again. I was forced to catch up.

"Richard . . ."

"What of your wife?" he interrupted. "How is she?"

I could not help but wince at the reminder, and Richard laughed.

"Oh, dear," he said, sounding entirely unsympathetic. "How old is she now?"

"Nearly seventeen."

"Almost an adult. You have a sister that is the same age, do you not?"

"I do, Agnes. She is in Greece. She left France seven years ago."

"Ah, yes. The empress." He frowned. "Seven years? How old was she when she was married?"

"Eight."

"Eight!"

"My father was eager to send my sisters away," I said.

We came to a bend. Instead of turning, Richard stopped. He leaned over the top of the parapets, looking across the countryside. He said, "Do you miss her? Agnes, I mean?"

Although his tone remained conversational, there was a new tension in his posture. I replied cautiously. "Yes," I said. "We were close."

"My parents had many children, you know."

"I know. You have six siblings."

"*Six*," he repeated. "Six, and yet one is dead, and the rest I hardly know. I have seen none of my sisters in years. Some I have met only once in my life."

I said nothing, observing him in the darkness. The air of restlessness he normally carried with him had calmed in the cold, leaving him still and pensive. "Most of my family are strangers," he continued, and then he fell silent.

I thought that perhaps he would say more, so I did not respond. Instead, Richard simply stopped speaking entirely. He clasped his hands together, resting his chin over his knuckles, digging his elbows into the snow atop the wall.

I walked to his side and peered into the darkness with him. With no stars nor moon, the night was startlingly complete; there was merely the black sky and the silence of the snow. The only sounds were our breathing, and the shuffling of our feet as we tried to stay warm. I could taste the cold on my tongue. I had expected Richard to radiate some sort of heat, as bright as he always seemed to burn, but he did not. The chill of the air would not allow it.

"Say something, won't you, Philip?" he asked.

"Say what?"

"Anything. I cannot stand silence."

"Well—I . . ." I searched myself for a suitably harmless anecdote. "I saw a gyrfalcon here, once."

He smiled at me, encouraging. "Truly?"

"Yes. In spring, when I was thirteen. I was standing in the courtyard, and I looked up to the battlements. There was an enormous gyrfalcon sitting on the parapets and watching me. I ran to tell my mother, but when we returned it was gone."

"A gyrfalcon?" he asked. "This far south?"

"Perhaps it escaped from a nobleman's estate."

"That seems unlikely."

"Yes, well, it was," I said. "My mother agreed with you. She said it was probably a hawk."

"I doubt you were ever foolish enough to mistake a hawk for a gyrfalcon."

I shrugged. "The only one who believed me was Agnes. She *knew* that the gyrfalcon was still on the castle grounds. If only we could find it, we could prove to everyone that I had been right. So she—" I stomped my feet against the ground, fighting off a shiver. "She went to the kitchens and stole two dozen sausages—"

Richard laughed. "Two dozen?"

"Near enough. I left my lessons that evening to find servants collecting sausages from every windowsill in the royal apartments."

"She sounds *marvelous*."

"She was, if a little foolhardy."

"Perhaps she was wiser than you give her credit for," he replied. "Gyrfalcons are good omens."

"Are they?"

"They symbolize victory."

"It was not a good omen for me," I said. "I got lost in the woods three days later, in the middle of a storm. I nearly died."

"But you survived, did you not?"

I rolled my eyes, and I said, "Yes, I did. How fortunate. But my father . . ."

I went silent. Richard repeated, "Your father?"

"He grew unwell."

"I heard of it, although I never saw him as such."

I rubbed my palms against the snow, concentrating on the sharp sting of the cold. I ought to have finished speaking there. The anecdote was no longer harmless: it was veering into territory I had long kept enclosed, a corner of my life reserved only for consideration during absolute privacy.

My eyes met Richard's. He was staring at me with utter concentration, as if I were something *important*, something to be studied and learnt.

The guilt I had borne with me ever since his departure grew suddenly crushing. I never had said goodbye to him that day, once my meeting with my council was done; but I was king, and I'd had a rebellion to deal with, and war does not wait for farewells. I did not regret my actions, except in my most shameful moments of desperation. Rather, I had regretted ever revealing to Richard how desperately I wanted him. I had hoped fiercely that I would be able to conceal myself again, once he returned. But clearly, it was still obvious how I felt. Otherwise, he would not look at me like that: as if we were inevitable.

I felt a sudden need to justify myself. I wanted to show Richard why I had made the decisions I had. I wanted to prove to him that I was not worth the devotion he afforded me.

"My father," I said. "He said strange things. Some days, he was present. Some, he was not. He would fly into fits of fear as I have never seen otherwise, shivering and pissing himself. He never told me what it was he was afraid of. He refused to wash also. My mother made me say good night to him every evening. The room always stank. It clung to me after."

"Philip . . ."

"I do not want your pity. I only wanted—I only wanted you to know. This is the legacy I carry. The blood in my veins."

"I do not pity you."

I turned so that my back was against the wall. I leaned against it, tilting my chin upwards. The cold curled around my exposed throat and skittered down my spine. Richard watched me.

"You were brave," he said. "You were a lionhearted child."

I almost laughed. "Certainly not. I was melancholy, anxious. I was *always* anxious. I could not sleep at night. I would go for days without sleeping."

"You have worked miracles to become as you are. I know how crushing the weight of a father can be."

"We are not the same, Richard," I said too harshly. "I live as I do, *despite* my father. You live as you do *because* of yours."

Richard went silent. His eyes narrowed, and his lips thinned. At that moment, he might have been a gyrfalcon himself, circling the sky and scrutinizing me with predatory focus; I tensed, preparing for the plunge of talons into my neck.

But then he gave me a small smile, forgiving me without words. "Speaking to you is like scouring myself with a pumice stone," he said. "I have never suffered such a flaying. Good Lord."

"You flatter me."

He laughed softly. When he fell silent, he was still smiling. I was struck with a sudden need for him to speak again. I wanted him to take his laughter away, breathe it back in and pull it out of the air. But he remained quiet, and I looked away from him. We were at an impasse until another breeze passed over us, causing me to grit my teeth against the cold.

Richard said, "You are shivering." I tugged my cloak tighter around my shoulders, even as I shook my head. "Shall we return?" he asked, and I agreed.

We walked in silence back to the courtyard, and then into the castle. In the hallway it was almost as cold as it was outside. I stomped my boots against the stone floor, staring down at them, and then I felt a hand run across the top of my head.

"You are covered in snow," Richard told me. He dropped his arm slowly, trailing his hand over the back of my neck. I gave him a skeptical look, which he ignored. "Forgive me," he said. "I insisted we stand in the cold."

"It was . . ." I began, and then I sighed. "I spoke too harshly."

"Speak as harshly as you like. I would rather know what you think of me, than have it obscured with platitudes." He paused, in an unusual show of hesitation. "I thought—well. It has been a long time, Philip, since I saw you last."

"It has."

"We parted on difficult terms."

"We did," I said. "No matter. We ought to move past it."

Richard nodded slowly, opened his mouth to speak, then closed it once more. He bowed his head and smiled softly, eyes half closed. In that smile I saw affection, regret, hope, resignation; I could not tell how far they were my own emotions, reflected back to me in the mirrors of his eyes. And if he had asked me then whether I still wanted him, if he had told me that he still felt the same—those words alone might have been enough to undo me. It did not matter how much time had passed. The flame he had lit within me had never darkened. It was merely a lantern hooded, and now the light had been exposed once more.

Richard stepped forward, and he bent down towards me. I was helpless; I could not have stepped away, even if I wished to. I nearly lifted my chin and offered myself to him. Instead, I remained frozen, paralyzed by indecision.

He stopped with our lips an inch apart. He smelled like snow and damp silk.

"It has grown late," he said.

"Yes, it has."

"Good night, then."

"Good night," I replied.

We stood in silence for a protracted moment. I could have moved forward, looped my arms around his neck, and finished what we'd started in my study a year ago. I did not. I did not move, and Richard lingered only briefly before he backed away and turned to leave. I watched him ascend the steps, his wet boots leaving dark imprints on the stone floor.

The snow on my cape had melted, leaving it sodden. Its weight felt as if there were a pair of hands gripping my shoulders, forcing me to watch him as he walked away. When he finally disappeared, I recalled the dark and dreary day after he'd left Paris the previous summer. I remembered the hours I'd thrown away arguing with my council; the smothered laughter of my courtiers that night when Blois had insulted me at the dinner table; the order I'd signed to send armies to put down a rebellion that—when my men arrived—had already dissolved into anarchy: torched villages, corpses in rivers, the tattered banner of the fleur-de-lis stamped into the mud. It had taken less than a month to resolve it, but in that time, I'd made a thousand sacrifices, large and small, stacked upon my shoulders until I ached with the weight of them.

Now, I had made myself yet another burden in Richard. I had been unable to forget him, and in that failure, I had created one more enemy to conquer. But it was a futile war, I feared. There were no soldiers to send, no battles to be won: just me, left alone in his wake, shivering from the chill and my own desire.

CHAPTER ELEVEN

𝕻𝔥𝔦𝔩𝔦𝔭

The next day, Geoffrey arrived in time for the morning meal; the herald allowed him entry through a shard of dawn light and a puff of icy air. As the door to the great hall closed, he swept a bow to Isabella and me. He was familiar enough with us that the movement was polite but not servile, and he approached with the confidence of an old friend.

Richard was not there. His retinue was absent also. I would fear he had left court entirely, but his horse was still in the stables. Either he was avoiding me, or he presumed that I wished to avoid him. I did not know which was worse.

"My liege, my lady," Geoffrey said in greeting. I gestured for him to sit, and he took the empty chair at my right. It had been reserved for Richard, although he had no way of knowing.

"My Lord Brittany!" Isabella said, pleased. She paused in filling her bowl to offer him a beaming smile. "I hope your journey was pleasant?"

"The snow was a bother, but we made good time."

"And your wife, is she well?" she asked.

"She is," Geoffrey replied. "The baby is healthy also. The baptism just passed."

"What have you named her?"

"Eleanor, for my mother."

Isabella cooed and poured him some wine. I glanced at Geoffrey; it was clear he was tired. "Have you eaten?" I asked him.

"Not yet."

"Please." I gestured to the table, and he nodded gratefully. I waited until he had taken some bread before I continued, "Richard is here."

He sighed. "I am not surprised he ran to you, after what happened in Rouen."

"You have heard?"

"Yes, I was there."

"In *Rouen*?" I said.

"Yes."

"Richard does not know."

"As I intended," he replied. "I stayed hidden. I was also there to see my father. Circumstances have changed."

"How so?" I asked.

He glanced around the room. Although it was early, some courtiers were present; Guillaume was standing in the corner, listing tasks to a pair of servants. At the end of the table, Blois was in conference with my chancellor Sancerre. They glanced over at Geoffrey and me with narrowed eyes. Geoffrey made a thoughtful noise, took his knife, and sliced his roll while it remained in his hand, bringing the blade treacherously close to his palm. He said, "We should discuss it in private."

"My study?"

"Somewhere else, where Richard is unlikely to find us. Where is he?"

"I do not know. Perhaps still asleep."

"Hm. He is best avoided, for now."

"The turf maze," Isabella said. We turned to her, and she raised her chin, unashamed at her eavesdropping. "It was finished last week. Have you seen it yet, Philip?" I shook my head. "The grass is all frozen now, but it is still pretty, I think. It is in the western courtyard. It is closed off, so no one else could enter."

"There, then," Geoffrey said, approving. "Thank you, my lady."

Proud, she took a voracious bite of her pottage. "I was the one who had it commissioned," she told him, mouth half full. "I drew it out."

"Isabella has a good mind for puzzles," I said.

"Oh, better than for stitching!" she agreed. "I've had to throw my butterfly away."

Geoffrey had begun to butter his bread now, with a thoroughness bordering on obsession. He stared at it ponderously. "A labyrinth," he murmured. "We had one in England also."

"Your father liked them?" I asked.

He snorted. "He hated them. The last king had it made. I used to run about in it with Richard and Harry, but Henry had it dug up, and he used the spot for latrines."

Geoffrey continued to butter his bread as I sought a reply, but the sudden frustration in his manner had created an awkward silence. Isabella, who had a greater gift for small talk than I, interjected with a question about his daughter. She carried the conversation for the rest of the meal.

Once we were all finished, I gestured for Geoffrey to follow me. "I shall show you the western courtyard," I said. "But if we speak for long, we may have to move inside. It is still cold."

"It shouldn't be long," Geoffrey replied, with a slow, triumphant smile.

Isabella's turf maze was a convoluted mesh of gravel and green. It was almost dizzying to look at, although pleasing; the grass had been tended to that morning, the snow cleared, but the blades were still whitened with frost, interlocking with key-like teeth in a confounding pattern of paths. Geoffrey made a sound of surprise and pleasure. "It is as good a maze as any I have seen," he said.

I stepped to the entrance and began to trace through the gravel. He followed, taking a different turn than I, and we ended up on different paths. I gave him a challenging look. "The first to the end," I said, "shall have first cut of the boar tomorrow."

Geoffrey nodded, and we set to work. I stared at my feet as I walked, tracing my turns. Once I felt confident in my strategy, I said, "What happened, in Rouen?"

Geoffrey, more distant than I thought he would be, replied, "Richard made a mess of things."

"For us?" I asked.

"For himself. Did he tell you what Henry offered?"

"He did."

"And did he tell you how he responded?"

"He refused him," I said. "He said it was—difficult."

"Difficult, indeed," Geoffrey replied. "They had a terrible argument."

"Was Henry angry that Richard did not agree?"

"Richard never would have agreed, and Henry knew that. It was intended to prompt another round of negotiations; to put our mother in play as an incentive."

"Did it not succeed in that?" I asked.

"Certainly not, thanks to Richard," Geoffrey said. "He made

our father so angry that Henry has ordered me to invade Aquitaine."

I stopped and looked at him. Geoffrey mirrored me, smirking and raising an eyebrow, as if to challenge me with his tranquility. He was only two paces away, but with the barrier of the turf between us, I could not reach him. "Pardon?" I asked faintly.

"Henry has ordered me to invade Aquitaine," he repeated.

"He knows that we are allied, the three of us."

"Yes."

"So why would he expect you to agree?"

Geoffrey did not clarify. He stared at me, unashamed, as he waited for me to understand. And then I did understand—like the tick of a water clock, the mechanism dropped, the hand moved. The knowledge dripped to the base of my stomach, where it sat rippling and cold.

"Henry has offered you Aquitaine," I said.

"He has." Geoffrey looked back to his feet and continued his path around the maze. I could not move, and so it seemed as if he were circling me, growing steadily closer.

I said, "But you already have Brittany. John . . ."

"John has the lands of a baron," Geoffrey replied. "Father might have liked to reward him for his loyalty, but, in the end, he is not a threat. He does not need appeasement, as I do. And he cannot provide the armies needed to defeat Richard."

I was horrified by my own naïveté. "You intended for this to happen."

"You could not have foreseen this, Philip," Geoffrey said, sympathetic. "*I* did not. I had considered it a possibility, I suppose, but I hadn't thought it likely. Henry hates me only a little less than he hates Richard. I remind him too much of Mother, I think. That he would allow me so much land? It seems madness, does it not?" He came to a dead end. Sighing, he spun around.

"But we underestimated Richard's efficiency, both of us. With one argument, Henry stopped caring who had Aquitaine, as long as it was not Richard."

Slowly, I began to walk the maze again, staring at the gravel. "You will do it then, I suppose," I said. "You will invade Aquitaine. The war will finally begin."

"Yes."

"Will Henry send his armies with you?"

He chuckled. "Not all of them. You would be pleased, I'm sure, if he left Normandy undefended. The bulk of his men will remain north; John and I will lead the invasion southward. I have already sent the word to begin moving troops."

"It will be a close battle."

"Richard has the advantage," Geoffrey admitted. "As defender, and as a greater general than I. Even with Henry's aid, I will struggle. But that would change, Philip, with your support."

"And why should I support you?" I asked. "Richard has promised me Anjou."

"As will I. It was a condition of mine that you have it, when I agreed to my father's plan. I knew you would not help me otherwise."

My feet hit the edge of the turf. The exit, infuriatingly, was on the other side of the grass, only a step away. Geoffrey was on the path towards it. As he walked languidly across the gravel, he continued, "Anjou, Philip, as you have always wanted. And Anjou *soon*, at the end of the war, delivered directly from my father's hands to yours. No need to wait until Richard is crowned."

"Richard promised me Vexin also," I said almost desperately.

That made Geoffrey falter in his gait—only slightly—and he stopped as he reached the end of the maze. He cocked his head at me. "Vexin is part of Normandy. That was to be my land."

"Will you lecture me on duplicity, Geoffrey? *Now?*"

"No, of course not. I am simply impressed. Well, I doubt I can offer you Vexin. But I don't suppose Richard would, either, once the throne was his. It is too valuable. An empty promise."

"You cannot know that."

"He is my brother," Geoffrey replied. "He is as much a liar as the rest of us. The only difference is that he tells himself he is not. If you want Vexin that much, I will not prevent you from taking it once I am Duke of Aquitaine, and Richard is king. I will no longer have interest in that land, after all. Until then, you will have Anjou as comfort, far sooner than you would have it otherwise. And, even better, you leave the lands split between my brothers and me. Richard will be far easier to deal with, once our father dies, if he does not have Aquitaine as well as England."

It was an arrangement undeniably superior to our current one. No wonder Geoffrey had strolled through the maze with such confidence; this was all as good an outcome as he could have hoped for. As *we* could have hoped for. I should have been overjoyed.

"Richard will be furious," I said.

"Of course."

"He will hate me. He will take the throne, hating me."

Geoffrey narrowed his eyes at me, clearly confused. "He will be king of England, and you king of France. Of course, he will hate you. He will hate you the moment the crown touches head."

I nodded in acknowledgment of this. Satisfied, Geoffrey stepped out of the maze. "First cut of the boar to me," he said, pleased. "But perhaps I ought to offer it to Isabella. It was a masterful puzzle."

"Indeed," I replied.

His smile faded. "You are nervous, which I suppose I understand. But I assure you, Richard is perfectly manageable, even when in a rage."

"I am not afraid of him."

"Then think upon my offer, Philip. You will realize there is no disadvantage to you. I would hear your answer soon."

"I know," I said.

"After the hunt tomorrow, perhaps."

"Very well."

He nodded and turned away, leaving towards the gate. When he saw I was not following, he stopped, and looked back to me. "My liege?"

I walked across the grass to reach him. At the edge of the maze, I glanced behind me; my boots had left a line of crushed grass. It was evidence of my defeat.

"It will regrow," Geoffrey said, and I followed him as he left.

⌇

I met with Blois in my study that evening. I had to, despite my reluctance; he was my martial, and if we were to go to war, he would be the one to command my armies.

He was delighted to hear of Geoffrey's proposal. Why wouldn't he be? Despite his gruffness and hostility, and despite the unspoken resentment that had wound its way between us, Blois and I had one essential similarity: we loved France. Our nation would be taking another step towards glory.

"We must take the opportunity as it is offered," Blois said to me, teeth bared in vicious excitement. We were looking at the map of Europe, laid out upon my desk. I had thought that it would provide clarity, but the ink on the page seemed to have no meaning, only letters and lines. Paper or soil, legacy, loss, reward: I could no longer tell the difference.

Blois clearly did not feel the same. He looked at the map and he saw his own name, soon to be carved into the annals of history. He had never married, never had children. It was a self-imposed solitude that I was envious of, in some ways: such a life would never be an option for me. But sometimes I wondered if he was lonely. I watched him as he described to me his battle plans, our inevitable victory, the blood that would wash the Loire red—and I was surprised by the desperation that commingled with the joy in his expression. Blois was only a handful of years younger than my father would have been that day, had he survived. This was a swan song for him. It was his last chance to seize greatness.

"I am not yet certain we should agree to Geoffrey's plan," I said to him. "If Richard—"

"We must agree," Blois replied, interrupting me. "There is no other option."

"It would be a great betrayal. A shameful one, by some standards."

He regarded me with a sneer sharper than the sword at his hip, and he said, "War is only shameful if it is lost."

"And what if we lose?"

He glanced back to the map, pressing his finger against the black line of our northern border. "We cannot lose," he replied, more to himself than to me. "This may be the final opportunity to regain what has been lost. We cannot even consider defeat."

"What has been lost? Anjou, you mean?"

"Our honor," he replied firmly. "Our legacy. Consider it, my liege. I was your father's martial also. I will not permit myself to be defined by his mistakes. You shouldn't, either."

I had no response to that. He bowed to me, clearly considering the conversation finished; then he left, and it was only the map and me, alone in my study.

I was utterly lost. I stood there and decided to decide something, anything at all: but although I could usually grasp at the torrent of thoughts, tug out words and meanings, there was now only a strange, disappointing silence.

After what felt like an interminable period, someone knocked on the door. I went to answer it and found myself face-to-face with Richard. He seemed painfully pleased to see me, his face softening as if in relief. He had a cloak pinned around his shoulders, and a fur collar at his neck.

"Philip," he said. "Good, you are here. I thought we might go riding."

"Why?"

He shrugged. "Why not? We ought to become reacquainted, after so long apart."

I could hardly bear to look at him. His presence felt almost mocking, as if he already knew about my conversations with Geoffrey and Blois, and he had appeared only to compound my guilt.

"I am . . ." I began weakly.

"Busy," he supplied. "Yes. I thought you might say that. But come, I braved seeing my brother to retrieve you." He peered into the room over my shoulder. "He is not here, is he?"

"No."

Richard grinned. "Perfect. Then you must come with me."

"I can't see how—"

He grabbed me by the shoulders and tugged me bodily into the corridor. He pulled the door shut behind me, and I was trapped. I pressed my palms flat against the wood, as if Richard were a cliff edge I was about to fall over.

"*Sincerely,*" I said, a little winded, "I do not have time to go riding. And I am not dressed for the weather."

He frowned, folding his arms. "You seem unsettled."

"Because you just *threw* me into the corridor—"

He shook his head. "Not that. What is it, Philip?"

"It is nothing."

With a noise of frustration, he grabbed my chin and forced my gaze forward, so that I was looking him in the eye. "Did something happen?" he asked.

"I—I cannot tell you."

"Cannot, or will not?"

"I do not know," I replied. "I do not know what the difference is. I do not know what I want. I do not know who to be."

Richard's face softened and he released me. He ran a finger across my temple, pushing some hair behind my ear. I could not bring myself to complain.

"I wish I understood you," he said. "Sometimes you speak, and I feel like a sailor navigating by foreign stars."

"I am nothing like the stars."

"You are," he replied. "You are as lovely, and almost as distant."

My throat tightened. I realized, with horror, that I was almost in tears, and I swallowed in a desperate attempt to keep them at bay. Richard took a step back. He seemed disappointed, but more in himself than me; he frowned at his shoes, and when he looked back at me his expression was almost apologetic.

"Richard . . ." I began, and he shook his head again.

"I will be in the training courtyard, if you have need of me," he said. "I will not force you to come. Perhaps we will go tomorrow, instead."

"There is the hunt tomorrow."

"Of course." He smiled without conviction. "I will see you then, I suppose."

"Yes, you will."

He nodded and gave me a short bow before he left. Halfway down the corridor, he looked back at me over his shoulder, and our eyes met; I turned around and opened the door. Once I was within my study, I found myself almost gasping with relief and shame. Unable to stomach more consideration of the map, I instead went to peer through the slats of the window shutters. I could see only slices of white light from the clouded sky, and the edge of a tree branch. It bowed and then sprang back. A bird was taking off, riding the southern wind towards Aquitaine.

I had never visited Aquitaine, nor, indeed, any lands outside my own. There had been a time when I had wanted to. When I was younger, I had dreamt of riding in a single direction until everyone lost sight of me; then, in the dark of the forest, I would become someone new. I had wanted to travel until I saw trees that could not grow in France, until I stood on foreign soil, until I heard words that I could not understand. I wanted to find a place where my name was not known, somewhere where I could be lost. There I would be anchorless, drifting: a sailor, navigating by foreign stars.

But I was Philip the God-given, after all, destined for the throne, destined for greatness. I would never be permitted to forget that. So, as I grew, I learnt authority, and I put aside compassion. I made myself a shell of steel, a plate armor of indifference, so that when it came to this—when it came to necessary betrayals—I would not suffer to make the choices I needed to. I would not be defined by the mistakes of my father. I would preserve my honor, preserve my legacy, and do the work my blood assigned.

Stay the course, Philip Augustus, I told myself, as I sat at my desk. *Prepare yourself for war.*

⁓

"Philip?" Isabella murmured. "It is late."

I pushed the covers up and crawled into the bed beside her. "Pardon," I said. "Go back to sleep."

"I haven't seen you all day."

"I spoke with Geoffrey."

She shuffled upwards, to sit against the headboard. She rubbed sleep from her eyes. "What did he say?"

"Many things. He . . . well . . ."

She waited, patiently, as I constructed sentences. I had spent the entirety of the day looking at papers, armies, accounts, and letters; designing a conflict I did not want to fight; trying to excise my guilt. Now it felt as if I had unlearnt speech.

Eventually—in a tone halting with shame—I managed to explain. Once I finished, Isabella was frowning. "I thought I liked Geoffrey," she said, "but he seems cruel. To betray Richard—to expect you to do so . . ."

"Geoffrey does not care for others," I agreed. "But I do not think he would be cruel for the sake of it."

"Does that make it better?"

"I think so."

"Hm." Isabella fell silent, thinking. "So, you will help him, then?"

"Yes."

"But—"

"I *must*, Isabella," I snapped. She flinched, shifting back on the mattress. Pulling the blankets up, as if to shield herself, she murmured, "Pardon."

An awkward silence fell. I sighed and pushed my hair away from my face. It fell back in front of my eyes. "Shall I fetch you a ribbon?" she asked meekly.

"No. We ought to sleep."

I extinguished the candle. We both lay down in the bed, pulling our separate sheets over ourselves. Isabella turned onto her stomach, and her side. She shifted to face me, then away again. There was quiet for a few minutes, before she flipped onto her back, and she sniffed defiantly.

I sighed. "I did not mean to upset you."

"Perhaps you should not *shout* at me, then."

"I know. Pardon."

Her hand stretched to squeeze my arm. "Do you feel ashamed? About Richard?"

"What should I feel ashamed of?" I asked. "It is only half a betrayal, really. He ought to be expecting such a thing. And I do not need his approval."

"But you want it?"

I did not answer.

"Richard is nice," she continued. "Funny. He carved me a snake."

"What?"

"I saw him this evening, in the gardens. He was with his friend, Sir Bergerac. I was with my ladies. We went for a walk. Richard found a stick, and he used his knife to make it all wobbly, and then he said it was a snake. It did not look like a snake. We all laughed over it."

"Was he at supper?" I asked.

"Yes, we went together. But you weren't, and neither was Geoffrey," Isabella said. "And Richard said that was a relief, because he was avoiding both of you. But still, he spent the whole evening talking about you."

"What did he say?" I asked, despite myself.

She replied, "He asked me if you had seemed sad last night, and I said I did not know. Then he asked if you had seemed happy, and I said I did not know. Then he said that he also found it difficult to tell if you were happy or sad. And *I* said that your sort of happiness is not the same as mine is, so I find it difficult to measure you against myself; and perhaps it was the same for him."

"What did he say then?"

Isabella replied, "He said that he would be very happy, if only he could know that you were happy also."

"Oh."

"Which I thought was *very strange*," she said. "*Very strange* indeed."

Richard had the subtlety of a ballista. "He considers us friends," I told her, in an attempt to salvage things.

She hummed in thought and fiddled a while with the edge of the blanket, rubbing it back and forth between her fingers. It was too dark to see, but I could hear her frustration in the rasp of skin and fabric, even though she did not speak.

When I thought the conversation might have ended, she said, "I saw you on the battlements."

"When?"

"Last night. I saw you through the bedroom window. I only saw your backs, standing next to each other, with your arms pressed together. And I realized I had never seen you do that. You hardly ever let people touch you. Always, you step away."

I couldn't say anything. I took a gulp of air.

"And how you look at him," she said. "I have seen that, too. I remember it, from when he last came to court. You looked at him like you could not bear it, but you needed to. As if you had no choice."

I could have denied it. I could have done so in a manner that would prevent her from ever speaking of it again. Isabella trusted me, in all her luminous certainty of my goodness; if I asked it of her, she would never again mention Richard, nor my need of him. She would allow me some measure of ignorance.

Instead, I said, "I have never wanted to look at anyone like that."

"Apart from him?"

"Apart from him."

"Not—other men also?" she asked.

"No. But perhaps that is because I never allowed myself to do so. I cannot be certain."

There was a pause as she considered this.

"I was upset, at first," she said finally. "And sometimes I wondered if I was imagining it. It wasn't—obvious. It is only because I know you, and—and because he looks at you like that, as well. Staring all the time. I suppose it makes sense now."

"Isabella, I am sorry," I said.

"Should I not be the one who is sorry?" She turned on her side to face me, and I did the same. We stared at each other in the darkness. "I can never be what you want. Not ever. Not even a little."

"That is not your fault."

"But I do not think it is your fault, either," she replied. "I realize that, now."

"I wish it could be different."

"I do, too. If only so that you might be less burdened. If only so that you would have one less reason to pretend."

"This is part of me," I said. "I could not change it for normality, and still be myself. I would become someone else."

"Would you want that?"

"I used to be certain that I did."

"No," she said. She threw her arm around my waist and pulled herself towards me, pressing her forehead against my chest. "I do not want you to be someone else. I want you to be Philip."

I returned the embrace. "I *am* Philip."

"I know. Please stay that way. I would prefer a Philip who does not love me, to a not-Philip who does."

"I do love you, Isabella," I told her. "Very much."

"I love you, too. So, you must stay Philip, promise me you will. If you do anything to change him, I shall miss him terribly."

"I won't."

"You must promise."

"I promise," I said, and then I lost whatever composure I had been able to maintain. I pressed my face against her hair as we both began to weep. It was the first time I had cried in a decade. My eyes stung with it and my throat closed; my breath became frantic. I was grateful for the darkness of the room; I had a sudden certainty that something was above me, approaching, ready to fall and crush me. I did not want to see it, whatever it was. I breathed in, breathed out, counting the breaths as Isabella rubbed my back.

She said, "I am sorry for upsetting you."

"You haven't—it isn't your fault."

"Will you be able to sleep tonight?" she asked.

"I shall try."

"You must rest. We have the hunt tomorrow."

"I know."

Silence fell. Isabella shuffled her feet under the covers. I was wide awake; my limbs twitched with some instinct of escape, and my mind was racing with words, images, fleeting notions of shame. I shuddered against the mattress.

"Philip," Isabella said.

"What is it?"

"I sing of arms and the man," she whispered in Latin, "fated to be an exile, who long since left the land of Troy . . ."

I smiled. "Your pronunciation has improved."

"Do you wish to hear it, or not?"

"I do."

"Good. Who long since left the land of Troy, and came to Italy . . ."

As she spoke, I allowed my neck to bow, my mind to clear. Calm settled, shallowly, but still real enough. Isabella made me Aeneas, even if only for that night: a wanderer tossed in the tempest, escaping the fickle hand of fate.

CHAPTER TWELVE

Richard

The morning of the hunt dawned light and clear. It was good weather for riding. I had almost wanted it to be raining, to cause some delay, which might have provided more opportunity to speak with Philip alone. But the sun seemed to welcome the excursion. It demanded blood.

Determined to get by on bluster, I came to the clearing accompanied by my men and a sort of fatalistic optimism. I beamed at the crowd of waiting nobles. Geoffrey seemed almost horrified by my supposed good cheer, and he approached me with a suspicious expression.

"Good morning, Richard," he said, as I dismounted my horse. I grinned at him, and his mouth twitched downwards. "I had expected you not to come, after your absence yesterday."

"And miss a chance at the kill?" I asked. "Never."

The air had the sort of bracing cold that came only with cloudless skies, and the ground was covered in fresh snowfall. In the light of the morning, it was blindingly white. The hunting party had gathered outside for breakfast, wrapped in their furs, jewel-toned banners fluttering in the chill wind. There was a small group of ladies nearby, intending to spectate. Isabella stood at their center, her small pink face crowned by red hair; it was braided with ribbons in an extraordinary confection of green, blue, and white. As I watched her, she tugged at it self-consciously, clearly proud of the effect. Our eyes met and she raised a hand in bashful greeting, although her gaze then dropped to the ground as if she were ashamed.

I could see Philip, too. He was crouching at the edge of the clearing, avoiding the chatter of the court. His hound sat in front of him, and he appeared to be talking to it.

Geoffrey followed my gaze. "I have told the king about Rouen," he said. It had been months since we had last seen each other, but clearly neither of us were inclined to share pleasantries.

"What was there to tell him about?" I asked him. "And how do you know of it?"

"I remain informed," he replied. "It is hardly as if you keep such things secret. You made Father *furious*."

"Father was already furious."

"Not this much, I assure you."

I made a dismissive gesture. "It changes nothing," I said. "He might attempt further negotiations, but by then we shall be prepared for war."

"I suppose so," he replied. He gestured towards Philip from across the clearing. "But I fear our young king is hesitant."

"Why do you think that?"

Geoffrey shrugged. "He mentioned a lack of resources. He might wish to delay the conflict."

"Why would that be?"

"The longer our argument with Henry continues, the less stable England becomes," he said. "And the less likely our father is to bother France."

I replied, "But Philip won't have Anjou until the war is over. Surely he would not wait longer than he needs to."

"Either way, we might consider reducing our garrisons. I suspect we shall be throwing money away, otherwise."

I frowned at him. "This is a change of opinion, Geoffrey, since we last met."

"We must adapt to the circumstances."

I scratched at my chin, looking back to Philip. He was crouched upon the balls of his feet, rubbing at the dog's ears. "I shall consider it," I said. "But I trust you as much as I would a snake in Eden."

"Colorful, as always, Richard."

I began to retort, but a horn blared, and then another, and another. Philip started and stood up. As he turned around, our eyes met, and he immediately looked towards the snow. I stared at him as long as I dared. The sound of horns fell away, leaving a hollow echo behind.

". . . like the time in Angoulême," Geoffrey was saying. I had not been listening. Watching Philip had entirely detached me from the conversation. "Promise me that, at least," he continued.

I made a noncommittal noise. An attendant approached Philip with his mount. Turning back to my own horse, I offered Geoffrey a grin.

"To the victor, the spoils," I said.

~ ∽ ~

Philip's hunt master was a skilled man, and he had driven the boar into our path by the time we were halfway down the trail. In my conversation with Isabella yesterday, she had mentioned that it was of extraordinary size; from what glimpses we caught of it, it was as big as she had said, perhaps even bigger. It made the trees tremble as it moved, hardly seeming like an animal at all: formless and frantic, a black cloud of bristles and the occasional gleam of a white tusk. Its bellows were like claps of thunder rolling through the forest. As the dogs were released along the relay, they snarled and tumbled over one another in their eagerness.

My horse, Rufus, was a palfrey of Berber descent. He was a gift from my mother, and his hide was a chestnut so saturated it was almost crimson. He cut a wound through the forest as we rode, a bloody slash in the pale flesh of the snow; there was an intoxicating violence to it all, and I was consumed by hunger and joy, grimacing and grinning in equal measure. Geoffrey remained at my heels, riding with his usual, singular intensity, and behind us Philip wove around the trees, content to follow and watch.

The chase was excruciatingly long. Steam billowed from Rufus's mouth, dragon-like; we roared after the boar until it finally began to slow. As we passed another bend in the trail, a horn sounded, and more dogs spilled onto the track. I saw a flash of familiar sandy fur as Philip's hound took the lead.

We rode only a few more paces before the dogs began to bark. A hulking darkness had paused in the gap between two pines.

"We have him!" I cried, slowing Rufus down to a trot; there was a great commotion behind me as the rest of the party did the same. Ahead, heaving and snarling, the boar had chosen to make its final stand. The dogs stood at some distance from it, baring their teeth, keeping it at bay. Philip and Geoffrey pulled up their horses to flank me.

I had never seen a beast so massive. It had an exceptional set of tusks, like a pair of ivory daggers. One was broken, snapped at its tip—this was a creature used to fighting for its life. You could smell the stink of it even from this distance. It was sour and earthy, dulling the cold.

Groaning, the boar took a step forward, as if to charge. We tensed as the dogs began to growl at it, readying our spears in front of us. It hesitated.

The reluctance lasted only a moment. More fury than sense, it threw itself forward. It caught a black hound with one of its tusks, throwing it sideways into a tree as it made directly for Geoffrey's horse. He danced his mount to the side with one hand, and brought his spear down with the other, catching the boar's back with the tip. The angle was wrong for a killing blow, and as the boar careened forward—missing its mark by mere inches—the spearhead sliced across its back, the shaft of the weapon remaining in Geoffrey's hands. Bleeding, but still alive, the boar came to a halt and turned around. The dogs surged forward to put themselves between us.

Breathing heavily, Geoffrey flicked blood off his spear, splattering the snow. "A good blow," I said begrudgingly. Philip made an approving noise, and I shifted my horse between him and my brother. The boar watched us, but it was clearly too injured to charge again.

"Extraordinary," Geoffrey replied, flushed with exertion. "It is enormous. I have never seen anything like it."

"It will soon die," Philip observed. "It is losing too much blood."

"My kill, then," Geoffrey said, pleased.

Philip gave him a sideways glance. "I suppose so. It is a slow end. A cruel one."

My eyes met the boar's. There was a sort of primal recognition between us. It shuffled back a little, and then forward, recognizing a challenger. The moment was stripped of everything but the blood on its hide, and the blade at my hip.

"Such a creature deserves a noble death," I said.

I pulled my leg over the saddle, dismounting my horse. Behind us, there was a cheer from the rest of the hunting party; there was nothing more chivalrous than dealing the killing blow up close. The pleasure of the crowd goaded me, and I drew my hand away from the shaft of my spear, reaching for my dagger instead.

"You will be killed," Philip said, alarmed. I looked up at him and grinned.

"For a worthy cause," I replied. "And God, how glorious it shall be."

He did not contest me further. His lips pressed together, in typical disapproval, but his eyes had widened with excitement. Even Philip was not immune to the joy of the hunt. Giddy, I winked at him, and then I moved forward, pushing through the dogs. With my dagger raised, I approached the boar.

It watched me without movement or noise, beady black eyes glinting behind the bristles of its snout. The stench of it grew greater as I approached, but it remained eerily silent. There was a grim acceptance in its stance. It knew that these were its final moments. I took a step forward, and then another; when it seemed as if it might have given up—as if it would allow me to butcher it where it stood—it let out a groan and made another faltering charge towards me.

It was slowed by its wounds. I sidestepped easily, and then bent my wrist, slashing my dagger towards it. The sunlight bounced off the metal—a beam of light passed across my face—and, almost too quickly to see, I passed the knife through its hide. It was not a deep blow, but the boar stumbled, all the same. It made another swipe at me with its tusks. Again, I dodged backward; again, the boar charged; and again, the dagger fell. It had been too long since I was afforded such a battle. I was limbs and instinct only, a flurry of constant, frantic movement. The achievement of each hit felt secondary to the momentum it provided me with, as I found myself spinning out of the boar's reach: I was a bear-baiter, a dancer, a jester. The hunt had become a performance.

There was blood on my hands where they held the hilt of the dagger. I was distinctly aware of every movement in my body, the shift of each muscle, the push and pull of tendons, even the thud of my pulse beneath my ear. The gaze of the crowd, the gaze of *Philip* watching me, gave the air behind my back a certain weight; I feared I might stumble into it, and be pulled down like an armored man in water. I could not risk the distraction, nor the loss of my prize. Soon, I reached the moment of quietude, where my joy concentrated into focus. My movements became more deliberate. I would dismantle my opponent, piece by piece.

The boar was insensate. It made no noises of pain or submission, only anger. I leapt backward as it made another rush at me. In a fatalistic, confused fury, it did not stop. Instead, it rammed itself headfirst into the pine behind me. The tree gave a weeping wail and bowed under the pressure. I turned to look at the boar as it trembled, groaning.

Its haunches slumped, and it kept its snout pressed against the wood. It did not move. It was alive, yes, but only barely; blood steamed on the snow beneath it. I approached slowly. It remained still. I came to a stop by its left flank, my knife gleaming eager in my hands. Glancing over my shoulder, my eyes met Philip's.

I had expected indifference, or even sorrow, some element of pity for my opponent: but I saw none of these in his expression. There was some surprise there, certainly; but in Philip's blown pupils, there was something else also. It was *desire,* as dark and sweet as a ripe plum. It was more than enough prize for the effort of my victory.

"I dedicate this kill to the king," I said. "Long may he reign."

This was an expected formality, but my voice was too satisfied to be servile. Philip inclined his head in acknowledgment. He did not look away from me, gaze steady, as I ended it. The boar twitched, slumped, and was still. The hunters roared. I stepped back and wiped my blade clean across its hide. As I approached, Geoffrey gave me a nod of reticent respect.

"A fine hunt," he said.

"Yes," Philip replied. He was not speaking to Geoffrey. His words were half a sigh, half a surrender. "Yes," he said. "It was."

<hr />

The boar was tied to the stick by its feet, and they carried it, swinging, back to the clearing.

"Most impressive, my lord," Philip said to me, demure under the scrutiny of the other hunters. Our horses, still recovering from the chase, picked languidly over crushed twigs and frozen leaves. His eyes were lowered, the dark fan of his lashes stark against his skin. "It is an honor, to be dedicated such a fine kill."

"I endeavor to serve, my liege," I replied.

"Hm." He surveyed the retinue, cautiously; we were a little ahead from the rest. Behind us, Geoffrey had become entangled in a conversation with a courtier. Deeming us in private, Philip said, "Yesterday . . ."

"You would not ride with me then," I replied. "Not alone."

"No, I would not."

"Would you now?" I asked.

He gaped at me. "With everyone following us?"

"Tell them we will meet at the clearing."

"I . . ."

"Philip, please," I said. "I want only a moment, to speak to you without the eyes of the court."

He shifted in his saddle, considering. My heart thrummed in my chest. I decided, at that moment, that if he said no—if he could not bear to be alone with me again, even for the sake of this single, desperate request—I would let him go. I would have to.

"Very well," he said, turning his horse around. "I will tell the others. There is a stream nearby. We shall speak there."

I nodded, mute, as he returned to the retinue. I had no plan as to what I would say to him. I only knew that, if he was never to be mine, I might at least lose him here: in the snow under blue skies, with only the cold as our audience.

～๑～

Away from the trail, the trees thickened. We traced around them on our horses, carefully avoiding the low-hanging branches. It took some effort, and little conversation passed between us.

The stream was frozen. It wove like a skein of silver thread between the trees, glittering in the light. Philip stopped his horse beside a pine tree. As he dismounted, she shook her white mane and gave him an accusatory look. I dismounted Rufus also, and he stuck his snout into the snow.

Philip approached the stream. I followed him. He stopped at the bank, clutching his cloak around him, staring at the refracted colors on the surface of the ice.

We considered it in silence. I thought to comment on the beauty of the place we found ourselves in, but I was surprised when Philip spoke before I could: "I thought that when you returned, Richard, I might feel differently about you."

"Do you?" I asked.

"No," he said, smiling bitterly. "And you? Do you feel the same?"

"Yes. I want you still."

Philip shook his head. "Does it occur to you that we hardly know each other, not really? That our shared circumstances make us feel more familiar than we are? If I weren't king—"

"If you weren't king, then—"

"Then things would be different," he said, and his eyes met mine. I had expected his expression to be cold, but instead it was strangely desperate; I could not tell if he wanted me to agree with him or prove him wrong.

"Things *can* be different," I replied. There seemed a crack, suddenly, in his composure—in that beetle-like shell that surrounded him; perhaps it was time to pry it apart. "We could be together, Philip," I continued. "We could try. You could come to Poitiers with me, and escape this court. I know you are not happy here. In my palace in Aquitaine, there is a hall my mother built; she named it the Hall of Lost Footsteps, as it is so vast you cannot hear people move inside it. You ought to see it. You would like it, I think. When troubadours play in the garden, you can hear it from within the hall. The marble floor is so polished that you can see yourself inside it, and when you dance it is as if twice the people are dancing."

"Richard—"

"There is something so *simple* about Poitiers," I said, "so easy and *good*. It is the farthest north of my cities, not far for you to travel. And the cathedral—Lord, it is the finest in Europe—there is a window there that glows every color under the sun, and the light that cascades upon the pews . . . it is beyond imagining. When you leave the church, the market is ahead, and on saints' days they bring out the relics. The entire town comes to see them. You should hear them shouting, during the parade, calling for Eleanor and Richard, for the glory of Aquitaine. If you were there, they would call for you also. We could go together, once the war is over, and they will call for King Richard and King Philip. Can you imagine? Two kings on progress through Poitiers. Such a thing has not happened for a hundred years."

"Stop, Richard, please," Philip said. "This is cruel."

"Cruel? Why?"

"Because it cannot *be*," he replied. He gave a shivering, warbling sigh, sending a puff of smoke from his mouth that dissipated in the frozen air. His eyes were watering, with either cold or sorrow, and he drew his finger across his lashes to collect a nascent tear. He hardly seemed real when he was like this, with the snow a halo around him and the reflection of the frozen water shifting across his skin. He looked as if he were under siege, as if the world were an army waiting for him to waste away. I had never known someone so captivating in his melancholy.

"It cannot *be*," he repeated. "Even if—even if we allowed it to happen, it would not last. You and I—we are France and Aquitaine, France and England. We can never be at peace."

Even I had to accept that there was some truth to these words, as stubborn as I was, as desperate as I was. "We could make our own peace," I said. "Even if only for a moment—we still could."

He made a frustrated sound. "You still don't understand. You should not *want* this, Richard. I will destroy you if you permit it. I am a coward, but I am also cruel. I will always prioritize my gain, France's gain. I am a throne wearing the face of a man. It is all I will ever be."

"I do not believe that is true. You are more than a king."

"If it is not true, then I will endeavor to make it so. I will spend my life making it so. I do not know how else to live. You wondered how I survived my father?" he asked. "This is how. I will not make his mistakes."

I replied, "You are not cruel, Philip. You are afraid. You are desperate, as I am. And perhaps I should not want you, but I still think of you constantly." I gave a small, helpless laugh. "*Ceaselessly.* You are my permanent passenger."

"You do not know how much cruelty I am capable of," he told me, voice wavering. "You—you do not understand how quickly things might change between us, once the crown demands it."

"Then, perhaps only here, by the river," I said. "We could pretend nothing will change, at least until we leave this place. Please, Philip. I cannot let it end like this."

He sighed again and said, "Richard," almost in accusation, which made me believe he was angered by the suggestion. I opened my mouth to defend myself, but then he stepped forward, took my collar, and pulled me down to kiss him.

It was only brief. His lips were very cold, but he was still soft, pliant; I tried to pull him closer, but he tipped his head back to look at me. He pressed his palm against my cheek and ran the tips of his fingers along my cheekbone, lowering them to dance across my chin.

"What are you doing?" I asked.

"Remembering," he said. "If we are pretending, only for a moment—if this is to be the last time—then I want to remember."

He kissed me again. It was slower, more passionate, but it still felt like a farewell. He used his hands to catalogue my neck and my shoulders before they moved up to my hair. He ran his fingers along my temples and behind my jaw. His lips shifted to the left corner of my mouth, then my right. I explored him in turn: I found a mole hidden behind his right ear, a tiny scar on the very edge of an eyebrow. I whispered his name against his neck. It felt real. I made it so. Briefly, I persuaded myself it meant something more than goodbye.

We remained there, anchored by the snow, until the cold finally forced us to part.

Philip took a step back. He was flushed and shivering. "I want you to know," he said. "I want you to know that—that I meant this. Whatever might happen."

"Whatever happens, I meant it also," I told him. "I always will."

"If that is true, then I have been a fool. Perhaps I shall be glad, for once, to be proven wrong."

I did not understand this. I wasn't certain that I wanted to. For a moment, Philip seemed as if he might approach me again. Then he turned away, and he went to mount his horse. I watched him silently.

"Will you come with me?" he asked.

"Later." I did not know if I could look at him for a moment longer, not without reducing myself to nothing. It felt as if every second that we were together, he was chipping part of me away.

"Very well." He settled in his saddle. "Richard," he said, "I am sorry."

"I am also," I replied. "Not for loving you, Philip. But for expecting you to feel the same, when it is impossible. I know it is impossible. Forgive me."

Something shifted in his expression. Another fissure, a dissolution, spring come early to thaw the ice. "I—" he began, and his voice broke. His hands tightened around the reins. Then he said, garbled and fearful, as if he feared someone might steal his voice from the air before it could reach me: "Come to the hallway behind the solar. Tonight, after supper. Wait there—do not enter."

This was so unexpected that I could not answer. The words seemed to rebound from me and fall to the snow before I could comprehend them.

Philip did not give me time to comprehend them. "Farewell," he said, and he turned his horse away.

Before I could reply, he disappeared into the trees.

CHAPTER THIRTEEN

𝕻𝖍𝖎𝖑𝖎𝖕

By the time I reached the clearing, there had been sufficient time to swallow my panic; not enough to make peace with my decisions—of course not—but to construct some scaffolding of control, as flimsy as it was. Still, though, I could feel the echo of Richard's lips against my own, and the warmth of his chest. It had been cruel, to force myself to remember these things, to take the time to commit them to memory. But it had felt as if I had no other choice. No choice but to want him, to compromise my own plans for his sake. I had acted impulsively. Now I would have to deal with the aftermath.

Geoffrey approached me as I was dismounting my horse. As my feet hit snow, he tugged at his earlobe, in an unusually transparent display of annoyance. "Philip," he said. "I do not know why Richard needed to speak with you, but—"

"It is none of your concern. Only a personal matter."

Geoffrey's lips thinned. "Time enough for personal matters, I see, but not for those of state. I looked for you this morning, but I could not find you."

"I was busy," I said.

"With Richard?"

"With my *wife*," I snapped, which was true; Isabella had spent the morning attempting to distract me from my anxiety with chess games and troubadours. Geoffrey's accusation seemed somehow an insult to her, and I felt suddenly and unusually infuriated. "I am king, Lord Brittany. Will you dictate the company I keep?"

Chagrined, he replied, "No, of course not. But Richard—"

"Richard is my guest, as are you. You are here on my invitation. Do not force me to revoke the privilege."

"Pardon," he replied, alarmed. "I did not mean to offend."

"You overstep."

"Yes, I know. Pardon," he repeated. "It is only that, Philip—my *liege*—time runs short. My father will soon demand my compliance. I must return to Brittany, and to Henry, either with your support or without it."

"I . . ."

I looked to the trees. No Richard, yet. The rest of the retinue was at the other side of the clearing, chattering excitedly around the boar.

Geoffrey and I were alone. Anyone who bothered to look at us would have guessed we were plotting betrayal. We were as natural a partnership as any: two politicians colluding together. Europe waited within our palms. All I needed to do was close my grip.

"Give me the afternoon," I said, "to check my accounts. I must know what I can offer you as aid. And then—we shall speak after supper."

He grinned, victorious, and he took my hand in his. His fingers were freezing cold, his palm dry. It was a gentle grip, a respectful one; the sort anyone might use in an expression of gratitude. His face, however, was utter savagery. It was the same as Richard's had been, when he had plunged his knife into the boar's hide.

"This is the beginning of our greatness," Geoffrey said. "With the continent between us, we can do whatever we please. We needn't think of Henry nor Richard. They can be forgotten to us."

"Not forgotten," I replied. "They are and will be the king of England, after all."

"Very well. Not forgotten, but often ignored." I nodded, mute. "Where shall we meet?" Geoffrey asked. "Somewhere private, I should hope."

I could have told him anywhere. The turf maze, my study; and yet, I still found myself saying, "The solar. Do you know where it is?"

"Yes. Your father once met us there. I did not know you used it."

"Usually, I do not," I said. "Be there after supper, once Richard is gone."

He nodded, primed to reply; then Richard and his horse broke through the trees. Geoffrey dropped my hand, although no one would have noticed us. Richard was the hero of the hunt, and the commotion was extraordinary as the retinue surged to gather around him. The air was filled with screaming, laughing, and whinnying. The noise worsened as two of Richard's men brought him the boar to inspect, hanging grim and glass-eyed from the stick. Richard swung from his saddle to the snow. He looked ruffled and victorious. His hair stood in every direction, and his ears were red-tipped from the cold. Isabella began to speak to him; she pointed at the boar, commented upon it, and he laughed in response.

"Tonight," Geoffrey said quietly.

"Yes," I replied, and I despised myself for it.

~∽~

I went to Louis's rooms that afternoon. I had kept my old chambers, even after being crowned, and no one had stayed in the king's suite since my father's death. All was clean and tidy—the servants ensured it—but it was a dead room, a blank one, just like the man who had once lived there.

I did not usually visit such places, nor wish to remember what had happened within them. But on that day, I felt an unusual kinship with my father. He had been desperately in love with Eleanor of Aquitaine, and he had suffered for it until he died. They were married when both of them were young. Nothing came of it. The match had been made by my grandfather—he had wanted her land returned to France—but a lack of heirs led to the relationship's steady unravelling. Eleanor could not stand Louis. She had left him in the middle of the night, and the Pope granted her a divorce three days later. She called him Louis the Monk, as many did, but not for his piety. Rumor tells he never managed a full night in bed with her. It was not because he did not love her; I knew that he loved her, for when he had been at his worst—insensate, dribbling, reduced to his component pieces—it was her that he called for. *Eleanor, forgive me,* he would whisper, lying supine on the bed. For the last two weeks of his life, that was what I saw of him: a dying man, whimpering for his first wife.

Love destroyed Louis. He had wanted to hurt Eleanor, for her abandonment. When she became the architect of the princes' rebellion, he refused to see her, even while he had her sons at our court, even as he gave them armies to lead at her bidding. Sometimes I wonder if he lost that war on purpose, merely to spite her. When she had left France, Aquitaine had gone with her. It would never be ours again, not unless I managed an extraordi-

nary feat of conquest. Louis knew that. It was an endless source
of flagellation for him. He had been a failure as a husband, failure as a man, failure as a king.

I once pitied him for it. I derided him for it, too. When I
stood over his grave, as the priest gave rites, I thought him lesser
than the dirt beneath my boots. After Eleanor, Louis the Monk
had permitted himself a life half lived. I could not conceive how
he had managed it. Kingship required such a consuming absence of self. It was extraordinary that he had so much to lose.

But I had been a fool not to understand. Little wonder my
father had wasted away, considering what had been taken from
him. I understood that now. If I caught light as he once had, if
I burnt and then faded; if I became ashes and soot, the dust in
the air; then certainly, I would be as he was. I would be the dirt
beneath another's boot. It was only natural to fear such a fate.
But I was wrong to think I could ever avoid it, once Richard
came.

～∽～

The solar was a long, narrow room, studded with windows on
either side. There was a door at the back—locked—and one at
the front, still ajar from my entrance. The space was sparsely
furnished, since I spent most of my leisure time in my study. The
only things of note were the large table in the center, and the
chairs surrounding it; my father had once met with his councilors here.

It was dark outside. The table was lined with lit candles, which
guttered at my entrance. They were reflected in the window-
panes, which themselves were reflected in the windows opposite. The result was a roaring multitude of candle flames,
shuddering in sync: an endless echo of light.

Geoffrey arrived soon after I did. I stood from the table to greet him, and he stopped to do the same, bowing shallowly at the waist. His smile was preemptively gratified.

"Well met, my liege," he said, his tone overfamiliar for the formality of the words.

I responded in kind. I did not sit down, and neither did he.

"I have thought upon your offer," I said.

"And?" he asked.

"I will send my armies to Aquitaine." His smile split, showing teeth. "In the invasion of Richard's lands," I continued, "my men will support Brittany's, in equal number to your own. Does this satisfy you?"

Geoffrey was so delighted, he laughed; his shoulders twitched as if he wished to embrace me. "I am satisfied," he said, "more so than I had ever hoped for. Philip, you will not regret this. Anjou will be yours. Vexin, too, once the duchy is mine. I swear it."

"You will pledge fealty to me also, once you have Aquitaine. To solidify our future alliance."

"Of course," he replied. "I will return to Rennes and begin preparations immediately. As long as Richard hears nothing of our intentions, we should have some time before the invasion begins."

"Before then, Henry must write to me," I said. "He must confirm that Anjou shall be mine."

"You do not trust me?"

I frowned at him. He chuckled. "A jest," he said. "Yes, I will ask him to write."

"This was not a decision made lightly, Geoffrey."

"I know. I am grateful. I half thought . . ."

He paused. Candlelight flickered across his cheeks, catching his eyes. In its curious clarity, their color changed with the reflection, from green to brown-gold. They were now almost Richard's eyes, but colder, sharper. They saw more and said less.

"You half thought . . . ?" I prompted.

"I thought it was possible Richard had convinced you otherwise."

"He did not."

"And I am glad of it," he said. "Whatever distraction my
brother might provide, he is that. A distraction. Until he takes
the throne, you needn't bother with him again."

I made a noise of vague agreement. Geoffrey extended his
hand. "An oath," he said. "A final bond between us. Your armies
with mine."

"In Aquitaine."

"In Aquitaine," he agreed. "We march together."

I took his hand for the second time that day. This time, I was
glad for the tightness of his grip; it concealed my trembling.
Every nerve within me was alight. Regret and triumph, unusual
partners, danced upon the ends of my fingertips.

Geoffrey released me. "We ought to celebrate," he said. "Shall
we call for some wine?"

"It is late. I have preparations to make."

"Surely they can wait a single evening?" he asked.

"Not if you are to leave tomorrow," I said, and he sighed.

"I suppose so. You are nothing if not thorough, Philip."

"I will do all I can to ensure our victory."

"And I am thankful for it. You are certain I cannot sway you?"

I shook my head. He said, "Very well," in a placid tone, but
then he leaned forward to watch me intensely, as if searching for
traces of a lie. I met his eyes, concentrating upon the reflections
within them, the glow of the candlelight. Geoffrey dropped his
head in surrender.

"I shall find you in the morning, to bid farewell," I told him.

"Yes, do. I intend to avoid Richard until I am gone. Afterwards, keep him at court for as long as possible. The longer he is away from Aquitaine, the better."

"I do not know if I can convince him to stay."

"I suspect you can," he said.

I raised a brow, challenging him to specify. He did not. He pushed my chair in by the table—it was still askew from my standing up—and rearranged his cloak around his shoulders, the sleeves at his wrists. Once he was satisfied, he bowed. "Good evening, my liege."

"Good evening, my Lord Brittany. Until tomorrow."

"Until then."

Since the back door was locked, Geoffrey turned to leave by the front. He was careful to shut it gently behind him, but the candles guttered, all the same. The sudden silence was unnerving. I waited a good while, listening for his receding footsteps. Eventually, his absence was certain.

I stood up, turned around, and walked three paces to unlock the door behind me.

It was so dark in the corridor that I thought he was not there. "Richard?" I murmured.

For a moment, there was no response. Then Richard walked into the doorway, parting the shadows. We were only an arm's span apart; he took a step into the room, and I took a step back.

Richard's face was usually so open. It was odd to see him like this, expression warped with confusion and anger. He took a deep breath and closed his eyes, curling his hands into fists. The muscles in his arms flexed. He seemed to tremble with whatever fury he was withholding.

"Was this what you wanted?" he asked hoarsely, as if the only way he could prevent himself from screaming was to whisper.

"I . . ."

"Was this what you wanted, Philip?" he repeated. His features began to deconstruct as his composure dissolved. His mouth curved, anguished, so that he was speaking through a grimace. "When you told me to wait behind the door. This was it? You wanted me to hear you and Geoffrey?"

"Yes."

"Why?"

"Why do you think?"

Richard strode past me. Pulling up a chair, he folded himself into it. He hunched over and sneered at his boots. "Out of cruelty, perhaps," he suggested. "How long have you known about this? This—this invasion?"

"Since the day Geoffrey arrived."

"Two days," he murmured. "Two days it took for you to choose him over me."

I took the chair to sit next to him, and I turned it in his direction. He did not look at me as I did so. "Richard," I said. "Listen to me. Invade Brittany. You know, now, that an invasion shall happen. Strike first. Bring your armies to him."

"Why should I do that?"

"Because then I *cannot help him*," I said. I wanted him to look at me, and I leaned towards him, attempting to attract his attention. His shoulders hunched further. "I did not lie to Geoffrey," I continued, pleading. "I told him I would move troops to Aquitaine. I did not promise to defend Brittany."

"What do you mean? You will not involve yourself if I act first?"

"I will not involve myself until *he* invades *Aquitaine*," I said. "That was the promise I made."

Richard did not respond. He tapped his foot against the floor. He was still trembling. He was still furious. Perhaps my gambit had failed. I could have betrayed him without warning, I could have kept him ignorant—but I did not. I was weak, and now I had made a certain victory uncertain.

"I suppose it is clever," Richard said, "to warn me. Perhaps you wanted to ensure my future forgiveness. This way, you will have Anjou no matter the outcome of the conflict. Anjou from Geoffrey and Henry, should they win. Anjou from me, should I defeat them."

His tone was low, controlled, an animal leashed. There was a sense of preparation—a willingness to escalate—that gave me a feeling of genuine unease. I had never fully understood why some were afraid of Richard, until that moment.

"That isn't why I told you," I said weakly.

"No? Then *why?*"

"I do not know," I replied. "Because I could not bear it otherwise."

"You have still betrayed me."

"Yes, I have."

"You might lead armies against me. You are willing to do so."

"I am."

"But—I would do anything for you, Philip." His voice cracked, and his eyes finally met mine. He made a choked sound, rage shattering into despair. I should have felt relieved, but it was somehow worse than his anger. "You know that," he said. "You know that I would do anything for you."

"Would you give up Aquitaine, if I asked it?"

"I . . . No. I would not."

"Then you understand why I am as I am."

"I do not understand. I never will. You do this because you stand to gain, not because you are at risk."

"I am at risk," I replied. "*Constantly*, I am at risk. I am not like you, Richard. I am not brave enough to live as you do."

He shook his head. "I do not want you to be brave. I want you to love me as I do you. I want—I want *anything* other than this. Are you not sick of it? This push and pull, these endless, petty games—this grasping, ravenous ambition. It is a plague. It will kill us all."

His expression was so sincere, so desperate; I had never felt so inadequate. "I have never known anything else," I told him.

"What if you could? What if we both could?"

"I have ambition only. I do not know what else there can be."

"I could show you," he replied, and he reached out, cupping my cheek. His thumb skimmed over my lips. "Please. Let me show you what else there can be."

Silence fell. His gaze dropped to my mouth. I knew, then, that he was going to kiss me; I offered myself for it, tipping my chin up to meet him. Richard surged forward without hesitation, and we collided. It was desperate, almost painful, his hand reaching back to pull at my hair, his teeth sinking into my lower lip. I could not respond with anything but immediate capitulation, opening my mouth to him and allowing him to hold me in place.

It lasted only moments before he drew away. He said, "I am angry with you; I remain so—"

"You ought to be—"

"But I want you still, I have no choice but to want you. And my anger seems only to make me want you more. It is as if everything I feel is *you*, Philip. You are my fear and my fury and my most fervent hope; and God, I—I cannot . . ."

Words failed him. His hand was looped around my wrist; he tightened his grip, my pulse thrumming beneath his fingers. He asked, "May I?"

I was uncertain what he was asking for. "Yes," I said. He let go of me. His hands curled around my thighs, and he hauled me onto his lap. Pulling me down by my shirtfront, he kissed me again. It was slower, this time, exploratory, his tongue soothing my lip where he had bitten it. His arms wrapped around my lower back and tugged me closer, so that our chests were pressed against each other. When we parted, I felt as if I were at a different axis to everything else. I closed my eyes and dipped my head, pressing my lips to his chin, his cheek, his throat. I knew nothing but the sensation of skin.

"I love you, too," I whispered against his neck. "Forgive me."

He shuddered in response, and his grip on me tightened.

There was little room for further thought. I moved my mouth downwards, preoccupying myself with his collarbone. His fingers pressed against my scalp. Our lips met, fell away, met again. My hips began to move against his, but it was without true intention. I did not know what I wanted. My skin was burning. I was burning, and I wanted him to keep me so.

"Philip," he murmured, once an unknowable amount of time had passed. I hummed in acknowledgment. He traced a line with his finger from my chin to the base of my neck, and I squirmed. "We ought to be somewhere else."

"Where?"

"In bed."

"Together?"

He huffed a small laugh beside my ear. His breath tickled, and I flinched. "Together," he agreed.

I straightened to look at him properly. "Why?" I asked.

"Why do you think?"

"I think we are at war," I said, "and I am taking as much as I am permitted, until you realize you are furious."

"I realize I am furious," he replied warily.

I pressed my face to his neck, to hide myself from him. "Then how can I allow it?" I asked, muffled. "How can I allow this, knowing what I have done, what I shall do?"

"I do not know. But for tonight, I wish to forget. If we are to part enemies—I want to have you, Philip, just once. You and I, as we are now, before it all falls apart."

"Are you certain?" I asked him.

"Yes," he said. "Are you?"

"Yes," I replied. "If you want me still—then yes."

"I will always want you. Enemy or ally, I always shall."

"That is a foolish promise to make."

He said, "Then I am a fool. You have made me so."

I did not know what would happen once the night passed; once he was gone, and our fragile peace finally shattered. But— for now—Richard was glowing like iron being forged, molten with his conviction in my worthiness. I could not bear to prove him wrong.

I slid off his lap. He reached out to pull me back. I shook my head and offered him my hand.

"Show me, Richard," I said. "You have made your promises, as I have made mine. Now you must prove them."

"I will," he replied. He stood, taking my hand. Tugging me towards the door, he pulled me into the corridor. It was darker there, cooler. Without the light of the candles we were un-moored, anchored only by the press of his palm to mine. "I will," he repeated; and, with my eyes half closed, I allowed him to lead me away.

Part Three

JEU-PARTI

CHAPTER FOURTEEN

Richard

I was a coward.

When I awoke, it was very early, only the beginning of dawn. Philip was asleep; he was as still and silent as stone. If it were not for the rise and fall of his chest, he might have been petrified. His face was turned to the side, his head resting on his hands. He was beautiful. And, as I watched him, I realized that I could leave him like this. I could ensure the last words between us were the night's whispers of devotion. I could forget that this Philip, and the one I might meet in battle, were the same person.

So, I left him there. I made the memory of him that morning an effigy in flesh: a monument to us, as we had once been. I knew him entirely now. I had seen him vulnerable; I had seen him flushed and bare and desperate and *mine*. He had made our night together as much an ending as a beginning, our peace dissolved, sending me to battle from his bed; but that was my fault as much as his, as I was too craven to bid him farewell. Too craven to request further apology or explanation, to plead for mercy or demand surrender. I simply brushed a kiss across his temple, left the room, and went to war with a man whose hips were still inscribed with the shadow of my fingertips.

It was foolish of me to mourn our parting. I would return to Paris eventually. I would be victorious in this war, no matter whose armies I faced. And regardless, I would be king of England someday. For now, Philip and I were France and Aquitaine, and even that was not enough to keep us from conflict. I would have to grow accustomed to this, eventually. I had been naïve to ever assume I could keep us at peace. Kisses do not a kingdom make, nor love a conquest end.

I loved him, but that was not enough.

Perhaps it never would be.

—⁊⁊—

Philip,

I am writing you these letters in case I am defeated, and my brother or father captures me: under which circumstances I expect I shall be imprisoned in England, and I shall not see nor speak to you again until Henry's death. I am giving them to Stephen for safekeeping, and he will bring them to you.

I left you one week ago, and since then we have been marching towards Brittany. It has rained every day since we left. I fear I shall drown. My army is quite soggy, you can hear them squelching from miles away. We took to the shore to avoid the mud. I saw a little pink shell on the beach that was perfect, not chipped or cracked at all: a small blushing thing. It went directly into my pouch. It is your fault I took it. It made me think of you.

Lord, I adore you. I despise you. You are haunting my every waking thought.

Soon Geoffrey will know that I am here, and he will wonder how I heard of his intentions. Do you think he will realize it was

you? I hope he will. I hope that he is angry at you, and he decides
he will never speak to you again. Perhaps then, you will always
choose me, and I needn't fear another betrayal.

There is something about the salt in the air here. It scrapes me
raw, batters me from within. I have been so nervous. I was not
like this, the last time I went to battle. Stephen says my confi-
dence shall return once the siege begins. I pray that it shall.

I pray that you miss me. I miss you. I wish I did not.

Sometimes it feels as if you do not exist. I invented you, the
Philip I wanted, and I still pretend that you are him, even
though you have betrayed me. Perhaps I should forgive you for
that betrayal—I do not know if I can forgive you for it—
nothing seems certain to me at this moment but my love of you,
and this torrential, ceaseless, accursed rain.

～∾～

It had been far too long since I wore anything but tournament
armor.

"Stop squirming, Richard," Stephen said. "I am closing a
buckle."

The wind howled outside the tent, and the walls shuddered.
The air was so damp I felt likely to dissolve. The fire was a whimpering runt; the brazier would have been better used as a soup
bowl. This was Breton winter, in all its glory. I had hoped I would
never experience it again.

As Stephen stood, I moved my arm back and forth, feeling
the slide of metal upon metal. "As it was," I said. "It fits the
same."

"Yes, it does. But it has been some time since you wore armor
in battle."

"It won't come to battle," I replied. "And if it does, it shall be
quick."

We were nearing Nantes. It was one of Geoffrey's largest cities, gateway to his duchy. We had set up our camp less than a
day's march away. Several thousand men were now sprawled
across the field in an anarchistic web of mud-drowned tents, like
flies on carrion, buzzing with the drawn-breath anticipation of a
fight. It would be a difficult siege if the city were expecting us, or
if its garrison were not depleted in preparation for Geoffrey's
invasion; but both of those things seemed unlikely. In Brittany,
there was little love for my brother, who was Duke merely by
marriage to their beloved duchess. I did not expect a zealous
resistance. Nor did I expect to remain in Nantes for long. I
wished only to pass through unhindered as we made our way to
the capital, so I could finish this fight as quickly as it had begun.

Stephen went to poke at the fire. "A murder of crows flew past
the camp last night," he said. "Some of the men thought it was
an omen of death."

"Our death, or our enemy's?" I asked.

"That is debated."

I crossed myself. "Pray it is a warning for caution," I said, "and
not a sign of things to come."

Stephen made a noise of agreement. His movements with the
poker became more combative; the fire sputtered and went out.

"Richard," he said, frowning at the ashes.

"Yes?"

"Why are we here?"

"Because we are invading Brittany," I replied. "Did you hit
your head somewhere?"

"Why are we invading Brittany?"

"Because we defend Aquitaine."

"Yes, but—" He stabbed again at the brazier, as if he could
revive the fire with annoyance alone. "Who told you to invade in
the first place?"

"...Philip," I said.

"Philip," he agreed. "I have thought upon it, and what you overheard—it might have been planned, surely? Could Philip have contrived this himself? To draw you further from Aquitaine, so that he could invade while you were away?"

My blood ran cold. I hadn't even considered this a possibility.

"He would not," I said, but my voice trembled a little. "That would be too far. Philip would not."

"Are you certain?"

"I have to be." I approached Stephen, pulling the poker from his hands. I used it to rearrange the logs; an ember glowed between them, and it seemed the fire might catch again. "I have to be certain," I repeated. "If he does such a thing—if he is willing to do so—then my war with him is done. I have already lost."

⁓

Philip,

We took the garrison in Nantes by surprise, and it was a pitiful one, too, with half the men gone. There was hardly a battle; we surrounded the walls, and they sued for peace less than an hour later. It was the easiest seizure of a city I have ever known. We will blaze through this land like a wildfire. The capital awaits.

Geoffrey must have realized that I am coming. It is pleasant to imagine the moment he found out; the moment he realized the advantage was mine. I never thanked you for what you did, and perhaps I should have. If you had not forewarned me, Aquitaine might be lost. As it is, Brittany has become nothing more than a series of conquests. At the end of them, Geoffrey shall lay surrender at my feet.

Stephen thinks I am a fool for my gratitude. He says that be-

*trayal is betrayal, no matter how well watered. I suspect you
would agree.*

*Nantes is beautiful, though I am loath to admit it. Now that
the snow is thawing, one can see the grass. Even in winter, it is
the greenest grass I have ever stepped on. The soil must be good
here. I found a tree that still had apples on it: winter apples, red
as blood.*

*I think of you constantly. You are the sky above me and the
ground below, you are the rain and the sun and the snow and the
grass. You are winter and you are spring. I cannot escape you.*

~ ⚬ ~

My siege engineer was a marvelously decrepit Basque who had
already been old when my mother appointed him. His name was
Marko, and his age was almost as inconceivable as his skills;
Eleanor had an exceptional talent for recruiting genius. I suspected he had contributed to the fall of Rome. He had no hair
and wore glasses like a monk. He could walk with little trouble,
but he liked to be carried around anyway. Where he learnt his
craft, or why he had left Basque country, were both lost to history.

We were a day from Rennes, the Breton capital. I stood with
him by the side of the camp. He was jabbing at the ground with
his stick, muttering to himself. After several minutes of this, he
finally said, "No."

"No?" I asked.

"Too much rain. The ground is soft. If we dig, the tunnel will
collapse. Is this what you want?"

"Of course not," I replied.

"Then no digging," he said.

"But—"

"Wait," he spat at me, through the three teeth he had remaining. "Hm? Sometimes, it is best to wait. The city will fall. No seaport. Blockading will be effective. Starve them out. No need to dig beneath walls."

"If you are certain."

"Your mother knew it was best to wait. In Aleppo—"

"Yes, thank you, Marko." I sighed.

He waved his stick at me. "In Aleppo she wished to wait," he said, "but King Louis took her to Antioch. And what happened then?"

"What?"

"Divorce."

I snorted in amusement, and he grinned. "Very well," I said. "We shall wait. But—if we were to assault the walls instead, would it be possible?"

He scratched at his chin. "Possible, yes," he replied. "And faster, too."

"It would prevent Geoffrey from escaping. Allow us to leave Brittany before reinforcements arrive."

"True, true."

"But our losses would be greater."

"Oh, yes."

"How much greater?" I asked.

He shrugged. "Greater," he said. "Certainly. Your decision, my liege."

"I would do it, if it were certain to win me the battle."

"It is certain to win you the battle. But the battle is not the war. And the war is not the conflict, I'd wager, not in the end; so what would be the point?"

"I—well—I suppose I don't know."

"Glory," he said, satisfied, and he patted my shoulder with twiglike fingers. "That would be the point. That is all it is. You choose if it is worth it. Not my place to decide."

I watched him as he hobbled away. "Glory," I murmured to myself with mounting excitement. I imagined myself tearing through Rennes's walls, assaulting the castle, and sitting on Geoffrey's throne. I was triumphant; then the scene shifted, and the ducal seat became that of England. For the first time, I pictured the crown upon my head, and drew pleasure from the image.

Then I remembered Philip in the clearing, telling me, *I am a throne wearing the face of a man,* as he brushed a tear from his cheek.

And the word *glory* became ash on my tongue.

~·~

Philip,

Long since I have written one of these. I thought to stop, but then I saw Rennes, and I saw the archers upon the wall. I realized that war is war, after all, and I want these messages on paper, in case they are the only part of me ever able to return from Brittany.

This is the worst sort of siege, a starving siege. A blockade, rather than a battle. We are well equipped for it, but I would rather batter the gates down and be done with it. I nearly did. Then I thought of returning to Aquitaine with half an army, and—for once—I allowed caution to prevail. So instead, we sit outside with trebuchets primed, while Geoffrey hems and haws in his palace. He sends me warnings about how Father will be displeased, and how you will march from France to enact revenge. He wants me to think that you will come after me; that you will arrive with ten thousand men and lay my armies to waste. It is a bluff, of course. I know that it is. I do not bother to respond. Instead I wait, camped outside Rennes, as my men eat their way through the surrounding countryside.

Geoffrey is a stubborn fool. Perhaps we are more alike than I would admit. I wish I could remain angry with him, but all I feel now is annoyance. I so strongly expected his betrayal that I do not feel betrayed by it. Instead, I am desperate for combat. It makes me twitchy. Last night a soldier outside my tent dropped his shield. The clang woke me up, and I leapt out with my sword drawn. I could tell he was trying not to laugh.

I cannot be faulted for it, really. There is something so shameful in fighting a battle this way. Stephen says I have bloodlust. I do not think it is bloodlust, but rather a desire for resistance. I wish to feel that there is a reason I am here, knee-deep in the Breton mud. Because if there is no reason but you, your betrayal and your sending me here, then surely I must despise you for it—and surely I must accept that you despise me also, that you hate me in the manner our blood assigns. But I do not want to hate you. I do not think I am capable of it.

I am becoming capable of nothing, I fear, except regret.

～⤳～

I would not be permitted a reckoning with Geoffrey, that much was becoming clear. We could not watch over every inch of the city. If he had not already escaped, he would certainly be gone by the time Rennes fell.

This infuriated me. I would walk the base of the walls at night—day was too dangerous, I would be too visible to archers—and I would crane my head upwards to see the tiny points of light on the battlements. These were the fires of the city's defenders. Beside one of them was Geoffrey: looking out over the dark mass of my armies, counting the days until his resolve would break.

He had spent so much of his life denying me victory. It was little surprise he would do so now, even as Rennes starved, and my hand closed around its walls. It seemed he would rather I crush him, than admit that he had lost. I began to wonder if his surrender would ever come. Perhaps we would invade a city full of skeletons. I would find my brother's corpse sitting on his throne: dead, but still the victor. It almost felt *likely*. The entire siege, the entire battle, futile and hollow. Victory or no, I'd find no reward but bones.

∼ᴏᴄ∼

Philip,

The siege has broken. We have entered Rennes. Geoffrey was gone from the palace when we entered; he escaped as our armies arrived. We knew that he would. No man would choose to be caged for so long, unless he was engineering an exit. But then we heard the news from Anjou, and we realized that he had delayed for strategy rather than stubbornness.

It is partly my fault. I knew that Henry might provide rein-forcements. I knew that assaulting the city might have prevented them coming in time, and it is my fault I chose instead to wait; but wait I did, and now John is leading our father's men towards Aquitaine, and Poitiers lies undefended.

Part of me wonders if you intended this all along. Perhaps you knew that I would lose, in the end, and you intervened because you wanted to ensure this conflict would be as lengthy and ruin-ous as possible. I can imagine you find it a fascinating puzzle, all of this: considering the scales, deciding which weights to place when.

I suppose such things are in your nature, as much as loving you is in mine. And I cannot judge you too harshly for it, Philip, when I have had a hand in my own destruction. But John's armies arrived in Anjou while I was walking through Rennes's gates. And although Geoffrey might have surrendered, the invasion is not over until Henry calls for its end. So now, where shall I go? East, to cut off my brother's armies? South to the border, where you might be waiting for me? I am a baited bear. I cannot remain here and allow John to walk into Poitiers. But the moment I turn back towards home, you shall be at the border to greet me. That was the promise that you and Geoffrey made. I want you to betray him for my sake, as you betrayed me for his, but it is not certain that you will. And if you do not—when I arrive, my army shall be exhausted, while yours is eager for battle. You will win the war in my brother's stead. Anjou will be yours, just as you have always wanted.

You warned me. You told me the invasion could not come to Aquitaine. I thought that it would not. It is astonishing that Henry has risked putting John on a battlefield. You have not met John, but he is as much a soldier as I am a ploughman. It never ceases to surprise me, how far my father is willing to go. And you are similar, in that manner; I still feel, even now, that I do not know what you are capable of.

But God, Philip, you have changed me, at the very least. I did not realize how much until this moment. Once I would have charged like a bull to Anjou, to meet John in battle. I would have defeated him, but it would have cost me my hold on Brittany, as I do not have enough men to leave a garrison here. What else would there have been to do? Out of spite, I would have flung my armies at my father, over and over, until there was nothing left. Then there would be no path towards Aquitaine, except for surrender; and I have always considered surrender a death for those too cowardly to die. But the path to Aquitaine might lead to you also, and I will have you in any way I can. I love you. I think I always will.

Perhaps you will march your armies through Poitiers. I sup-

*pose that you will not. It is faster to take the river west. But I
imagine it, all the same. I imagine that we will meet in the city,
in front of the cathedral. I will kneel to you there, in the market
square, and give you my heart to bury.*

~⁊~

The siege of Rennes had broken, the garrison surrendered, but
some enemy soldiers had lingered hidden in the city. In my fury
and my sorrow, I forgot what small semblance of caution I had.
The morning after my victory, I went to walk the walls. I was an
easy target.

I saw the bolt before I felt it. In the time between a step, my
foot still in the air, there was a tooth-jarring impact that sent me
spinning into the dirt. Flat on my back, I looked at my shoulder.
It was an impressive wound, and the bolt jutted from it like a
nail half hammered. Blood spurted in stuttering gushes to fall
upon my sleeve. Then, finally, came a blinding pain, across my
cheek and my shoulder, as if the skin there had fractured like
glass.

Stephen fell to his knees beside me, pressing his hands around
the bolt. The pressure made the pain worse. I gave a garbled yell
of protest. He began to shout things at the men around us. I
could not follow his speech. He was already dissolving into the
ground, streaking like ink beneath the rain. I saw my own reflection in his dark eyes. Black shapes floated indolently in the grey
sky above us. My head lolled against the mud.

I closed my eyes and saw Philip behind them.

Forgive me, he said.

CHAPTER FIFTEEN

Philip

When Geoffrey learnt that Richard was in Brittany, he sent me a letter.

It is a troublesome thing, sending messages in an invaded land. The courier travels by night to avoid interception. There is a chance that he will never arrive, having been attacked or captured on the road; often, multiple copies are sent for security, each with a separate messenger, each by a different route. Geoffrey did not send multiple copies. Geoffrey sent only one. The courier arrived, having survived two hundred miles of potential battlefields, to deliver a piece of paper that read only: *Well played*. It was an extraordinary display of Angevin pettiness. I threw the thing in the fire, and I found myself laughing at the flames.

As months passed, more couriers traveled by night, and more paper fell into my hands. Each missive was burnt with progressively less amusement. News came from Brittany: Richard had taken Nantes. News came from Brittany: the siege of Rennes had turned to Richard's favor. News came from Brittany: the city had fallen, and Richard had been wounded. *A crossbow bolt to the shoulder. A maiming, not fatal,* said the letter. And then—on another line, as if an afterthought—my spy had added, *Not yet.*

"Not yet," I murmured to myself that night, a prayer to my pillow. Not yet.

The next day, I moved court to Orleans. It was closer to Aquitaine, and Brittany. The rain there was torrential, as it was across the entire continent. That spring was to be a season of storms. Three couriers followed that night; they all brought the same letter. Sat upon my desk, they were near-perfect triplets, each sealed with the same wax. One was soaked too badly to read— that messenger had been caught in the gale—but the others remained in perfect condition. I recognized the seal. This time, Geoffrey had taken no chances.

I sat down to read. I had not heard from him since Rennes had fallen.

Richard was victorious, the letter said. *But not soon enough. John has reached Le Mans. I march to meet him there. Richard will head south. Cut him off at Nantes.*

Make good your promises, my liege, and I shall make good mine.
Geoffrey.

I put the letter down with trembling fingers. I broke the seal upon one of the others; it was identical, of course. Even the sodden letter, ink too wet to read, had once clearly contained the same. I pushed them all away from me to the edge of the table, and I covered my face with my hands.

"What are you doing?"

I nearly yelped in surprise. I looked up at the doorway. The room was dimly lit, and the figure at the threshold was impossible to distinguish; it was only her voice that made me realize who it was. "Very little," I said. "Should you not be in bed, Isabella?"

"Only as much as you should," she replied, shuffling into the room. When she saw Galahad lying on the rug by the fire, she went to crouch beside him. His tail thumped against the floor. He rolled to his back to expose his belly.

Isabella used the hand that was not petting Galahad to rub at her eyes. "I woke up, and you were gone," she said, her voice still drowsy.

"I received a letter."

She glanced at the desk. "Several, clearly."

"They were all the same."

"What was it?"

I went to sit next to them, clutching the most legible of the letters in my hand. I passed it to her. She scanned it blearily. Comprehension dawned, and she dropped it.

"Oh no," she said.

I collected the letter from the rug. "It is as it is," I replied. "Richard did not take Brittany fast enough, and now the invasion travels to Aquitaine."

"You speak as if it is nothing. But you will *lead armies*, Philip. Against Richard." She paused and then repeated, "Against *Richard*!"

I said, "I have led armies before."

"Those were petty wars, against vassals! Ones where you did not have to fight!"

"Isabella, no one will insist I fight on the field. Richard is his own general because he is talented in combat, and because he is reckless. I hardly need to—"

"Philip, you might *die*!" she cried.

At this half shriek, Galahad rolled over and stood. Disturbed by Isabella's distress, he poked her face with his nose, whining.

I stroked his back in comfort. "I will not die."

"How do you know that?"

"How can one know anything? I will do all I can to prevent it."

She made a frustrated noise. Galahad whined again. "I hate you," she said. "You will leave me here, won't you? All alone."

"You know I cannot bring you with me."

"If you die, I shan't ever forgive you."

"I know."

"I cannot understand it," she said. "Neither you nor Richard wish to fight. Why not make peace?"

"It isn't as simple as that."

"I don't see why not."

"The conflict must end," I said. "Richard's opportunity for victory is gone, and I have ensured that Geoffrey's is, as well. As it stands, the two of them will continue to occupy each other's lands, in constant exchange; they will do so until they are so weakened that their father can do as he pleases."

She considered this. "Is that what Henry wanted, when he started the war?"

"It is possible."

"So—what will you do?"

"Richard must surrender," I said. "That is why my armies must meet him at Nantes, and stop him before he reaches Aquitaine at all."

"But then he will lose Aquitaine," Isabella replied.

"That is likely, yes."

Eyes half closed, she bent to look at Galahad. The fire cast gentle light across her face. Meanwhile, I sat in the shadows, grey-blue and blurred, like a phantom come to haunt her.

"Will he surrender, before the battle?" she asked me.

"He—he could."

"But he won't."

"No," I said. "I do not think he will."

She asked, "Surely, you are scared, Philip? That you will be hurt? That *he* will be hurt?"

"I am constantly scared. Always."

"I do not know how you can bear it."

"Often, I am uncertain I can."

"It is as if there are two of you," she said. "I used to wonder why. Sometimes you are Philip, and sometimes you seem like someone else; someone who is willing to do the things that Philip is not. But now I understand. It is because there is too much burden for you to carry alone."

I pressed my arm against hers, laying my fingers against Galahad's paw. My throat was closed tight; when I spoke, the words were almost whispered. "Yes. I suppose that is why."

"But I think Richard could share that burden," she told me, frowning. "He understands. He could help."

"What we have, it . . . I cannot come to rely upon him, as you wish me to."

"Why?"

"Because one day I will lose him."

"One day you will lose everything," she replied. "We are human. That is what happens. Nothing is permanent."

"But this, least of all. He knows that as much as I do, even if he denies it. We will always be enemies. It is inevitable. It is *ordained*."

Isabella scowled and opened her mouth to reply, but her protest was interrupted by a wide yawn.

"Go to bed," I said, shoving her shoulder.

She sighed. "I shall," she told me, "but only because you are impossible to reason with, when you are in one of these moods."

She stood up. Galahad rolled over and gave me an accusatory look, blaming me for her departure.

"Are you coming?" she asked.

"After I have put my documents away."

"Then you'll sleep?"

"Yes."

"Promise?"

"I swear, Isabella."

She nodded and walked to the door. Away from the fire, she was once more obscured by shadow. "Good night, to both of you," she said. As she walked into the hallway, she was entirely swallowed by the darkness.

Galahad whimpered. I frowned at him. "Go with her, if you like," I said, as if he could understand me. But he simply stared at me as I stood and returned to my desk. I folded the letters as precisely as I could, resealing them. Then I realized they had to be burnt. I threw them into the hearth, wax and all. They fell apart amongst the flames.

I stared into the fireplace for a good while, and I continued to do so, even as my eyes began to sting with exhaustion. My vision blurred, and the fire became an indistinct glimmer. It reminded me of sunlight glittering across frozen water, and Richard whispering my name against my throat, his voice a brand upon the cold-white silence of the forest. I felt his absence like an ache, like a hunger, like a breath I could not breathe.

Eventually, Galahad made for the door. I went to let him out, standing at the threshold in indecision before going to take a candle with me. The hallways seemed alien this time of night. I followed the route to my chambers more by memory than sight, trailing my fingers on the wall, until I came to my bedroom door. Inside, I could hear Isabella's soft breathing, and I could see her under the covers. Snuffing out my candle, I crawled into bed.

Isabella shifted. "You came," she said.

"You made me promise."

"I did, but I thought you would fall asleep at your desk. You always do."

"I am sorry for waking you."

"No matter." She turned to face me. "Philip," she said.

"Yes?"

It was too dark to see anything, but I felt her breath over my face as she spoke. "What if you do not come back?" she asked.

"I will."

"But what if you do not? I would be alone," she said. "Useless. I am nothing without you."

"That is not true, Isabella," I replied.

"It is. I am hardly anything at all, even when you are here. I am hardly your wife—"

"You—"

"Hush. You cannot pretend otherwise. Do not insult me by pretending otherwise."

"You are dear to me," I said, feeling utterly inadequate. "I am sorry that I cannot give you more than I have."

"It is not that I want you to be in *love* with me. But it hangs over me, that we cannot have a child. It is all anyone thinks I am meant to do. It follows me everywhere. Doesn't it also, for you?"

It did. Of course, it did. My dynasty was two hundred years old, and it lay across me like a shroud. The weight of my blood was suffocating. My father had gone half mad in his search for a son to continue his lineage. Now that son could let the lineage die out, in all his cowardice and insufficiency.

Isabella did not deserve such a husband. She did not deserve the accusations that would be levied against her, should we grow old without an heir. If we had a son, the weight would be lifted.

I said, "Perhaps someday. Perhaps—"

"Stop. I do not expect your promises. And I do not blame you for it. I swear that I do not. But I would ask you for at least one thing."

"Anything I am able to give, I shall."

"I ask that you consider happiness," she said. "We have both made sacrifices, I know that. But I have been forced to make mine, and, often, you have *chosen* to make yours. I understand that sometimes it is for the best. But sometimes—sometimes you could choose happiness instead. You have a choice, Philip. It hurts that you do not choose the things I would, if I were ever permitted them."

"Like what?"

"Like *love*," she said. "One of us has to fall in love, at least once."

"You might fall in love one day, Isabella."

"Maybe so. But you could do so now, if you wanted to. You have been given the chance." She reached under the blankets to take my hands. Her grip was desperate. "When this is over— when the fighting is done—allow yourself to fall in love. Even if it is not Richard, even if it is someone else; if the chance comes again, please, take it. I cannot forgive you, Philip, if you refuse it. You cannot fall in love with me, I know. But you can show me that someday I might be loved, as you will be." I did not reply, and her grip tightened further. "Is that selfish?" she asked. "To want it for my own sake?"

"You should be selfish. You deserve to be."

"I deserve nothing," she said, and she released me.

I sought her hands again in the darkness. I could not find them. "Isabella, you are my wife," I told her, "through no choice of our own. And what that is, for us, will never be as it is for others. But it is just as important. You are as beloved by me as any wife is to her husband, if not in the same way. You are my dearest friend, and I love you for it, and in all that we have endured—all that we will endure—I am grateful that it is you beside me."

She reached for me. I hugged her, pressing my hands into her back. I could feel her shoulder blades shifting as her posture slumped, and my nose pressed against her cheek.

"Me, too," she replied.

"And you deserve happiness also," I said. "So if—if having a child would make you happy . . ."

"Oh. You do not have to—"

"I will have to, someday."

"I know. But I meant, not *now*."

"If not now, when?" I asked her. "I am about to go to war. It is possible I might not return. And besides—how long will I leave you to suffer?"

She pressed her face into my chest. I tightened my grip around her. She had become so familiar to me, and I did not know if that made it easier or more difficult. "I am sorry," I said. "I am so sorry. I have been selfish."

"No, you haven't, Philip."

I released her. "Give me a moment," I said.

"You do not have to," she replied. "Are you not tired?"

I was. In a way, it made things easier: the haze of it, the sensation of detachment. "Are you?" I asked.

"I am completely awake now."

"This is—" I smoothed a hand over my face. "This—"

"I am so embarrassed. I have never been so embarrassed in my life."

I began to laugh. "I feel the same, good Lord."

She sat up. "I have known you too long, Philip, to be uncomfortable around you any longer. If—if we have decided it must happen, it must happen. We will do all we can to make it easier.

Then, come morning, we will say absolutely nothing of it, and I will pray a lot and then all shall be well."

"It is likely that . . . I mean, we will have to try more than once."

"All shall be well," she repeated. "We will do what we must, as much as we need to. We can imagine it is someone else. We can—we can pretend that things are the same."

"Things will be the same," I said. "I would never allow this to change us, Isabella."

"Good," she said, and she moved back towards me.

We both fell silent. Then there was no sound but the shifting of sheets, and the soft hiss of the wind outside. There was no light, either; and it might have been better if there had been, so that I could have seen her face, pale and moonlike, gentle eyes half lidded in concentration. I should have seen it. I should have reminded myself it was her. The ghost of Richard remained with me, even at that moment. He made it possible, but he also made it more difficult. To imagine him there was to remember how much I missed him. At that moment, my very existence felt pulled taut, like the webs of skin between grasping fingers; it was as if a single surge of emotion, too raw, too real, might split them apart. No measure of planning or ambition could prevent it. I could only hope I remained in one piece.

~∞~

I approached conflict the same way I did taxes: with extensive and brutal bureaucracy. I was not a general, so I found those men who were, and I gave them armies to lead. My father had made our troops a hoard of prestige for anyone willing to pay enough tribute, sacrificing competency for coin. I could not afford such tactics in a war against Richard the Lionheart.

We came to Brittany by ship across the Loire, which extended like an eager artery from Orleans to Nantes. We crammed thousands of men into hundreds of ships, a shoal of silver-plated soldiers glimmering upon the water. The journey was quick but arduous, as the weather was terrible. I was woken each night by the rocking of the boat, slamming my head into the hold with each new gust of wind. I slept little. My men quickly learnt to avoid me, and I was of little use to them, regardless. Most of the combat strategy was being handled by Blois.

I knew that there was no earthly way Richard could have reached Nantes before us, but it was still eerie to see the walls unguarded, with the banners of Aquitaine left abandoned at the gates. We had thousands of men in our fleet who would need to be fed and housed, and we had expected some resistance to our entrance. But we could see no garrison. If Richard had left men here, there were too few to prevent our occupation. It seemed as if we could simply wander in and take the city without complaint.

I came to the deck to see the place up close; my officers were gathered there, staring up at the walls. They bowed when they saw me.

"Nantes is ours, my liege," said the Count of Sancerre. "It has been left unguarded."

Blois gave me a thin-lipped smile, and added, "I've taken the liberty of instructing a small force to remain here. I suggest we continue farther north, to meet Aquitaine's armies as soon as possible."

A wet wind struck my face. I pulled my cloak around me, scowling. "A small force?"

"A few hundred men."

"A *skeleton* force, then," I said. "It seems a great risk. What if Richard passes us by, and takes the city?"

Blois shook his head. "He cannot pass us by. Our numbers are too great. You are cautious, my liege, but there is little need for caution with so great an advantage. Best to confront him while our men are still fresh, with the river behind us."

"What if he fords the river farther east?" I demanded, irked by his supercilious expression. "If he circumvents us, and reaches Nantes? Or even ambushes us from behind?"

There were skeptical sounds amongst the other men. Blois cleared his throat, as if to prevent a sigh. He scratched the top of his head, his hair falling limp and damp over his brows. "It would be impossible to ford the river with an army that size. And to bring a smaller force would be suicide. Such recklessness is un-imaginable."

He did not know Richard, clearly. "It is possible," I said.

"My liege, in battle, all things are *possible*. We must act in anticipation of what is *likely*."

I narrowed my eyes at him, digging my nails into my palm. The other men were looking at me with a mixture of amusement and concern; I imagined some felt great pity for me, the young king whose mad, incompetent father had failed to school him in war.

I could have demanded we remain in the city, and they would have been forced to oblige. Had I been a man like Rich-ard, who held a sword more naturally than a quill, they might have done so willingly. But they did not trust me—why would they, when I was so inexperienced—and any further insistence would have fomented resentment. I was not prepared to have them hate me. I still wanted them to respect me, as futile as such an ambition was, with Louis's blood running through my veins.

Blois took my silence as acquiescence. "We prepare for battle, then," he said.

I had no choice but to agree.

That night, I had my armor fitted. The tabard was my father's, navy with fleur-de-lis stitched in gold. It was old-fashioned in style, cut long enough to touch my ankles. With my mantis-head helmet on, I could have been Louis exactly. We had the same build, and the same slightly cowering posture, beneath the weight of the chainmail.

I pulled the helmet off, and I told the servant to have the tabard shortened. "Are you certain, my liege?" he asked, shocked by the very suggestion. The cloth was worth its weight in silver. I was trimming away half its value.

"Have it shortened," I repeated, "to my knees."

"Shall we save the fabric, sire?" he asked.

"Make it a gift to the mayor of Nantes."

He bowed. "As you wish," he said, and he departed to find a tailor.

I was left alone in the tent. There was a flash of light behind the half-open entrance, and a rumble of thunder. I had my sword at my hip; I drew it from its scabbard and held it up to the light of the brazier, staring at my hands around the pommel. My fingers were spindled, bird-boned things, as if sucked clean of flesh. The more anxious I was, the less I ate, and this had been a fasting month for me. I felt dizzy, and I stooped under the weight of my armor, sword wobbling uncertainly in my grip.

This blade had never been used in battle. I doubted it ever would. When battle began, I would remain at the camp with my archers, sending orders ahead. This was not atypical of a king—at least, any king that was not an Angevin—but that made my cowardice no less cowardly. Richard of Aquitaine would howl through the battlefield like a gale, and Philip of France would hide behind a thousand men's shields.

I wondered what Richard was like at war. I had seen him hunting, but this was not the same. That was a pursuit. This was destruction for destruction's sake, until one side could not bear further violence. Perhaps Richard treated the battlefield the same way he did a bed; I still remembered our night together with shameful clarity. It had not been a gentle thing. It had felt like combat, but not between us. Our enemy had been some nameless force that Richard wished to shelter me from. He had held me as if I were in danger of disappearing, as if someone were trying to drag me away from him. He had left marks on me in his desperation. I had welcomed them, staring at them after he was gone. I needed to do so. He had not said farewell to me, that morning, and they were the only reminder that it had all been real.

Now I would return those marks to him, with crueler intention. I imagined them with terrible clarity: scratches on his back, scored with swords rather than nails; bruises on his thighs from the pommel of a weapon; gasps of pain, my name spoken with desperation, as I had once spoken his. He might find himself at the point of a blade, pleading for surrender, while I would be across the field, in the safety of my camp. I would stand there, watching the battle from a distance, waiting for the flag to raise. If I had to, I would learn to live with his blood on my hands.

CHAPTER SIXTEEN

Richard

The crossbow wound had left a scar: a puckered line from my left cheekbone to beneath my ear, culminating in a mottled circle on my shoulder. My beard parted to accept it like banks of a river. I had grown fond of it, and I had taken to pressing my fingers against it as I spoke, feeling the tightness of new flesh, the faint twinge of pain as my mouth moved and pulled at the skin. It was like carrying part of the battle with me.

But the scar was the least of my injuries. My shoulder had yet to fully heal, and I was still having trouble with my sword arm; the wound flared up intermittently, twinging with pain and causing my hand to spasm. Meanwhile, the march south was grueling, the mood dour, since we knew what was waiting for us. Intelligence drifting north told us that Philip had arrived in Nantes, greeted with pleasure by a city that had no loyalties but to my brother's wife. Brittany, once a French duchy, had little attachment to Angevin hegemony. The people were certainly joyous to see us leave Rennes. While now nominally in my possession, the capital had been scoured bloody by our siege. The local nobility would have tossed me out by my collar, if they could have. We had no choice but to leave as soon as we could.

So, we marched. I was blades and boots and mud, as I had been constantly for the past few months. There were no battles to show for it, nor glory for my name. I was angry with myself, and I was angry with Philip also. He had seen fit to go past the border and take his armies to Geoffrey's lands, after all. My frustration's source was only a meaningless technicality—what difference would it make, if we were to meet twenty miles farther north? But his agreement with my brother was that he would invade Aquitaine, not defend Brittany. It was further confirmation of his betrayal.

I was furious with him, that much was certain. But I had mastered that contradictory position in which I adored him simultaneously. I pictured him in ridiculous and impossible fantasies, wherein he was instead a baron, or a count's son, a vassal of mine who would come to Poitiers for the season. Most things would be the same—the tense arrangement of his shoulders; the careful sweep of his dark hair; the way he said my name, that breathless sort of scorn—but there would be no Brittany, nor England, nor France to come between us. There would be only Aquitaine in summer, where we could live entwined until we died.

It was not reality. Reality was the endless march south. It was blades and boots and mud. It was a dawn so clouded the sun hardly rose at all, leaving us in watery darkness as we reached the outskirts of Nantes. And as we crested the hill, so came the scout returning to us, raising his voice to shout a warning: the French army was ahead.

~⚬~

They had stopped even farther north than we'd expected, leaving Nantes largely undefended. A calculated gamble, and one I might have taken also, considering how much larger their army was.

We camped at an elevated position, overlooking the farmland that stretched before the river. We could see the French, but they could also see us. Philip's army was near double the size of mine, and that was without whatever men remained within Nantes. We were in a good position to defend, but so were they. There was the Loire at their backs, and the melting ice had left it a treacherous crossing, a weeping wound of water that tore through the valley with a constant, torrential roar.

Stephen could see it was hopeless, as much as I did.

"Send an emissary," he told me. The march here had made his dark skin ashen with exhaustion. He stood uncertainly, as if the ground were shifting beneath him.

"Yes, I will," I replied.

"Surrender," he said.

"What, before the battle has begun?"

He flung his arm out towards the French. "It will be a massacre, Richard."

"For them also," I said. "Our position is strong."

"I think Philip can stand to lose a few men."

"Philip will be willing to negotiate."

"Can you be certain of that?" he asked.

"No, I am not *certain*, Stephen," I snapped at him. "I can never be certain. Does that satisfy you?"

He scowled, but said, "Pardon."

Our nerves were frayed. Such as it was, to fight a battle you knew you were losing. I sighed and put an arm around his shoulders, in silent apology.

"I will send an emissary," I said. "There must be *some* way to prevent a battle."

"What if he refuses to parley?"

"He will not."

Stephen made a skeptical noise.

"He will not refuse," I repeated. "I swear it."

Despite these words, I spent the next few hours in tense anticipation. The sun seemed to rise slowly, as if in warning, as if offering time to retreat. Still, we remained, and once the day had fully arrived, we sent the emissary waving the flag down the hill. He was only a boy; it was a dangerous task, but he had flung up his hand to volunteer, wide-eyed with devotion. When I had asked him his name, he had said "Arnaud, sire," with tearful reverence. He was too young for a beard, and too trusting for fear. We sent him to the jaws of the enemy.

We had given him the slowest horse imaginable, no armor, nothing to indicate hostility. It would have been supreme cruelty for the French to attack him. But it was terrifying, all the same, to see his tiny figure become gradually more distant, until it was subsumed by the tide of foreign soldiers, drowned in navy and gold.

"What if he does not return?" Stephen asked me.

"Then we prepare for battle," I replied. "We have nowhere to run to."

We sat by the fire to wait. Although it was almost noon, the light remained dim, and many men bore torches as they made their way around the camp. The clouds only thickened as the time passed, but it refused to rain; it lent the air a heady, expectant quality. I began to panic. By the time the sun had sunk halfway to twilight, I was pacing around the fire, digging a trench in the soil with my step.

"We should prepare the men," Stephen said.

"It is too dark. It would be suicide to attack, for either side. Best to wait longer."

We waited. The day dimmed, and more torches blazed. The camp became a collection of half-lit stars. In the blue hour be-

fore the sun disappeared, I returned to overlook the battlefield: I
saw a matching cloud of light on its other side. One of those
lights was Philip. And one of them was breaking apart from the
rest, to return across the field.

I shouted for Stephen. He was brought to me just as the emissary reached us. The boy slipped off his horse and bowed,
thrumming with excitement. "My liege, the king wishes to speak
with you," he said.

"When?" I asked.

"The morning."

"What took you so long?" Stephen demanded. "It required a
day to hear an answer?"

The emissary shrugged. "I believe there was some argument,
between the king and his vassals. But I was not privy to it."

I asked, "Did you see the banners of his generals?"

"I saw those of Blois, my liege," he replied, "and Sancerre."

"Blois," I muttered, and I scowled. To the boy, I said, "Philip
will parley in the morning?"

"Aye, at dawn."

"Then we hold fast for the night."

He nodded, bowed again, and went to repeat the order to
another, who would then repeat it to another, as links in a chain;
soon all my army would know. As the camp fell to a frantic defensive effort, Stephen trailed with me back to my tent.

"Will you sleep?" he asked.

"Shall we take shifts?"

"Yes. I do not trust this peace."

"Me neither," I admitted.

"Would Philip—would he go against his word?" Stephen
said. "Assault at night? Is he capable of such a thing?"

"Capable? Yes."

"Willing?"

I could not answer that. Stephen waited as I considered it. When I gave no response, he prompted, "What if it were not you, Richard? What if you were there with him, by the river, and this was Geoffrey on the hill?"

"Then I am certain he would have suggested it," I said.

"So, we should prepare for an attack."

"But I am not Geoffrey," I told him. "I am Richard."

"Will that make a difference?"

"I certainly hope so," I said. "I have to hope. There is little else to be done."

~⁊~

Stephen took the last shift before dawn, so I would wake up rested. I was not rested; my sleep had been fitful, as was to be expected. But no assault came overnight. I assumed that Philip was hoping for an easier victory, one offered rather than taken. I did not know how I would react when I saw him, whether my anger would outweigh my relief.

There was no time to eat. I had to get dressed; armor would be expected, even for parley. My chainmail was polished to the quality of a mirror, and I wore my best tabard, with lions stitched in gold across its front. It was one usually reserved for the victorious march home. Once I was sat upon Rufus, I tucked my helmet beneath my arm, and I kept it there as we made our way to the camp's edge. We were ten of us, in all: Stephen and I, as well as my commanders, who followed in a chaotic crowd behind us. They hissed between themselves in constant, petty argument. I had learnt early in my dukedom that it was best to leave them be, when such tensions rose. They knew who they answered to, in the end.

"Will you wear it?" Stephen asked, voice muffled from beneath his visor.

"What, the helmet?" I replied. "No, I shan't."

"What if you get shot in the head?"

"Then Philip does not wish to parley, and we are all dead, re-gardless."

We soon left the safety of the camp. In the open vastness of the field, there was a sudden feeling of nakedness, of vulnerability. Even the quibbling nobles behind me fell silent. Albret, who had been put in charge of the flag, started waving it about with such desperation I had to turn and tell him to stop.

"Look," Stephen said, as I faced forward again.

A group of men were approaching us from the direction of Nantes, waving the fleur-de-lis. Leading them, I saw a figure on a white horse, with a navy tabard. It was the king, my enemy, my heart: the sole obstacle between myself and home.

Inches by inches, the gap closed. Philip came closer into view. Once we were near enough for it to be reasonable, he removed his helmet. He was thinner than I remembered, dark circles around his eyes. His hair had been cut short in preparation for battle—I preferred it long—and armor did not suit him. The sword at his hip had an intense wrongness about it. It bumped against his leg with the movement of his horse, like an awkward, unwanted limb. I ought to have kept some measure of anger about me, to call him out on his forgotten promises; but instead, all I wanted was to fall to the ground, and take him with me, and put everything back in its place. I wanted to tear away the armor and the sword and make him Philip again, while ten thousand eyes were watching.

Our gazes met. He winced, as if in pain, before he became impassive once more. Perhaps he had seen the desperation in my expression.

"My Lord Aquitaine," Philip said, as our horses came to a halt. There were but ten paces between us.

"My liege," I replied.

"My congratulations for your victory at Rennes. Are you fully recovered from your wound?"

No need to inform him of my arm. Instead, I craned my head, to show him the scar. He made a sound of surprise. "God was with me," I said. "It might have killed me, otherwise."

"Perhaps," Philip returned, "if God had been with you, you would not have been shot at all."

This provoked some amusement from his commanders, who laughed in a restrained manner at the comment. Still, some cast me apprehensive glances, and I supposed that my reputation as short-tempered had preceded me. Swallowing my annoyance, I gestured to the ground. "Are we to speak on our horses?" I asked.

"After you."

This was a pointless display of superiority. I had thought we were past such things. I slid from my horse to the grass, which was damp with dew. After a moment of looming above me, Philip followed. My men prepared to dismount; I gestured to stop them. He did the same to his. We were the only two standing.

There was new intimacy to the conversation, now that we faced each other on solid ground, our audience watching from above. "You are here," I said. "In Brittany."

"I am," Philip replied.

"Did Geoffrey ask you to come?"

"He did."

That was enough to cause my anger to return. I sneered at him. "I see your promises meant little."

"I meant all of them, Richard," he said quietly. "But I came here because I have no choice. Someone needs to put an end to this."

Philip gazed up at me through his eyelashes. There was something hopeful in his expression, something tender, that was exceptionally disarming. My shoulders dropped. "I want it to end also," I murmured.

"Good. Then we ought to discuss the terms of your surrender."

I laughed loudly. There was some uneasy shuffling from the lords surrounding us. "Shall I surrender?" I asked. "I have thousands of men at my back."

Philip rolled his eyes and gestured towards his own army. He did not bother to point out its comparative size. "The invasion has come to a standstill, you must realize that," he said. "Even if you win this battle, what do you intend to do? Trade cities with your brothers until you are all destroyed?"

"What you offer instead is losing Aquitaine," I replied, "which I will not abide."

"That is between you and Geoffrey."

"A surrender to you, Philip, is the same as a surrender to him. Geoffrey will only give you Anjou once he has Aquitaine. We both know that."

Philip folded his arms. A cloud passed over the sun. It left a shadow over us, and an unbidden understanding of silence; no one spoke again until light had returned.

"You are risking your life," he said, "for your land—for your stubbornness—"

"Are you not doing the same?"

"Not to the same degree. I am not a fool; I do not lead my own armies."

"That is a shame," I replied. "I would rather fight a fool than a coward."

Philip flinched. He glanced between me and his men nervously, as if my very presence were a secret he had failed to keep. When he looked back at me, I expected him to say something harsh or contemptuous. Instead, he bowed his head, and said, "Please."

"I—pardon?"

"Please, Richard. Surrender, I beg of you. Otherwise, it will come to battle. And I . . . I cannot risk such a thing."

It was clear that he meant *I cannot risk you.*

If the crossbow in Rennes had been aimed at my heart, it might have been less of a blow; I had convinced myself my affection was mostly one-sided, sometime during the mud-soaked siege, or on the grueling march back south. This proof he felt the same was as visceral as any wound. "I cannot," I said, but I nearly choked on the words. "I cannot lose Aquitaine. It is all I have left of my mother, her legacy, my home—you know that."

"There must be some way," Philip said, pleading. He paused, and doubt shadowed his expression. "Perhaps, if I were to . . ."

He trailed off. I took a step towards him. "If you?"

Philip glanced up at his men once more. All of those surrounding us were utterly silent. His face twitched with uncertainty and fear; he said, "Perhaps, if we—"

Above him, sneering down at us from his horse, the Count of Blois interjected, "If you will not surrender, my Lord Aquitaine, then I am certain there is little else to discuss."

The tension was broken quite abruptly by this. The rest of Philip's men hollered in agreement, startling their horses; in response, my own vassals began shouting in consternation, and soon a great argument had erupted. Philip and I watched each other in a terrible moment of inaction. I took another step closer, almost reaching for his hand. At the last moment, I prevented myself from doing so, and I said to him, "Surely we can—"

He shook his head and stepped back. "No," he replied. "I should not have—I cannot."

"Philip—I will forgive you anything, *everything*, if only you would listen—"

"I do not deserve your forgiveness. Save it for a better man."

The other men were still screaming at one another. None of them could hear us. I wouldn't have cared if they had. "I love you," I said to him.

"And I you," Philip replied. "But that does not matter. It never has."

I fisted my hands and bowed my head. There was nothing left to say.

Philip mounted his horse and then spoke louder, his voice cutting through the fray. "If we do not have your surrender by sundown, my Lord Aquitaine," he said, to bellows of approval from his vassals, "then we shall meet you in battle."

I was defeated. I nodded curtly, and I watched him ride away.

~⚬~

A few of my commanders were in favor of surrender, but just as many were not. They were loyal to me, and they trusted my authority. To them, and to all Occitans, I was my mother's son above all else. To betray me would be to betray Eleanor, the duchess who had made their lands some of the greatest in Christendom. She had named me her heir, and they would die by my side before they let her word be betrayed; just as I would die by theirs.

But the battle would end in carnage. We were too greatly outnumbered. Instead, we could turn back—into the welcoming arms of my brothers and their armies—or we could attempt to ford the Loire River and pass Philip by. Both possibilities promised disaster.

"The water flows too fast, and we are too many," I told my

commanders, when the river route was first proposed. "We will be caught by the French before we are able to pass."

And yet, despite this, the Loire began to seem a tempting prospect as the sun continued to sink. There were stories that my family descended from Mélusine, a river spirit who fell in love with a human man centuries ago. If I were to fling myself into the half-frozen waters, perhaps she would deliver me from disaster. More likely I would meet my end. It would be a death less glorious than one on the battlefield, but it would deny Philip the chance to kill me by proxy. It would prevent the guilt he would feel, once he did.

As darkness fell, I sat half submerged in mud on the banks of the Loire, watching the shattered reflection of the sunset on the river. I wondered what Philip would do, if he were me—would he have surrendered already? Almost certainly so, but only in the knowledge that with patience, he would eventually find Aquitaine returned to him. He would have a dozen contingencies already in place, all prepared before he'd even set foot on my brother's land.

But I was not Philip, and there were no contingencies. This was a war, his and mine, and it was Philip's life or my own. The only way this battle would be won would be if his alliance with Geoffrey was broken and France no longer had a reason to fight; and that would only happen if Philip were captured or killed. But Philip would be far behind the front lines, sheltered by his armies at his front and the Loire at his back. No man had a chance of crossing those hungry, furious waters with an army behind him. They would be too visible, too vulnerable, a target for a thousand archers' arrows. A lone man perhaps could cross, accompanied by only a few soldiers, with the rest of the army distracting the French elsewhere. But it would be a great risk, and for what? To steal into a foreign camp and raise a blade to the man I loved? To capture him and threaten him with death unless he surrendered? Or—simpler still, smarter still, to kill him and leave France in chaos?

It would be a brutal solution, duplicitous too. Such a strategy would be madness, or suicide, even, considering the danger. An act of supreme desperation. The Richard I had once believed myself to be would have never done such a thing—Richard the noble, the knight, the lionhearted—but that man did not exist, not really. He never had.

The river roared. I pulled the letters I had written to Philip out of my pack. He would never read them, now. They were epitaphs: for him and I, for all we were, for all we could have been.

I flung the letters into the water. They were quickly swallowed by the tide.

~∞~

I returned to the river that night, my men with me. It was only the first month of spring, and the Loire was frigid with the lingering grip of winter. It was cold enough that it burnt to touch, a paradoxical sort of heat; the skin on the tip of my finger flushed red with blood as I tested the water's edge.

We had scant hours before dawn. My men had managed to requisition less than a dozen fishing vessels. The bulk of my armies had been sent towards the French camp; less than a hundred of us now stood at the river's banks, considering how best to cross. There was not enough room in the boats for more than a handful of men in each. And the more men were visible, the more likely it was we would be seen by the enemy's archers.

"We have no choice," I said to Stephen. "We cannot swim, but we cannot all fit into the boats. We must lash ourselves to them and be dragged across."

He blanched. "It is freezing. Your men are loyal, but . . ."

"It is cold enough to hurt, perhaps, but not to harm," I replied. He gave me a doubtful look. "I will go first, then, and prove it to them."

"What? Richard, you needn't—"

"If I am to ask it of them, I should be willing also. Fetch the rope."

Stephen recognized the determination in my expression, accepted the futility of further protest, and did so. The soldiers surrounding us watched in silent horror as the rope was tied to the stern, and then looped around my waist and wrists. I looked like a prisoner, I supposed, with my hands clasped and bound; but looser restraints would have risked being lost to the tide.

Stephen helmed the ship. As they prepared to cast off and row into the darkness, I stood at the water's edge. It lapped hungrily at my feet. This time of night, it was too dark to see my own reflection, except as a blurred silhouette; I imagined, absurdly, that if only I could see it, the figure in the Loire would have Philip's face, mirrored back to me instead of my own. And so returned an unwanted memory: I remembered him in the clearing that day, months ago, when he had given me a warning I ought to have listened to. For a moment, the night withdrew, and I saw the sun that morning bouncing across the snow, falling upon his hair, so that it went from black to brown to bronze at the edges; his skin almost glowing with it, and his eyes almost blind with light. I should have looked at him, then, and known that he would destroy me, just as he said he would. I should have known all along.

I could kill him, if I had to. I would resent him, and allow that resentment to guide my hand. I would make my memories of him wounds, and keep them bleeding; and once it was done, once he was gone, once my father was dead and this war was finished, I would be grateful to wear the crown upon my head. I would be anointed at Westminster, and when I returned to Poitiers, to walk through the Hall of Lost Footsteps, empty but for the throne that my mother built—I would sit upon it and know that God was with me, for I was the chosen king of England, Duke of Aquitaine, and *I would yield to no man*—

"Richard," Stephen said. He was watching me from the front of the ship, a concerned shadow in the dim light. "We need to go."

The ship was still tied to its moorings. I looked again at my bound hands, and my certainty faltered. Did I really believe I could kill Philip? Was I truly capable of such a thing? If I didn't, we would grow old together, just as I had sometimes imagined. We would never be rid of each other. We would always be England and France, only ever a sliver of sea apart. I did not know if that was better than his permanent absence. I did not know if I could ever be thankful to have him as an enemy.

Perhaps, then, it was time to bury my principles, as my brothers had. Time to accept reality, as Philip did. I loved him, of course. I always would. But it was as he said: that did not matter, not anymore.

I stepped into the water, and I ignored the ice it carved into my skin. I did not know what I would do when I saw him; but I would accept my fate, and Philip's also. There was never really a choice. It was always going to end in this, with steel and blood, with fury and regret. It was always a war that neither of us could win.

CHAPTER SEVENTEEN

Philip

Night fell, the sun departed, and with it went any hope that Richard would surrender.

I hadn't expected differently. I knew he would rather die than lose Aquitaine. Richard was my heart, he had become so long ago, and just as stubborn as that organ was, he would beat, beat, beat until there was no blood left to spill; to cease would be to kill us both. If such an end was to come, he would not greet it willingly.

I had wanted to make peace with him during our parley, but it was impossible. Blois would have almost certainly rebelled, and the entire kingdom would have fallen into chaos. Besides, I had warned Richard what would happen if he did not take Brittany in time. If I peeled back the past—counted all my regrets— I could still easily prove my actions reasonable, merciful even. If I had refused to aid Geoffrey, Richard would simply be fighting his brothers' armies here instead. And if he won such a battle— even if he won this one—it would only delay the inevitable surrender to his father. Eventually, Richard would find another glorious death on another muddy field. That would always be his fate, and he knew that as well as I did.

But it was still my fault. It was all my fault.

I would never forgive myself for it.

~

Any reasonable general would have waited for daybreak before mounting an attack, but Richard was desperate, and reason was no longer relevant. I realized this, so I advised my commanders to keep the army at the ready overnight. But Blois considered this unreasonable. We had the better defensive position, after all, so we could fight on our terms. Better, he argued, to have the men fresh when they were needed. The meeting between us had resolved uncertainly, and I was not confident, when I retired to bed, that Blois would follow my instructions.

I did not sleep. It seemed pointless to remove my armor, so I lay awake on the pallet for what must have been hours, tossing and turning. I reached a point of almost meditative terror, where all I could concentrate on was the tightness of my chest and the churning of my gut. Then, gradually, I began to hear the sound of shouting outside, and the clinking of metal.

I stood on trembling legs and went to peer outside the tent, sword jutting awkwardly from my hip. It was very dark, the stars scattered thinly above us. The only illumination in the camp was their wavering light, and the dim sputtering of dampened torches. Everything was in disarray. Hundreds of men were hurling themselves through the mud, bearing arms and equipment. They hollered at one another, straining to be heard over the roar of the river behind us. It was so loud my skull seemed to echo with it.

I saw Sancerre and Blois in conference at the edge of the

camp. I waded towards them, the sod gulping hungrily at my boots.

"What is happening?" I demanded. "An attack?"

Sancerre bowed. Blois did not bother. "The western flank," Blois said. "A good number of Aquitaine's men, unprovoked and without strategy. It seems they have no intention at all except to cause chaos. Quickly put down, but . . ."

"Odd," I said, frowning. "Why would Richard do such a thing?"

He shrugged. "Perhaps his men have taken matters into their own hands. I fought alongside Aquitaine during the princes' rebellion; he was a direct leader. Such a strategy does not seem his work."

I considered this. It seemed to me there was something more to the attack, something I had failed to anticipate. Still, there was little to be done except ask, "You will deal with it?"

Blois pursed his lips. "Yes, my liege," he said. "As always."

It was clear to me Blois had ignored my earlier instructions, and many of the men were clearly still asleep. I had tolerated my share of insubordination from him, but at that moment, exhausted and terrified, I felt little inclined to leniency. I fisted my hands at my sides. "Actually—my Lord Blois, I wish to speak with you in private."

Alarmed, he replied, "If I am required by the men—"

"It will take only a moment. I'm certain Sancerre is competent enough to oversee defense."

Sancerre bowed again, pleased. Blois shook his head and said, "But I am needed here. I am your marshal, my liege."

"And I am your *king*," I snapped. "Come with me."

He followed reluctantly behind me as I made towards the main tent of the camp. Inside, there was a roaring brazier, as well as a large table that had been set up with a map of the countryside; three of my generals were standing over it and arguing about where to place our archers. I gestured for them to leave. They bowed hurriedly and went, cowed by my furious expression.

I stood by the brazier and turned to Blois. He was taller than me by only an inch, but he was stocky, scarred by battle; when he folded his arms, it felt as if he towered over me. For a moment, my confidence quailed, and then I forced myself to remember who I was. This was my army, and my war. He was the weapon, not the hand that wielded it.

"Enough," I said.

Blois raised a brow. "My liege?"

"If I give you orders, I expect you to follow them. You do not accept my authority—that much has always been clear—but you no longer have the excuse of my youth. I have been king for years, and I have proven myself competent. I am your ruler. You must permit yourself to be ruled."

Scowling, he replied, "My liege, you are king in Paris, but—"

"But what?"

"You are no warrior." He squared his shoulders, straightening his posture. "You remain your father's son, Philip, though others may have fooled themselves otherwise."

"I am not my father," I said.

"As the tree, so the fruit. I saw what Louis did to France. I remember. I will ensure it does not happen again."

His expression was one of open disgust. He was making no attempt to hide his derision. I realized that he had been long prepared for this confrontation.

I had been naïve. Blois had threatened rebellion against my father many times, and I had always presumed that Louis had simply failed in the art of appeasement, as so many kings did; I thought of diplomacy as a matter of balance, giving so one might eventually take. But I had failed to realize that Blois's hatred of me was so innate. I had given, and given, and given to him, and now there was no limit to what he felt he could demand.

There were fresh yells from outside. I presumed more men were being moved to deal with the attack. Blois turned his head, frowning, and I took a step towards him. He looked back to me.

"I could have you arrested for speaking to me like that," I said. "I would have fair cause to."

"If you wish the rest of the council to rebel, then certainly."

"They are so loyal to you?"

"They are loyal to France," he replied.

"*I* am France. They ought to trust their king."

"And their *king* ought to trust his elders. Their *king* fears war and kneels to Angevins; according to some, he permits them into his bed."

"That is absurd," I said. "You would dare accuse me of such a thing?"

"Whether or not it is true, it does not matter. They are our enemies, and you ought to treat them as such." There was a further chorus of yells outside, and Blois scowled, rubbing the back of his neck in frustration. "I must attend to the men."

"You will attend to nothing, unless I say so. Blois, *listen* to me. You must accept my authority, or your own authority is threatened. I am king by blood, as you are count by blood; if my title means nothing, then nor does yours."

He paused at that, pressing his lips thin. It was clear he had never considered such a thing. So few do. They ascribe their power to God and to fate, and they fail to realize how fragile the foundations of our sovereignty are.

The flap of the tent was pushed aside, and a soldier entered. "Leave us," I said harshly, turning to him; then I saw that it was Richard.

He was soaked with what I presumed was river water, red tabard darkened to the color of dried blood. He had been in a fight: a scarlet line was scored and weeping across his temple, and his right cheek was swollen. If he had ever been in possession of a shield, it was long gone. In his right hand, his sword was held ready, and in his left, he had the same dagger he had used to kill the boar last winter.

Blois cursed and drew his sword. I ought to have done the same, but I could not. I simply stood there, silent and astonished.

"An ambush," Blois said.

"An ambush," Richard agreed. His eyes were glazed, almost feverish; the excitement of the battle lingering, causing his chest to shudder with the speed of his breaths.

Blois cursed. "How?" he demanded. "How did you manage it?"

"The river."

"You crossed the river? But—"

"I swam," Richard said.

"You swam," Blois echoed.

"Yes. We tied ourselves to fishing boats so we wouldn't be seen. There aren't many of us, you know, and yet we got through the guards easily. You really ought to have kept more of your men here, instead of sending them all to the western flank." Richard looked at me. Some of the triumph in his expression faded. "Hello, Philip."

"Hello, Richard," I said.

He leapt forward. I had never seen anyone move so fast; he lunged with the desperate, feral movements of a predator. There was no time to react. Richard was at the entrance of the tent, and then he was behind me, having shoved Blois aside. An arm wrapped around my abdomen, knocking the breath from my chest, and something cold and glinting was suddenly at my throat—the dagger, clean and damp from its trip through the Loire.

Blois had almost fallen to the floor with the force of Richard's shove, but he recovered admirably, scrambling to stand. He held his sword in front of him in a ready stance, watching us warily.

I could feel Richard's breath against my neck. "Are you here to kill me?" I asked him.

"Well—" he said. "I—I do not know."

"You could take me hostage."

"I could. But then I'd have to get you out of the camp, and through the river."

"Troublesome," I said.

"Yes."

I ought to have been panicking, but I almost felt grateful; here was a *solution,* finally, to all of it, and it was one I had never considered possible. How clever Richard had been, how reckless. I admired him for it. If he managed to kill me now, if he could really bring himself to do it—then at least I would die in his arms. There were worse endings. It would be less a tragedy than a relief.

I raised my chin to stare up at him, the back of my head brushing against his chest. The movement exposed my throat, bringing it closer to the dagger, but I did not hesitate. He looked down at me. Our eyes met.

I said, "Blois, if I am killed"—Richard made a choked noise; I ignored him—"then my cousin Angoulême is next in line. You must move east immediately. Ignore Aquitaine and Brittany. The new king *must* be anointed before England can gather its troops. My wife will be regent until he is of age. Do you understand?"

Blois made an incredulous sound, and replied, "Your wife?"

"Yes."

He would be a thorn in her side. I wished I could do more. I should have already done more than I had, permitting Blois and my council their liberties. I had been weak, cowardly, and it would be Isabella and France who would pay for that. But there was no longer time for regret.

Richard said, "Philip." The dagger wavered in his grip. His right arm, still woven around me, clenched tighter; the sword it held glinted in the light of the brazier.

"How long before my men return to camp?" I asked him. "You ought to do it now, if you are going to."

He did not respond.

I wanted to live, of course, but I also felt at peace with my possible death. That was what ruling was, after all. It had always been more backgammon than chess. For all my dedication to strategy, there was still the roll of the dice. I had made my moves correctly, but fate had given Richard the victory. There was little injustice in that.

Richard groaned. His head bowed forward, so that his nose was resting against my temple. I felt a droplet land against my cheek, and I did not know whether it was a tear, or the river dripping from his hair.

"Give me a reason not to do it," he said. "Please."

"Will you trust any promise I make you?"

"I do not know. I shouldn't."

"No," I agreed. "You shouldn't."

His arm tightened around me. "You are a liar," he said. "You lied: you said you would not come to Brittany, and now you have. You have lied to me before, and you would lie to me again."

"I know."

"You are a liar, Philip," Richard repeated, "and you have betrayed me. You have raised armies against me. I hoped you would not. I hoped you would not come here, but you did."

"Yes, I did."

"If you had a knife against my throat, would you hesitate?" he asked, voice strained. "Do you think you would?"

"I do not know."

"Nor do I." He shuddered, and repeated, "Nor do I."

Blois had told me, *As the tree, so the fruit;* and perhaps we were the proof of that, Richard and I, reduced to daggers and accusations and regret. We might as well have been our fathers, or our fathers' fathers: meeting beneath the elm at Gisors, declaring war or demanding surrender, staining ourselves with each other's blood.

But we were not our fathers. In the tremble of Richard's grip, the stuttered movements of his breath, I knew whatever roots my betrayal had planted were shallow still. He loved me, far more than I deserved.

"I am glad it is you," I told him, for no reason other than it was true; I had no more moves to make, no more dice to roll, no recourse but honesty. "If I am to die at another's hands, Richard, I would rather they be yours than anyone else's."

He did not reply. The dagger shivered in his grip.

"And I forgive you for it," I said. "I forgive you for this, and for anything else. I pray, one day, that you shall forgive me also, for all that I have done."

"I cannot forgive you," he replied. "I realize that now. There is nothing to forgive; I love you too much to blame you for anything. You won this war long ago, I think. There is nothing I can do but surrender."

The arm around my waist fell. Richard stepped back from me. He looked at the dagger in his hands, and he dropped it to the ground.

"Richard . . ." I said, reaching for him, offering my hand. He ignored me. With a small, fatalistic gasp, he fell to his knees, gripping the pommel of his sword with both hands, as if he were praying around it. Outside the tent, the waters of the Loire seemed to grow louder, filling the sudden silence.

I wanted to fall to the ground with him. I had told Richard I would use him, that he would suffer for my sake, and now that promise was fulfilled. My chest filled with a starving, serrated sort of emptiness. I could neither cry nor speak. I felt undeserving of my own sorrow.

Behind us, Blois made a contemptuous sound, and he stepped forward. He still had his sword raised, and he pointed it towards Richard. "Enough," he said. "It ends here."

"Leave him be," I said.

"Why? With Aquitaine dead, we could easily push west, and take his lands for France."

"He has surrendered, you cannot slaughter him where he sits."

Blois said, "It would be a kindness. No one but us would know; we could say he was felled in battle. Besides, when will such an opportunity present itself again?" He gestured to Richard with his blade, waving it insolently through the air. "He is wounded—can't you tell? He can barely lift his sword. I see no reason not to act. You stay my hand for sentiment's sake, but sentiment should play no part in war. Surely even *you* ought to know that."

Unable to reply, I looked back to Richard. He showed no reaction, his head lowered, hair falling in front of his face. His shoulders were hunched. He did not seem to care that his life was at stake.

Blois took another step forward. "Stop," I said, and then, "Stop" again, as the gap between them closed; I drew my own sword from its scabbard, and I held it between them, as if to prevent Blois from proceeding farther. The blade wavered in my uncertain grip. It carved sweeping lines through the air, like waves upon sand.

"I gave you an order," I said to him.

Blois looked at my sword and snorted. "You will thank me for acting, my liege, once you are older, and you understand the threat he poses."

"I understand the threat."

"Not enough, clearly."

"Perhaps you ought to allow it, Philip," Richard said, his voice hoarse. "Little is left to me."

"Don't be absurd," I snarled at him. "I cannot permit—"

"It is war; blood will be spilt."

"But not *yours*. Not—not like this."

Shouts came from outside. "We are losing time," Blois said. "My Lord Aquitaine, surrender your lands to France publicly, accept exile, and perhaps you might be spared."

Richard grinned mirthlessly at him and replied, "I would rather the blade."

Blois stepped forward again.

"Stand down," I said to Blois. He ignored me. "Stand down," I repeated. But then he lunged, sword raised, expecting I would lower my own weapon rather than wound him; Richard flinched, awaiting a blow that would never come; and I—without thought, without strategy, without logic nor reason—gave a cry of horror and raised my blade to meet Blois as he moved.

The metal flashed in the light of the brazier, a sharp-edged flame that burnt silver then red. I pulled back, but it was too late. Across Blois's stomach, his tabard blossomed crimson. He gasped, hunched, and fell to his knees. It was a clean blow, a merciful one, upwards and into the heart. He made very little sound; no cry of pain, only a momentary choke of alarm, and then he pitched forward, face-first. I watched him fall.

I looked at the sword in my hands. I dropped it to the ground. My ears roared; perhaps it was the blood rushing to my head, the blood pouring out of Blois, the Loire behind us—

I turned and ran out of the tent, ignoring Richard's garbled shout to wait. Outside, the camp was largely empty. The fighting had shifted towards the battlefield. I wove, gasping and stumbling, through the tents, until I reached the banks of the river. Hunching by the water, I watched it froth and tumble, feeling my stomach roil and wondering if I would vomit. I had not eaten enough the previous day to do so. Curling my arms around myself, I swallowed a sob.

Someone approached behind me. I whirled around—reaching for the sword I no longer had—and I saw that it was Richard. I said his name. He said mine. Then he reached for me, and he had his arms around me, his palms pressing into my back, and he was saying, "My love, don't think of it. All is well. All will be well."

I pressed my forehead into his chest, nearly unable to breathe with shock and terror and terrible, terrible relief.

"It is a war," Richard said, once my trembling had abated. "Such things happen. No one will know except us."

I pressed myself further into his arms. It was almost painful to be so near to him now, after months of absence; I could smell the Breton mud on his clothes, and beneath, the salt-sweet scent of his skin. I could hear the stutter of his breathing, the rasp of chainmail against his back. He was a real man, as real as I was, flesh and bone.

I loved him. I could not regret saving his life.

Richard reached for my face, tipped my chin upwards, and kissed me. I gave a small gasp, reaching up to meet him. My heart was pounding, breaths still short; I could not separate my panic from the sudden and entirely inappropriate rush of lust that swept over me in reaction to the embrace. I pushed my hands up, under his shirt, under his armor, and I pressed them against his bare back, pulling us together. I bit his lip and raked my nails against his skin. He groaned.

I heard a shout in the distance, and I flinched, pulling away. "There is a battle nearby," I said. "We are at war, still."

"I wish we were not."

I replied, too exhausted for denial or deception, "As do I."

"Then let us end it, Philip, please."

"How can we?" I asked. "After all this?"

"How can we not?" Richard kissed my throat, in the same place he had pressed the dagger, not minutes before: an apology, or at least an acknowledgment. "What other choice do we have? Each of us has attempted to sacrifice the other, and we have failed. I could hold another knife to your neck; I do not want to. I never want to hurt you again."

I pressed my lips to the scar on his chin, and said quietly, "Nor I."

"I love you."

"And I you. If—if you had died—if I had—neither of us would have survived it, I think. I realize that now. I cannot lose you."

Admitting it felt like removing shackles from my wrists, and I nearly collapsed with the relief. Richard stepped back from me. I reached for him, bereft; he took my grasping hand and held it in both his own, raising it to brush his lips across my knuckles.

"Tell me what you need," he said. "For us to end this war here."

"Without you losing Aquitaine," I replied, skeptical.

"Yes."

"You ask too much."

"I know."

I shook my head. "If we make peace now, I will be betraying Geoffrey—"

He smiled wryly. "Yes, you will."

"And my vassals will be furious. They will be angry enough about Blois."

"War has casualties," Richard said. "Blois was a soldier. His death was not unexpected."

That was little comfort, but my thankfulness for Richard's continuing survival was still enough to assuage my guilt, and I suspected it would be for some time. Still. "You ask the impossible," I said. "After all this—to simply *undo* what we have done—"

"You are king," Richard replied. "As I shall be one day. Who else could achieve the impossible, except us?"

I paused to consider, and Richard watched me, his thumb rubbing circles at my wrist. "I suppose I could change sides," I said, wincing a little at the absurdity of the proposal. "It would be foolish for both of us, but—we could form a new alliance. Then the invasion would become a stalemate; the two of us in Brittany, John and Geoffrey in Aquitaine. Your father will have to respond."

"We will fight him?" Richard asked. "Finally?"

"We will propose a truce," I answered. "We need peace, if only a temporary one."

"I do not want peace, I want victory. This has already taken far too long."

"It does not matter what you want. This is as much as we can achieve. Your men are exhausted, diminished. They have marched to Rennes and back."

Richard narrowed his eyes at me. He knew as well as I did that, with both our armies at our disposal, we might have been able to defeat Henry for good, even with his men depleted; but I could not bear more battles so soon. We were broken and bloodied, both of us. I wanted, desperately, for all that had passed between us before that moment to be undone. I wanted to return to the herb garden in Montlhéry, rosemary and mint and the overcast light of a peaceful spring, no wars between us, no demands, no regrets.

Perhaps we could. Now that Blois was gone, if I could appease my vassals—find terms favorable enough—then . . .

"You must give me Anjou," I said. "Anjou and Normandy, the entire duchy. Since Geoffrey is no longer relevant."

Richard's eyes narrowed. "Oh, is that all?"

"I want Auvergne also."

He winced. "Come, Philip," he said. "*All* of it? I could offer you everything east of the Loire."

"Auvergne," I repeated.

"I shall have no kingdom left," he said tersely, "by the time I take the throne."

I stepped closer to him, looking up at him pleadingly. "But Aquitaine shall still be yours," I said. "Aquitaine, and England."

"I know. Still, if our positions were reversed, I would not make such demands of you."

I nodded in acknowledgment of this. "Because you are a better man than I am," I replied. "I have always defined myself by my achievements. Restoring the land my father lost—my legacy, my nation." A small, hysterical laugh bubbled in my throat. "It is all I have ever worked for. If I fail in that, what am I worth? All I have done—this war, Blois's death—it will be meaningless. My *life* will be meaningless."

"You mean everything to me, Philip, regardless of your borders," Richard said. "But I will give you what you request, if you think it so necessary."

My shoulders slumped in relief. "Thank you."

"Anything. Always."

"I hope so," I replied, "for there is something else I must ask."

"What is it?"

"A show of loyalty, to appease our vassals. If we are to end this war now, you must pledge fealty to me. Kneel to me, on the battlefield, in front of our armies."

"I shall," he said without hesitation, and I smiled. He continued, "On one condition."

"Yes?"

"That you do the same. Swear your loyalty. Even if it is only here, in private. Even if it is only a promise, without ceremony. I would like to know . . . I would like to know that you are mine, Philip, as I am yours."

Oath or no, it would be a pointless gesture without an audience. And yet, I understood why he felt it was necessary. I had betrayed him before. His distrust was well founded.

I fell to my knees. I raised my hands towards him.

He blinked at me, shocked. "You will pledge fealty?" he asked.

He still had a cut on his face, a growing black eye, and he wore armor covered in my men's blood. I was kneeling partly submerged in the mud of the Loire. It was an absurd setting for formality, but nothing about the night felt normal enough for that to matter. "I might as well do it properly," I said.

"Philip, you needn't—"

"Promises are not enough. I owe you this."

"Very well." He placed his hands on either side of mine, also facing upwards, so his palms bracketed my own. I had been in his place many times. Usually, the man kneeling was a count, or a baron, not a king. "Philip, king of France," he said. "Will you submit yourself to me, as my vassal?"

"I will."

He flipped his hands inwards, so they were holding mine. "Then so swear," he told me.

"I, Philip," I said, "king of France, so swear that present and future, I shall to my lord, Richard of Aquitaine, be true and faithful; and love all which he loves, and shun all which he shuns, according to the law of God. I submit myself to him, and I will never with will nor action, through word nor deed, defy his wishes. I swear this oath, in the witness of—" I paused; what witnesses could I name? "In the witness of God," I finished. "In the witness of my heart, which is his."

He pulled me up and kissed me. "I accept your oath," he said against my lips. "And I will serve faithfully as your lord, as long as you will have me."

"And I you," I replied.

I kissed him again. Behind him, a pinprick of light appeared on the horizon. The sun, perhaps, or the torches of two armies soon to be reconciled; either way, the night had ended. I had blood on my hands and an oath newly sworn. There was no path left to us but peace.

~ ⚬ ~

Richard knelt to me on a field outside Nantes, with a pair of armies watching. He knelt to me on damp grass in the sunlight, and I felt the very moment that we were bound. It was not the sort of binding that could be undone. It might change its character—unspool, or become tighter—but these were threads of iron around us, and they would remain there until we died.

"Richard, Duke of Aquitaine," I said. "Will you submit yourself to me, as my vassal?"

"I will, my liege," he replied.

And ten thousand voices roared.

Part Four

CHANSON DE GESTE

CHAPTER EIGHTEEN

Richard

We stayed in Nantes until Geoffrey and John sued for peace. We had three weeks there, together. They were some of the most perfect weeks of my life.

News of what had happened spread through Europe with the fury of a hurricane. Christendom was in chaos. My father howled and clawed at his borders with his armies like a caged dog, but there was little to do except instruct my brothers to stand down. He sent messengers, diplomats, generals, every man he could. He begged Philip to reconsider our alliance. Philip did not. Many of these visitors, we did not even bother to see. We were busy with other things. Everyone must have known the nature of our relationship, as we could hardly bear to be outside the same room. It drew some disdain from our vassals, but there was little they could do to stop us. Besides, with Blois's death, the gristle had been carved out of France's court. He had been at the heart of its discontentment; with him gone, Philip's gambit went remarkably unchallenged—perhaps because many suspected Blois had not been killed by the rogue soldier their king claimed.

"They are afraid of me now," Philip admitted to me. "A bloody solution, but an effective one. I have always avoided doing diplomacy with swords, but perhaps, sometimes, it is necessary."

"In future, I shall be your sword, my love," I replied. "You needn't wield the blade any longer."

We were in bed, our clothes in a heap on the floor. We had been eating honey wafers. Philip had crumbs on his lips, and I began kissing them away. He kissed me back—leaning into the embrace, without hesitation or fear—and I realized I had never been so happy. In my euphoria, I had a moment of inspiration, and I stopped to say, "We ought to have a tournament."

"What?" Philip asked, a little dazed. "A tournament?"

"In celebration of our alliance. Next spring, perhaps. We could organize it together. We could even have it in Paris, so you do not need to travel."

"Tournaments are loud, Richard," he said.

"Yes, they are."

"Lots of people."

"That is the *point*," I told him. "Come. Wouldn't you like to see me joust?"

"Well—I would," he said. "But . . ."

"And Isabella would enjoy it."

He sighed. "Yes, that is true."

"So?"

"Perhaps," he mumbled. In response, I shoved him down into the mattress, and he wheezed in complaint.

"Most magnanimous, my liege," I said.

"Yes, it is, actually, and I—"

I ran my fingertips across his sides. He started laughing, trying to bat my hands away, garbling, "Richard, stop—stop that— *stop*—"

I slowed, bending to replace my fingers with my lips. I pressed kisses to his stomach, his hip bone, his inner thigh. As I moved further, his giggles became whimpers, and then gasps. He curled his fingers in my hair.

A knock on the door interrupted us. We groaned in unison, and I sat up. Still lying down, Philip called, breathless, "What is it?"

"Pardon, my lord," came the reply. It was Stephen. He was the only one with enough bravery to interrupt us while we were in Philip's rooms. "A missive has arrived, from Lords Brittany and Cornwall."

"Together?" Philip asked.

"Yes. They request a truce."

"I shall be there shortly."

"If you happen to see Richard, you could tell him he ought to come also."

"Thank you, Stephen," I said.

Stephen made an amused noise, and his footsteps receded. Philip sat up with some speed. He nearly knocked me under the chin with his foot, and I fell back from him. "It is time," he said, eyes flashing. "Richard, it is time."

"I suppose so."

"Henry will call you for negotiations. He knows he faces defeat."

"Yes," I replied, displeased. "And so, I shall have to leave."

"You can return to Aquitaine once it is done."

"That is true." Mollified, I pulled him forward to sit between my legs, his back against my chest. I kissed his shoulder. "Will you visit?" I asked him.

He leaned against me. "I wish I could. Perhaps I shall find the time, but it is difficult to leave my lands when I am not at war. I need an excuse for it, or my vassals will be displeased."

"You are king. Tell them you wish to go."

"That would be easier if the threat of rebellion were not so high. I risked much for this, Richard."

"Was it worth it?" I asked.

"Yes."

I pressed my face into his neck. "I shall miss you desperately."

"I feel the same."

"Shall I come to Paris for Christmas?"

He nodded, and added, "And in spring. Since we are having a tournament, apparently."

"Yes, we *are*," I said, delighted. "Lord, it has been too long since I jousted. When I was young—very young, in England—Geoffrey and I would run at each other with sticks, playing as if we were at the tiltyard. It was the only time we ever got along, those pretend jousts."

"Perhaps a real one would do something similar," Philip suggested. "Soothe your tempers."

"Perhaps," I replied doubtfully.

Philip sighed and disentangled himself from me. "We should meet the emissaries," he said. He stood, lifting his shirt from the floor, frowning at the creases.

"Let them wait. I was occupied, before Stephen came, and I intend to finish what I started."

"It would be rude to be late. John and Geoffrey are no longer our enemies. We should extend them courtesy."

"They are my permanent enemies," I said, "even if they are not yours. What matter is it, how long they wait? Peace is peace. The truce will hold."

"Peace is fragile, Richard," he corrected. "Let us not shatter it before it is made."

"Nothing could prevent it, not now. My brothers *must* accept surrender. I do not care if I offend them."

Philip bent towards me. "Not all hearts are as resilient as

yours," he said softly, trailing his fingers along my jaw. "Some are more moldable. Someday, you might reconcile."

"Reconciliation has never been the way of my family."

His lips quirked. "Neither is loving the king of France; your mother can attest to that. But here you are."

"Here I am," I agreed. "And I am your humble vassal, my liege. Allow me to swear fealty once more."

Then I pulled him back into bed, and I swallowed his protests with a kiss.

⁓

Henry wanted the peace talks in England. The journey would be a difficult one, and I delayed it more than I should have. After my time in Nantes with Philip, my departure felt like an expulsion from Eden. The arrival in London was the worst moment. The weather had begun to warm, the air was humid, and the heavy stench of the city mocked me as I passed through it. The smell seemed to cling to me even as I was swept up the river, away from the crowds, and into the grounds of the Tower.

I did not know why this place was chosen. I suspected it was because England was troublesome to reach for all of us, apart from my father. But even Henry himself usually avoided the Tower. He preferred his castles on the continent, particularly those from which he could cast a jaundiced eye south over Aquitaine. London had not seen its king for many years.

And yet, despite its neglect, the fortress was as intact and as imposing as ever. There was a scrubbed-bare starkness to the stone walls that seemed defiant, that spoke of a stubborn sort of English hostility. This vindictiveness extended to the weather: the moment I entered the courtyard, it began to rain. In this heat, the water came in bloodlike, lukewarm droplets. When I went inside, I was dripping wet. I climbed the stairs and entered the great hall with a trail of water marking my path, but there was no Philip here to chide me for it. Instead, I was greeted only by John. He was pacing by the hearth, muttering to himself, his hands laced behind his back.

The dim light of the fire gave his angular features a ghoulish quality, as did his hunched shoulders and the spindled lengths of his fingers as they interlocked. His face was haggard, his hair now grown so long it brushed his shoulders. He recoiled at the closing of the door. As he saw me, his posture became defensive, his back curving so that he was stooped over.

"My lord—Richard—" he said, aghast, and it was obvious that he was genuinely shocked.

"John," I replied, attempting to mask my discomfort. Neither the anger I usually aimed towards my brothers, nor the affability I affected amongst strangers, seemed appropriate in the face of his earnest expression. "Where is our father?" I asked. "Geoffrey?"

"They are having a *private discussion*," he said, biting his lip. "But they do not know you have arrived. You were supposed to come a week ago."

"I was occupied," I said.

"Occupied with what?"

"Traveling."

"We have traveled farther than you."

"I was busy with court matters."

"In Nantes?" he asked.

"Did Father leave you here to interrogate me?"

"What?" He grimaced. "I—no. Pardon."

Scowling, I took a seat on one of the benches by the fire. John shifted awkwardly.

"Are you angry?" he asked.

"What?"

"Are you angry? That I—"

"That you sieged my land? That you tried to take my duchy from me?"

"Yes."

"I am exhausted," I said, "and I am angry also. But not at you, John, because you had little choice in the matter. Really, I pity you for it."

"Pity me?"

"It isn't as if you had anything to gain from it," I told him. "You simply did as Father bid you to. As always."

It took him a moment to digest these words, and then John sneered. It was a true Angevin sneer, cruel and reflexive. I recognized it well. All his repressed fury had risen to the surface, looking for someone to direct itself towards. I watched him and hoped I would not become a target; I had to smother a sigh of relief when he said, snarling, "I would pity myself also, when my loyalty has been repaid with—with—"

"Shackles?"

He nodded emphatically. "*Shackles*, yes. Father has *shackled* me. I did not—I did not want this, Richard, you must believe me."

I did not know if I believed him, but I was glad of this faltering attempt at reconciliation, all the same. It was a relief that there remained at least one man in my family who was not resigned to our mutual resentment. And I appreciated, also, how afraid John was, seeming to shrink within himself as he looked at me. It gave me hope that I still had a presence of some sort; that my father had not succeeded in trimming me down, like a candlewick, until there was nothing left of me to burn.

I said, "I believe you, John." His shoulders slumped, his back straightening. I realized he was not quite as short as I had thought, certainly a little taller than Philip was. And yet Philip always held himself with perfect posture, whereas John looked as if a pair of bellows might tip him over.

The door behind us slammed open. It shuddered against the stone wall as my father walked in, Geoffrey following at his heels. I stood up out of reflex. The last time I had seen Henry was in Rouen, little more than a year ago, and yet he seemed to have aged a decade. His eyebrows were streaked with grey, and his jowls were prominent beneath his chin. The sagging skin gave a new softness to his face, in almost comedic opposition to the strength of his scowl.

Behind him Geoffrey was as he ever was. His face was like carved quartz, glancing between Henry and me with polished concern. I had wondered if he might permit himself some anger, after Philip's betrayal, but displays of such emotion would have been far too inconvenient. Instead, he was as composed as if our conflict had never happened. He said nothing and did nothing in greeting, and neither did I, nor John, nor our father; a silence descended upon us as—for the first time since we were children—King Henry and all his living sons stood together in the same room.

"You are late, Richard," Henry said to me.

"I was otherwise occupied," I replied, and Geoffrey gave a small, contemptuous laugh.

"Were you?" Henry asked. He approached one of the tables, reaching for the wine jug. He did not look at me as he continued to speak. "I heard you have been courting Philip in Nantes."

My eyes narrowed. "Courting?"

"It is a fool's errand," he said. "He will offer you Christendom, but he will give you ashes. Such is the manner of his family. You have been wasting your time, and mine."

Through my teeth, I replied, "I am here now, *Father*, as you have bid me. I will submit to your truce. There is no need to speak of other matters."

"You will not apologize, for your foolishness?"

"I should have arrived sooner. That is all I will concede to you. You will get no apologies for anything else. Aquitaine is mine, and Philip aids me because he knows this."

Henry finished pouring the wine. He still did not look at me. "Is it yours? Your mother and I agreed that the same son would never have Aquitaine and England."

"That was before Harry died," I said.

Geoffrey said dismissively, "Circumstances change."

"Death cares not for promises," Henry agreed. "You are not immune to fate, Richard."

He strode towards us. Although his cup was full, he held it as an afterthought, dangling at his side. "I will repeat my offer to you," he said to me, "although this shall be the last time I do so. Concede Aquitaine to your mother, and I will name you heir. I will forget our differences."

"No," I replied.

He nodded, unsurprised. "So be it. We will announce our truce tomorrow. You may use this peace to consider your current position, and how long you shall be able to maintain it. My patience wears thin, and you will not find me so amenable in future."

Geoffrey said, "Do you *really* think he will change his mind, Father? After all that has happened?"

Henry gave him a thunderous glare, and he stared back at him, placid. "I merely think it a little naïve," Geoffrey continued, "to expect Richard to give way, when you have offered him everything you have but Aquitaine, and seen him refuse it in turn."

John took a step back, regarding Henry nervously. "This is a reconciliation, that is all, Geoffrey," he said. "We ought to—"

"Are you not sick of this?" Geoffrey asked. "All of you? It would be easy enough to finish it."

"I will not give you Aquitaine," I snarled.

"Fine!" Geoffrey returned, exasperated. "Then—since you are *so* resistant to anything else—we ought to leave Richard his duchy and pass the throne to me."

John gawped at him. "You cannot have England! Richard is the oldest!"

"He was born only eleven months before I was," Geoffrey replied. "Besides, it is hardly as if Richard *wants* England, anyway. Much would be resolved, were I to have it instead." He looked at me. "You could keep Aquitaine," he said, "and you could keep . . . anything *else,* that you would lose once you took the throne."

My eyes widened. I glanced to Henry, who was frowning in thought. For a moment, it seemed as if he were entertaining the idea; then he shook his head. "I cannot set a precedent in which the heir is uncertain," he said. "The dynasty would suffer for it."

Geoffrey shrugged and replied, "Very well."

The absurdity of this exchange, and the situation, struck me all at once. It seemed to do the same to John. Our gazes met in a fleeting moment of camaraderie.

"But certainly," Geoffrey continued, "we should not allow our inheritance to be determined by the king of France. Such as it is, for the moment."

Henry made a dismissive gesture. "Philip is young and fickle. I shall steer him away from Richard, if need be."

Incredulous, I replied, "And how would you do that?"

"It would not be difficult," Geoffrey said, sneering. I raised an eyebrow at him; his composure was cracking. "He goes to the highest bidder," he continued, "or rather: the man most willing to *kneel*."

"He is my ally," I replied in a low, threatening tone.

"*I* was his ally," he said, with what sounded like genuine resentment. "Then he realized you were easier to walk over. The moment I can make him a better offer, he will leave you in the dirt."

"Are you jealous, Geoffrey?"

"If you think that I would even *consider* such lengths as you have gone to—"

"Enough," Henry said in a voice that would have cowed a mountain; but Geoffrey was now focused so entirely on me that he ignored it. His eyes were fevered, pupils blown in the dim light; although his expression remained controlled, his hands were curled into fists, as if to prevent himself from tearing me apart.

"You never wanted to be king, Richard," he said. "You were happy enough as you were, before Harry died. Do you know why you think you want it now? Because Philip and I *made* you want it. Because we knew we could gain from it."

"England is my right, as heir," I said. "Neither of you could contrive that."

"Your right?" He laughed viciously. "Your *right* only matters as long as it aids France. Do you think that Philip will not discard you the moment you have outlived your usefulness? He did so to me."

"Do you envy me that much?" I took a step towards him. "Are you so angry, to have spent your life as a last resort? You will always be the third son, called upon when all others have failed. Philip chose me over you. Even Father prefers John to you, and Mother—"

"Mother!" he echoed. "Must it *always* return to her? The only reason she likes you best is because you are the most easily controlled—and the only reason Philip has chosen you over me is because he likes to *spread* his *legs*—"

"Enough!" Henry shouted, but I surged forward at the same time as Geoffrey did. We crashed together, hitting the floor heavily. Geoffrey scowled at me as I fell beside him. He did not attempt to stand up, or cower away. I did what we both expected me to do: I sat up, and I hit him.

He might have been able to roll out of the way, but he did not. When I pulled back to punch him again, he grinned at me, wide and wild. I faltered. His lip was split, and there was blood on his front tooth.

Geoffrey began to laugh at my hesitation, and Henry howled incoherently at us, pulling at my shoulders. He did not have the strength to move me, and he fell away quickly. John had backed up in front of the fireplace, casting a long shadow over us all, and Geoffrey was still *laughing;* I made a noise that might have also been a laugh, perhaps a sob. I rolled over so that I was lying on the floor beside him, and I covered my face with my hands.

Then there was silence, except for Geoffrey, whose laughter slowly grew quieter and quieter until he was simply breathing too loudly. No one moved; there was the sound of footsteps, and across the room I heard the door slam shut.

Once the echo had faded, John said, "This was supposed to be a *reconciliation*," with such genuine grief that Geoffrey laughed again. I did also, my hands falling away from my face.

I did not stand, but I craned my head up to peer around the room, ensuring that Henry had left. I lay back on the floor, groaning.

"I lost my temper," Geoffrey said wryly. "Perhaps, Richard, we are more similar than I thought."

John sat on the bench. He stared down at us, frowning. "This is awful," he said. He opened his mouth again, as if he had more to say, but then he realized that he did not. He scuffed his feet against the rushes.

"It is," I said.

"It could be worse," Geoffrey replied.

"Could it really?" I asked.

"Yes." He stared up at the ceiling with a furious sort of concentration. I had never, before that day, seen Geoffrey furious about anything. "Every day," he said, "I thank God that you are my brother, Richard."

"What?" I asked, incredulous. "You despise me."

"*You* despise *me*. I have neither the time nor disposition to despise anyone. But I resent you, certainly, for you have been given everything that I have ever wanted."

"The crown?"

"No," he replied. "Priority. I live my life as an afterthought, trying to claw myself to relevance. I hurt people, in the process, and I will not apologize for it. But nothing I do is out of hatred. I would like you to know that. You too, John."

I considered this. Then I said, "Very well." John echoed me, confused.

We all fell quiet. The wind wailed outside, and my wet clothes pooled around me. "Look," I said, on a strange, sudden whim; perhaps the intensity of our argument had inspired some rare desire for compromise. "Philip and I are having a tournament, next spring."

Geoffrey snorted. "What? Together?"

"Yes," I said, "in honor of our alliance. You both might come, if only—if only to get away from our father."

From above us, John said, "Richard, are you inviting us to a celebration of our own defeat?"

"I suppose so," I replied, and Geoffrey chuckled.

"Well, certainly I will not come," John huffed. "I will only embarrass myself."

"That is true, John," Geoffrey said. "And, Richard, you are a fool. But perhaps I should come. It would show the world we are reconciled."

"Are we reconciled?" I asked.

"Whether we are, or we are not, it does not matter," he replied. "Nothing matters, except what we can make others believe."

I had no response. Silence returned, and I closed my eyes. My thoughts were muffled and slippery. I imagined that Harry was there with us, sprawled on the chair by the fire. He would be wearing the crown of England on his head, rolling his eyes at our arguments, and I would be only a duke once more. Returning to the continent with the sun on my shoulders, I would spend my life on the road between Poitiers and Paris, following my heart from east to west and back again. Harry would come to the tournament, and Geoffrey, too, and even John; there we would bicker and compete as we had when we were children, when our arguments had only shallow foundations.

My throat grew tight with unshed tears. When I opened my eyes once more, I saw John staring at me. Embarrassed, he shuffled so that he was lying on top of the bench. Then I realized that all of us—Geoffrey, John, myself, even Harry in Rouen—were in the same position, laid flat and staring upwards. I wondered if any of us would find something worthy above us, some escape from our cages; something apart from a stone ceiling, and the patient drumming of the rain.

CHAPTER NINETEEN

Philip

I did not have the opportunity to visit Aquitaine that year, but such a trip had become unnecessary; Richard was a constant presence at my court. I was glad to have him there, and Isabella was also. They became good friends. I think his company was a comfort to her.

Our continued efforts to conceive took a toll on my wife's well-being. We did as little as we could, when we felt we needed to, and I believed that was enough. But it was not enough for her. Isabella fixated on the issue; she wore symbols of Saint Anne, the patron of the childless, and she clutched them in her fingers as she prayed. She took tinctures and read medical books and performed strange exercises in the mornings. Eventually, I told her she was doing too much.

"I am not," she said. "I am doing exactly what I must. Kingship is your burden, Philip. This is mine."

Eventually, however, she seemed to realize she was doing herself harm; her mood settled, and she ceased in her efforts. A month went by without mention of it, from herself or me. It almost felt as if we had managed to forget the obligation entirely—

and then one winter morning, as we were eating breakfast, she said, "I am pregnant."

I dropped my roll onto my plate. "What?" I replied, voice faint.

She gave me a look of mild amusement and repeated, "I am pregnant, Philip. You are to be a father."

I was to be a father. Shocked and confused, I went to embrace her. I ought to have felt joy, but there was only a familiar fear, stomach squirming in anxiety. Still, when I looked at Isabella, she seemed delighted, so I did my best to hide my terror.

After the meal, I went to find Richard, who often skipped breakfast in favor of eating a lunch big enough to feed an army. He was in the library, flipping through a book near the easternmost shelf.

When I entered, he looked up from the pages, smiling. "Your poetry collection is lacking," he said. "All Latin; surely, a little Occitan wouldn't be remiss— You look upset. Has something happened?"

"Isabella is pregnant," I said.

"Congratulations."

"She told me this morning," I continued, "and it was so sudden, I—oh. *Congratulations?*"

"Yes."

"I thought you might say something else."

"Would you like me to say something else?"

"No," I said.

He smirked. "Would you like me to be jealous that you are sleeping with your wife?"

"*Richard,*" I hissed. "Of course not."

"Philip, you know I do not mind. It is merely duty."

"Yes, it is."

"It *must* be merely duty," he said, a small frown now shadowing his brow. "She is so young. Well, she *was* so young; I suppose that now she is not. I suppose . . ." Seeming suddenly uncomfortable, he put the book back on the shelf, clearing his throat. "I suppose it is perfectly normal."

"It does not seem normal to me," I said. "None of this is normal. I have caused her so much suffering, and yet she is so happy, so relieved to be carrying the child of someone who is—who is as I am."

"As you are," he repeated. "But there is nothing *wrong* with you."

"I—I am sorry," I murmured. "It feels as if I should be glad, but I am not. I am to be a *father*—but there is so much I have done, so much I will do—Blois—the war—and I—"

I was beginning to panic, and I desperately measured my breaths, hoping to maintain some semblance of control. Richard stepped closer to me. "Philip," he said, slowly, "it is to be expected that you might be overwhelmed."

I closed my eyes. "I am afraid, Richard."

"I know."

"So much could go wrong. I know that Isabella needed this. I know that *France* needed this. But I am terrified."

"That is to be expected," he said. "I would be frightened, too."

"Childbirth is dangerous—and I—what if she—"

Richard embraced me. "She won't."

"You cannot know that."

"She won't," he repeated, stubborn. "Look at me."

I looked up at him. He kissed me, cupping my cheek in his hand.

"Isabella is strong," he said. "As are you. All will be well."

"All will be well," I repeated. And I buried my face in his chest, so that he could not see the uncertainty in my expression.

As time wore on, and winter became spring, both Richard and Isabella became more involved in tournament preparations. I was put in charge of the budget and nothing else, which suited me well. I did not want to be reminded of the event's existence. The closer it loomed, the more I felt there was something foolish in it. It seemed such a performative sort of happiness, such a naïve display. Isabella's pregnancy, the fragile truce—so much could potentially go wrong. It was as if we were courting disaster. Each moment of joy Richard and I shared, each kiss and embrace, seemed permitted only by some temporary accident of fate; and I dreamt, sometimes, of Isabella pale and bloodless in the bed, our child quiet, Paris made silent with grief.

This sense of unease grew when, a few weeks beforehand, Richard told me he was needed in Poitiers. "Only until the tournament," he said. "I will return before it begins, my love, I swear it."

He did not return before it began, as he was delayed by a flood near Tours. Instead, I was sent headfirst into the tempest. Clearly neither Richard nor Isabella had understood the meaning of moderation. It was the largest tournament held in Paris for over a century, gutting my court of its order with the efficiency and speed of a fishmonger. Life became a constant cacophony: the clang of plate armor, the snorting of horses, thousands of knights hollering and squelching sabatons in the mud. Richard's absence meant that, at first, all responsibility fell upon my shoulders. I was obligated to personally greet every visiting noble, regardless of whether they owned half of Aragon or a square mile of English bog.

The day before the first events was spent smiling and nodding to arriving guests. Isabella and I had been set up in a grand pavilion, the walls a cloth of green and gold. Attendants plied us with wine and pastries, while a group of musicians in the corner strummed softly at their lutes. The weather was balmy and comfortable, but it did nothing to improve my mood. Ever since the guests had arrived, my general sense of unease had become an acute anxiety. Isabella had noticed this, and she was frowning at me from her seat as yet another knight backed out of the tent.

"What is the matter?" she asked. Her feet were propped up, shoes off—a grave impropriety, but her ankles had swelled, and she was understandably unwilling to suffer the discomfort.

"I do not know," I replied. "I only—I feel as if something bad shall happen. As if I ought to be preparing for it."

Her expression became sympathetic, and she reached to lay her hand over my own. "Richard shall arrive soon."

"I hope so."

"He will," she repeated, squeezing my fingers. "And then, all will be well."

Before I could respond, an attendant poked his head in through the tent's entrance. He said, "My liege, the Duke of Brittany requests an audience."

I stiffened, as did Isabella beside me. She turned to me, her eyebrows raised. "Geoffrey?"

"Apparently so."

"I thought he might not come," she said. "Richard said he was uncertain."

"Yes, I know." I looked back to the attendant. "Very well. Bring him to us."

The attendant bowed and disappeared once more. Isabella took my arm, as if to prevent me from leaving. I cast her a chiding look, and she stared back, defiant.

Geoffrey entered the tent. He had a woman with him whom I had never seen before. She was unusually fair, her hair almost white-blond, blue eyes pale and clear; she was tiny also, especially when she stood next to Geoffrey. He removed his cap immediately at seeing me, offering a practiced bow at precisely the same time she curtsied.

"My liege," Geoffrey said, "my lady, I am glad to see you well. My congratulations, of course."

"My Lord Brittany," I replied. I did not know whether to stand to greet him; I could not tell how angered he was by my betrayal, even a year later. His expression was composed, but he made no move to approach. Isabella nodded at him and looked purposefully over his shoulder.

If Geoffrey was affected by the awkwardness of our reunion, he did not show it. He smiled cordially and gestured to the woman beside him. He said, "I am glad to finally introduce my wife: Constance, Duchess of Brittany and Countess of Richmond."

Constance curtsied again, gazing at me through pale lashes. "I am honored to meet you at last, my liege, my lady."

She spoke with perfect elocution, each syllable neat and clipped. As she straightened, she reached for Geoffrey's arm at exactly the same time he offered it to her. I had never seen two people move with such symmetry.

"It is a pleasure, my lady," I said. I looked at Geoffrey. "Do you intend to participate in the tournament, Lord Brittany?"

"I shall joust, yes," he replied. "And yourself?"

"I am afraid not."

This answer was what Geoffrey had expected, and he allowed a small smirk in response. "A shame," he said, launching into an elegant but impersonal speech complimenting the tournament preparations.

The conversation that followed was stilted and uncomfortable, the result of two men determined to make a show of their own indifference. He did not mention what had happened in

Nantes, and neither did I. It might have been an attempt at reconciliation, in that manner, but there was a forced distance in his
politeness. We would never again be close enough to dispense
with ceremony.

The meeting lasted only briefly before he made his excuses
and left, his wife's footsteps perfectly measured to match his
own. It was only once he was gone that I allowed myself a moment of grief: mourning the sudden shallowness of what had
once been a friendship, as conditional as that friendship had
clearly been. I did not regret the decisions I had made, to lead us
to this point; but I did regret that it seemed this new distance
would be a permanent one. I now realized how much I had once
liked Geoffrey, for all his cruelty and his disdain. I had never
truly considered how much we had in common. He too thought
of life as a sum, as gains and losses, cost and benefit. I wondered
if it gave him as much sorrow as it did me.

"Are you well?" Isabella asked, concerned. "It was odd to see
him again."

"Odd, yes," I agreed, and I swallowed the knot in my throat.

～∽～

Richard arrived that afternoon. He was delighted by the tournament, by the guests, the sport, the pageantry; he wore full armor
like a knight sent to quest, and he insisted upon inspecting every
inch of the grounds on foot, as he would inspect an army camp
before battle.

"It is about *precision*, really," Richard said to me. We were
standing on the grass of the lists, where the jousts would be held
the next day. The tilt rail was still being finished, and his words
were punctuated with the rhythmic sound of hammers on wood.
With his free hand, he gestured at the field. "Precision, not only
in the strike of the lance but in the path of the rider, the speed

of the horse, the distance between you and your opponent—all these things must be considered and controlled."

"I still think it is absurd," I replied. "Tantamount to idiotic. The risk of injury is so high."

He sighed. "Accidents happen, as they happen during any sport. But as you have already banned the use of sharp lances, as well as dueling once a contestant has been unseated—"

I interjected, "Because I would rather no one be *murdered*—"

"—then I am quite sure we are safe." He tugged my earlobe, and I swatted at him weakly. He laughed in response.

I wanted to mirror his joy, to be glad of the tournament, and glad for the opportunity to celebrate. It was unlikely that Richard and I would ever be allies again, once he was king. This was our shared victory; it always would be, even once he traded me for his crown. I should have been glad to memorialize it, but it felt like mourning something not yet dead.

Richard glanced to the side, and his expression darkened. I followed his gaze to see an auburn-haired figure seated in the stands on the other side of the field.

I raised a hand to acknowledge him. Geoffrey stood and began to approach us. Richard groaned. "We could have ignored him," he said.

"We couldn't have. You know that."

As Geoffrey neared us, he seemed uncharacteristically nervous, straightening his green cloak around himself. With his rigid posture beneath it, there was something pauldron-like in its square shoulders. He was prepared for conflict.

"Please, pardon the intrusion," he said.

"What is it?" Richard asked.

"I wished to speak with you in private. I have a message for you—both of you." He inclined his head towards me. "Forgive me, I thought it ought to wait until Richard arrived."

"Go on," I said.

"Father wants to meet with you this summer. At the elm."

At the elm. Gisors, then. Each time Henry had met with Louis there, my father had lost something to him: land, men, his own wife. I wondered what he would take from me.

Richard threw his hands up in frustration. "Am I not permitted even a moment of peace?" he demanded. "One *hour* without politics?"

Rolling his eyes, Geoffrey said, "Of course not. Especially not now. Henry is desperate. He knows this is a war he cannot win. Negotiation is the only tactic remaining to him."

"He ought to surrender, in that case," I said.

Geoffrey shook his head. "He is too stubborn. He decided John will have Aquitaine, and so he will insist upon it until he dies." He glanced at Richard, and said, with dry humor, "A family trait."

I expected Richard to contest this, but he did not. He simply stared at Geoffrey with a resigned sort of frustration, as if he could no longer bring himself to muster genuine anger.

"You act as Henry's messenger," I said to Geoffrey. "You side with him still?"

Geoffrey shrugged. "You will have a letter, too, no doubt. But I thought I would forewarn you."

"Why?"

"Goodwill? Regret? I do not know." He glanced warily between us. "In truth, you have both thrown me into a great confusion. What happened with the invasion—I cannot fathom it. I thought I understood you both. I thought I had your measure. But, Philip, when you changed sides, I could not reconcile that with what I knew; and I admit that I do not—I—well . . ."

I had never seen Geoffrey at a loss for words, and it was fascinating, in a macabre fashion, to watch the slow dissolution of his composure. His face twitched with displeasure, fingers flexing and contracting by his sides. "I struggle to understand it," he said finally. "I do not understand what the outcome of this *entanglement* is expected to be, for either of you. Once you are at war with each other—once Richard wrenches France from your hands, Philip, or you wrench Aquitaine from his—what will be left to you but regret? You have built yourselves a throne of glass, and you cannot share it. Someday the weight will be too much, and it shall shatter beneath you."

Shaken by this, I looked desperately to Richard. His expression was unreadable. "You will never understand, Geoffrey," he said. "What we have—you are incapable of understanding. I am sorry for that."

"I do not want your sympathy, brother," he replied. "I never have."

"Would I offer it, if you did?"

These words seemed to provoke a moment of grim amusement between them. They both smiled, brief but genuine; then Geoffrey cleared his throat, and he turned his head away. "A final warning," he said. "Henry still has our mother. He will use her, if he must."

"Use her how?" Richard demanded. "If he threatens to hurt her . . ."

"Doubtful, although possible, I suppose. But there are other ways. I do not know." He glanced to me. "No matter. I have detained you long enough, my liege, and I must attend to my wife. May I be excused?"

"Of course," I said. Geoffrey nodded, bowed with his usual precision and purpose, and turned to leave the field.

Left in his wake, Richard and I stood side by side at the half-finished tilt. Richard ran his hand across one of the hitching posts and sighed, the sound half swallowed by the wind.

"It is not true, Philip," Richard told me. "What Geoffrey said, about . . ."

He trailed off. Even Richard, in all his desperate and stubborn conviction, could not prove his brother wrong.

"What he said makes no difference to me," I replied, which was true enough. He had told us things I already knew.

"Good," Richard murmured, frowning. "Then let us put him out of our minds. Gisors awaits, and then a battle, if need be, to put my father down for good. We shall soon be free of this uncertainty."

"Yes."

Relieved, he took my hand in his. "I love you," he said.

"And I you." I tightened my grip on him, feeling the press of his palm against mine, committing it to memory, as I did all things belonging to Richard the duke, before he became a king. This was *my* Richard, Richard before the glass shattered. I would keep him with me always, even if an enemy someday took his place.

〜༄〜

The jousts were the first event the next day. Jousts are always first, before the pandemonium of the melee. It is considered the civilized sport, as civilized as two people flinging themselves at each other can be.

Richard was concerned about the competition. "I must return to Poitiers with the prize," he told me. "And I must beat Geoffrey, too, or I shall live my life in shame."

"Is he as good as you are?" I asked him, to which Richard responded only with a grimace.

By the afternoon, the crowd had become a swarm. We took refuge in the royal box in the stands. Richard came with us and deemed the view acceptable. He coaxed me into providing him with my cloak pin as a token, which I made him wear underneath his armor.

"Now no one can see it," he said, displeased, but I felt it a fair enough compromise. He strode away with a thoughtless confidence, and I watched him leave with the same nameless terror that had gripped me for the past few days. As he took the field to joust, I found myself leaning forward in my chair, nails digging into my palms. Isabella watched me with graver and graver concern.

"Philip," she murmured, "he will be all right—"

She was cut off by the blast of the horns. Richard and his opponent charged forward on their horses. The thunder of hooves and the slam of wood against metal immediately devoured any pretense of civility. The moment of impact was brief and vicious. Richard's lance met the knight directly in the shoulder, while the other man's aim went wide. The knight bowed backward but remained seated; he dropped his lance to concede as his horse reached the other end of the field.

I found I was almost standing up, and I dropped back to my seat. There was a polite smattering of applause, but the result was as expected. As Richard dismounted and took his helmet off, he seemed dissatisfied. Perhaps he suspected—as I did—that his opponent had hoped to lose. He threw his helmet to a squire and nodded to the knight. Turning to me, he bowed, placing his hand on his heart, directly above where my brooch was pinned. Then he marched away before I could congratulate him.

"He seems angry," Isabella said. "He won, surely he should be pleased?"

"It was a shallow victory," I replied. "That is worse than a loss to him."

The jousts continued. Richard soon joined us again. His armor was off, but his forehead still had a sheen of sweat. Scowling, he slumped onto the bench and ran his fingers through his hair.

"Congratulations," Isabella said cautiously.

"No need to congratulate me," he replied. "I could have hit him with a spoon and he would have thrown himself into the stands."

Isabella giggled at this, but then cut herself off with a small "Oh." She shifted in her seat with nervous excitement. "It is Geoffrey," she said.

Geoffrey cut a severe figure in his monochrome livery, an ink stain on the field in his black doublet. As his horse was led forward, he raised his head to look at me, and he bowed, quickly and neatly. His helmet was still tucked beneath his arm. His lance had a handkerchief tied to it; I supposed it was his wife's.

The other competitor was an English count. He entered the field with his helmet's visor already closed, and he offered me an awkward bow before going to mount. I acknowledged both of them before I glanced to Richard. He was now hunched forward, hands on his knees, frowning at the field. Our eyes met, and he offered me a small, uncertain smile.

My anxiety returned. Attempting to distract myself from it, I swept my gaze to the stands on the other side of the field. Something shifted at the corner of my eye. I glanced to the right of the crowd, where a wooden stake had been driven into the ground as a hitching post. On top of it was a large bird, feathers white as bone. At first, I thought it was only a hawk, but then it stretched its folded wings: black shapes swirled across them, and the dark lines seemed to hold some meaning, like an unfamiliar alphabet. As I stared, it tilted its head towards me, tipping open its hooked beak.

On the field, Geoffrey mounted his horse. A squire checked for the tightness of the saddle straps.

Richard noticed my unease. He placed a hand on my arm. "Philip?" he asked. "Is something wrong?"

"A gyrfalcon," I said.

"What?"

"There is a gyrfalcon. There. Do you see it?"

Richard turned to look, and he said, "I cannot—wait!"

The horns blared, signaling that the competitors were ready. When the noise ended, Richard said, "It is gone," as the sound had startled the gyrfalcon away; then all was consumed by the cacophony of shouts and hooves and flying dirt, as Geoffrey and his opponent hurtled towards each other.

And so they jousted, in the same manner as all those before them: lances were lowered, knees locked in place. The figures in the metal masks aimed for impact, braced for impact, and impact occurred. But there was nothing here of Richard's victory, a weapon glancing against the shoulder of an unwilling opponent. Instead, there were two symmetrical and solid hits directly to the chest. Both men were pushed from their seats with equal speed and opposite direction, flying towards the ground.

Isabella surged to her feet. Richard's hand dropped from my arm. The horses continued to the ends of the field, as if steered by phantom riders. Both men lay flat and unmoving.

A great clamor came from the stands as physicians and squires began to swarm the grass. Isabella clapped a hand over her mouth. Through it, almost inaudibly, she said, "Are they hurt?"

"Perhaps a little," Richard replied, even as he stood. He peered over the crowd. "Geoffrey is an excellent rider," he said, more to himself than to us. "He knows how to fall."

The throng on the field was too thick to see through, and another minute passed before anything happened. Geoffrey's opponent, groaning and battered but otherwise unharmed, was pulled away from the crowd.

There was a gnawing in my stomach. It was not hunger, but instead the emptying sort of dread that precluded comprehension. I found I could not look at the field any longer, and I cast my eyes up to the sky, blue and empty and indifferent. I could see only a small white dot that might have been a bird, or perhaps the remnant of a cloud.

"He is an excellent rider," Richard said again. But the crowd continued to seethe around Geoffrey's body, and the minutes passed; with them, Richard's silence grew heavier and heavier, until it filled my throat and lungs and mouth, and left me mute with realization beside him.

CHAPTER TWENTY

Philip

The days after the tournament were a strange, unreal mass of existence. I felt almost disembodied, as if I were spinning up in the ether. Meanwhile, everyone else continued living beneath me, as small and unfeeling as ants.

Richard shut himself inside his rooms for the remainder of the week. I sent food to him, and I came to speak with him twice. He turned me away both times, yelling at me for coming. I tried not to be injured by it, but I was. What had happened at the tournament had been enough to endure, without losing him also. Geoffrey was gone. I needed to know that his brother still remained.

The funeral would be held in Brittany. Constance, Geoffrey's wife—Geoffrey's widow—came to request permission to leave. She wanted to bring the body back with her. She bore her grief very differently from Richard. There was no fury, nor frustration. Instead, she had almost gained transparency, pale and weightless, like paper held up to light. She spoke so softly I could barely hear her. Her gaze, unfocused, seemed to be constantly fixed upon something that did not exist.

I offered her my blessings, and as large a guard as I could afford. Constance was too distracted for gratefulness. The day before she was to leave, Richard called on her, and he spent the entire day in her chambers. He told me, afterwards, that they agreed Geoffrey's heart should be buried in Rennes.

"And if my father tries to put it in Rouen," he snarled, in sudden anger, "I shall tear his own heart out of his chest and bury them in a pair."

We were both exhausted. I was utterly overwhelmed by attempting to contain Richard's moods, which swung wildly with the intensity of his grief. I had never seen him like this. Perhaps Geoffrey's death had been the final shattering of something long repressed. He looked to me for constant reassurance. When we spent the night in the same bed for the first time since the tournament, he had held me so tightly I could hardly breathe. As two weeks passed, and then three, he would constantly take my wrist and tug me downwards, as if to anchor me to the earth. He seemed to think that if he did not, I would float away from him and disappear into the clouds.

I could not tell if I felt my own sorrow at what had happened; all my emotions seemed to have become parasitic to Richard's. I fed from his anger, and I allowed it to hone my own mood into something determined, something purposeful. I became extraordinarily productive, in a manner that was, perhaps, almost callous: I spent my time preparing resources for our impending conflict with Henry, and for all that would come after our victory. I found a good candidate for Constance's inevitable remarriage, one who would bring Brittany back to France. And I began to plan, also, for what would happen once Richard was king. He was a warrior, after all, as his father had been in his youth. With him on the throne, France would no longer be able to rely on an old man's weariness. It might have been years before that happened, but I needed to prepare for it. I moved money to shore up defenses in the north. It felt like a betrayal. I did it still.

I awoke each morning feeling frayed, like rope snapped from strain, with all my limbs clenched stiff and my breaths short and stuttered. I told myself that my condition was merely the result of shock, that the intensity of this anxiety would pass. But it was difficult to remember this once I saw Richard's face, and I stared into the dark caverns of his eyes.

Isabella did as best as she could to play at normalcy, even as her confinement loomed ever closer. The tournament had to end, obviously, but she continued to invite minstrels to court, and pageant players, and poets. These were distractions that worked only in half measure. I had little interest in any of it, but I attended these events for her comfort. Richard usually did not bother; the troubadours were the only thing that made him emerge from his rooms or return from one of his endless solitary rides. He would sit and listen to the songs in perfect silence, clap politely, and then leave.

After the last of these performances, however, he merely sat there, staring at the floor. I waited until everyone else had left before approaching him.

"Richard," I said. I sat beside him. "What is it?"

He shook his head. "That was a song my mother favored. It is nothing."

"It is not nothing."

"I fear I am going mad, Philip. I hadn't expected to feel so—so— I do not know what to do."

I stared at him. It was raining outside—Parisian spring—and the grey light made his skin sallow. I almost did not recognize him.

"You should leave," I told him. "Return to Aquitaine; we can meet this summer, at Gisors. You are suffering by remaining here."

"Come with me," he said desperately, and he turned to grasp my hands. His grip was viselike, his knuckles like jagged teeth beneath his skin. "Come with me," he repeated. "Philip, *please*."

I had work to do, still. Europe was in disarray after Geoffrey's death. The argument over Constance's marriage was already spiraling into threats of war. I needed to prepare my armies, in case Henry decided to attempt invasion; besides, I felt uneasy about leaving Isabella unnecessarily.

"I cannot," I said weakly. "I wish I could, but—my court— Isabella—I . . ."

Richard's grip on me loosened. "I should not have asked."

I tried to meet his eyes, to say something to mend the sudden absence in his expression. But his gaze skidded over me, passing to the middle distance.

By the evening, he was gone.

～⚬～

"What happened?" Isabella asked me the next morning, at breakfast. She glanced at the empty seat beside me. "Where is Richard?"

"He left," I said.

"What do you mean?"

"He returned to Poitiers."

"What?!" she snapped too loudly; we both flinched, looking down the table to see if any of the nobles present had noticed. They were all staring studiously at their plates. Voice lower, she continued, "Why?"

"He needed to be in Aquitaine," I said. "It is his home."

"Yes, I know. Why didn't you go with him?"

I glanced down at her swollen stomach, and then back to her face.

"We have months yet," she said. "You'll have to leave at some point. And he is *grieving*, Philip, for God's sake."

"If something happens—"

"You are a coward," she told me. "He needs you."

"He does not need me."

Exasperated, she replied, "Of course, he does. He loves you."

"It isn't that simple," I said.

"It is exactly that simple." Dropping her fork to her plate, she narrowed her eyes at me. "You wanted him to leave without you, I think. You wanted him to resent you for remaining here."

"What? Why would I—"

"We have been married for years, Philip, and all this time, you have flinched away from happiness. You are so afraid of it. You seem to think it might sting you, like an insect."

"I do not—"

"You have begun to distance yourself from him, I think, ever since the tournament. I do not understand it; frankly, it infuriates me. You have something good, something precious, and you *insist* upon destroying it."

"Its destruction is inevitable," I said, although I heard the uncertainty in my voice just as well as she did. "Someday, Richard shall also be a king, and when that happens—"

"You are Philip!" she replied, exasperated. "He is Richard. England and France may be enemies, but you needn't be."

"That is naïve."

"Perhaps so. But he loves you, and you love him. And he needs you. So go."

"Go," I echoed, dumbfounded.

"To Poitiers." She shoved at me with her foot. "*Go,* Philip. I will watch the court while you are away."

"But you ought to be resting."

"I am pregnant, not a leper. Go."

"What if he does not want me there?" I asked. "What if—"

"Listen to yourself," she said. "All these endless questions you ask. They are constant. You demand so much of yourself. I understand that it is overwhelming to have so many choices. But you must choose still. Go to him; I will never forgive you if you don't." She leaned forward, her expression hard as steel. "Some things are more important than the crown."

"I am a king," I said. "What could possibly be more important than that?"

She laughed, and she picked up her fork once more. "Anything, Philip," she said. "Almost anything else."

⤙⤚

I went.

The journey from Paris to Poitiers normally takes a week; I managed it in four days. But however fast I traveled, Richard was somehow faster. Our paths did not cross until I reached the city itself.

I had never seen Poitiers. I had only ever heard Richard speak of it, with frantic, ardent affection. To be there, finally, felt like an intrusion on something intensely private; the breach of some final barrier between us I hadn't realized existed. It was a small town, much smaller than Paris, but far more colorful. Flowers crawled between the cracks in the paving stones, and many of the windows had red banners flung across their windows, Aquitaine's lion livery snarling in threads of gold.

The streets were already busy. Crowds had emerged to greet

Richard, who I later learnt had arrived just before us. When I showed up, there was a great deal of confusion. The already assembled populace watched my progress from windowsills and cobblestones, following us with silent, curious gazes. It felt more than enough of a greeting, considering the circumstances.

One man, clearly drunk, stumbled out of his house to yell, "God keep Duke Richard! God keep King Philip! God keep our land of Aquitaine!"

I found myself smiling at this, and I pulled the procession to a halt to greet him. The man was so astonished by my attention he threw himself to the ground in obeisance.

"Rise," I said. He stumbled to his feet and bowed, but the bow was violent enough in character that he tipped over and sent himself back to the pavement.

I waited for him to stand once more. After a largely unintelligible conversation, conducted in what little Occitan I could muster, the man agreed to lead us to Richard. He took us through a set of winding, narrow streets, down to the cathedral square.

The cathedral itself was an extraordinary construction of spires and pale stone, of a size to rival anything in France. My retinue was content to wait outside; when I entered the church, I first assumed that it was empty. It was a vast space, clearly still under construction: the columns remained unpainted, and most of the windows lacked glass, permitting sunshine and a light breeze to flit across the white floors. But across the nave, behind the altar, a single window was completed and stained. Beneath it stood the figure of Richard, staring up to the glass.

He was utterly enraptured, and he did not notice my entrance. As I approached the window, I understood why. It was astonishingly beautiful. I found myself smothering a gasp. I was moved not by the images—crucifixions and saints, things I had seen countless times before—but instead by its colors. It was jewellike, with blues and greens and reds of a vibrancy that seemed almost impossible. When I looked away from it, the rest of the cathedral was entirely leached of its tint.

Richard turned his head to look at me. His eyes widened.

"Philip," he said, astonished. "You—what are you doing here?"

"I followed you," I replied.

"Why?"

"You needed me; I ought to have come with you when you first asked. Forgive me."

Richard's expression softened, and he offered me his hand. I placed my palm in his, and he drew me towards him.

"I am so glad to see you," he said. "I—I owe you an apology also. I have treated you terribly these past few weeks. I was angry. I should not have been."

"You are permitted anger."

"Not towards you. You have done nothing wrong."

I gripped his hand more tightly in my own. He looked down at our linked palms; when our eyes met once more, his expression was desperate. He continued, "It is only that—I am *so* angry, Philip, all the time. I am angry at Geoffrey, and I am angry at myself."

"I know," I replied.

"All the arguments we had, all the wars we fought—the battles, the petty insults, and yet—in the end, it was so easy. It was so *quick*. I cannot stop thinking about how quick it was."

"I know," I repeated.

"In the end, it is so easy, isn't it?" He glanced back to the window and breathed a deep, shuddering breath. "I have begun to wonder— Do you think that I caused it?"

"What?"

"I invited Geoffrey to Paris," Richard said. "He came to the tournament because I asked him to. And I have often wished he were dead, Philip. Perhaps I even meant it."

"You did not kill Geoffrey, Richard," I replied, reassuring myself as much as him; for if he were somehow responsible for it, then surely I was, too. "Sometimes people die," I said, "and once they are dead, you cannot kill them, and you cannot save them, and you cannot forget them, either. They are beyond our reach. We must accept that, or else hate ourselves."

He made a broken sound. "I feel so powerless. I do not want to lose you also. And I feel as if I might lose everything, at any moment. I feel as if it will all suddenly disappear."

I did not know what to say in response. I often felt the same. I felt certain that everything was fragile, everything was going to shatter. Some part of me would always believe that the very moment the crown was on Richard's head, he would leave me.

But I loved him. He loved me, and he needed me. Perhaps it was as Isabella said: it could be that simple. For once, I could permit it to be.

"You will not lose me," I said. "I swear."

"I love you," he replied, and he pulled me into his arms. "I am sorry. I am so sorry."

"You needn't—"

"You are my question and my answer, Philip," he said. "My everything. I have been treating grief as an argument to be won. But I must make peace with it, I think. As I made peace with you, and with Geoffrey. As I will with even my father, someday. I am so sick of being at war."

I brought my mouth to his, and he sighed, leaning into the embrace. He had never kissed me so gently before. It made me feel as if I might dissolve, as if he had found something tangled within me and untwisted it.

When we parted, the clouds had shifted, and the sun was

filtering through the window. We were standing within the panes of color the light laid upon the floor. I lifted my hand to see my skin cast in emerald, the metal supports of the window forming veins of shadow across my sleeve.

Richard reached again for my hand, his arm stained red and gold. He lifted our linked palms into a diamond of blue, pressing them flat. And for a moment, I believed that the window really was sacred; I imagined it expanding around us, so that all the white stone of the cathedral—every bonelike arch and altar—would be replaced by stained glass. Loss became a distant memory. Here, in Poitiers, we were bound together. Not shattered. Not yet.

~

The palace in Poitiers was nothing like the castle in Paris. It was newer, brighter, wider. No memories haunted its corridors.

On our first day in the city, Richard had the Hall of Lost Footsteps emptied of all its furniture. We spun around in an unstructured, swirling dance, as troubadours played outside. The singer, Beatriz, had come all the way from Andalusia to perform at Aquitaine's court. She sang in Occitan, as well as Arabic and Spanish. Many of these songs I did not understand, but it did not matter. The hall was rightly named: we could hear nothing but the music and our laughter. Our feet hardly seemed to touch the ground.

Each day we spent there, Richard seemed partially reconstructed. My own mood brightened in return; still, my return to Paris became more and more pressing. I did not want to leave, but Isabella awaited me. France awaited me. We had less than a month before we were to meet Henry at Gisors, and the confrontation that had circled us like a scavenger for years would finally occur. I had to prepare.

On the morning of my departure, I wandered the halls of the palace, as if to say goodbye to it. The walk was little comfort. Each feature of the corridors seemed to recall a battle: the iron bandings on the windows cast thin shadows on the stone floor, like the arcs of arrows overhead; the marble tiling echoed against my boots like the beat of a war drum; when I went to the Hall of Lost Footsteps again, its vast emptiness seemed to promise armies might clash within it, colliding as Richard and I had once met in dance.

It suddenly became clear how foreign I was here, how little I belonged. In Paris, it was as if walls were fixed together with my family's blood, as if I myself was a necessary component of its construction. If I were ever to leave permanently, the building might starve and fall away, like a dead leech. But it was not so in Poitiers. This was Angevin country. It was white corridors and large windows, sunshine and plum trees. This was enemy territory. Once Richard was king, I would not be permitted here. I would be an invader. It might be years yet, before Henry died, but our meeting at Gisors was the first step towards that inescapable conclusion.

I went to the gardens, and I stood beneath the plum tree, pressing my hand against its trunk. Someone called my name. I turned to see Richard approaching. He was weaving around the flower beds, the sunlight laid like a cloak around his shoulders. Watching him, I allowed myself a moment of comfort. *I will remember him like this,* I thought, as I returned his smile. *Even if it ends, I will always remember him like this, and then it might not matter that he is gone.*

CHAPTER TWENTY-ONE

Richard

Philip left Poitiers a scant three weeks before we were to meet Henry at Gisors. I kissed him farewell with such desperation I suspect it hurt him, but when I looked at his face after, I saw only apology.

"I shall soon return," he said.

That afternoon, I discussed strategy for the coming conflict in my study with Stephen, considering the movements of troops. With such an advantage as Philip and I would have over my father in numbers, it almost felt a pointless effort; regardless, it was something to occupy myself with, something to make me feel useful. Still, by the afternoon my head was spinning with strategy, and I was grateful for the reprieve of the messenger's knock on the door.

"It is a visitor," he said to me, with wide, startled eyes.

"What visitor?" I asked.

"It is—it is Eleanor, my liege."

I frowned. "Pardon?"

"Your mother."

"My mother," I repeated, incredulous. "She is here?"

"Yes, my liege, at the entrance. She refuses to get out of her litter until you—"

I elbowed him out of the way. Stephen called after me and jogged in order to keep pace as I charged through the palace. We reached the great doors in record time.

There was a great crowd gathered at the base of the front steps. At their edge, a two-horse litter was set upon a pair of poles. The litter was covered by a wooden frame, and there was fabric draped over it to form a ceiling, providing shade from the sun. The fabric obscured the passenger from view. In front of the litter stood a pair of ladies in court dress.

One of the ladies was my mother's favorite, Adelaide. She was radiant in pale blue silk, her dark hair coiled upwards in a complex braid. I looked at her and felt nothing but a small stab of amusement; although they resembled each other little, she reminded me of Philip, with her aloof expression and rigid posture. I had never noticed these similarities before. I might have expected it to provoke some sort of mislaid affection for her, but it did not. It served only to remind me of how much I missed him, despite mere hours of his absence.

I approached them, and Adelaide curtsied. "My liege," she said, as a pale hand emerged from the litter. The other lady reached to take it. With her help, my mother pulled herself down. She stood before me, looking as she always had: elegant, self-satisfied, and achingly familiar.

"Richard," she said. "Dear heart."

"Mother," I replied, too astonished to say anything else, to make any action except a halting, stumbling step forward.

She embraced me. "I am so glad to see you," she murmured into my ear. "To return home. This moment is the greatest happiness I have ever known."

I tightened my grip around her. She allowed me to cling to her for a moment longer, and then she pulled back.

"We have much to speak of, you and I," she said. "It has been so long since I last stood on Poitevin soil."

"Mother, *how*—"

"Richard, I have been traveling for hours. I am in need of a drink and some rest. All shall be explained, I promise."

"Of course," I replied, mystified. I felt equal parts joy and confusion. Offering her my arm, I began to lead her up the steps.

She noticed my perplexed expression. "Are you not pleased to see me?" she asked. She smiled, to show she was jesting, but I still winced with guilt.

"Of course I am, Mother. I am merely surprised. The palace isn't prepared. I shall have to arrange quarters for you—but *how*—"

"Hush," she said, and I sighed. "I hardly expect you to have everything ready. There is the rest of the day to see to such matters." We came to the door, and she hummed in thought, tilting her head upwards to gaze at the sky. "Let us go to the courtyard. Is the plum tree still there? The one as tall as an oak?"

"Yes, it is."

"Wonderful." She clasped her hands together at her waist and smiled approvingly. "We shall sit beneath it," she said. "Have the servants bring a blanket."

"Very well," I replied, my voice faint.

She led me through the palace with the confidence of someone who still ruled there. She trailed her hands along the stone walls as if greeting a lover. Her face was serene, but behind the expression I could tell that she was overcome. There was a slight tremble to her fingers and her voice, a sense of wistfulness in her polite comments that betrayed her profound relief. Her joy suffused the air, and I became dizzy with it, trailing at her heels as I had when I was a child, when she had first shown me this place. I recalled my tiny hand in her own, as she said, *It is all yours, Richard, my gift to you: Aquitaine, Poitiers, home.* It was as if we had regressed to some halcyon moment of our past, before we had both been ruined by my father's resentment.

She took me to the plum tree, and we settled in the mottled shade of its branches. The boughs were heavy with ripening fruit, but they were still too small to pluck, egg-shaped and matte blue in color as if covered with frost. Mother trailed a finger along one of the roots in affectionate greeting.

"Geoffrey was born here," she said to me. "In the same room as you. Did you know that?"

"I didn't."

"Aquitaine was never his, but it ran in his blood, just as it does in yours. This palace has his ghost, now; many places do."

"I am sorry, Mother," I said. "I would have saved him, if I'd had the chance."

"I know. Do you think of him, Richard? Do you remember?"

"I do."

"As do I," she said, and she sighed. "We must remember him often. Harry, too. If we do, we keep them alive, if only a little."

We fell silent. I stared at my mother with my eyes watering. Seeing her here, free of her prison, was such a relief—such a shock—that it was almost unbearable.

"I am very glad you are here, of course," I said to her, "but I do not understand— Did Father release you? Did you escape?"

"He released me," she replied.

"*Why?*"

"Why do you think, dear heart? We made a deal. Henry has made me duchess once more. Before his court, he has revoked your title and passed it to me. I came as soon as I was released."

My heart stuttered, the air caught in my throat; the breeze itself seemed to pause, as if to commiserate with me. "Oh," I said. "Of course."

She laid her hand over my own. "I ought to be glad to have Aquitaine returned, and my freedom also. Still, I cannot help but be jealous that his resentment towards you, dear heart, has finally exceeded his resentment towards me." I managed a short snort of amusement at that, and she patted my hand before she continued. "This was the only recourse he had left, to ensure that you did not declare war. In exchange for my liberty, I swore before God that I shall demand my lands back from you. He expects that you will give them up, rather than go to war with me."

"A fair enough expectation." I bowed my head and pulled up a tuft of grass with my fingers. "I suppose you must make John your heir?"

"I must, yes. Don't do that, darling, you are making a mess of the blanket."

"I apologize. I—" Frustrated, I tipped my head back, staring up at the tangled mass of the plum tree's branches. "I did not expect this."

"Of course you did not expect it," she said with a note of irritation. "Henry has made an extraordinary gamble, the sort he has not made in a very long time. You should be proud that you have driven him to such lengths."

"A gamble?" I asked, and she leaned back onto the heels of her hands. The shadow of a leaf fell across her face, and her lip curled upwards; she looked so much like Geoffrey in her disdain that I was momentarily unsettled, and I tightened my fingers around the wool of the blanket.

"He has gambled that I value my happiness over his sorrow," she replied. "He believes that I would rather have my land than my revenge."

There was a promise in her voice, a righteousness, a fury—and I realized what she intended to do almost immediately. "*Mother,*" I said. "You do not have to—"

"I do not do this for you, darling, as much as I wish I could tell you otherwise. I do this because I will not allow Henry a victory, even if it is one that I share. I swore to myself that I would never do so, the moment he locked the gates of that tower and left me there to decay." She squared her shoulders and raised her chin. She looked like an empress declaring war. "And so, Richard, I will make you Duke of Aquitaine once more. The land is yours. Defeat Henry, claim the crown; all that I ask is, if you are given the chance, that you imprison him in the same place as he did me. Nothing else would give me a tenth of the satisfaction."

"But—if I do not defeat him—you swore. This is treason. Your life will be forfeit."

"You will defeat him," she said. "You must. I want to see him admit surrender."

"You really are giving me Aquitaine out of spite," I said. "Is that truly the only reason?"

"Yes," she replied, and I frowned. She smiled and covered her mouth—not to hide her amusement, but to draw attention to it. "Dear heart. You are so charming when you are confused. I know you do not understand. It is good that you do not."

"What do you mean?"

"You cannot know the depths of my bitterness. That is only natural, at your age. Each time you love someone, you carve part of yourself away, so that they might have it. There is very little left of me. I have been butchered quite thoroughly. But you—" she sighed. "You have so much of yourself still."

I said, strained, "I am sorry, Mother, that I could not help you. I am sorry that I left you in England."

"Nonsense, Richard. You did what had to be done. I have no regrets, and you should not, either."

"What about Father?" I asked her. "Surely you regret him, after all he did to you?"

It was an impulsive question, and I half expected her to react with anger; instead, she made a thoughtful sound. "I do not regret loving him. To regret love for its ending is like regretting that flowers bloom, once winter comes. But I do regret the trust I placed in him, and he in me. I regret . . ."

She paused to consider. Her eyes, which were the same spectacular green that Geoffrey's once had been, had always had a curious, mirrorlike quality to them; I could not tell if she was saddened, or guilty, or frustrated. She seemed only to reflect my own face back to me.

"When I first saw Henry," she said, "I was still in Paris, still married to Louis. Louis had always been . . . peculiarly obsessed with me, but he hated me also. He thought his love of me was a weakness, and he grew angry that I might dare to be a duchess, rather than only his wife." She sighed. "I was not afraid of him, but I was afraid of what he represented. I hated my life with him, in that gloomy court he kept, fasting and praying and weeping as I slept. The future haunted me. I saw it skittering in the dark like a roach."

"I cannot picture you afraid."

She laughed at that. "But I was, dear heart, and suffering for it also. So, I had begun to plan my escape. Some might credit my leaving to Henry; it was not so. I would have run had I known him or not. But when I did meet him; when, one day, the Duke of Anjou came to court? It was as if my life had begun anew. He found me after supper, ambushing me in the corridor—he took me in his arms—I said to him, 'Who are you, to take such liberties with the queen of France?' And he replied, 'the king of England.'"

"He was not king yet," I said.

"Exactly! And I told him so. But he said, 'I will be. I will be, and you will be queen of England, Eleanor. You will be my wife.'"

"*While* you were married to Louis?"

"Yes. He had decided the moment he saw me. Henry loved more intensely than any other man I have met, and more quickly, too. He was fickle. Quick to fall, and quick to fall away."

"What about you?" I asked. "Did you love him?"

"Of course," she replied. "How could I not? But I loved differently than Henry did. Never with such strength, such fervor; but the moment I knew, I knew it was forever." She gave me a small, bitter smile. "That is the trouble," she said. "That is why my resentment for him is so great. I love him still. I always will."

I did not know what to say. I took her hand in my own.

"I am in love also," I admitted to her. "Desperately. And sometimes—it is frightening. I fear we will grow to resent each other, as you resent Father."

She cocked her head at me, brows raised. "Is it Louis's son? Philip?"

"I—how did you—"

"Richard," Mother said, "I have heard the rumors. All of Europe has. It gave Henry much cause for concern, and it improved confidence in your alliance. I thought you were both quite clever. It did not occur to me that the rumor was true."

"Why wouldn't it be?" I asked her. "Why couldn't it be true?"

"Because of who you are, who you both are. To share a bed—as, clearly, you *have* done—would be utter foolishness."

"Yes," I said. "Perhaps it is foolish. Sometimes I wonder if we ought to end it now, before we come to ruin."

"Do you wish to end it?"

Fervently, I replied, "Of course not. I would die before I lose him. But—I do not know if Philip feels the same way. I fear, often, that he does not. I fear he will leave me, because he believes we cannot remain together."

She shrugged. "Perhaps that is a reasonable position for him to take."

"But I hardly see how—"

"I am not finished," she said. "It is perfectly reasonable. But that does not matter. You are in love. Clearly, reason became irrelevant long ago."

I nodded slowly. Seeing the lingering uncertainty in my expression, she gave me a pitying smile; another one of Geoffrey's controlled, supercilious expressions, transplanted to her own face. "Richard, I have been a queen for fifty years," she said. "A duchess, longer than that. I have seen kings dead and kings born, I have witnessed the rise and fall of empires; I have won wars and I have lost wars; I have traveled from Poitou to Antioch; I have led armies; I have worn a hundred crowns upon my head. I have gained all the glory there is to be gained. And there is one thing, above all else, that I have learnt."

"And what is that?" I asked.

"That none of it matters," she said. "None of it has ever mattered at all. That is what is so extraordinary about it, this game we all play. In the end, the winner is of no consequence. All we can hope for is that we are entertained in the process; and that, perhaps . . ." Her smile blossomed wider; it was no longer Geoffrey's, but my own, crooked and earnest. "Perhaps," she said, "we might find something of meaning, in the moments in between."

My mother made me Duke of Aquitaine again that afternoon, before all the court. She smiled as she gave her land away with such satisfaction and viciousness that I felt a thrill of fear as she placed the coronet upon my head.

Afterwards, I returned to the plum tree. It was a magnificent thing—as my mother had said, as tall as an oak, and as wide besides—but it was nothing compared to the elm at Gisors. That tree had always towered above me with such height it tore through the sky itself, like a needle through fabric, or an arrow through flesh.

I had not seen the elm since my rebellion, years ago, when myself and two of my brothers had negotiated peace with our father. Now both of those brothers were in tombs. I wondered if Geoffrey had ever returned to it. It was likely he had not. He never would. The tree had outlived him, and it would outlive me also.

When I was young, my father had spoken of banding the elm in iron, to ensure it always remained standing. But the plan had never come to fruition, as such measures were unneeded. Stoic and eternal, it was a ceaseless presence at the border. The wall between two empires: Angevin and Capet. England and France. One day, Philip and I would face each other beneath its branches as a pair of kings. Another step towards history. Another link in an unbroken chain.

I pictured myself all those years ago, standing beside the walls of my mother's prison; before I had met Philip, when all I had ever wanted was revenge. Briefly, I tried to become that Richard again, the Richard who would consider a victory over my father a meaningful one. I wanted to be the Lionheart once more.

But the thought of Henry's defeat brought me no joy. And it

was then, for the first time, that I forced myself to accept it; I accepted that it did not matter what I did. I would be king of England someday. My father was no longer my greatest enemy, and he had not been for some time. Nor was it Philip, despite our inevitable rivalry. It was the man I could become, years from now, sitting on the throne with hatred in his heart. I had to prevent his arrival. I had to ensure I did not let myself become as my parents were, embittered and resentful.

I did not know if I could, but I had to. If I did not, I would lose Philip; and if I lost him, I would lose myself.

CHAPTER TWENTY-TWO

Philip

Early one morning—while it was still dark—I was awoken by a desperate knock on my study door.

I had fallen asleep at my desk, clearly. I lifted my head and rubbed at my cheek, to see that the visitor had entered. It was Marie, one of Isabella's ladies. She was pale and wide-eyed.

"My liege, it has begun," she said. "The midwives are with her."

It took me a moment to understand what she meant. "But—" I said, alarmed. "I—it is too soon, surely."

Marie's hand fluttered over her chest, and she glanced anxiously to the door. "Yes," she said, "it is."

I stood up. "What of Isabella's mother?" I asked as I made for the exit. "She was supposed to arrive tomorrow."

"We expect her soon. My liege, the labor will take hours yet, and you cannot come inside the room—"

"I wish to wait outside the door."

Marie frowned. "Very well," she said, and she followed me begrudgingly as I hurried to Isabella's chambers. We stopped in front of the door. I could hear voices inside, and then a shout of pain.

Marie gave me a cynical look. "Are you certain you will wait?" she asked.

"Yes," I said. "Will you tell her I am here?"

She nodded curtly and slid inside the chamber.

I waited. I was so nervous I felt as if I might cough up my stomach. It was too soon—a month too soon, at least. Birth was dangerous enough when it was *expected*, let alone when it was early. It was certainly more dangerous than any battle I had ever fought. I had armies to hide behind, fortresses to run to. Isabella did not. My father had lost his second wife to the childbed, and the thought that I might lose Isabella in the same way filled me with terror.

Hours passed. As I waited, I became so insensate that I actually *prayed* for the first time since my childhood. Once the sun rose, a servant took pity on me, and he brought me a pillow for my knees. I ended up sitting on it, cross-legged, as I heard Isabella scream behind the door. Galahad came to stand beside me, whining and pawing at the threshold, but I could not allow him inside.

If she survives this, I told myself, *I will do anything she asks of me. I will listen to her. I will tell her that I love her as often as I can. I have not told her enough.*

I have not told her enough.

I pulled my knees up to my chin and held them there. Every so often, Marie emerged to give me news, but it was not enough. There was no distraction. There was only time passing, and the sun lowering, and the screams behind the door.

～❧～

At sunset, the door was flung open. It was a midwife. She curtsied to me. "My liege," she said. "You have a son."

"And Isabella?" I demanded, standing up. "Is she well?"

"Exhausted, but as well as a new mother could be. She was very brave."

I burst into tears. The midwife stepped back in shock. I had made no sounds of distress, but I could feel the wetness on my cheeks. I can only imagine how alarming it must have been, to see the king in such sudden disarray. "Pardon," I said with as much composure as I could muster. "I am only relieved."

"Would you like to come inside?" she asked.

I nodded and followed her into the chambers. The light inside was still dim, the air stale and sour. Isabella was sitting up in the bed, holding a wailing bundle in her arms. She looked up at my entrance, and our eyes met. She saw that I was crying, and then she began to cry also.

"Philip, *look*," she said, smiling through her tears. "Look at what we did."

I came to look. She showed me the bundle. My screaming son was thumb-like, his skin red as a radish; he was entirely bald, and entirely furious. "He is perfect," I told her.

"He was silent at first. Silent, but—" She sighed, pressing a kiss to his forehead. "Then I held him, and he began to cry."

I sat with her. Midwives and maids came and went. They lit candles and drew curtains. Isabella fed our son and he fell asleep. She followed soon after. There was enough space on the bed, so I lay beside them and listened to their breathing.

Pressing my arm against hers, I wondered what Richard would think of this new Capet. I wondered how he would have reacted to my panic as I had waited outside the door. Had it been like this for my own father? Had he held me in his arms and bemoaned the fact that Eleanor was not there with him? I looked at the minute slant of my son's nose, and the pink bloom of his cheeks. I told myself that I would never be as Louis had been. Whatever I felt for Richard, whatever happened between us, I would never permit it to ruin me.

Still, in all the exhaustion and relief of the evening, I could not help but imagine him with us as I began to drift to sleep. I pictured Richard standing beside the bed, one hand on my shoulder, one hand on Isabella's, smiling down at my son.

He is beautiful, the illusion said. *I cannot wait to see him grow.*

~⚬~

He was christened Louis, as was customary; it was either to be my name or my father's, and neither I nor Isabella wanted a second Philip in the family. Despite his early arrival, he was healthy, much healthier than I had been as a child. Isabella glowed with happiness and pride. I wanted to remain in Paris with her for the rest of the season, to share in her joy, but I could not. Gisors awaited.

We left early in the morning, but not early enough to escape the summer heat. The sun was merciless as we made our way north. As we rode, I remembered the last time I had come to the elm: I had been only a child, and Louis had taken me with him to observe his negotiations with Henry. They had gone badly. We had lost Anjou, and Louis had been so furious he had spent the night whipping himself in penitence.

I had Anjou now, but I was not naïve enough to be certain I would keep it. If I ever did lose it, that loss would be to Richard; and as Paris disappeared behind us, I wondered if he feared the crown that awaited him as much as I did. He might come to regret all that had passed between us, once he took the throne. I might also.

But I knew, even as I asked myself the question, that I could not regret it. To regret Richard would be to regret the very act of existence. We had always been inevitable. For the rest of our lives, we would be as dusk and dawn; one's ascendancy would cause the other's fall. Perhaps, in that way, we could never truly part.

~⁊~

The elm at Gisors straddled the border between my territory and Henry's. To the north, there was Normandy, and south, there was Paris. At the center of it all, a tree had teetered on its hill for centuries, and it seemed likely to do so for centuries more. It was a slender thing, its trunk bent with a subtle eastward curve, and it bowed in the breeze with a sort of ceremonial sway. Its height was that of at least a dozen men, perhaps more. At the very top, its leaves were crushed flat, as if the hand of heaven were pressing down upon it, or the wind had sliced part of it away.

When we arrived, Richard and his retinue were already there. They were wading in the stream at the base of the hill; unsurprising, considering the heat. Richard was at the center of the stream, speaking with some of his men. As I approached, he grinned at me, waved, and then crouched to cup some water in his hands, pouring it over his head.

"Will you speak to your father like that, dripping wet?" I asked him, raising an eyebrow.

"It is hotter than hell itself, Philip, have mercy."

Richard's men made their excuses and waded away. I watched them leave, then said, "Where is Henry?"

"I have buried him beneath that elm." I laughed, but nervously. Richard gave me a reassuring smile. "My congratulations, by the way."

"Oh—thank you."

"Isabella is well?"

"Yes, she is." I rubbed the back of my neck, narrowing my eyes at the water. "It is too damned hot."

"It is," Richard replied, amused. I toed off my shoes and pulled off my surcoat, stepping halfway into the stream, movements tentative. The water was lukewarm but still some relief from the sun.

Richard rolled his eyes and tugged me forward. I stumbled farther into the water, scowling at him. His smile widened, and his eyes dropped to my lips. I could not kiss him, not with so many others watching, so instead I pressed two fingers against his lips. He did the same to me.

"I am late," I said as I dropped my hand. "Pardon."

"I admit, it is unusual, for you. But I suppose it was to be expected, considering you've just had a son."

I sighed. "Everything comes at once," I replied. "My son; Henry—we are to be at war with him again, soon; everything is changing."

"I know."

"And once it changes . . . I do not know. Sometimes I fear that you will be gone."

"I will be gone?" he asked. "Philip, I do not intend to leave."

"I know you do not. But I am so frightened that once you are king, Richard of Aquitaine—*my* Richard—will disappear."

Richard looked bereft. "I shall always be your Richard. Richard of Aquitaine, Richard of England. It makes no difference."

"Perhaps." I stared down at the water. He moved to comfort me, but I shook my head. There was no time now for doubts, not when Henry was nearly arrived. "No matter," I said. "I love you."

Richard smiled, flushing slightly—it was rare I managed to fluster him, and I felt inordinate pride at the sight—before he kicked again at the water. I snorted and aimed a kick at him in return; we were dangerously close to trading splashes when more figures peaked at the horizon, shifting gauzily in the hot air. I stiffened and stepped out of the water, beginning the reconstruction of civility as I tugged my clothes straight and patted my face dry. Richard did the same, with some reluctance. We stood together at the bank of the stream, staring at the approaching cloud of the foreign retinue.

"Henry," I said.

"Yes," Richard agreed, with all the animation of a Gregorian chant. The shimmer of the army in the heat formed a sort of visual echo, a duplication of each rider and horse; the line of the retinue seemed endless, stretching from one end of the horizon to the other. "God save us all," he said, grim-faced, and I rolled my eyes.

⁓

Henry had brought John with him. I had never met the youngest Angevin, and although I greeted them both as politely as possible, I could not help but stare at Richard's brother. I sought something familiar in his features, but he had little of Geoffrey in him, nor Richard, nor Henry; really, he didn't look like an Angevin at all; he was as short as I was and as slender besides. As I watched him, he seemed intimidated, and he nearly stumbled as he bowed. He hovered at Henry's shoulder, darting his gaze between Richard and me, over and over. It felt almost absurd that someone might be frightened of me, and yet the fear was plain in his eyes.

Henry seemed disinclined to greet Richard, and he spoke to me alone as we ascended the hill. "I often met with Louis here," he said to me after the usual pleasantries, and there was something of an accusation in the words. He wanted me to recall my father's failings, before we started negotiations; an intelligent enough tactic, I supposed.

I had not seen the king of England since my coronation, and I was shocked by how much he had aged. His voice had a harsh gravel that spoke of years of shouting; his hair was combed back, crow's feet sprawling to his temples like varicose veins. He seemed in contention with his own age, movements frustrated and combative. When I did not reply, he continued, "The last meeting we had ended with Anjou mine, and him surrendered. You were there, were you not?"

"Indeed, my lord," I said, as cordially as I could. "I remember."

Henry gave no response to this but a grunt. We continued to walk in awkward silence until we reached the top of the hill. In a moment of ill-timed deference, I allowed him to pull in front of us; he positioned himself where the shade of the elm began, his guards behind him. We were forced to stand at his front, directly in the sun.

John shot Richard and me a nervous glance. I wondered if he wanted to apologize for the rudeness, but then Henry snapped "John!" and he moved to stand behind him.

Keeping my tone measured, I said, "Perhaps you might shift a little, my lord, so that we might move to the shade."

Henry ignored this. Richard—who had thus far remained entirely silent—made an aggravated noise, scowling at him. Then he glanced nervously to me. I had already spent hours traveling in the heat, and no doubt he could see I was suffering in the sun. "Perhaps some water, Philip," he suggested.

I shook my head. "We ought to hear the king's demands."

"Demands," Henry echoed, disdainful. "They are concessions. It is a *concession* to be meeting with you here, to be making you an offer I have made a dozen times before, when you have dismissed it for nothing but pride."

It was certainly not a concession, considering we all knew we were about to enter a war he would lose. But the intention of the

comment was to anger Richard, and it worked. "Pride!" Richard
cried. "You would call it *our* pride!"

"Pride and foolishness. Consider, Richard, what has driven
you to this. Once you were your own man. Once you were a
prince. No longer." Henry sneered at me. "You answer to the
whims of another now."

Richard sneered at him in return. I coughed politely. "To the
matter at hand," I said. "You have yet to acknowledge Richard as
heir."

"Richard has yet to give Aquitaine to John. I released his
mother—she *broke* her *vows*—and still, he makes no attempt to
compromise."

Richard said, "I have no need to compromise. If we go to war,
you will lose; we all know that. You must abandon this ridiculous
demand before it ruins you, and acknowledge me as heir. It is
absurd that you have waited this long."

"I have been *waiting* for you to come to your senses," Henry
replied. "A futile task, it seems, but one I am destined to continue."

"You will keep waiting until you are dead," Richard said.

"If that is the case," Henry snapped, "then that is exactly what
I shall do."

I made an astonished noise. "But that is absurd," I said. "You
must name him heir before you die. Otherwise, succession will
be chaos. You invite civil war."

"Then ask Richard to stand down," he told me. "Have him
cede Aquitaine."

"Richard would never give up his duchy on my account," I
replied, lips thinning. "Your obsession with taking it is nothing
more than a false crusade. We are offering you peace, instead of
fighting a war you are destined to lose; and yet still, you refuse. I

will not support you in this matter, and I never shall. I hope that is quite clear."

"Certainly, it is clear," he returned. "You are exactly as your father was, Philip. There is too much bile in your blood. Cowardice and confusion. I will not waste time forcing you to see sense."

I could not help but flinch at that. Richard took a step forward, and said, darkly, "Father—"

"Silence, Richard. Do you think you are any better? Reduced from duke to catamite? You ought to be ashamed. You bring ruin to the family name."

"The only person ruining anything is you," he said. "Every action I have taken, everything I have sacrificed—"

"Sacrificed? Perhaps that is how you think of it; perhaps you think your cause worthy enough to warrant the cost." Henry laughed coldly. "Perhaps you think yourself a Solomon, sitting in judgment, tearing the kingdom in two. But I will not surrender to you, even if you cause England's destruction. You can be sure of that."

"You care more about yourself," I said, utterly perplexed, "and your petty grudges, than you do your throne—"

"I *am* the throne!" Henry cried. "As are you, Philip; you will learn that soon enough. The crown is worth only as much as the head it sits upon. We are kings because we believe we are, and because we have made all others believe it. Those who threaten that belief are the greatest threat of all. *That* is why Richard must pay for his rebellion, even now. *That* is why he must accept my authority. Until he does, the monarchy itself is at risk. There is no crusade. There is only the struggle for survival."

I opened my mouth to reply, but the words caught in my throat. I had no rebuttal.

Richard said, "You can hardly claim this has all been *necessary*—"

"Can I not?" he asked. "Whatever you do, Richard, the land shall remain. This elm shall stand and shade kings for whom we are but a distant memory. All that matters is our claim to authority. Until you surrender, that is what you threaten to take from me."

Now—finally—I understood every decision Henry had ever made. I had once believed myself to be a throne wearing the face of the man; Richard had proved me wrong. But here was a king who embodied that. He was a crown and nothing more.

"I will take it," Richard said, "if I must."

"And you shall succeed; we both know that. This war is not one I can win." Henry's shoulders dropped, and he leaned upon the tree. There was suddenly an almost tragic exhaustion to his posture. I had never imagined he could look so frail, and I was reminded, for a moment, of Louis. When he continued to speak, his voice was lower, resigned. "My son, you will know, in time, why I cannot forgive you. For a king, personal loyalties are only a passing distraction. There is a reason why we are taken apart when we are buried: the heart must be separate. The heart must always be separate." His fingers splayed across the elm's trunk, in an almost reverent gesture. "One day, you will both put your sentiments aside. Then the two of you will meet beneath this tree, just as we have, and mark my words: you shall despise each other as much as you do me."

"Never," Richard said.

"It is inevitable," Henry replied. "That is the curse of your kingdoms. That is the curse of your blood."

I wanted to speak, but I could not. I drew in a deep, shuddering breath, my hands curling at my sides. I rippled my fingers against my palm, over and over, attempting to echo the movements of my lungs; I could not panic, not here.

Richard gave me a concerned look. "Philip—"

"Is there anything else you wished to discuss, my lord?" I asked. Despite my anxiety, my voice remained cold. A small mercy.

"I believe I have made myself clear. Aquitaine for John, or it will come to war. I have no choice."

"Then war it is," Richard said.

"War it is," Henry agreed.

~⚬~

We slept that night in an estate within walking distance of the elm itself. We were close to the commune where I had been born. The room was stuffy and hot. We lay above the covers, blinking at each other in the low light, exhausted but unable to sleep.

"He is a horror," I said to Richard. The warmth of the air seemed to stifle the words, making them quiet and difficult to grasp; Richard shuffled closer as if to catch them.

"Henry?" he asked.

"Yes. It is difficult to believe that you share blood."

"We look similar enough."

"You are different creatures entirely," I said. "Except, perhaps, for your stubbornness."

Richard reached for my hand. "What he said—what Henry said—it is not true."

"Some of it was true."

"Some of it," he admitted. "But not—I shall never *hate* you, Philip."

I closed my eyes. The words were some comfort, of course, but

I could still feel the heat of the sun that morning lingering upon my skin, still see the dappled shadows of the elm behind my eyelids. "You are always so certain. You are so certain of everything."

"Because I know that it will never happen. What Henry said—that someday, the both of us, by the tree . . . It will never happen."

"But how can you *know*? What has *convinced* you of it?"

There was a long pause, then Richard sat up.

"Richard?" I said, confused, propping myself up on my elbows.

"It shall never happen," he said, his voice alight with conviction. "France and England, beneath the tree—it cannot happen again. I will not allow it. I will not become my father."

"What do you mean?"

"If we are to stand in the sun, then so shall he."

"Richard . . ." I began, and then I understood.

"I have seen it so many times," Richard said. "The elm, I mean. It is always the same. But now, I would not have *anything* stay the same, not if it would mean losing you. I think I would raze all of Aquitaine for you, Philip, if you asked it of me."

"I would not ask it of you."

"I know that," he said, "but I would."

"Does it worry you?" I asked. "The destruction we are capable of? For each other's sake?"

"It is no more destruction than my father would cause, in the name of his crown. Who is to say his reasons are better than our own?"

I should have convinced him otherwise. It was foolish, impulsive, and yet—it was hope. Small as a mote of dust, but hope, all the same.

"I do not know whether I am your cause, Richard, or your

excuse," I said. "But your reasons have become my own. I cannot separate us."

Richard grinned, turned around, and pinned me to the bed. I went willingly, arching into him. His skin was tacky with sweat, as was mine; we did not care. Richard's hand slid down my front and pressed against my stomach, fingers teasing lower, and I whimpered.

"For you, Philip, I shall," he murmured. "I will cut the elm down. And you would do the same for me. Wouldn't you?"

"Yes," I gasped.

"When it falls, think of this; think of my touch. I want everyone to see it fall. I want everyone to know the way I touch you."

"They know. They look at me and know, they must. It is all I can think of."

He bent to hover his lips above mine. I tried to lift my head, to meet him, but he pulled back, smile widening. "We should leave soon," he told me, but he did not move.

"Yes," I repeated. He shifted his hand lower, and I gasped again, managing to stutter—"Before—before the sun rises."

"And when they come, there will be nothing left."

"Nothing but us," I said.

"Nothing but us," he echoed.

I surged upwards, then, taking him off guard; he laughed as I flipped our positions and pushed him down to straddle him. His hands fell to my hips. Despite the heat, I pressed my mouth to his neck, so that I could taste the salt of his skin.

"I love you," I said, muffled, "I love you, I love you," and then a fourth time, and then a fifth, because perhaps if I said it enough times the words would somehow gain new meaning, and cease to be so desperately inadequate.

I was certain of so little; my fear was nothing less than a disease, it had been my entire life. But I loved him, and that was enough. King or no—it no longer mattered. I needed to be nothing but his. And, for a moment, every possibility, every choice I once thought I could never make, bloomed before me, stretching upwards around us; reaching up, up through the roof of the building, smashing through the tiles, bursting into the sky. Hope grew anew, untethered and unrooted, like the branches of the elm we would now cut down.

CHAPTER TWENTY-THREE

Richard

The men were disgruntled that we were leaving so early, but once we arrived—once they were told of their task—they took their axes to the tree with vindictive pleasure. They had seen Philip and me standing in the sun the day before. To them, our reasoning was nothing more than a repayment of a discourtesy, but that did not matter. As we stood there, watching the elm shuddering with each blow, there was the sense we had accomplished something greater. We had pulled something ancient from the land, and left the earth itself disfigured. The stump that remained was a gnarled whorl of flesh, the distorted corpse of a titan.

Once they were finished, the tree was dragged away. Philip had been sitting in the grass. When he stood up, he had a daisy-crown in his fingers. He placed it upon my head, smiling. "Isabella taught me how to make these," he said. "It suits you."

We climbed the hill and I stepped onto the elm's stump. Beneath my feet, the tree's rings rippled outwards, wood tinted saffron-yellow in the rising sun. Philip circled slowly around me. He had to step very high to avoid tripping on the roots.

I clapped and stamped down upon the stump. Philip looked up at me and frowned. "What are you doing?" he asked.

"Dancing," I said. "With you turning like that, it is a little like a dance, is it not? You clap also, and spin."

"There is no music."

"Very well." I began to hum tunelessly, stamping a beat. Philip smiled, and to my delight he began to spin around the base of the tree trunk, clapping along.

"You are utterly tone-deaf," he said, breathless, as he passed by.

"I know," I replied. "It is the only thing preventing my career as a troubadour."

"I can picture it," he replied, still spinning. "You as a troubadour. I imagine you visiting court . . ."

"My liege," I said in an Occitan accent. "If you would permit me to play you a short *canso*"—here I clapped to exaggerate the words, and Philip laughed—"in *private*."

"In private! I think this troubadour very bold, to take such liberties with his king."

"But how can I resist, when my king dances so prettily?" I reached out to catch his arm. Laughing, he spun away.

"This troubadour is rather slow, I fear—" Philip said, and then he squealed as I threw myself at him. I caught him at his back, winding my arms around his waist. The momentum was such that we both stumbled, nearly falling halfway down the hill. "Richard!" he squawked, squirming. "Release me at once—"

"I shall, my liege, but I will ravish you quite thoroughly first—"

"If you *dare,* I shall have to—"

I kissed him quiet. He responded briefly, and then he put his hand on my chest, pushing me back. He glanced a warning down the hill, to our men by the stream. None of them were watching us, and I rolled my eyes at him. He sighed, kissing my cheek in appeasement.

He stepped back from me, and for a moment we watched each other, lit gold by the rising sun. Philip turned to stare at the tree stump. "It hardly seems real," he said. "It feels as if it should grow back at any moment."

"I know. I feel the same."

"We are about to go to war," he told me. "With your father. With *England*. I know we will win, but . . . Sometimes, victory seems as frightening a thought as surrender."

"Yes, it does."

"I am scared," he said, and he sat down on the stump.

I sat beside him. "I am scared also," I replied. "I do not know what will happen. You asked me once how I can be so certain of everything, but I am not certain. Everything in my life is uncertain, except how I feel about you."

It was true. There was no other constant in my life, not anymore; no mark upon its landscape but him. Everything I did, everything I wanted, was bound irrevocably with him. Where the elm fell—where there had once been something unchangeable—there was now only the recollection of Philip and me, dancing around its stump. It would remain there for the rest of my life.

"I love you," Philip said. "Ceaselessly. And I—I am trying to be less afraid. I do not know yet if I can be. I cannot promise that it is possible. But I can promise that I will try. And if my fear ever comes between us, if I do leave—I can promise that I will return to you, Richard. I always will."

I cupped his cheek and pressed my forehead against his, staring into his eyes. The thought of him leaving me, even temporarily so, filled me with a terror that was almost indescribable. I searched his expression, wondering if I could see hesitancy there, if I could sense him drawing away. But I saw only Philip. He was *my* Philip, whose smiles were as rare as summer in spring; who was often fearful and cruel and cold; who kept his heart caged in iron, but who sometimes—in the quietest hours of the evening, or while the sun was still rising—would let me reach through the bars to feel it beat beneath my fingers, thrumming and bloody and real. In that moment, he was real, and he was mine. That was all that mattered.

I stood from the stump and offered him my hand. He took it, and I pulled him up to face me, his left hand in my right.

Philip reached up to touch the daisies he had placed upon my head. "Long live King Richard," he said, smiling.

"Long live King Philip," I replied, throwing the crown to the ground so I could bend and bring his lips to mine.

And all my life, in the search for something remarkable—something extraordinary—I had never imagined something such as this; something so solitary, this private and flawless moment. Once, before I had known Philip at all, I had wanted to be the subject of songs, a hero in poems. I had wanted to be like Richard the Lionheart, like Philip Augustus. These were the men who would be chanted of, who would be immortalized in their castles and their cities, in the soil of their kingdoms and the white stone of their effigies. But those men were not real, and they never would be. We were real, he and I, and I was glad that no one else would ever know Philip as I did in that moment, nor know me as he did. We were only for each other.

All of what we had fought for now became secondary. It seemed our wars and our lands existed only to bring us together. And beneath our outstretched arms, where the elm had fallen, there was England and France, Paris and Poitiers and the Pyrenees; under our feet, the kingdoms we had carved, their roads and rivers all a path for us to follow. And we would follow them, I knew. We would follow them, until, as always, we would find each other once again.

AUTHOR'S NOTE

I had largely abandoned history by the time *Solomon's Crown* was finished. The true story of Philip II of France and Richard I of England is fascinating, dramatic, and more than worthy of its own retelling; but it is, in many ways, a tragedy. In real life, the two men had a tumultuous relationship, and by the untimely end of Richard's reign—he died at age forty-one from a battlefield wound, a crossbow bolt to the shoulder—they were undoubtedly enemies.

I first learnt about Richard and Philip's relationship in James Reston Jr.'s *Warriors of God*, one of the few histories I've read that lends the rumors of their romantic entanglement credence. The concept of two kings so destined to rivalry falling in love utterly captivated me. Further inspiration came from the perfect 1968 film adaptation of *The Lion in Winter*, in which a young Timothy Dalton made Philip dark-haired and blue-eyed in my mind forevermore.

Five years before this book's publication, I visited Poitiers, and there I saw the window at the cathedral commissioned by Eleanor of Aquitaine that Richard and Philip meet beneath in

Chapter Twenty. It still survives today in the exact state it was created, and it's one of the oldest stained-glass windows in the world. It's a testament to the beauty, hope, and ingenuity of a period so often defined in the modern imagination by its brutality. For all the blood and grime and suffering of the past, people loved one another just as much as they do now. I think that's wonderful.

When I wrote the first chapter of this book, years ago, I was a teenager struggling with my mental health and coming to terms with my own identity. The story I initially envisaged was one much truer to history—darker, grittier, and ending in tragedy. But eventually, as I grew older, I realized that I wanted something more joyful. So, accuracy fell by the wayside, and I wrote a romance instead. I hope others find some joy in it, too.

ACKNOWLEDGMENTS

This book wouldn't exist without my marvelous agent, Tara Gilbert, whose passion and dedication never cease to inspire me; and my editor at Dell, Jesse Shuman, whose love for this story made *Solomon's Crown* what it is today. I can never thank either of you enough.

My deepest thanks also to my team at Dell: Kathleen Quinlan, Megan Whalen, and Melissa Folds for their amazing work bringing this book to readers; Rachel Ake Kuech for her beautiful cover; Kathleen Reed and Nancy Delia for their exceptional editorial work; Kara Cesare, Kim Hovey, Jennifer Hershey, and Kara Welsh for all their support.

Evangeline, Hannah, and Susie: you three sat through endless drafts and gave me endless encouragement, I adore you all for it. To Grace, Margarida, Oscar, Rebecca, Saint, and all the others who read and provided feedback, I am also indebted. And Omar—for loving this book, and being in my life—thank you, always.

For my family, who have always supported me, I am both privileged and grateful. My sincerest thanks to my godmother,

Belinda—your advice and support was invaluable; my father, Kim, whose excitement about my achievements has never ceased; my brother, Jonas, whose kindness, intelligence, and bravery astonish me every day; dear Estela; my aunt Alex, uncle Jonathan, and my mormor Danielle; and my mother, Caroline, to whom this book is dedicated. Mom, you've never allowed me to give up on writing, and your imagination and love made me who I am today. I'm so grateful to you, and to everyone else who helped make this book a reality.

Solomon's Crown

Natasha Siegel

A BOOK CLUB GUIDE

SECTION TITLES:

A BRIEF EXPLANATION

The four sections of this book (Parts I–IV) are named after forms of medieval poetry popular in Europe during the twelfth century. Eleanor of Aquitaine was a well-known patroness of the arts and the granddaughter of William IX, the supposed "first troubadour"; the real-life Richard Lionheart was a poet himself. Much of the poetry the characters would have encountered in this period would have been set to music, and written and performed in Occitan, which was—as it is today—a distinct language with a rich literary tradition, entirely distinct from the French Philip would have been speaking to Richard.

DESCORT

The *descort* was an Occitan lyrical form that was used to express a story of discord or disagreement—in particular, unrequited love. Its structure is chaotic and disparate, with variable numbers of lines and syllables between verses. Part one is named after this form, from the moment of Philip's coronation until his disagreement with Richard and their subsequent parting.

Salut D'Amor

Meaning, literally, "letter of love" in Occitan, these were written from the point of view of the narrator to their beloved, often exalting the beloved to return their affections or to reconcile with them after an argument. The first *salut* we have on record, by Raimbaut d'Aurenga, frames love as a battle, in which the poet has now surrendered: "*Ves vos mi lais vencut e domde,*" he sings, or: "I bow before you, won and subdued." Part two is named after this form, spanning the length of time Richard is at Philip's court before the war begins.

Jeu-Parti

The *jeu-parti* is composed and performed by two troubadours, rather than one, taking the form of a debate. It is a combative genre—the beginning of the poem presents a dilemma that the two performers are arguing over; most surviving examples discuss love, but other topics may also have been considered. The answer was usually not given within the poem itself, but instead left for the audience to discuss afterward. This form is the namesake of part three, which deals with the war between Philip and Richard.

Chanson de Geste

Part four breaks somewhat with the previous three; it's named after an epic, narrative poetry form, rather than a lyrical form favored by troubadours. *Chanson de geste* is old French for "A song of heroic deeds," and these poems tell the stories of legendary kings and knights, dealing particularly with Charlemagne and other important figures in French history. The majority were written in French, although there are Occitan examples, too. They are celebratory, extravagant works of imagination, which present entirely fictionalized versions of their historical characters; they have magic, monsters, and—of course—romance, too.

QUESTIONS AND TOPICS
FOR DISCUSSION

1. Natasha Siegel tells readers from the start that "This is not a historically accurate novel." Instead, she has chosen to reimagine history through a more optimistic lens, to create a version of it that is less tragic. How did this blurred boundary between fact and fiction affect your reading of *Solomon's Crown*?

2. "I wondered if any of us would find something worthy above us, some escape from our cages," remarks Richard. How do the constraints, or "cages," of one's position and birthright define the various characters in the novel— Richard, Philip, Isabella, Geoffrey, Henry, John? How do they deal with the pressures and expectations foisted upon them?

3. How do Richard and Philip change during their time with each other? Do the lessons they learn from each other continue to be guiding forces in their lives?

4. "Isabella made me Aeneas, even if only for that night: a wanderer tossed in the tempest, escaping the fickle hand of fate." How does Philip's predicament mirror that of Aeneas? What is his "exile" and his "tempest" in this case, and does he *ever* escape "the fickle hand of fate?"

5. What parallels do you see between the characters and conflicts of this novel and today? What pieces of Richard and Philip's story can be universalized?

6. Which is more important: love or duty? How do Richard's and Philip's sense of duty and ambition get in the way of their love? How does their love usurp their sense of duty? Is love worth pursuing if you know it will lead to heartbreak?

7. "Our family trees are as tangled and thorny as a briar patch. . . . It is impossible to unpick one thread without the entire thing coming apart." Philip remarks that he can pick at those threads and cause the "tapestry" to unravel. How does he do so? What are some of his most cunning political moves?

8. Discuss the women of *Solomon's Crown*—Isabella and Eleanor of Aquitaine. What roles do they play in the story? How do they exercise their power?

9. What is the significance of the titular Solomon's crown? Why do you think Natasha Siegel chose this as her title?

10. Which of these characters is the most flawed? What is their hubris?

11. How do the section titles mirror the events of the book? How do ideas about courtly love and chivalry fit into *Solomon's Crown*?

12. "The elm at Gisors straddled the border between my territory and Henry's. To the north, there was Normandy, and south, there was Paris. At the center of it all, a tree had teetered on its hill for centuries, and it seemed likely to do so for centuries more." Discuss the implications of chopping down the elm tree. What do you think the future holds for Richard and Philip? Do they *really* get a happy-ever-after?

13. What makes a great king? How would you have dealt with the complicated political situation that Richard and Philp both find themselves in?

14. You're casting for an adaptation of *Solomon's Crown*. Who's your perfect Richard? Your perfect Philip?

PHOTO: © ALEX STEVENS

NATASHA SIEGEL is a writer of historical fiction. She was born and raised in London, where she grew up in a Danish-Jewish family surrounded by stories. When she's not writing, she spends her time getting lost in archives, chasing after her lurcher, and drinking entirely too much tea. Her poetry has won accolades from *Foyle's* and the University of Oxford. *Solomon's Crown* is her first novel.

natashasiegel.com
Twitter: @NatashaCSiegel
Instagram: @natashacsiegel